ALSO BY

ROBERTO TIRABOSCHI

*The Eye Stone*

# THE APOTHECARY'S SHOP

Roberto Tiraboschi

# THE APOTHECARY'S SHOP

A NOVEL OF VENICE, 1118 A.D.

*Translated from the Italian*
*by Katherine Gregor*

Europa
*editions*

Europa Editions
214 West 29th Street
New York, N.Y. 10001
www.europaeditions.com
info@europaeditions.com

Copyright © 2016 by Edizioni E/O
This edition published in arrangement with Grandi & Associati
First Publication 2017 by Europa Editions

Translation by Katherine Gregor
Original title: *La bottega dello speziale. Venetia 1118 d.C.*
Translation copyright © 2017 by Europa Editions

Library of Congress Cataloging in Publication Data is available
ISBN 978-1-60945-417-3

Tiraboschi, Roberto
The Apothecary's Shop

Book design by Emanuele Ragnisco
www.mekkanografici.com

Cover photo by Franco Gatti

Prepress by Grafica Punto Print – Rome

Printed in the USA

# CONTENTS

To Roberta and Sebastiano.

But, my dear fellow, nothing in the world that ever you have heard of Venice, is equal to the magnificent and stupendous reality. The wildest visions of the Arabian Nights are nothing to the piazza of Saint Mark, and the first impression of the inside of the church. The gorgeous and wonderful reality of Venice is beyond the fancy of the wildest dreamer. Opium couldn't build such a place, and enchantment couldn't shadow it forth in a vision. All that I have heard of it, read of it in truth or fiction, fancied of it, is left thousands of miles behind. You know that I am liable to disappointment in such things from over-expectation, but Venice is above, beyond, out of all reach of coming near, the imagination of a man. It has never been rated high enough. It is a thing you would shed tears to see.
—CHARLES DICKENS,
*Extract from a letter to John Forster* (November 1844)


Resplendent daughter of the dawn,
To whom all men bow in love;
Your winds, the sirocco and the bora,
Are like a breath from heaven above.
Golden lady reigning over us,
O Venice, O Queen, O Venus.
—ANDREA ZANZOTTO, *Recitativo veneziano*

# THE APOTHECARY'S SHOP

# I.
## METAMAUCO

The twisted form emerged from the water like a swollen, fleshy root that had been borne up somehow or other by the slimy mud of the lagoon.

Alvise did not linger on the strangeness of that sight but dragged the *scaula* ashore and got ready to hunt.

The muddy expanse was swarming with tasty crabs that scurried out of his way, terrified. He plunged his hand into that living, repulsive carpet, grabbed a handful, and stuffed them into his net.

A male crab suddenly ran out of a spongy rock. A huge creature with a hairy back and silver nippers, and the *garzone* chased after it, provoking myriad splashes that, hit by the pale winter light, were transformed into iridescent splinters.

The frightened crustacean found refuge under a tangle of gray filaments undulating like a sea anemone.

Alvise bent down and reached out with his hand to drive out his prey.

It was then that his mind became a blur and the features of his face twisted into a grimace of horror.

That which he'd taken, at a first, absent-minded glance, for a lump of wood abandoned by the tide turned out to be a face wrapped in a shawl of sand.

It was sticking out just above the water surface, like a flower that had survived salt corrosion.

The young man vomited an acidic sound, a cry for help nobody could hear in that watery desert.

He took a few steps back and considered running away, pretending he hadn't seen anything. However, something stopped him from acting on his intention: a morbid curiosity, a pleasant weakness that horror often triggers in men's bowels.

He looked again at the macabre remains.

He noticed that, as well as a head, still mainly immersed in the mud, lay a body caressed by the slow undulating light—a woman's body. Her legs were tucked up under her chest and she was holding a fist up to her mouth, as though to stifle a final cry. She looked like a sleeping fetus.

She was completely naked. There was a metal thread around her neck, with a series of glass beads that, corroded by the salt, had lost their sheen.

Operating its nippers adroitly, the crab was feasting on the flakes of skin collected in her hair.

The young man picked up a piece of wood, struck the crustacean, and sent it flying into the distance.

It was that very gesture that made him think.

It was perfectly obvious that he was in the presence of an extraordinary event. Despite having been immersed in water, the body was perfectly preserved in all its parts.

The skin had kept a delicate shade of amber that in no way evoked the pale image of death. The vitality of the features was still intact: sensual lips, rounded cheekbones, delicate earlobes, a mane of hair that had only barely faded to an ashen tone. Even her full breasts, round belly, buttocks, and thighs, although half submerged, looked as firm as those of a young woman in full bloom. Only her eyes, which he could glimpse through the half-open lids, had lost their original glow, and were dimmed by a dull, melancholy veil.

She seemed to be oozing a kind of supernatural energy.

How could she be so well preserved after being at the mercy of the fish and the force of the waves?

Alvise knew very well that when flesh is immersed in water,

it soon turns mushy and rots. Perhaps the body hadn't been abandoned long. But then how come it was trapped in the sand?

This section of the lagoon had been totally submerged for over ten years, and it was only the recent exceptionally low tide that had cast ashore what was left of that which had once been the island of Metamauco, an important and industrious part of the duchy until the Year of Our Lord 812.

Twelve Lent seasons had passed—Alvise was but a child then—since the most devastating storm Venice had ever experienced had obliterated islands, districts, harbors, and *fondamenta*.

She had lain buried in the abyss for all that time and yet was still intact. It was a miracle.

He remained motionless, as though stunned, gazing at the image of what must have been an extraordinarily beautiful woman. Then he reached out and gently touched her shoulder.

A sudden gust of icy wind rustled the reeds, rippled the water, dug a furrow around the limbs, head, and hair, and swept off the layers of sand that were still keeping her imprisoned.

The sliding beams of the vanishing sun quivered on the wet skin, then exploded in a whirl of sparks, and the body rose as though traversed by superhuman energy.

Thus it remained, suspended in the void, lapped at by the spray of the waves and a bed of algae.

Overwhelmed by the demon of fear, losing all control, Alvise ran to his *scaula* at breakneck speed and began rowing with all his strength, not turning back once.

Later when, still stammering, he told the city authorities what had happened, he swore repeatedly that, when he'd seen the woman's corpse rise from the bed of sand as though animated by divine power, he was certain it had come back to life.

Conflicting rumors spread regarding the interpretation

Venice residents gave to this extraordinary event, which took place the day after the Ides of February in the Year of Our Lord 1118.

Scholars and God-fearing individuals claimed that it was the body of a resident of Metamauco, and that the fact that it had been perfectly preserved for twelve years after its death was clear evidence of a miracle of the Almighty, who wanted to remind the people of Venice of His omnipotence.

The common folk simply added it to the list of unusual events, a quirk, an exception that merely confirmed nature's rule that a body submerged in mud at the bottom of the sea rots and becomes an excellent meal for fish as early as three days after its death.

Some people of uncertain birth and dubious morals let slip the odd incomplete word that secretly alluded to the sublime power of the King of the Underworld.

Since we are humbly and diligently about to recount events that occurred so long ago, we do not feel inclined, given the lack of documentation and solid evidence, to embrace any of the above-mentioned theories. We will therefore give up trying to distinguish lies from truth, surrender to the impossibility of representing reality just as it appears, and choose instead to trust the visions of the night, the blurred images, the intangible apparitions that come to visit us at almost every dawn, in the hope of succeeding in creating a completely illusory, unreal world that may nonetheless become imprinted in your minds as something truer than truth itself.

# II

## CA' GRIMANI

Close the windows immediately, hurry. Shut and lock everything up! It's after Vespers, night is falling. How many times do I have to tell you that when the sun sets I want everything to be closed? Nena? Did you bolt the front door?"

"Yes, Signora."

"Then why are the windows still open?"

"They're too heavy, Signora, I can't manage them on my own."

"Get your son Alvise to help you."

"Alvise's not back yet, Signora."

Nena saw an uncontrolled tremor creep into her mistress's orderly, haughty face and instantly dissolve her imperturbable features: a blend of terror and anger transfigured her dignified face into a distorted mask. Nena got frightened.

"When the master is away traveling," Magdalena shouted, "am I the only one in this house who worries about our family's safety? Can't you see the dangers all around us, can't you hear the commotion every night, the rattle of men murdered in the *calli*, the screams of girls being raped? Don't you care if you die?"

Her hoarse, harsh voice was a perfect match for her gaunt, highly strung body. She ended every sentence with a deep inhalation, like a swimmer who catches his breath after being deep under water for too long.

The mistress's face was like a thicket of thorns. Nena stared at her blankly.

"Is there nobody to help you? In that case I'll do it. Come with me, let's go."

They went out into the inner courtyard and climbed the stairs to the main floor.

Obsessed with the dangers that could come in from out-side, Magdalena Grimani had persuaded her husband to have heavy stone shutters fitted, which sealed all the windows in the house hermetically.

She had first noticed them in the Basilica of Santa Maria Assunta in Torcellus and thought they were an essential defence against the risk of raids by thieves, cutthroats, and rapists.

With great difficulty and Nena's help, she closed the slabs and leaned against the windows the panels, coated in oiled parch-ment, which shielded the house against the freezing winter wind.

"Where's Costanza?" Magdalena suddenly asked as soon as they'd finished.

"I don't know, Signora, I haven't seen her, honestly."

"What do you mean, you don't know?" The Signora grabbed Nena by the arm and shook her small, delicate frame. "How many times have I told you that my sister must always be watched and followed? She's a sick, frail girl. She must never be left alone, do you hear?"

"Yes, Signora, I understand."

Magdalena let go of Nena, pushing her into a corner. "Is the front door bolted?" she asked, rushing to the loggia again.

"Yes, it is, Signora."

Nena tolerated these fits of anger good-naturedly. She had been a servant in the Grimani household since before the mas-ter had married and owed him a debt of gratitude.

She was only thirteen when that Slav boatman had caused her belly to swell, but the master hadn't kicked her out, and instead carried on feeding both her and her child, even though Alvise ate as much as a boar.

The issue of safety had become a nightmare, and Magdalena saw dangers and enemies everywhere. As soon as night fell, a cloak of anxiety would wrap around her, almost suffocating her.

Her peat-colored eyes, one of which glistened with golden flecks that gave anyone looking at her a sense of unrest and instability, would turn into bleeding wounds.

Terror gave her face an ambiguous charm, a blend of salvation and perdition: the trunk of a tree stifled by ivy in a stretch of ice.

There was a stench in the city that gnawed away all hope from even the most God-fearing folk.

In just over a year, Venice had been shaken by catastrophic, mournful events that had debilitated it, crushed it, and deprived it of its lifeblood.

Three days before the Nones of January in the Year of Our Lord 1117, a terrible earthquake had struck churches, towers, and houses with such violence that many buildings had collapsed, banks had cracked, and the church of Saint Ermagora and Saint Fortunato had caught fire and been totally destroyed.

The burgeoning city had been left balancing on the waters, as though about to sink forever. It was only thanks to the work and love of its people that it had been able to get back on its feet. However, four seasons later, the ruins of that terrible cataclysm could still be seen on the islands, the fords, and along the canals.

Just when the city seemed to have recovered its stability another disaster struck its long-suffering residents: at the end of 1117, during the war against the Hungarians, the illustrious doge Ordelaffo Falier had been killed near Zara while fighting bravely in battle.

Thus the city of Venice was facing dark times, without the guidance of its doge, and without a steady government.

Cutthroats, thieves, and murderers took advantage of this atmosphere and walked around the *calli* undisturbed, masters of the night, ready to kill, rob, and rape.

The district gastalds had repeatedly complained to the Great Council, but no solution had been found. Until a new doge was appointed, nobody was under the illusion that any laws would be enforced to guarantee more safety for the residents of Venice.

Overwhelmed by irrational agitation, Magdalena Grimani searched all the rooms on the main floor, hoping to see the diaphanous figure of her sister Costanza appear out of thin air.

Increasingly out of breath, when she realized that there was no sign of her, she went down into the inner courtyard, onto which gave the kitchens, various storerooms, and a shelter for the horses.

Sometimes, Costanza liked to seek refuge in the oven room, to keep warm whenever the icy north winds swept across the lagoons and penetrated the gaps between the larch wall paneling, not giving humans a chance.

"Costanza! Costanza!" Magdalena shouted.

A servant came out of the woodshed and stared at her blankly.

"Have you seen my sister?'

The man shook his head and grunted something.

God almighty! Where could she be? Magdalena walked across the porch as far as the flight of steps that connected it to the canal at the back of the building.

A lonely *scaula* moored to a pole was rocking on the surface of the putrid water, which was stained with mud dumped in the lagoon by the currents of the Medoacus, the Silis, and the Plavis after heavy rain.

There was no sign of Costanza.

She flung open the door of the storeroom where goods awaiting voyages to the Orient were kept. The only living thing she saw was a huge rat that ran past, holding the head of a new-born kitten in its mouth. She shut the door, horrified.

She suddenly wondered whether Costanza had ventured outside on her own, unaccompanied: that would have been pure madness!

All that was left was the part of the house known as "the pantry."

That was what Tommaso, her husband, called the space he had organized in the mezzanine, beneath the apartments. A seaman and a navigator, he'd wanted to recreate on dry land a corner of his ship, specifically the pantry, which is what the Genoese called the section of the hold where food provisions were kept.

It consisted of a narrow corridor that could be reached by means of a few steps, onto which gave two cabins, one used as a study and the other, to which nobody had access, her husband's exclusive refuge.

The floors and walls had oak paneling, and all the furniture, in every detail, reminded one of a ship ready to sail across the seas.

She went up the steps reluctantly: whenever she approached that part of the building, she felt an uncontrollable tremor start in her heart, the diseased memory of a terrible grief that rotted her soul.

She went in. The wood creaked under her steps and a sickly-sweet smell of wilted flowers took her breath away. She felt dizzy and weak at the knees. She leaned against the wall. There was a spongy lump in her throat. It was as though she was being sucked into a vortex of pain. She thought she might faint.

She noticed a faint light through the half-open study door. She took a deep breath and stepped forward in an unnatural silence that was broken only by a screeching that reminded her of the grinding of her husband's teeth as he slept. She flung the door open.

She saw a shapeless form undulating on the wall: a creature with two heads and an enormous body. She half closed her eyes to get accustomed to the semi-darkness.

Only then did she recognize, lit by an oil lamp, hunched over the scriptorium, the spindly form of her sister Costanza. Bent over like a sick weeping willow, she was dragging a goose quill across parchment, copying with meticulous care a manuscript that lay open before her.

"You're here!" Magdalena exclaimed. "I've finally found you, sister. I was worried."

Costanza neither replied nor looked up, her mind intoxicated by the magic signs formed with ink on the rough surface.

A voice emerged from the shadows and slid from the dark corner of the little room toward the intruder. "We're copying Severino Boezio's *De Consolatione Philosophiae*."

Like the sudden blow of a saber, the fire cast a light on a creature with a twisted body, which seemed to have lost its life force to the devil in a game of dice.

The suffering face, concealed by a neglected beard, the vacant eyes, and the mass of red curls that fell over his brow gave the impression of a bundle of old, scorched clothes that had formerly belonged to a wealthy prince. What made that form even more unusual and unnerving was the bump protruding from the sternum, under the cloth jacket.

"Oh, it's you, Edgardo d'Arduino—I hadn't seen you," Magdalena whispered, trying to conceal her unease.

Although Edgardo, the scribe, had been known at the house for many years, she still wasn't fully accustomed to his mysterious presence, which she found unsettling. A man of thirty-seven who kept intact a diseased youthfulness. A tile she was unable to fit into the mosaic of her soul.

She harbored conflicting feelings toward him: her respect for the inspiring spirituality he radiated and his gentle manner were sometimes counterbalanced by a sense that this man's soul was in the grip of deep torment, an open wound the origins of which nobody knew and which, someday, could become infected and spread death all around it.

"Costanza is an attentive and accurate pupil. There's a delicate touch in her writing that only women possess. She'll be a model copyist," Edgardo added calmly, putting the miracle contraption he always carried with him back into a leather case.

"The pupil is a mirror of the master," Costanza replied.

Only then did the young woman lift the goose quill from the sheet and raise her head, her face lighting up with a faint smile of gratitude.

Magdalena couldn't help giving a start of anxiety. Never had she seen her so pale and thin. Their mother too had suffered from that same exhausted pallor, but in Costanza's case, the illness had reached its peak, giving her skin an ivory transparency through which you could see the path of her veins, the relief of her bones, and the texture of her flesh.

A pair of liquid eyes protruded from this evanescent mask adorned with fine hair the color of dried grain.

Notwithstanding all that, the young girl, who had recently turned seventeen, emitted an air so gentle and serene that it would envelop and conquer everyone's spirit. People were charmed and surprised by her body language, the warmth of her voice, and the tenderness flowing out of her eyes.

Ever since, left alone after their father's death, Costanza had been welcomed into their home, Magdalena lived in a permanent state of anxiety about her sister's health. When she herself had arrived from Bruges, in the far north, she had found it difficult to get used to the customs and the climate of this city risen from the swamps, suspended over the waters, which every day fought hard to snatch land from the marshes and canals that ate away at everything, including your will to live.

When she thought she was succumbing, Costanza had

found salvation in her curiosity for learning and writing; thus, with stubbornness and after much insistence, she had managed to gain the right to dedicate herself to an art to which very few women were allowed access.

Tommaso Grimani, a rich and powerful merchant belonging to the influential class, had agreed, albeit reluctantly, to deprive the crews aboard his ships of Edgardo d'Arduino, the administrator scribe, and keep him ashore so that he would teach his sister-in-law.

"Honestly, what do you think?" Costanza held out the parchment to Magdalena, who took it closer to the lamp.

"It looks very tidy, the signs are clean and sharp, but you know very well that unfortunately I can't read." She looked up at Edgardo, almost as though she held him somewhat responsible for not having included her in that fascinating, inaccessible journey.

"If you wanted to, I'm sure you'd learn quickly," Costanza said. "It's not hard."

Edgardo nodded, thereby signaling he would be ready to teach her too.

"No, it's too late." Magdalena regretted arousing her own hopes. "Besides, I wouldn't have the time. I have too many chores, the responsibility for our home is such . . . " She sighed. "In any case, Tommaso wouldn't allow it."

She leaned toward her sister, and as though afraid to damage the perfection of that absolute pallor, gave her face a light caress.

"My heart is full of joy that you, sister, should become the family scholar."

A loud knock echoed through the small study. A boat was mooring in the narrow canal. There was a screeching of ropes. A hastily abandoned oar rolled on the bottom of the boat. Someone leaped from one bench to the other. There were hasty footsteps.

"What's this racket?" Magdalena rushed to the steps, followed by Edgardo and Costanza.

They found themselves facing a frightened-looking, glassy-eyed young man, covered in mud.

"Alvise, where have you been? Your mother needed you," Magdalena said, annoyed. "When my husband returns, I will tell him how you behaved."

"Forgive me, Signora, something's happened. I got the fright of my life." He stood there, mouth open, looking breathless.

Edgardo intervened. "Come, tell us."

"I went crabbing and stopped in a patch of shallow water."

"And?" Edgardo said.

"And . . . And . . . instead of crabs I caught a human—a woman, in fact."

"A woman?" Magdalena said.

"A beautiful woman."

Costanza approached the boy. "Was she alive?"

He shook his head. "No, no, God bless her soul, she was dead, she'd been dead a long time, or at least so it seemed . . . except that later—how can I put it?—the lagoon gave her up again and she rose once more, perfect, as though preserved in brine. She was even wearing a little glass necklace. Alive and as beautiful as a young virgin."

The young man looked at Costanza and gave her an apologetic smile.

They had all fallen silent. Everybody was studying Alvise's face, unsure as to how to interpret what he had just said: whether it was the imaginings of a fool, the hallucinations of a drunk, or the tall tales of a youngster.

Magdalena broke the silence. "So what did you do?"

"I ran like a bat out of hell and went straight to tell the gastald. I don't want people to think I'm crazy."

"Alright, alright," Magdalena said abruptly. "Go to your mother now. It's past Vespers."

Alvise gave a little bow, stole another glance at Costanza, and was about to run away when Edgardo stopped him. "Wait. Where did you find this beautiful woman?"

For a moment, Alvise seemed not to understand, then he lit up. "In the new marshes, the ones that came up in front of the mouth of the Medoacus. Where there was once the wonderful island of Metamauco."

Magdalena and Costanza had already walked away, so neither of them noticed anything. Only Alvise saw Edgardo's expression change, his face ravaged by a spasm, his body crumpling and shaking.

The young man thought the scribe was about to collapse, so much so that he put his arm out, ready to support him. "Are you alright, Signore?"

Edgardo did not reply. He was panting, a faint hiss escaping his lips. His mind was being dragged down a vortex, to the seas of a distant past, tossing him about among recollections he wanted to erase. All it took was that name, Metamauco, to reawaken within him a boundless sense of longing.

"May I go?" Alvise asked.

Edgardo could only muster the strength to make a gesture with his hand, then he closed his eyes in the hope that his memory might dissolve the dreadful image he had been carrying around for over ten years. A woman's body emerging from the sands of the muddy sea. A ghost returning.

# III.
## THE APOTHECARY'S SHOP

He couldn't get to sleep. His mind was possessed by the image of that woman who'd emerged intact from the depths of the lagoon. One question had been haunting him since he'd heard Alvise's story: was it her? Was it the only woman he'd ever loved, who'd vanished in the waves during the storm?

If the body that had appeared amid the ruins of Metamauco was that of his beloved Kallis, he would have solid proof of her death: this would set him free and, after so many years, allow him to cast away the ghost eating at his soul.

But what if this wasn't Kallis's body? It could be anyone, a stranger; after all, so many people had perished in the cataclysm that had erased the island of Metamauco from the lagoon. In that case, he could carry on hoping, dreaming that she was still alive.

And yet wasn't this possibility even more devastating? It would keep him chained to the past, and take away all desire to live, all hope of picturing a future. The diseased thought that had never left him surfaced again. Once before, in Bobbio, while he was still a clerk, he'd considered putting an end to his torment with death.

He turned over in his bed, trying to banish this nightmare. The boards under the straw mattress emitted a grim shriek. The bells of the church of San Leonardo rang Compline, the final prayer before nighttime.

Edgardo thought back with longing on all the years he'd

spent at the abbey before relinquishing the habit. How calm were his days then, punctuated by prayer and his work as a copyist. Everything made sense, everything followed a higher order that was now irremediably lost. Now, his soul wandered through a hostile universe, unable to find a glimmer of light, tormented by remorse.

He threw off his damp blankets covered in mold and picked up the clothes strewn over an old trunk that, together with a worn lectern, made up the sparse furniture in the loft. He was about to reach out for the leather case he always kept nearby, but stopped. No point. He wouldn't need it.

He'd promised himself over and over never to give in to temptation again, but the weight oppressing him was becoming unbearable.

He quickly got dressed.

The house was plunged in silence. Nobody would notice anything. He went downstairs in the dark: he knew the way. Down in the internal courtyard, he walked up to the front door. There was a creaking sound by the well. He froze and waited a moment before pulling open the bolt. He heard more rustling, followed by a dry, wheezing breath that grew closer.

The back of his neck was soaked in cold sweat. Finally, he sighed with relief. It was a piglet wandering about undisturbed, perhaps after escaping from an enclosure in the *campo* behind the church of Saint Ermagora and Saint Fortunato.

As soon as he breathed in the soggy night air he immediately felt better. The sky was low and black with rain.

Turning his back on Ca' Grimani he made for Rivoalto. It wasn't far, he'd taken this route so many times, yet he had to walk with care. The *calli* had turned into rivers of slime, the rotting planks of the bridges would split under every step, the support poles would sway, shifted by the canal currents that had swollen during the winter. He hadn't brought any light: it was safer to walk around unseen. Not a single glow came from the surrounding homes—wretched, single-story, little wooden huts. He was immersed in a thick, dark liquid that slowed down one's movements and clouded the mind.

Every night, Venice would turn into a sleeping octopus, cloaked in a huge jet of ink.

It was only the surrounding sounds that reminded him that he was going through a stretch of real life and not a nightmare. Ever since his eyesight had become so unreliable, his ability to pick up even the softest noises had sharpened.

He walked along a canal, allowing himself to be led by the swishing of the waves lashing against the bank, followed the rustling of a bed of reeds, and realized he'd arrived at a *campo* that, owing to the dirt track, had withstood the devastation of the rain better, because he heard that the gurgle of his footsteps in the slime had given way to a more echoey, more solid sound.

When he thought he'd already reached Rivoalto without encountering any danger, the black world around him was suddenly filled with a deep, dark cry, and a sharp pain pierced his chest like an incandescent needle. A powerful scream that enveloped the whole of Venice, echoing from district to district. The torment of a soul that doesn't want to leave its body, he thought, the sound of life's desperate struggle against death.

He hid in an archway, waiting for the evil of the world to calm down, and for anxiety—his constant companion—to allow him to resume his journey.

Silence returned. He left his shelter. After all that, he had arrived. Just a few more steps and he would reach oblivion: torments, memories, and ghosts would be erased, forgotten, at least for a while.

The front door of the Crowned Wolf was shut, but Edgardo knew how to be let in even at this time of night.

He picked up a pebble and threw it at the planks covering the second-floor windows. No result. He tried again with a larger stone. In the end, he heard noises coming from inside, a creaking sound, and a shadow looked out.

"Who in hell is coming to break my balls at this time of night?" It was a deep, fat voice, like a rumble of thunder.

"It's Edgardo. Open up."

"It's you, Signore, God bless your soul."

"Leave God alone and open up, Sabbatai. Hurry up, I need you."

"It's impossible, Compline rang ages ago, it's forbidden, Signore, we can't."

Edgardo's tone brooked no refusal. "You'd better open up, apothecary, or I'll kick the door down."

There was some rough grumbling, like hazelnuts shuffled together, then the moan of a bolt, and a ray of light slid out through the lower edge of the front door.

"Quick! Quick, Signore! Before someone sees you!"

Edgardo bent down and slipped inside. As always when he went into the apothecary's shop, he had to defend himself against the attacks of the shadows of pottery vases, phials, and stills that, from the shelves, like a fragile army, seemed to want to assault the visitor at any moment.

He was enveloped by a disorderly multitude of vapors and scents that took his breath away.

The essences, tinctures, and herbs that were calmly resting inside bags hanging from the beams in the ceiling gave off fumes that had totally impregnated the walls, counter, and even the bare floor, intoxicating the mind of every customer.

The acidic fragrance of aloe vera, mixed with the tangy whiff of black mustard, was battling with the spicy aroma of ginger, diluted in the cool field of saffron and poppy.

After a little while, Edgardo's torpor dissipated, and he approached the counter behind which the apothecary had meanwhile sought refuge.

"How can I help you, Signore? Do you need a purge, a pack, or a poultice?" he asked in a unctuous voice.

"Don't play games, Sabbatai, you know perfectly well what it is I want."

"At this time of night? But Signore, in the name of all the saints, it's a concoction that requires time, knowledge, and skill."

Edgardo leaned toward the apothecary, whose head only was visible behind the counter, and poured out a few coins in front of his face. "Perhaps these will help you find your skill."

Sabbatai considered the money with a sideways glance. "You can't buy skill, but in the case of time and will . . . Come back early tomorrow morning, and you'll have what you yearn for."

Edgardo lost his temper and grabbed Sabbatai's hand, which was already sneakily picking up the coins.

"Tomorrow'll be too late, I'll have been eaten alive by nightmares by then." Edgardo stared into the cerulean-blue eyes of the malformed man. "Nature hasn't been kind to either of us, so let's at least help each other."

A soundless laugh that revealed a set of horse-like teeth shone on the shopkeeper's face.

"Even put together we wouldn't make a proper man. And, in all honesty, I'd rather keep my dwarf's body and big rod than have an average body with a hump right in front in full view."

"Don't be insolent, Sabbatai." Edgardo let go of his hand. "So?"

The apothecary sighed. "Alright, God give me strength, wait here."

Edgardo heard some bustling and saw the man's head run down the counter. Then, after a little leap, the rest of the body appeared.

It looked even smaller in the faint light. Sabbatai was Venice's most singular dwarf. Not just because of his height, just over three feet, like so many other dwarves, but because of the disproportion between the head and the rest of his body, as well as the structure of his face.

The body, arms, and legs were still those of a six-year-old child, while the head had grown into that of a thirty-year-old adult.

His oblong, misshapen face emphasized a series of deformities that were, in their way, unique: there was a large growth hanging over his left eye, like a ripe plum, that significantly impaired his vision, his nose was retracted like a frightened snail, and his mouth, framed by a wormy beard, formed a permanent laugh produced by unnaturally swollen lips that forced him to display his large, sparse teeth.

Sabbatai went down a narrow corridor and vanished into the backroom. Edgardo knew of the existence of the secret room but had never been lucky enough to visit it. He knew that back there the apothecary made up his concoctions, prepared the medicines prescribed by physicians, and shielded from curious eyes the equipment necessary for complex procedures aimed at producing remedies for ailments.

After what felt to Edgardo like an interminable wait, Sabbatai reappeared, holding a cinnabar-colored glass urn closed with a lid.

"Here you are."

"Is it the usual recipe?"

Sabbatai rolled his eyes. "This is an even better one. I've concocted you a paradise that would make Our Lord envious."

Edgardo did not like the comment, which he considered blasphemous. He took the urn and left hastily.

Shortly afterwards, he was back in his room, sitting on the bed, holding the glass container in his lap. He stroked it with his finger then slowly lifted the lid, raised the urn to his nose, and inhaled deeply.

The substance inside gave off a vapor with a slightly bitter smell. Edgardo brought the container even closer to his nose and took a deep breath that filled his chest.

The concoction was beginning to have an effect. Sabbatai hadn't lied, he'd done good work.

The opium vapors were beginning to take possession of his mind. He breathed in one final illusion to fill his soul, then fell back on his pillow, his eyes fixed on the ceiling beam.

A knot protruding from the wood, deep as a cave, started to move, to turn on itself, dragging Edgardo into a whirlpool in the midst of a tempest at sea. Clinging to his oar, in a boat, he was trying to reach Kallis's *scaula*, which, tossed about by the waves, kept disappearing and reappearing amid the billows.

He thought he heard her voice echoing beneath a black sky, calling him, begging for help—that gravelly voice he could not forget, just like the taste of her skin, cool as spring water, smelling of myrrh.

He heard her cry that she had returned, risen again in that semblance of life, in that intact body resurfaced in the fords of Metamauco. She was calling him, repeating his name, imploring him to look for her. She had returned. She was waiting for him.

# IV.
## THE MERCHANT

The fluctuating crimson glow that quivers on the surface of the waters at sunset.

The silver reflections that creep in among the reeds, mixed with the soft shadows of oak trees kneeling majestically on the shores. The sinuous cobalt fluids that, vanquished by the heat of the sun, bathe beaches lush with cordgrass, and soft land swollen with salt.

The blinding glow of the sea that can suddenly rebel and plunge into the leaden darkness of a tempest, and the shining wonder of light in the marshes that plays among holm oaks and pine trees and caresses bushes of sea-lavender and Venetian dogbane.

The voice of the lagoon as it blathers while slamming against the *fondamenta*, the water smacking between the wooden boats that were bumping against one another. The secret undertow on steps and banks.

This was enough for Tommaso Grimani's soul to feel restored whenever, after a long absence, he returned to his Venice.

When the cog came out of the mouth of the river Medoacus into the lagoon, and, beyond the fords and sand banks, Tommaso saw the fairy-tale skyline of the domes of San Marco and the towers of the Doge's Palace emerge, he knew that no other place in the world—be it Constantinople or Alexandria, or other cities in ice-covered countries—could ever rival the splendor of this new city that had the sea for a floor, the sky for a roof, and water for walls.

He was returning from Bruges, in the cold land of Flanders, with his freight of cloth, linen, and amber. He'd travelled across plains, forests, and impassable mountains.

As a merchant, he felt he belonged to a wider Civitas Veneciarum, one formed by three Venices: the dry land that went as far as the river Adda, the one bordered by the lagoon and protected by islands and water, and the one in the east, made up of sailors who founded self-sufficient communities overseas. As a man, he felt at peace with himself only when he was held in his city's belly of light.

The transport barge entered the Viganò canal, skirted Spinalunga, and arrived within sight of the watchtower standing tall near the Basilica

Outside the dock, which lapped the crenelated north walls protecting the Doge's Palace, and stretched as far as the west door of San Marco, an impressive number of galleys, dromons, and chelandions were anchored, ready to sail out in a convoy, the seasonal fleet that left for the Orient in the spring.

Trade was growing relentlessly and the city was now struggling to fit in all the ships that arrived from every port of the East and West.

Tommaso knew these ships well—where each of them came from and who owned it. They were mainly at the service of Venice's most powerful families, like his own, heirs to the old tribune families that had contributed to electing the first doge, Paoluccio Anafesto, in the Year of Our Lord 697, and were now the proud holders of the title of *boni homines*, members of the Great Council of that governed the city alongside the Doge.

Making their way amid the forest of masts and oars interwoven in the bay, they managed to moor the cog along Riva degli Schiavoni, where the Grimanis owned warehouses.

Tommaso was eager to go home and embrace his wife again, ask after her health, and see if . . . he was obsessed with this thought that had never left him during his voyage. After over a month, perhaps Magdalena would have good news for him, perhaps the merciful God, who drives all and sees all, had heard his prayer.

After the trial He had submitted them to, after all the grief, the day of rebirth would come, and he and Magdalena would see the light again.

When he reached his house, it seemed to him that the enormous winged lion over the front door of Ca' Grimani was welcoming him back with a smile. He took it as a good omen.

The Istrian-marble-clad façade shone with glaring whiteness. Tommaso was proud of his mansion, one of the first stone and perforated brick buildings in Venice.

Since it was nearly dinner time, he found Magdalena in the salon, in front of the fire. She was not alone. Costanza and Edgardo were with her.

Tommaso greeted everyone kindly, concealing his irritation, and everybody paid his and her respects. He wanted to breach the subject immediately, ask questions, find out, but was prevented from doing so by the presence of strangers. Several times, he tried to catch his wife's eye in the hope of reading in it the answer he so longed for.

However, all he received was perfect proof of a woman's ability to resort to any subterfuge in order to flee the direct and silent communication of the secret language between a husband and wife.

As though in a high state of excitement, Magdalena was addressing now Edgardo, now Costanza, inviting her husband to tell them about his journey, about the places he'd seen, especially her beloved Bruges and the relatives she had left behind there.

Tommaso replied wearily, trying to satisfy her request with brief, disappointing sentences.

At the dinner table, where Nena served two huge platters of

game, wild duck, and stuffed thrushes, the conversation revolved exclusively around Flanders cloth, which, in Magdalena's opinion, had no equal, not even among the silks that came from the Orient.

She and Costanza could wear only Flanders linen, or run the risk of their delicate skins breaking out in pustules and terrible itching.

"It's what we've been used to ever since we were children, so our bodies know immediately if we're offered cheap fabrics woven who knows where, pretending they're from Flanders."

Edgardo listened politely to the chatter of the gentleman and lady who had generously welcomed him into their home, and noticed the looks of impatience Tommaso couldn't conceal.

The meal was over soon, and the master of the house announced his wish to retire immediately.

Magdalena left before her husband, as though eager to flee.

When Tommaso caught up with her in the bedroom, he found her hunched over the prie-dieu, absorbed in praying in a loud voice.

It was a new barrier, an escape route to avoid the subject. Tommaso couldn't hold back. "I beg that you cease your prayer, Signora."

Bowing her head and speeding up the pace of her litany, Magdalena gave a clear sign that she did not wish to grant her husband's request.

"*Sub tuum praesidium confugimus, Sancta Dei Genetrix. Nostras deprecationes ne despicias in necessitatibus . . .* "

"I've been away for over a month," Tommaso said again, "which is long enough for an answer . . . So, what is your response?"

"*Sed a periculis cunctis, libera nos semper, Virgo gloriosa et benedicta.*"

"Signora, I command you to speak." Tommaso's tone intimated that he would tolerate no delay.

"No, Signore, I'm not pregnant." Magdalena's voice came out like a hiss, interrupting the smooth flow of her prayer.

Tommaso sank into the high-backed chair by the window. "What wicked deeds have we committed? Why has our Lord decided to punish us like this? Doesn't the Bible say be fruitful and multiply?" His voice resounded in the room. "Thou hast already taken one child away from us, in two months, suddenly, without a reason. A sweet, innocent boy . . . Now we ask Thee to fill the void he left behind in this house with the joyful cries of a new life. God, why art Thou not listening to me?"

He clenched his fists and punched the paneling on the wall.

Magdalena leaped up and threw herself at his feet, hugging his knees. "We will have a child, you'll see, I'm sure of it, I can feel it, you must be patient and trust me. My belly isn't barren, I've already given birth. It's been only a year, we must give the bad humors time to dissipate and make way for the good ones."

Tommaso took her in his arms and held her tight. "I wish it more than anything else in the world."

"So do I, husband, you know that . . . I'm willing to do anything." She took Tommaso by the hand and led him to the bed. "Sit here and listen to me. I've heard of a physician from a city in the South who has recently taken up residence in Venice. He studied at a world-renowned school, in Salerno, which is consulted by popes and kings. They say this physician has studied mainly remedies for illnesses that affect women . . . "

Tommaso stood up abruptly. "More physicians . . . Haven't we had enough? Charlatans and crooks only interested in becoming rich. How many did we see for our son Luca? How many?"

"You're right, I know, but—"

"Bloodletting, poultices, enemas. It was all useless . . . he died after two months, remember? Your physicians were unable to save him. Enough, I know what to do, you'll see!"

"This one is different," Magdalena insisted. "He knows remedies against barrenness, everybody in Venice says so. I'm only asking you to try, to have a consultation. What do we have to lose?"

As though a demon had taken possession of his mind, Tommaso was pacing up and down the room, waving his arms, talking to himself. "He was only six . . . he was my light, my future. Then, in a matter of days, I lost him. Merciful God, why hast Thou put me to the test?"

"I beg you, stop, what's the use of tormenting yourself like this?" Magdalena stroked his face, his coarse hair. "We'll have another child. You'll see. Let's just try it, let's meet the physician, then you'll tell me the impression he makes on you, and you'll decide." Magdalena pressed her pale lips to his neck. "Say yes, I beg you."

Tommaso stared at her defiantly, then began unfastening the cloth jacket that contained a torso that was growing bulkier. Without a word, he pushed his wife's frail body onto the huge oak bed, and carried on undressing.

The nakedness of this man she knew so well suddenly appeared to her as though for the first time. Magdalena studied him with great attention, assessing the features of the coarsely-chiseled face, the square jaw, the hooked nose, that cheeky lock of hair over the forehead, which made him look like a hawk. And those hips made heavier by the weight of the mourning that had altered his body and left visible marks on it. Also, his obsessive way of rubbing his eyes when he was lost in his nightmares, almost as though he was trying to chase away a ghost flashing before his eyes.

With a solemn gesture, Tommaso took his penis in his hand and looked at it with pride, as though it were spoils of war requisitioned from the enemy. It had a funny, arched shape and a long, purple vein running the length of it, throbbing like the breath of a dying salamander. Magdalena had always felt a certain degree of unease at the sight of this piece of living flesh that would swell without restraint, burst its banks, and invade every cleft of her body.

She slipped off her tunic and linen shift, and remained naked, ready to surrender.

Her pale skin turned almost transparent. It seemed its way of rebelling against the coarse body of that being come from unknown lands. Irreconcilable worlds that could never merge.

Magdalena considered her small, silly, impoverished breasts, and the bone structure of her delicate belly, incapable of containing a new life. Then she parted her legs as far apart as she could, hoping that her invitation would entice the conqueror.

Instead, as usually happened, the man declined the offer. Tommaso grabbed her by the hips and turned her over with an abrupt, decisive gesture, the way one saddles a horse. He lifted her behind just as high as he needed to in order to glimpse the entrance to her vulva and, with a sharp, definitive thrust, pushed his penis all the way in. Like a bull with his cow, or a boar with his sow. He had always taken her like this, from behind, without so much as looking at her. She was attacked from behind, secretly. Ambushed.

She couldn't remember ever seeing his face, the color of his eyes, the sweat on his brow.

Always with her head stuck in the mud, worn out by thrusts that broke her heart.

Tommaso had never seen the tears she shed, scattered amid blankets and dried amid sheepskins.

This time too Magdalena heard the grunting buried in her hair and, in the final wheeze, felt the sack of bitterness empty and flood her indifferent, distant body, and the semen run between her buttocks and down her thighs.

Tommaso came away from her, mumbling something about her inability to keep the precious fluid inside her, and Magdalena immediately turned over, trying to limit the loss, closing her orifice with her hands. But the humors seemed not to care and overflowed, trickling out, as though refusing to follow the correct path.

"Fear not, it's all inside me, I can feel it," Magdalena whispered. "I have enough semen for a soul to be born again, the miracle of creation is already in my belly, I'm holding onto it tight."

But Tommaso, overwhelmed by the muffled torpor of oblivion, wrapped her words in a sigh and blew them away in the darkness of the night.

## V.

## MAGISTER ABELLA

M agister Abella'—don't you think it's an unusual name?"

"Everybody knows physicians are a little odd, Signora."

Magdalena was wearing one of her finest tunics, the indigo one, embroidered with turquoise stones. She wanted the Salerno physician to understand from their very first meeting that he would have to speak and act with the respect and deference appropriate when dealing with a lady of high rank. She checked her reflection in the panel of polished steel that mirrored a distorted, blurred image. The Venetian ceruse she'd put on her face gave her a regal pallor. She spread a light dusting of saffron over her cheekbones and rubbed her lips and gums with walnut root.

"What kind of a man is he? Have you heard anything around? Is he handsome?"

"He hasn't been here long, so I don't know . . . " Nena hesitated. "They say . . . They say that . . . "

"What is it? Come, speak out."

"I don't know if I should . . . but they say he can tell everything from piss, that he looks at it sideways, studies it with his eyes, then tells you all the ailments."

Magdalena seemed very impressed by Nena's words. "Let's hope that's true and that God hears my prayers."

"Yes, of course, Signora, you'll see, you'll soon be pregnant."

At that moment, Alvise came in, somewhat agitated.

"Signora, Signora, there's that person you made me go fetch down in the courtyard."

Magdalena's lips quivered. "He's here. Quick, let him into the salon."

The *garzone* was about to go.

"Wait," she added, "do you know where Costanza is?"

Alvise trembled as though caught red-handed. "I think she's with the scribe."

"All right. Now go, hurry up."

The young man ran off and Magdalena lingered while fixing her dress. She wanted him to wait a little while. Then she slowly walked to the loggia.

Immersed in the half-light of a morning suffocated by fog, what appeared before Magdalena's eyes brought back the gruesome recollection of a fox, skinned and dripping with blood, nailed to the door of a stable, which she'd seen as a child.

An explosion of scarlet was throbbing in the middle of the room. It came from a large, regal robe, which came down to the floor, trimmed with a fur collar, dominated by a wide-brimmed hat with a cone, also bright ruby.

The physician was standing with his back to her and, under his robe, there was the suggestion of a strong, sturdy body.

He radiated a vibrant aura and exuded authority. Magdalena took a couple of steps forward, in silence, then resolved to speak. "Welcome to my home."

The contours of the blood-colored mass shifted and produced a warm rustle. The body spun around, swelling the cloak. In the uncertain light, Magdalena couldn't immediately make out the lineaments of the face. She approached and the vague idea that had already taken root in her mind became more defined.

"Greetings, Signora. I am very honored to be received in your home."

Oh, merciful God. There was no doubt. The physician, Magister Abella, was a woman!

Magdalena tried to restrain her astonishment and bowed her head in a sign of greeting.

"Please don't concern yourself to conceal your surprise. I am accustomed to it." She had a gentle but very authoritative voice, and a plump face with rosy cheeks, like a ripe peach. "Would you still like to use my services? I shan't be offended if you've changed your mind," Abella added.

Nobody had ever spoken to Magdalena so frankly and directly. She took time to reply. "They say astonishing things about your skill as a physician."

"Rumors grow in size as they travel from mouth to mouth, like an echo, and quickly scatter in the wind. Don't believe what they say. For me, it's only the facts that speak the truth." She had the tone of a knight.

"Please, sit down." Magdalena made a sweeping gesture with her arm, implying that her soul had opened up. "You have an unusual name—"

"Magister Abella. The common people cannot accept that a physician should be called Magistra, so I've had to make do. I studied at the School of Salerno, and was a student of the great Trotula de Ruggiero during the final years of her life. No doubt you've heard of her."

Not wishing to disappoint her, Magdalena nodded. "The reason I called for you—"

"No, wait, don't say anything, I don't want to know."

Magdalena looked at her, surprised.

Abella stood up. "Do you have a chamber pot?"

Magdalena staggered. "What do you mean? A—what?"

"A chamber pot, a bedpan, a pisspot. I need to examine your urine."

"Oh, a chamber pot, yes, of course . . . I think it's in . . . Nena. Nena!" she called out loud. She'd never been in this kind of situation before, and was struggling to contain her embarrassment. Nena promptly arrived.

"Magister Abella . . . the physician," Magdalena stammered, "needs a chamber pot."

Nena opened her eyes wide. That word was never used in the Grimani household, especially not by the masters. "A pisspot?"

"Yes, yes, go fetch it."

The servant sneaked away.

"If you find this embarrassing, you can do what you have to in your chamber," Abella said.

"Yes, perhaps that would be more befitting."

"But you must bring it to me right away. It must be fresh and warm."

"As you wish," Magdalena replied, and immediately vanished like a deer hiding in the bushes to escape the ambush of a wolf.

Quicker than it would have taken to skin an eel, Magdalena returned, followed at an appropriate distance by Nena, who was carrying a steaming bowl.

Abella parted her robe, revealing a light-colored shirt, fastened with a belt from which hung a pod-shaped, green glass container with a wide opening secured with a cork top. "Pour some into the bottle. I want to examine it in my own time, later . . . "

Nena obeyed.

"*And ora in primis the inquisitio.*" Abella lifted the chamber pot to her nose. "*Urina exquisita est per substantiam, colorem, copiam et materiam.*"

Her soft feminine features, deep, dark eyes, and her full, glowing face tensed up in an inspired expression. She inhaled a vortex of air through her delicate nostrils, which sucked up the flatulent scent that floated over the pale yellow liquid. Then she shook the container in a rotary motion and bowed her head even closer to it, studying its consistency, clarity, and transparency. She remained in this adoring posture for a while, then, as though waking after sleep, dipped her thumb and index finger into Magdalena Grimani's noble humor and rubbed her fingers hard.

As though watching a witch casting spells, Nena was staring, entranced. Overwhelmed by the astonishment that her body fluids should be worthy of so much attention, Magdalena collapsed into a high-backed chair.

Magister Abella gave a deep sigh, almost a wheeze, then looked up from the chamber pot and pronounced her verdict. "Sharp smell, inflamed, purulent, like overcooked cabbage. Cloudy, dense, frothy, with traces of sperm at the bottom. The color is pale, like overcooked meat; shiny like a polished white horn, with a vaguely citrine tint. Quantity: as plentiful as cow piss."

Abella stopped. Magdalena leaned toward her, waiting. "So, Magister?—"

The physician silenced her with a commanding sign of the hand. She took out the bottle and, with a calculated gesture, raised it to her lips and took a small sip, as though it were a good-quality, sweet Provence wine.

Nena couldn't repress a kind of gurgle in her mouth. Magdalena hid her face in her hands.

Heedless of the reactions provoked by her sampling, Abella starting swishing the urine around her mouth, whipping it from her palate to her teeth, licking it with her tongue, while making deep, guttural sounds, before performing a general rinse that took up her entire mouth and throat.

Nena feared the worst but then saw Abella spitting the delicious beverage back into the chamber pot.

It was only then that Magdalena found the courage to look into the Magister's face, as though that exploration had revealed her body in its most intimate details.

Abella sat beside her and, sounding like a good mother telling a story, began. "Your urine speaks loud and clear, and says everything about you. It's obvious what your problem is: barrenness, but not congenital barrenness. You have already given birth, your child died prematurely, and now you can't get pregnant again."

Magdalena leaned her head back and closed her eyes, overwhelmed by a wave of emotion, while Nena couldn't suppress an exclamation of surprise.

"You've seen all this in my . . . in my humor. How did you do it?" Magdalena asked with a thread of voice.

"God, in His generosity, chose to bless me with a supreme gift: an almost supernatural sense of taste. Through sensations triggered by various substances, my mouth sends my mind a series of clues that help me decipher every illness, every imbalance that torments the human body and soul."

Her admiration for knowledge and astonishment at Abella's powers of divination convinced Magdalena that the physician was a messenger God had sent her to bring comfort to her broken body.

"Do you think my wilted belly can be given new vigor?" she asked, hopeful.

"I want to be honest with you, Signora, and not give you false illusions. I could promise you miracles with magic potions but I believe neither in spells nor in talismans." She took Magdalena's hand with maternal gentleness. "Before suggesting drugs, ointments, decoctions, compresses, mustard plasters, or bloodletting, we must investigate, explore and . . . *rationes malorum pervidere.*"

"You're right." The frank authority of Abella's words made Magdalena glimpse a ray of light. "When can we begin? My soul is anxious and above all else my husband wishes for a new heir."

"When the full moon is in Aquarius it's not a good time to

examine the genitals, so let's wait for it to go into Pisces. Then I'll return and we'll carry out an in-depth examination."

"May God bless you. You have given me so much comfort."

At that moment, the sound of footsteps came from the loggia. Costanza rushed in and almost collided with Magister Abella. The young girl's enthusiastic expression and cheerfulness immediately faded. "Forgive me, Signora, I didn't know—"

"Let me present you my sister, Costanza."

The girl bowed.

"Magister Abella is an illustrious physician from the School of Salerno," Magdalena said.

Costanza stared at her, bewildered. The glow of the ruby-red robe created a vibrant, demonic aura around the body, in marked contrast to the cheerful, almost peasant-like face. The women's features froze in almost unreal stillness, as though they'd been surprised by an unexpected danger.

Abella assessed the girl with a detachment and precision that were almost unhealthy, invasive, without uttering a word, so that Costanza, crushed by this investigative vortex, was forced to take a step back and seek refuge at her sister's side, as though taking shelter from an attack. She felt stripped naked and penetrated through a cruel act that barred all escape. Then, in the time it takes for a breath of air to fold and extinguish a candle flame, the tableau returned to life.

Abella made a greeting sign and Costanza sneaked away to stand next to Nena.

"Come, I'll see you out myself," Magdalena said.

Going down the large staircase that led from the loggia to the ground floor, Abella let a few words slip with studied carelessness. "Your sister is very pale."

"Yes. She's always been like that, ever since she was a child. She's of a sickly constitution." Then, suddenly realizing that the comment had been uttered by a physician, she added, "Could you find a cure for her too?"

Abella shook her head. "Pallor is not an illness. Humors vary according to age and time of life. She narrowed her eyes at Magdalena with an expression of complicity. "Often, in young girls who are virgins, the phlegm takes the upper hand over the blood. But then as they grow up, and male humors penetrate the female uterus, blood, phlegm, yellow bile, and black bile recover their balance, and the body achieves harmony. Find her a husband soon, and she'll be cured."

Whenever the Magister spoke, Magdalena felt enveloped by a wave of warmth that filled her with calm and trust.

They reached the internal courtyard. Abella walked with a decisive step, showing surprising agility despite her stout body. Magdalena tried to work out how old she could be. Young but not too young, older than her but not so old she couldn't have been her sister. She decided she must be about thirty.

Alvise was waiting astern the *scaula*, clutching at the oar, ready to take her back to Torcellus.

The Magister was about to take her leave when the thud of the front door closing made her look around.

As soon as he noticed them, Tommaso's eyes cast aside the presence of his wife and lingered on the dominating, full-bodied scarlet mass next to her. The typical physician's outfit left no doubt as to her profession.

A few steps away, in the semi-darkness of the colonnade, Edgardo had stopped too.

"Signore," Magdalena said readily, "I'm happy that you should be here in time. Magister Abella, physician and scholar of the School of Salerno, has done us the honor of visiting our home."

Abella took a step forward and stood right in front of Grimani. "May God bless you," was the first thing she said to him.

Not a single muscle in his face, or crease in his mouth, or anything in the shape of his eyes betrayed the astonishment and anger that were swelling in Tommaso's chest. The illustrious physician was no more than a large woman with the features of a peasant. There was something outrageous about her presence.

"I've truly never seen a physician like her," Magdalena carried on. "She possesses surprising qualities. You know, she told me everything about myself before I'd even explained anything . . . and just by studying my—" she stopped.

"The Signora is too kind. I only applied the instructions I learned from my teacher, Trotula de Ruggiero, *Magistra mulier sapiens*. The art of medicine tolerates no lies."

Tommaso's voice came out refined and cutting. "Unfortunately, Signora, your so-called art is practiced by quacks, barbers, soothsayers, crooks, forgers, converted Jews, and Saracens. And now also by women, I see. Only a year ago I lost a son of a tender age and nobody could save him with your art. As you can understand, the trust I place in your profession at the moment weighs as much as a feather."

Magdalena had the impulse to intervene and put an end to the useless argument. Why offend someone you didn't know, why act on a whim? However, she held back out of respect for her husband.

She was surprised to see that Magister Abella didn't seem at all ruffled.

"I am sorry you've lost confidence in our art, Signore," she replied, keeping a celestial calm. "It's true that there are many charlatans around who pass themselves off as physicians but, as you've noticed yourself, they're all men. The women who practice this art are rare, and since they must allay the suspicions of the incredulous, they're obliged to be much more expert and knowledgeable—more so than men."

Heartened, Magdalena managed at that moment to intervene and support her protegée's arguments. "I haven't been prescribed useless potions. Magister Abella has promised to come and see me again in order to discover the cause of my ailment before she administers any remedies."

"Of course, a large number of reasons can cause sterility, both female and male," Abella added.

"What do you mean?" Tommaso felt as though he was being entangled in a viscous trap.

"I mean that a man too can harbor reasons why a woman cannot procreate. Already as far back as in the writings of Paul of Aegina, the latter mentions the weakness of the male sperm as a proven fact."

A voice emerged from the semi-darkness. "Excuse me, Signora . . . "

Edgardo's presence had until now gone unnoticed by Abella, who turned around, irritated.

"In the past, when copying scholarly texts was my only reason to live, I had the honor of transcribing Constantine the African's translation from Greek of Paul of Aegina's *De Re Medica*, and I don't recall any passage about male infirmities."

Abella's face suddenly altered. Her chubby cheeks stiffened and her mouth took on a twisted fold: who was this red, hairy owl come out of the blue who dared question a Magister's words? "Perhaps your memory is letting you down. It's a well-known fact that a copyist's mind often strays, and that many can't even tell what they're transcribing."

"You're right, our memory can sometimes fail us," Edgardo readily replied. "I have copied so many manuscripts about the medical arts, from Salerno, Baghdad, and Toledo, that my mind is probably confusing the various writings. However, I seem to remember that it wasn't Paul of Aegina who addressed male infirmity in procreating, but rather Trotula de Ruggiero, your teacher."

"Allow me to present Edgardo d'Arduino," Tommaso said arrogantly, "talented copyist from Bobbio, scribe, and a tutor in our service."

"I am honored," Abella said. She saw that it was better to walk away from the skirmish. She must be careful. This strange, ageless being was not a man like all the others: certain of his own superiority, he could write, and more manuscripts had gone through his hands than an ordinary physician could have dreamed of. As a matter of fact, he had been to the library of Bobbio Abbey, one of the largest in the Western world, and probably met a few disciples of the Salerno School. She put on a polite smile and said nothing else.

Tommaso looked at his wife, gloatingly: Edgardo had taught that arrogant woman a good lesson. "I would be happy to postpone this argument between scholars until a more appropriate occasion," he said.

Trying to defuse the tension, Magdalena gave Abella a friendly bow, and indicated the boat waiting at the bottom of the steps. Abella made her way there.

"You will be hearing from me," Magdalena concluded.

"I hope we meet again, Signora," Edgardo said in a very cheerful tone. It did not go unnoticed by anyone that he hadn't addressed her as Magister, as appropriate to her role.

"In that case I hope you remember me," Abella hissed back, "because it seems your memory is playing bad tricks on you." Then she leaped into the *scaula*, causing poor Alvise to clutch at the oar even more tightly to avoid falling into the water.

# VI

## THE CONVENT OF SAN ZACCARIA

Framed in a white veil, Costanza's face seemed to have lost substance, consumed by deadly pallor; her eyes had dark purple rings and her forehead was moist with sweat.

Sitting opposite her in the *scaula*, Edgardo was trying to give her courage with a slight smile that gradually waned as they cut through the layer of mist above the muddy waters that a taciturn Alvise stirred with his oar.

They left the narrow canal alongside Ca' Grimani and took the wider Rivus Altus that divided the city in two, already crowded with gondolas, *sandolos*, and cogs loaded with timber, Istrian marble, cows, pigs, and geese, as well as fruit and vegetables from vegetable patches scattered amid the islands in the lagoon.

Everything was enveloped by a mother-of-pearl light, softening the wooden outline of the houses that alternated with tree-lined gardens, beds of reeds, and grassy campi.

A scribe should have been able to find the right words to give her courage, but despite all his efforts, Edgardo couldn't find a reason to justify this visit.

It had been discussed for several days. Not even Magdalena's insistent begging could make Tommaso relent in his decision: Costanza had to consider the possibility of withdrawing to the Benedictine convent of San Zaccaria. There, she could continue with her studies, surrounded by the heiresses of Venice's most illustrious families. Supported by prayer and faith, she would find her way to glorify and serve Our Lord.

Costanza had tried to resist and begged her sister, but Grimani was adamant. In the first instance, she would have to visit the convent, meet the Abbess Contarini, talk with her, then they would discuss it further. Tommaso was certain that the conversation with the abbess would enlighten her.

They went past Rivo dei Santissimi Apostoli. In the *campo* outside the church, there were two horses tied to a fig tree, quietly grazing, not the least troubled by a flock of seagulls shrieking over a feast of a black goby's guts.

In Rivoalto, the number of boats that shuttled between the shores of San Bartolomeus and San Giacomo had grown out of all proportion, making it almost impossible to get through the tangle of wood, cables, and hawsers.

There were various barges on both shores of the canal, where carpenters were working on a solid bridge of boats to join the two branches of the city, to facilitate travel and exchange, and therefore stretch the limits of Venice, which was increasing in population and size year after year.

Alvise steered left to extricate them from that bustle, and took a narrower canal that ran alongside the convent of San Salvatore.

"Tell me honestly, Edgardo," Costanza suddenly said, "do you think I'll really be allowed to choose? Will the noble Tommaso respect my decision if I don't want to enter the convent?"

The hollow sound of the oar slapping the water filled the void Edgardo would have liked, instead, to replace with words of comfort. Costanza trusted him fully, so he couldn't lie to her. There was no hope for a young woman in her position. Her sister would never oppose her husband's decision.

"For a long time I lived in an abbey. Life in a convent can be very full and rewarding."

"But you had your writing and even despite that you gave up the habit . . . Why did you do that if life there was as full and rewarding as you say?"

Edgardo wished he could be frank and shout out, "Because of love for a woman! No writing can resist love, and even faith falters," but he kept his lips closed tight, swallowed his words, and just made a vague gesture that referred to a distant, now forgotten past.

"You see," Costanza said, "you have no answer."

The *scaula* went into a narrow, smelly canal than ran between single-story huts crowded together, rickety, clinging to unsteady *fondamenta* of poles corroded by sea salt.

Excrement and leftover food that had been thrown out of the windows had formed a hard, mottled crust on which merry bands of enormous rats ran around. Brandishing the oar like a weapon, Alvise hit them flat out, sending many flying into the water.

When they reached the canal of the alley, they were violently struck by a white light that forced them to half close their eyes.

They'd entered Rio Batario and the *brolo* of San Marco spread before them in all its vastness.

The waterway cut right across this green field, luxuriant in vegetable patches and fruit trees, and passed, to the east, the brick façade of the basilica named after the patron saint, and, to the west, the little church of San Geminiano.

On the pier outside the dock, like every morning, there was a crowd of *garzoni* and servants busy unloading goods, sailors directing pilgrims bound for the Holy Land, and slaves for sale at the market of Constantinople toward moored galleys.

Tied to a pillar outside the Doge's Palace, a recently executed cutthroat was on display: after gouging out his eyes as a lasting warning against his terrible crime, they'd quartered him from the throat down with a *bec de corbin*, so that his intestines were dangling between his legs, providing two cats with a lavish meal.

The man, a dyer of Albanian origin, had been guilty of the unnatural rape of a twelve-year-old girl, the daughter of his master's slave.

Despite being used to such sights, Costanza turned away just in time before one of the cats staged a final attack on the gentleman's guts. Having torn off with its paw a decent helping of shit storage, it scurried away amid people's legs, its daily meal between its teeth.

When they came out into the open lagoon, among moored galleys and chelandions, Costanza took a deep breath and let the sea breeze blow over her.

Just beyond the towers delimiting the Doge's Palace, the walls of the convent of San Zaccaria were already visible.

The Benedictine convent had been erected after the church of San Zaccaria had been built, when, in the Year of Our Lord 800, the doges Angelo and Giustiniano Partecipazio received the saint's body from the Byzantine Emperor Leo V.

After the terrible fire of 1105, in which many nuns died, asphyxiated, the convent was rebuilt and extended, and acknowledged by all the people of Venice as a most holy custodian of relics.

Alvise tied the *scaula* to an iron ring by the steps leading to the entrance.

The door knocker made a deep, loud noise. Costanza threw one final glance at Alvise, as though looking for support. He bowed his head.

There was a squeak of hinges and an attractive nun appeared, smiling, elegantly dressed, more akin to a lady than an anchoress.

"I bring madonna Costanza Colyn, sister of the noblewoman Magdalena Colyn, wife of the most illustrious Tommaso Grimani," Edgardo announced.

The nun gave a sign of greeting. "Our devoted and most holy Abbess Contarini is expecting her."

Costanza staggered forward and gave one more look of profound despair. Edgardo squeezed her hand and went with her as far as the front door.

"Have courage. I'll wait for you here," he whispered.

The door closed and Edgardo felt as though it would never open again.

Alvise was turning the oar nervously. "Maestro, I must deliver a message to the master's friend, in the bay of the shipyard, then I'll come back and pick you up."

"It's all right, you can go fishing," Edgardo replied. "We'll walk back."

Alvise, who had been hoping to hear precisely that, untied the rope in the blinking of an eye, and pushed the boat into the middle of the canal. Two strokes later, he was already in the bay, swallowed by the glow of the lagoon.

All that was left for Edgardo was to wait. His hip was aching, so he sat on the steps. A *sandolo* steered by an old man was approaching the shore, solitary, a little boy at the prow leaning out dangerously over the water, dragging a net. Edgardo wanted to shout at him to be careful but his attention was caught by the loud swish of large waves.

A shadow had suddenly appeared in the slightly blurred and distorted image conveyed by his ailing eyes. Silent, as though weightless, a large, round vessel, painted totally black, was gliding over the water, pushed by two boatmen wearing long, dark tunics.

Astern and on the bow stood two wrought iron crosses, and two ivory skulls of a heavenly whiteness were set in the side of the boat.

In the center, on a catafalque, there was a box, like a coffin, made of green, young wood.

The *sandolo* with the old man and the child halted, as though bewitched by that mysterious cargo.

Edgardo realized that the vision was penetrating his heart. He didn't know why. "What are you carrying?" he shouted at one of the boatmen.

The man didn't even turn around. "It's the virgin of the beads, the one they found . . . preserved in brine." He burst into a coarse laugh.

"Our illustrious bishop wants to see her, so he can act all scholarly and decide if it's a miracle or a big trick."

A vortex, a chunk of heart torn out of his chest . . . The body of the woman Alvise had found in Metamauco was there in that box, a few steps away from him.

One thought only, an obsession: to see that face and find out if it was Kallis's body.

Throwing all caution to the wind, as though spellbound, he followed the boat, keeping alongside it for a long stretch, as far as the spot where the canal took a left toward the basilica; there, the *fondamenta* flanking the convent walls stopped, and he found himself in front of nothing but water. He was blocked.

He considered walking around the convent and waiting for the boat near the palace. He could watch as they unloaded the box. Perhaps he would get an opportunity to see the woman's body!

He was about to go when, abrupt as the blow of an ax, a thought brought him back to reality.

Merciful God . . . Costanza! He had to go back immediately, before the girl came out of her meeting.

Magdalena had asked him to stay close to her, to protect her, and he had neglected his duties to chase after an illusion.

When he reached the gate of San Zaccaria, he saw that it was bolted. There was no sign of Costanza. Perhaps she was still at her meeting. He hadn't been away that long. An uncontrollable agitation was growing in his chest, and he couldn't refrain from knocking.

The same nun who had received them opened the door.

"I beg your pardon, sister, the young lady I accompanied here is still speaking with the Abbess, isn't she?"

The nun took a step back, almost as though to keep her distance from the question. "No, the meeting is over. I thought the young lady was with you, Signore."

"With me? No . . . "

"The abbess dismissed her almost immediately because she had to attend a service, so I accompanied her into the crypt and left her there to pray, alone, as she'd asked me to. When I went back to pick her up shortly afterwards . . . " the nun hesitated, "the girl wasn't there anymore. So I thought she might have left on her own, because you were waiting for her. I came to the gate but there was no one outside. So I assumed you left together."

"No, no . . . I didn't see her come out."

"How is that possible?"

"Perhaps she went out through the main gate, toward San Marco?" Confusion and panic were taking hold of Edgardo's mind.

"Strange. She knew you were waiting for her. Are you sure you haven't seen her? You've been outside the gate all the time, haven't you?"

There it was, the question he'd been expecting. An abyss opened before him: he was an idiot, unreliable, incapable of completing any responsible task.

"Yes . . . No . . . I walked away only a few steps while waiting . . . " he stammered.

The nun's look of contempt went right through his chest. That feeling of alarm Edgardo knew only too well swept over him. The nun kept staring at him, motionless, with almost cruel enjoyment, waiting for an explanation. Then she felt sorry for him. "You'll see, she probably went straight home when she couldn't see you."

"Alone?" The very thought was inconceivable. But it was the only hope.

"Go, I'm sure you'll find her at home," the nun said, trying to comfort him.

"May God hear you." Edgardo bowed and stepped back.

The door closed again and, for the duration of a heartbeat, Edgardo was left stunned and dazed, then he shook himself and, seized by an uncontrollable agitation, broke into a demented run.

Flashes of light, dark corners, splashes of mud, a heavy, threatening sky hanging over his head. A disorganized, desperate run through streets, canals, huts, and bridges, surrounded by a world that seemed about to crash on him, and a blind crowd that couldn't see his mortal anguish. His bones were aching, and sweat was pouring down his face and into his eyes, making everything transparent.

On many occasions, he thought he saw her: an opaque shape on a swaying bridge; surrounded by toothless crones who were pushing her into a dark cave; abducted by a Saracen slave on a cog transporting hay; dragged by force into a tower by a drunken soldier: images of Costanza generated by his weak mind accustomed to visions and nightmares created by opium. Nothing but ghosts, but expressions of his guilt. There was no sign of Costanza.

He reached Ca' Grimani exhausted, his veins swollen with blood, his head throbbing.

He saw Nena drawing water from the well.

"Have you seen Costanza? Is she back?" he asked, panting.

She looked at him, astonished, and shook her head. "No, Signore."

Climbing over sacks of flour, merchandise, and baskets of vegetables, he rushed into the study. Empty. He ran up to the main floor and looked into the salon.

Magdalena was sitting by the window, embroidering a piece of Flanders cloth.

"God bless you, madonna," he said, trying to control his agitation. "Is your sister Costanza back? Have you seen her?"

She slowly looked up and studied him with that fleeting expression that always seemed to be chasing after a secret thought. "She went to the convent of San Zaccaria with you," she said.

"Yes, madonna, but then at the exit . . . " Edgardo stammered a few unintelligible words before adding, "We lost sight of each other."

Magdalena leaped to her feet. The cloth fell on the floor. Her voice burst out, shrill. "What do you mean? What are you trying to say?"

"I waited for her outside the front door. We agreed she'd come and find me after the meeting with the Abbess."

"Where is she now?" Magdalena shouted.

Edgardo wished he could vanish. He barely found the strength to reply, "I was hoping to find her here. I haven't seen her."

"What are you saying? Are you insane?" Magdalena crossed the salon, stopped, then returned. "Did you ask at the convent?"

"They say she left . . . They thought she was with me."

"And where were you?" Magdalena screamed, out of her mind.

"I walked away just a few steps, long enough to get some water." And he was left with a sickly sweet taste in his mouth, surprised by how easy he'd found it to lie.

"Did you look for her in the surrounding area, along the way back?"

"Yes, but in vain."

"And where was Alvise?'

"I'd let him go. We'd decided to walk back."

As though only then becoming aware of the abyss into which she'd fallen, Magdalena let out a scream that echoed throughout the entire building and swept over Edgardo with all its might.

"Tommaso, Tommaso, merciful God, come, come quickly!"

Tommaso came out of the storerooms in the courtyard, accompanied by two porters. He saw his wife leaning over the balustrade, as though looking for something to cling to.

"She's disappeared . . . they can't find her . . . Costanza . . . Costanza . . . oh, my God!"

Tommaso rushed upstairs while Nena came out of the kitchen, ready to go up to her mistress. She froze. Next to the well, a grass snake was eating itself. A fatal omen, the diseased breath of the lagoon slithering into the home of her masters.

Tommaso hugged his wife. "How did it happen? That's impossible." He glanced at Edgardo, who appeared behind him.

Not waiting for an answer, he immediately gave the order that the whole building be searched, from the loft to the well, even the boats moored along the canal that ran near the fondamenta. Then he asked Edgardo to tell him everything in minute detail.

"I will never forgive myself for this negligence and God will punish me for it. I left for just a few seconds, I can't understand how this could have happened . . . Please forgive me, Signore."

Edgardo felt the sense of guilt and the torments that had accompanied him his entire life surface again. So this was his destiny: to be an incompetent, a coward constantly on the run from himself. Tommaso glared at him sternly, then turned to his wife. "We must beat the entire route between here and the convent, and search the narrow canals . . . "

Magdalena hid her face in her hands. Tommaso realized he'd gone too far.

"We must consider every possibility, even an accident.

Today I will go to the convent and ask to see the Abbess. Perhaps she'll give us more information. We'll get a better idea of Costanza's state of mind when she left the meeting."

Magdalena interrupted him. "What do you mean? What difference can it possibly make to know what my sister's feelings were at that moment?"

"It's no secret that the girl was opposed to the idea of going to the Benedictine nuns."

"That doesn't mean she would actually consider—Merciful God, I can't bear even thinking about it." Magdalena clutched at the hem of her tunic.

Tommaso tried to calm her down. "That's not what I said. She could have left of her own free will, perhaps with someone's help. I will report her disappearance to the district gastald today, so they can start their enquiries. We'll find her, you'll see."

Edgardo had been thinking while listening. The way things had played out, anything could have happened to Costanza. The time he was away hadn't been long, but enough to make a few theories plausible: she could easily have left but only by boat because, otherwise, he would have met her at the end of the *fondamenta*, or she could have been abducted . . . or an accident . . . Finally, and the very thought made Edgardo's heart sink, she could have taken her own life to avoid being shut away in a convent. In any case, all these theories came down to the responsibility of just one person: the one who'd been unable to watch over her.

Aware of the load weighing on his shoulders, he went up to Magdalena, head bowed, like a penitent. "I'm deeply sorry for what's happened. You know how fond I am of your sister," he said, raising his head in search of forgiveness, but in Magdalena's eyes, so full of pain, there was a stretch of ice. "If I have erred, I submit myself to God's judgement, but as far as human justice is concerned, I swear to you, Signora, there's nothing I won't do to bring Costanza back home safe and sound."

He completed his oath by kneeling before Magdalena and kissing the hem of her dress. Only then did he sense a shudder go through her body and feel her thin, pale hand being laid on his shoulder. An invitation to stand up.

Tommaso nodded, satisfied with this proof of loyalty and honor his retainer was showing.

The scribe raised his crippled body, which had earned him the nickname of 'Edgardo, the Crooked,' and left the salon.

A deep, repetitive voice kept echoing in his head: "You must find Costanza, you must find her! You can't fail again this time!"

## VII.
## A SILK RIBBON

He woke up oppressed by the bitter aftertaste of opium essence in his throat. Wracked with guilt, he'd once again gone to Sabbatai's apothecary shop in the middle of the night, in search of relief.

In the pale light of a dawn liquefied by steady rain, the image that had tormented him all night was still floating before his eyes: Costanza's naked body lying on a bed of yellow leaves, a pained expression on her face, her eyes, full of deep sadness, seemingly imploring his help. Her right hand was lying at her side, while the left was indicating an etching, like an embroidery, on her stomach, a kind of Arabic pattern, beautifully crafted, embossed, with an obscure significance.

He threw himself out of bed to get rid of that vision.

The mansion was still silent. The bells of San Leonardo had only just rung Prime.

A blurred, twisted recollection of what had happened instantly flashed back to him.

Hoping to find some relief, he went out. The pelting rain and cold wind partly dissipated the effect of the opium vapors still clouding his mind. The rain had turned streets and banks into a single soft, sticky marsh. His boots sank in the mire that seemed intent on swallowing him at every step.

He wandered aimlessly, although he knew there was only one place where he could find some peace.

He found the front door of the convent of San Zaccaria shut.

Edgardo stared at it in a daze, as though expecting Costanza to appear at any moment, refreshed after a night of restorative sleep.

Why had he come back here? What was he hoping to discover?

He tried to reconstruct all the stages of that ill-fated visit: every move, timing, and precise location. He tried to organize his mind according to a design, as he had read in Aristotle's *Ars Vetus*.

If Costanza had left of her own free will and walked, he would certainly have met her, since there were no other exits on the bank of the canal. If, on the other hand, there had been a boat waiting for her, then the perspective altered: she could have taken the opposite direction and disappeared toward the open lagoon, though it was very crowded at that time, or else have gone toward San Lorenzo and slipped inland, into the maze of narrow, ramified canals where it was easy to hide.

Who would draw advantage from abducting a young girl from one of Venice's most illustrious families?

He remembered the *sandolo* with the old man and the little boy, but couldn't see that man as the abductor of a young girl.

Maybe she had left of her own free will with someone's help. He hadn't heard anybody scream or cry for help.

He tried to follow a coherent logic but his thoughts seemed to run together like dyes that ended up forming a tub of dirty water.

Along the canal, there were timber huts with thatched and reed roofs, occupied by craftsmen and those who worked in the slipways that had sprung up around the bay of the new shipyard.

He came across a few women sitting on the doorsteps, mending nets while their children amused themselves hunting large rats, then cutting them up and feeding them to the pigs.

He went up to them and asked if, the day before, they had by any chance seen a well-dressed young lady pass by on a boat

from San Zaccaria, or if they'd heard any cries for help coming
from there.

The women exchanged suspicious glances, in part also
owing to the strange appearance of that twisted, tousled creature with that evident bump on his chest, so much so that
Edgardo was forced to explain that he was a scribe, and that
he was looking for his recently vanished pupil.

One of the women said, "We hear clamoring, screaming,
and weeping every day around here . . . all we do here is yell
like lunatics—what else are we supposed to do with this
wretched life?"

The others laughed and the children joined in, rolling in the
mud. Another woman got up and rushed to her door just in
time to punch a sow before it entered the hut.

"We know nothing about any missing girls," another
woman said. "We've seen nothing."

Along the shore, at the very end of the *fondamenta*, right in
front of the grassy *campo* outside the church of San Lorenzo,
there was the only brick and Istrian marble building in the
midst of timber huts: a two-story patrician home with a large
loggia, made even more genteel with phiales, reliefs, and coats
of arms.

It occurred to Edgardo that from that loggia one could
keep an eye on the entire canal as far as the entrance to San
Zaccaria and beyond, all the way to the open lagoon.

"You know that palazzo at the end of the shore?" he asked
the women again. "Do you know who lives there?"

"Nobody," one of them replied.

"Is it empty?"

"It might as well be."

Edgardo waited for an explanation that wasn't coming.
"Doesn't it belong to anyone?" he insisted.

A skinny, toothless old woman who'd kept quiet until now,
and who had been concentrating on stroking a rabbit on her

lap, made up her mind to satisfy his curiosity. "It was Matteo Mazzolo's house—a very wealthy merchant, a real gentleman. Then, one of his convoys, poor thing, there was a tempest and he lost everything—ships, merchandise, and even his son. So he had to sell the house to pay off his debts. Then he and all his family—or what was left of it after such misfortunes—went to the Orient." The old woman stopped speaking and spat on the ground.

"And who bought it?" Edgardo asked.

"Nobody knows. They say it's a merchant from the Orient but no one ever sees him, might as well be a ghost. We often see a little man around. He goes in and out, opens up and locks up, knocks around, does something or other in there."

Edgardo looked at them attentively, then, without saying anything, walked toward the entrance to the palazzo. For a reason he couldn't fathom, the old woman's story had made him feel anxious.

The front door was bolted, as were the windows on the main floor and the loft. On the front door architrave, wedged in the wall, was a beautiful bas-relief representing Jonah being saved from the stormy sea.

Without any particular motive, he cautiously approached the grating that acted as a vent to the storerooms, and peered inside. In the moldy semi-darkness, at the end of the room, there was a well stifled by a wisteria that was climbing along the internal staircase. The doors were shut, and there was no sign of life.

A cold draft that smelled of hay edged through the gap with a sharp, unattractive-sounding hiss.

An undefined feeling, akin to revulsion, made him take a couple of steps back.

The wide stairs leading down to the canal showed no sign of any recent docking, and the poles and steps were covered in red algae and moss.

Feeling downhearted by his fruitless search, he was about to walk away when he was struck by something glimmering through the dark mass of algae. He bent down but his unreliable sight didn't allow him to make things out up close. He took the leather case he always carried with him from the bag under his tunic. He opened it with care and delicately lifted out the miracle contraption: a wooden wishbone-shaped device that widened at the tips to contain two very clear pieces of glass: the eye circles that Maestro Segrado had crafted for him, thus giving him once more a reason to live.

It was a true piece of devilry that nobody in Venice owned, and the origin of which Edgardo had kept secret, giving vague replies even to the questions of the Grimani family. Where that device had come from, and how it had come into his possession, nobody knew.

He pulled open the wishbone and placed it against his eyes. The crystal glass, which had the extraordinary power to magnify everything, immediately unveiled the mystery.

They were long, narrow, straw-colored threads of oakum, like those used for making beds for horses. Edgardo picked one up and examined it: they were fresh, not yet rotted by water. That meant they'd fallen there not long ago. He followed the path from the steps to the front gate and noticed others, abandoned here and there, on the way. So somebody had gone into the building carrying stubble. For whom or what? He hadn't seen any animals or smelled any stables from inside. He stared at one thread of stubble, which, seen through his glasses, had transformed into the memory of sun-kissed fields of wheat. He couldn't account for why this useless discovery had made such an impact on him. What did it have to do with Costanza's disappearance?

When he returned to Ca' Grimani, the house was plunged into an almost unnatural silence, as though all activities had been suspended and its inhabitants had fled in a mad rush to avoid some catastrophe. Magdalena received him in the salon. The layer of ceruse on her face was so thick, it had smoothed away all her features. Only the gold-flecked eye was radiating with a rigidly cruel life force. Nena sat by her side, looking even smaller, crushed by recent events.

Magdalena raised her head slightly and looked at the scribe. She said nothing, asked nothing, but stared at him, waiting.

Edgardo felt deeply uneasy, and wished he could be the bearer of good news. Instead, he had nothing concrete to report. "I asked the people who live by the convent. Nobody saw anything or heard any screams or cries for help," he murmured.

Even Nena didn't even deign acknowledge him with a sign. Luckily, Tommaso walked in, filling the room with renewed energy and a semblance of vitality. Magdalena mustered the strength to go and meet him.

"I spoke with the Abbess Contarini, and she sends you her blessing," Tommaso said, trying to sound reassuring. "She confirmed what the novice had said. After the meeting, Costanza expressed a wish to go pray in the San Zaccaria crypt, and the nun left her there. When she didn't see her come out, she went to fetch her but she'd disappeared. So she went to the front door, where Edgardo was waiting, and, not seeing him there, assumed they'd gone back home."

The scribe felt as though a thin, sharp blade had slid in through his ribs: Magdalena's eyes were upon him.

"I also went to the Dogado," Tommaso continued, "and reported what happened to the palace judges. They promised they'd order the gastalds to widen the search to include every district. They've assured me that they'll do all they can. The city is in a state of alert. Young boys and girls go missing more and more frequently. Only a few days ago, a young *garzone* from Amurianum disappeared. There's no news of him, it's as though he's vanished into thin air."

"Do you think the two occurrences can be linked?" Magdalena asked, devastated.

"So far, there's nothing to suggest it. I'm sure we'll soon have news of Costanza. I trust in God's mercy."

Almost as a countercheck that the prayer addressed to Our Lord had been promptly heard, one of the *garzoni* Tommaso had unleashed to search for the girl burst into the salon, evidently shaken.

"Master, master, we found something!" He stopped in the middle of the room, breathless.

"Speak."

The young man took something out of the pocket of his breeches. "Here . . . it's this string." He held out a shiny, periwinkle-blue silk ribbon.

Magdalena immediately took it from his hand and studied it carefully. She turned it over and smelled it. "Yes, it's Costanza's. I'm certain of it. She used it to tie her braid," she said, excitedly.

Finally, a ray of hope, as though that piece of cloth represented the first step to solving the mystery.

"Where did you find it?" Tommaso asked.

"In the *scaula*."

"Which one? Where?"

"Downstairs. The one tied to the steps."

"Our *scaula*?" Magdalena said.

"Yes, Signora, ours."

Hope vanished in a second. Magdalena abruptly turned away, as though to flee from the disappointment.

"It's the boat we used to take Costanza to San Zaccaria," Edgardo commented, thinking it made sense. "She could have lost it on the way there."

As though a realization had suddenly crossed his mind, Tommaso took the ribbon, walked up to Edgardo, and stuck it right up against his nose. "Try to remember: was Costanza wearing this ribbon when she got out of the boat outside the convent?"

It was hard for a clouded mind that tended to confuse dreams with reality to remember, to etch a detail in its memory. Edgardo made an effort. "I can't say for certain."

"Think carefully," Tommaso insisted, "because if Costanza lost the ribbon before leaving the boat, then finding this proves nothing." He sighed deeply and rubbed his eyes. "If, on the other hand, she was wearing the ribbon when she went into the convent, then she lost it later." He looked at his wife. "In other words, it means she got into the boat again after the meeting, once she'd left."

The time for a bell to toll, and Nena grasped where this was leading. She slammed her hand over her mouth to stifle a cry.

That same instant, Magdalena's hoarse voice boomed across the salon. "Bring Alvise here immediately!"

He was shaking without knowing why. His arms, too long, hung down his hips, his flat face was colorless, his lips pale. Nena was fussing around him, as though to form a loving shield of good intentions. What did her son have to do with Costanza's disappearance?

Tommaso and Magdalena silently examined the lanky figure that had always been a part of their home, considering for the first time that they were before a being capable of thinking and taking initiative. They felt forced to admit the possibility that even a *garzone*, and a servant's son, could have a will of his own, and perhaps evil intentions. Only Edgardo tried to give him some confidence with a helpless smile that Alvise didn't even notice.

Tommaso went on the offensive. "What did you do after you left Costanza at the convent?"

A stammer. A soft, slimy mouth like the insides of a rotting fish. "As you ordered, I went to the shipyard to give your message to the master carpenter."

"And then did you come back here?"

"No, Signore, I went fishing for gobies. This gentleman had given me permission."

"Where did you go?"

"Between Burianum and Torcellus."

Tommaso pressed him. "Did you meet anyone? Speak to anyone?"

"I didn't see anybody. Nothing but water, reeds, and sky."

Slowly, Magdalena approached, almost wrapping him in the net of her grief. "So you didn't see Costanza again after you left her at the convent?"

"No, Signora, I swear."

Edgardo looked at the boy, pleased with his answer.

"They found a hair ribbon in your boat." She waved it before Alvise's eyes. "It's Costanza's. Do you recognize it? Did she have it in her hair when you went to the convent?"

Alvise stared at his mother, lost, looking for an explanation. "I don't know anything about ribbons . . ."

Magdalena went and stood behind him. "Tell me the truth, Alvise. Have you ever spoken with Costanza? Perhaps she confided her thoughts, her intentions . . . her suffering . . ."

"Did she ask you to help her? Did she want to run away?" Tommaso asked.

Alvise opened his eyes wide, confused, unable to make a sound.

"If you saw or heard anything unusual, boy, you'd better speak out," Edgardo said, trying to encourage him.

"As God is my witness, she never told me anything, and I never saw her after I left her at the convent. The ribbon . . . I don't know . . . I can't remember . . . I swear on Saint Mark and the Blessed Virgin Mary, I know nothing about Costanza."

Magdalena seemed satisfied with his answer, turned to

Nena and gave her a nod. What Edgardo couldn't work out was Tommaso's attitude: he kept rubbing his eyes, his limbs so tense he looked about to pounce, tormented by a doubt he couldn't express. His voice was to Nena like a raft on a stormy sea. "Alright, go. Do you know what the punishment is if I find out you've lied?"

Alvise lowered his head. Nena grabbed him by the jacket and dragged him out of the room.

## VIII.
## THE MOON IN PISCES

O n the eleventh day before the calends of March, the moon came out of Aquarius and went into Pisces. As agreed, Magister Abella arrived at Ca' Grimani and Magdalena received her, even though her mind was very troubled and her pain over her sister's disappearance had dried up all desire in her.

However, she felt she could not neglect her principal duty as a wife: to procreate, notwithstanding grief, notwithstanding suffering, and provide the Grimani family with an heir.

Two nights had passed since that unhappy day, and Costanza seemed to have vanished into thin air. The search had yielded no result, and every hypothesis was still being considered: abduction, escape, accident.

When she arrived at the palazzo, Abella immediately smelled the sickly-sweet, nauseating scent of death reigning over every room. Already during her first visit, she had felt crushed by a thick cloak, a sirocco carrying ghosts and mournful events. Now, if such a thing were possible, the air had become even more unbreathable.

When she was told about what had happened, she suggested postponing the consultation, but Magdalena asked her to stay. Life had to go on and she couldn't give in to calamities. Her desire for motherhood was stronger than ever; what God takes away He always makes up for with His mercy. The birth of a new heir was her husband's principal reason for living. Therefore, every action must be taken to make this possible. Including such an embarrassing exploration.

"I've never had this kind of examination," Magdalena announced, self-conscious.

"I understand and I'm sorry to have to put you through this ordeal. However, it's essential that I investigate and check the condition of the vital organ, so that I can pronounce a verdict and, consequently, propose a remedy."

Magdalena clutched at her dress, obviously deeply uneasy.

"Let me reassure you, Signora. It's not the first time I have conducted this kind of examination. In Salerno, it's a procedure we use regularly with pregnant women and those who complain of uterine problems."

"Alright, let's proceed," said Magdalena, agreeing.

"Please have a long bench and two tall stools brought here."

Magdalena called Nena and the order was promptly obeyed.

The bench was placed by the window, and the two stools arranged with a little space between them, then Abella asked her to lie down on the bench and put her legs, spread out, on the two stools. This position allowed the physician to kneel between the patient's thighs and easily reach the entrance to the collum vaginae.

She pushed back the Flanders cloth dress, then the fine linen undergarment, and finally saw the cleft: in truth, it looked like a rather shabby area, with a faded, poor growth of tufts of hair here and there.

"Now I have to examine the internal organ, but don't be afraid, my fingers are as gentle as crocus stems and my skin as soft and slippery as the body of an eel. Moreover, I have the terrible habit of biting my nails, a fault much appreciated by my patients."

"I have total trust in you, Magister Abella, but please hurry, because this is a very uncomfortable position."

The fingers parted the sparse hair and edged their way into the cavity.

"As you may know, the unity of life is created by the marriage of four elements: fire, air, water, and earth. The human constitution can be hot, cold, dry, or humid. Women are mainly cold and humid. A body is healthy when there's a balance between the four humors, blood, phlegm, yellow bile, and black bile. If one of the humors prevails, then there's an imbalance and the organ gets sick.

"Reproduction occurs when the male sperm, emitted by the two testicles through the vasa seminalia joins the female sperm. Is my exposition clear?" Abella's voice was booming from under the dress.

Magdalena agreed with a weary sigh.

"Now," the Magister continued, "as my teacher Trotula taught me: *causa infecunditatis est aut sanguinis eruptio est rara; aut profusio est miserrima, aut multa copiosa. Aut.*" At this point, Abella raised her voice to make sure she was heard, "*si orificium est impeditum, idest nimis calidum aut nimis frigidum, aut nimis aridum.* So let's have a look . . . *Qua de causa.*"

Having said that, she pushed deeper. Magdalena gave a start. Magister Abella brought her face close to the cavity and remained breathless: she had not expected this kind of sight, and yet many had been her journeys into the female organ!

The entrance was wide and smooth, well-protected by soft, velvety folds that tempted one to explore further and discover all the wonders of this exotic place. She was immediately struck by the fresh, crisp scent she'd smelled from the outset. There was no suggestion of staleness, filth, or fish that had gone off, as she had often experienced in many other examinations. None of that. On the contrary, it was a gentle, clear breeze, an invitation for playing and enjoyment. The passage was wide, well put together, and so clean that it made one feel like setting the table there and then, and eating that manna from Heaven to your heart's content. The soft walls were dripping with honey and cider, and bunches of grapes hung here and there, as though inviting one to suck their fullness. The dominant color was a nice, bright ruby, shiny and sanguine, with dazzling, pomegranate tones. Anyone afraid of sinking into grey, pale, dull depths could draw a sigh of relief. Inside here all was joy, vitality, and a cheerful disposition.

Going further in, her fingers slipped down a slight slope coated in soft moss that led to an opening where one could easily lie down by a stream of transparent, gelatinous waters, and wander off to admire unusually-shaped, extraordinary swellings that emerged from the folds of the walls: one looked like the head of a unicorn, another like the trunk of an elephant, and yet another like the wings of a mallard.

Every so often, the patter of fluid dripping from the walls all around was joined by the gurgling of liquids coming from the depths of the cavity.

The climate was mild and healthy, perhaps a little humid. Nevertheless, it invited one to rest one's weary limbs and restore the mind in an atmosphere of true enjoyment. It was hard to imagine a more welcoming, more heavenly place for finding peace and serenity, so much so that one began considering the possibility of establishing a permanent home there.

The idyllic atmosphere was interrupted from above by a sudden, violent cascade of straw-colored liquid that flooded the cave, making the hapless visitor risk drowning in its billows.

Abella immediately rushed for the exit.

"I beg your pardon, I couldn't hold it in," Magdalena apologized, embarrassed.

"Don't worry, sometimes, the stimulus caused by a well-carried out, in-depth examination prevents the bladder from telling the difference," Abella explained. "Alright, you can now get up from this uncomfortable position."

She gave Magdalena a hand and the latter grabbed hold of

it. Her cheeks were slightly flushed and there was a mischievous twinkle in her eye.

"My dear lady, from the examination I've conducted, in keeping with the teachings of Trotula de Ruggiero, *mulier sapiens*, I can state with certainty that there is nothing in your female organ to prevent another pregnancy. There are in you none of the possible causes of barrenness," Abella announced with authority.

"Your answer fills me with confidence . . . But then how come no life is blossoming in my belly?"

Magister Abella wrapped herself in the wide scarlet robe, as though to gather her thoughts. "Numerous reasons can act negatively on the balance of humors: first of all, the stars, since there's a strong connection between the human body and the universe. Some give a lot of importance to magic and spells, but the School of Salerno has never given any credence to this tendency. There is, however, in your case, a factor we can't neglect, if we want to investigate in depth the reasons for your sterility." She approached Magdalena and dropped her voice. "If the cause isn't in the uterus, then it's possible that the fault lies in the male humor."

Magdalena seemed not to understand. "What do you mean?"

"As I've explained, reproduction takes place when the male sperm joins with the female sperm deep inside the uterus. So if there's nothing broken in the female organ . . . "

Magdalena swallowed her astonishment. Never would she have considered this possibility. "We've already had a child," she replied.

"Humors change and lose energy. Powerful grief or mourning can drain even the most resistant organs of their strength. In order to have an answer, I'd need to examine your husband's sperm."

Magdalena jumped. "Merciful God, he'll never agree to this kind of examination."

"There's no need for his consent. All you need to do is bring me a fresh sample of his humor."

Never had Magdalena found herself in such an embarrassing situation. Abella gave her a reassuring smile. She was so frank and authoritative that she managed to give a tone of domestic simplicity to even the most thorny subjects. Magdalena raised her eyebrows so high that one of her eyes seemed to travel up to her forehead. "I'd need to find a subterfuge . . . I wouldn't know how . . . "

"I'm sure your experience as a woman and your imagination will work out a suitable way."

Magdalena concealed a complicit smile with her hand.

"Women are infinitely resourceful," Abella continued. Think, just for example, of the various solutions Trotula suggested as a remedy for lost virginity: starting from alum-based astringent rinses with egg white dissolved in rain water; or introducing red grapes and animal blood into the vagina. Or else applying a leech to the vulva which, by causing a wound, will create a crust that breaks during intercourse and so bleeds. And then there's the extreme measure: putting glass powder into the vagina, that will make the vulva bleed."

"I had no idea people went to such lengths," Magdalena exclaimed, horrified.

"Don't be surprised, Signora, these are very common practices. When a woman wants to reach her goal, sooner or later she always finds a way to cheat her man . . . After all, they're naive and simple, even though they pretend to be knowing and authoritative. I'm sure that you too will find a secret way to steal a few drops of your husband's sperm."

Magdalena nodded. "Maybe you're right. I'll try."

"As soon as you have it, pour it into a flask and get it to me as soon as possible, while it's still warm."

"I will."

"Only before I complete all my examinations, make sure

you abstain from all drugs, be they mineral, animal, vegetable, or composites. No suppositories, no poultices or any other medicines, and make sure your husband doesn't take any either. That would be useless and even damaging. *Remedia antecedentia causae perniciosa sunt.*"

The pale light of day, stifled by night's dark embrace, was slowly losing its strength. Magdalena interrupted her. "You must get back quickly. It's Vespers soon, and it's dangerous to walk around alone. You heard what happened to my sister. Venice has become dangerous. Come, let me see you out."

They went down into the courtyard. Nena, who was drawing water from the well, stopped and rushed to open the front door. Abella was saying goodbye when she noticed a shadow appear behind her. She instinctively turned around and saw the tousled, crooked frame of the scribe, who was walking with his head down, muttering to himself.

"I'm sorry I frightened you," Edgardo said as soon as he noticed her.

"Not at all. I don't get frightened that easily," Abella promptly replied.

"Any news, Edgardo?" Magdalena anxiously asked.

"Unfortunately not, Signora. But I've made a promise and I will keep it. The *garzoni* have searched the canal around the convent walls. There's nothing, thank God."

Magdalena sighed. "I keep thinking about that *garzone* from Amuranium who disappeared a few days ago. There could be a link."

"Do you know where he disappeared?" Edgardo asked.

Magdalena shook her head, then turned to Abella. "It's awful. My sister seems to have vanished into thin air."

"*Substantia non vanescit.* In nature, every single thing— even when it appears to vanish—leaves a trace behind. And that's what you must look for," Abella said, like a sentence.

"And this is exactly the direction we've taken."

Edgardo couldn't bear the invasive manner of this large, peasant-looking woman who made herself out to be a scholar.

"Tell me honestly, Edgardo," Magdalena continued. "Do you think Alvise is somehow involved in Costanza's disappearance?"

Edgardo gave the stranger an assessing look.

"You may speak freely. Magister Abella is my physician. She's very discreet and I have no secrets from her."

You've misplaced your trust, Edgardo wanted to reply, but refrained from doing so. He swallowed his aversion. "Alvise is a simple soul, with no malice. I really don't think he would have done anything improper."

"Not even if driven by a feeling of affection toward the girl?" Abella butted in.

Nobody had asked for her opinion. Edgardo bit his tongue, then said, "Love, as Our Lord has taught us, leads only to honest, merciful actions."

Abella frowned. "This is a universal principle. But if you go into detail, you can clearly see from Avicenna's teachings that love acts differently according to which humor is prevalent."

"Yes, I know the theory of the four tempers: sanguine, choleric, melancholic, and phlegmatic," Edgardo replied.

"Then you'll also know that in a melancholy temper like that of young Costanza, which is obvious from her congenital pallor, the feeling of love can lead to extreme actions."

This female quack was an annoying pedant. "I'm impressed with your sagacity," Edgardo hissed. "If I'm not mistaken, you've seen Costanza only once, and yet you've managed to see into her soul more than I have, although I've known her for years."

"That's why I am the proud holder of the title of *Magistra medicarum*. Our Lord has seen fit to bless me with sharp senses."

"It's true," Magdalena intervened. "Magister Abella managed to diagnose my ailment at first sight."

"I'm pleased for you. Our Lord has been truly generous with you," Edgardo added with a venomous smile.

"I don't wish to interfere in your search."—This matron always had to have the final word—"May I humbly suggest you don't waste time investigating too much outside, but concentrate inside, and search among the people who are closest to the girl, those you trust most?"

Thoughtful, Magdalena turned to Edgardo. "Maybe Magister Abella's right. So far, all our search outside has proved totally fruitless."

There it was, the pseudo-scholar had butted in once again. Edgardo bowed his head respectfully and was about to take his leave, but Magdalena stopped him. "Wait. May I ask you a favor, Edgardo? Would you be so kind as to escort Magister Abella as far as the shore of Santa Maria Nova, from where the *sandoli* for Torcellus depart? It's getting dark and the city isn't safe."

She replied even before Edgardo had had a chance to open his mouth. "Thank you kindly for the thought, Signora, but I have no need of an escort. I'm not afraid of attackers and in any case I can look after myself." Then she stared intently at Edgardo's hump.

"I must insist. I'd be worried. Please."

Magdalena made an eloquent gesture. There was nothing to do but obey. Abella forced her lips into an empty smile, and walked away decisively, without waiting for Edgardo to precede her.

The moon, shrouded by milky vapor, barely lit their way. The first impalpable shadows were floating in the air. With a quick and assured step, Abella slipped into narrow *calli*, crossed bridges, and walked around pools and ponds, careless of the fact that Edgardo struggled to keep up with her.

"Mind the trunk." "Let's go through the *campo*, it's less muddy." "Watch out, this area isn't very safe." Abella gave strict orders, and Edgardo patiently kept quiet.

"How are you going to get back without a light?"

"I'm used to walking in the dark. My eyes have been sick for a long time. I follow my intuition and I'm usually not wrong."

"Don't trust intuition too much. Better follow reason and logic." Abella's tone grew softer, less commanding. "It can't be easy for you. A scribe with sick eyes . . . "

The conversation seemed to have taken a different turn. Edgardo decided to go along with it. "I've seen better days. When I was a copyist at Bobbio Abbey, my sight was excellent."

"How long were you a cleric at Bobbio?" Abella asked, slowing down.

"For many years. I copied Greek and Latin texts that came to the library. I've also copied medical texts by Avicenna, and those translated by Constantine the African. You must know him. He attended the School of Salerno."

"I know Constantine the African very well. He's a great scholar."

Her voice cracked and this didn't go unnoticed by Edgardo.

"Trotula, your teacher, must have certainly studied texts translated by him," he insisted.

"So how come you left Bobbio Abbey and moved to Venice?"

The sudden change in topic aroused Edgardo's suspicion, but he decided not to insist.

He'd never told anyone about his trials and tribulations. Not even Tommaso Grimani knew exactly how events had brought him to live in the city born of the waters, and the time certainly hadn't come to open his heart to a stranger. He didn't reply, just as Abella hadn't replied. They walked in silence, accompanied only by the thud of their footsteps in the mud.

By the time they'd reached Santa Maria Nova, the night had already slithered into the maze of the city. There was a *sandolo* tied to an oak, knocking against the rustling reeds. The boatman was asleep. Abella woke him up and jumped into the boat, causing it to rock frighteningly. Edgardo couldn't help remembering how light Kallis had been, that first time he'd seen her rowing Segrado's *scaula* toward Metamauco.

"It really wasn't necessary, but thank you anyway for escorting me."

Edgardo thought he detected a subtle scorn in Abella's words. Perhaps he was wrong, and had become embittered and suspicious. He bowed his head in farewell.

The boat plunged amid the threads of fog over the waters.

"On your way back, trust me, follow reason and not instinct," Abella shouted before vanishing in the darkness.

She always had to have the final word.

# IX

# AMURIANUM

Plotinus claimed that intuition represents a superior level of logical and rational knowledge, contrary to Abella's argument that it belongs to an inferior class. And his intuition, stimulated perhaps by opium vapors, was telling him not to limit himself to searching among the people closest to Costanza. On the contrary, it was prompting him to push himself further, and widen the range of his investigation. Since his reconnaissance near the convent hadn't yielded important results, except for the unexplained presence of threads of oakum, he had to look where others wouldn't be able to see: through cross-references, connections, and similarities.

Edgardo had been deeply struck by Tommaso's news of the other disappearance, that of the young man from Amurianum, that had occurred a few days earlier and had similar characteristics to that of Costanza.

Reluctantly, since the place brought back memories he would have preferred not to reawaken, he asked to be taken to the island of glassmakers, an increasing number of whom were moving their foundries there from Venice.

He hadn't been there since that time. The first time he'd set foot there, he was still wearing the habit. Over ten years had passed since then.

In Amurianum, he found the same old chaos of cogs and other freight ships moored while waiting to be loaded with beads, vases, bottles, glasses, cups, and the traditional *murrine*:

vases, dishes, and bowls coated with mosaic paste—all bound for the Rivoalto market.

Porters and *garzoni* were running in and out of foundries, carrying merchandise among a crowd of negotiating merchants, while noble ladies and gentlemen walked in and out of shops, accompanied by their servants. Here and there among the crowd flashed the shiny silks of young women with ceruse on their faces, their lips dyed with walnut root. In comparison with his first trip here, he got the impression of excessive movement, a senseless frenzy, voices, a mishmash of shouts that made up an incomprehensible language. There were a larger number of foundries, and the glare of the fires painted the banks with a demonic glow. The celestial vault, crossed by low clouds, crushed that useless swarm, stifling any hope of a life dedicated to nurturing the soul.

He made his way as far as the vintner's shop in the *campo* of the Basilica of Maria Santissima, where the men of the island would usually gather.

He asked the landlord if he knew where the missing young man's family lived. The man gave a suspicious grunt and ducked under the counter. Edgardo then explained that he'd been sent by the Grimani family to investigate a similar case, the disappearance of a young woman.

It was extraordinary how all you needed to do was mention the name of an important Venetian family to see a fierce expression turn into a toothless smile. With just a few gestures, the landlord showed him the road leading to the north of the island, where the poorest families lived.

The woman who agreed to speak with him looked eaten away by suffering. Edgardo couldn't tell if she was the boy's mother or grandmother. Her face was marked by a thicket of wrinkles that dug deep furrows, and yellowish scabs had sprung up among her sparse hair. She was surprised that noble people should take an interest in the fate of a common *garzone*.

Usually, nobody cared when one of their lot disappeared, and no investigation was carried out.

"We're just dried shit, only good for fertilizer. It's the second son I've lost, and nobody cares about us."

She told him how, on a morning like any other, Giacomo had vanished into thin air after going to work. He hadn't returned home, and nobody knew what had happened to him.

"If you want to find out more, try his master . . . "

"Can you show me where Giacomo used to work?"

"Of course. Everybody in Amurianum knows him. His name's Tataro."

The name went through his head like a knife.

"Tataro the glassmaker?" Edgardo asked, struggling to keep calm.

"Yes, that's him, the most talented glassmaker in Venice. Giacomo had been working for him as a *garzone* for two winters, he'd learned quite a lot, he could have become his assistant, but . . . "

Tataro . . . Tataro . . . The name twisted around his tongue and constricted his throat until it was difficult to breathe. He thought he'd never have to deal with that man again.

"Do you know where his foundry is?" the woman asked.

Edgardo nodded. "I know it well." Then he stood there, staring at a dark cloud that was drifting quickly across the sky.

The twelve winters since those tragic, terrible events burned away in a second, and carried him back in time.

Odd, how in just a few days, ghosts that had long been kept stifled should have all woken up at the same time: the woman found intact in the ruins of Metamauco had reawakened the memory of Kallis, and Costanza's disappearance had taken him back to that man, Tataro, who'd played such an important part in his painful story.

He thanked the woman and went toward the watchtower, next to which the glassmaker had his foundry, wondering how he'd be received: had Tataro forgotten all or was the past still an ongoing game?

He didn't expect to find him there, just as he was back then, in front of the fire, surrounded by the naked bodies of his assistants, drenched in sweat, scorched by the unbearable heat of the reverberating flames. He was blowing through the blowpipe, inflated like Aeolus himself.

Edgardo thought he looked even skinnier than before, with leather-colored skin and no lips or hair on his head or body, as though it had been burned off by a sudden gust of fire. Only his pale, liquid eyes seemed to be darting signs of life.

He approached. He thought he wouldn't recognize him. A long time had passed, and Edgardo had much altered.

After he'd finished blowing, Tataro put the blowpipe down and took a sip of water. That's when he saw him. He half-closed his eyes, and took another sip.

"My hour must have come. The ghosts have come to settle accounts with the past," he muttered in a tired voice. He'd lost the boldness and arrogance he'd once had, and there was a sad weariness in his voice. "What do you want from me, scribe? Have you come to confess your sins?"

"Only Our Lord is in a position to judge our sins."

Tataro wiped his bare chest with a dirty cloth. "My heart is weary. It doesn't have the strength to rush around after a buried past any longer."

"I haven't come here to talk to you about the past, Tataro, but about the present."

The glassmaker gave him a suspicious look.

"I know that a young man disappeared, who used to work for you—someone called Giacomo."

Tataro bowed his head and went to the door to take a breath of fresh air. Edgardo followed him.

"It's true. He was a talented boy, precise, capable, and promising."

"I'd like to know the circumstances in which he disappeared."

"Why are you so interested in him?" the glassmaker asked suspiciously.

Edgardo told him of Costanza's disappearance.

"How old was the girl?"

"Seventeen."

"Giacomo too was seventeen. He could have been my son. I was fond of him. I often dispatched him to Venice when I had to send new and particularly precious pieces to a merchant. I trusted him." The sweat was freezing on his chest. He coughed, then continued. "That day, he was supposed to meet a gentleman who'd asked to see some glass pieces, cups and dishes inlaid with gold. I watched Giacomo leave in the *scaula* at dawn from this very shore. He never came back."

"Didn't you ask the gentleman he was supposed to go see?"

"Of course. He said he'd never arrived at his house."

"What about the boat? Did it disappear with him?"

"No. It was found empty near the convent of San Zaccaria."

Edgardo smiled, pleased. Sometimes, intuition and visions triggered by opium vapors produce better results than any strict logic.

"San Zaccaria?" he asked. "Maybe Giacomo was in cahoots with that man, and made himself scarce so he could keep your pieces without paying you."

Tataro shook his head. "No, I trusted Giacomo blindly. He was an honest *garzone*. And the gentleman in question is the steward of a very wealthy merchant. He's no chicken thief."

"Could you give me this steward's name?" Edgardo asked.

"He's called Jacob Lippomano, a Jew with a goatee. He lives in the merchant's palazzo, opposite San Lorenzo."

"Very well, I'll go see him. If you don't mind."

"You can try if it's that important for you, but he's often

away traveling. The merchant he works for lives in the Orient, in Alexandria. The glass pieces were for him."

Edgardo's face lit up. He was on the right path: the *scaula* found at San Zaccaria, where Costanza had disappeared, the palazzo opposite San Lorenzo, everything seemed to revolve around that area.

"Thank you, Tataro. I hope I can bring you good news."

The glassmaker looked at him in silence. Edgardo thought he detected in his expression the cloud of unresolved resentment.

She finished applying a thick layer of ceruse. Making her face so waxen lent it a severity that instilled confidence in her. Magdalena tried to see her image in the distorted reflection projected by the panel of polished metal. She thought she noticed the outline of her eyebrows, which were growing back, breaking up the wide, rounded line of her forehead. She should pluck them, but it was very painful. She tried concealing them with an even thicker layer of rouge. Then she took a pinch of saffron powder, so rare and expensive that you had to use it sparingly, and smeared it on her cheekbones to add a breath of life to the salt mask. She needed one more touch. She picked up the walnut root and rubbed it on her lips and gums, brightening them up. Her hair, in a knotted braid, was gathered in a headdress with a turreted crown, a circular band with an appliqué of pearls and gemstones.

Through the brocade tunic, with long splits on the sides, you could glimpse a periwinkle-blue undershirt. She slipped on the ground-length dress, open on the front, with wide, fur-lined, drooping sleeves. The wooden clogs secured to her shoes with colored ribbons, the *patitos*, gave her an imposing, regal demeanor.

She looked at herself again. She was ready to go out. She called Nena, so the latter would accompany her. Although it was still daylight, a noblewoman seldom ventured through the streets of Venice without a male escort. But this was a special occasion. The mission she had to carry out could not admit prying eyes.

She used a light veil to conceal her face and, preceded by her female servant, took the least frequented route.

She managed to reach Rivoalto without anyone recognizing her. Despite her heart brimming with sorrow for her sister Costanza's fate, she could not neglect Abella's instructions.

She sent Nena ahead to the Crowned Wolf, the apothecary's shop, to check that there were no other customers.

As was habitual at certain times of the year, at that moment, Sabbatai was trading outdoors, displaying to his customers the ingredients used in the miraculous and highly-expensive medical concoction called Theriac.

Outside the entrance, various porters wearing white smocks, red breeches, and yellow shoes were pestling the substances necessary for the medicine in brass mortars, singing in unison, "Against poisons, flatulence, and other ailments, Theriac is the first remedy amid these canals."

Sabbatai's Crowned Wolf was renowned for the quality of the materials used: adder flesh, opium, liquorice, gentian, black pepper, saffron, ginger, cassia, chamomile, cardamom, acacia, chili, resins, and vegetable gums, mixed with wine and honey.

To the traditional recipe, Sabbatai would secretly add an animal-derived medicine that rendered his mixture unique and infallible: a dog testicle dissolved in billy goat blood, then boiled in snake broth.

People came from afar to acquire the famous Venetian Theriac, and Sabbatai took advantage of that.

Nena approached the apothecary. "My mistress wants to speak with you, but in secret, without anybody else around," she said pointedly.

Sabbatai's deformed mask opened up in a smile that attempted to look angelic. "I shall be very honored to receive your mistress in my humble abode, and converse with her. We'll shut the door, so no one will come in."

Nena looked around suspiciously, then went back to get her mistress, who was waiting, concealed in a portico. "The coast is clear. You can come in."

They went into the shop. The dwarf welcomed them with a ridiculous bow that, because of his disproportionately large head, nearly made him capsize. He shut the door immediately and rushed behind the counter.

"I will do all I can to fulfil your every wish, most illustrious lady."

Magdalena couldn't stop herself from turning up her nose. There was an indefinable stench in the small shop, which made her stomach churn: it reminded her of the stinking, sickly-sweet mushroom found in the woods around her home in Flanders, in the summer. Sabbatai must have noticed, because he hastened to close the door that led to his laboratorium at the back. Then he smiled again, smoothly.

"I can offer you every kind of medicine, *simplex aut compositum, minerale aut vegetale.* Or perhaps cosmetics and essences to add even more glow to your beauty?"

"None of that," Magdalena replied abruptly. "I've carelessly injured myself and the nasty wound won't heal. I therefore need a cotton wad to stop the purulent fluid that's coming out in large amounts."

Nena stretched out her neck like an inquisitive goose.

"If you will allow me, illustrious lady, even better than a wad, I have a miraculous medicine for curing wounds." Sabbatai turned to the shelves, climbed on a stool, and took out a terracotta vase. "It's an ointment made from a blend of rotted lizards and earthworms, mixed with urine, incense, rosin, turpentine, and various herbs. After being left out in the sun for three days, it's distilled and kept in a vase under manure for thirty nights." The apothecary licked his fingers. "*Est mirabilis et sopraffina per piaga purulenta.*"

"Thank you, but I only need a wad."

"As you wish, your every desire is my command. What size wad would you like?"

A flash of uncertainty forced Magdalena to glance at Nena, who was unable to help her. "Medium size . . . for quite a deep, wide wound," Magdalena said.

"Of course, of course." The apothecary started rummaging under the counter.

What yarn was the lady spinning? A wound, she said? He knew very well what women did with those wads. They'd soak them in honey and a pinch of acacia and stick them up their cunts to stop the man's sperm so their bellies wouldn't swell.

"Here it is. A nice, pure cotton wad made of medium size. Soft as a fox's fur." He placed it on the counter with an innocent smile.

"Thank you," Magdalena said nonchalantly. "Nena, put it in the purse and pay the apothecary."

"I beg your pardon," Sabbatai interrupted. "You're the wife of the illustrious nobleman Tommaso Grimani, aren't you?"

"Yes, that I am."

"Forgive me for being so forward. I heard of the disappearance of your sister Costanza, a very beautiful young lady. We are very sad and aggrieved. Every day I pray to Our Lord and to the Blessed Virgin that she may return home safe and sound." And, as he said this, Sabbatai joined his hands together and placed them before his heart.

"Yes, we're all praying for her safety," Magdalena echoed. Then she gestured at Nena.

Sabbatai ran to open the door, and the two women plunged back into the Rivoalto crowd.

"Grimani's wife is buying wads to block her uterus," Sabbatai said to himself. "How odd. It's the kind of news many would like to hear shouted by the town crier outside the Doge's Palace." His sneer, as he said this, had nothing angelic about it.

# X.
# HUMORS

ope had given way to faith. At this point, they were hoping for a miracle.

Tommaso had ordered that everybody be present at the church of San Leonardo: Edgardo, Nena, Alvise, the servants, the warehousemen, all gathered around the Grimani family to attend mass and pray to God, so that He might hear their plea and let them find Costanza alive.

During the service, Tommaso had been approached by a corpulent man Edgardo had never seen. They'd started confabbing in dropped voices. Grimani looked so upset, he seemed unable to control his legs. He'd suddenly leaned down toward Magdalena as she was kneeling and whispered something to her. Bewildered looks. Agitated gestures. A second later, the Grimani family had left the church, followed by that man, and gone back home. Edgardo scrutinized the master's face, trying to detect a sign that would shed light on what was happening.

They were all gathered in the inner courtyard. Magdalena was staring at her husband, annoyed at being treated on a par with a servant, kept in the dark until the very last.

"I've just discovered new and decisive elements concerning the disappearance of our beloved Costanza," Tommaso began.

A shudder went through Magdalena's chest.

"I've assembled you here because I want you all to know."

He signaled at the man, who approached and handed him a leather bag. Tommaso opened it and pulled out a long lock of hair tied with a thread of hemp. He held it up, then went up to his wife. "Do you recognize it?"

Magdalena brushed it gently with her fingers: it was fine, stringy, of a pale blond that looked like silver.

"Yes—" she stammered. " . . . I think it's Costanza's."

"That's right. I also recognized it. Nena, come closer. Look at it carefully."

The servant woman dragged her feet a few steps, then looked up. "I think . . . My eyes, at my age . . . " she mumbled.

"Is it Costanza's, yes or no?" Tommaso boomed.

Nena nodded. "Yes, yes."

"Where did you find it?" Magdalena asked.

"While we were all at mass, I gave the order to a person I trust," he indicated the man, "to search the whole building for a sign or a clue. He found this lock of hair."

"Where?" Magdalena prodded.

Tommaso looked up to the sky, as though to find inspiration. "In Alvise's room." Then he turned his head toward the servant boy with deliberate slowness, like a long, nauseating wave advancing inevitably toward the line of the horizon.

"It's not true!" Nena cried out on impulse, but no one listened to her.

"Did you find anything else of interest in the boy's room?" Tommaso asked the man.

"Stuff of no consequence: fishing threads, bird beaks, nets, glass beads, rosary beads."

"Alvise, I want an explanation." Tommaso uttered the words with unnatural calm.

It was the second time Alvise had been accused. Edgardo saw in his face the expression of a hunted animal.

The servant boy swallowed the excess saliva generated by fear, then, in a barely audible, broken voice, said, "She gave it to me."

"Costanza? Costanza gave it to you? That's ridiculous," Magdalena burst out. "Why would she do that?"

"I don't know. She said it was a little gift, because we were friends."

"Friends!" Magdalena screamed. "What are you saying? How could you be friends?" Her lips suddenly contracted with suspicion. "You've been meeting alone. Where? When?"

Alvise was more and more confused, feeling surrounded. "In the bed of reeds at the back of the house . . . sometimes."

"Then why did you lie that first time, when you said you didn't meet with her?" Tommaso intervened.

The young man gave his mother a look of despair, seeking an answer. "I don't know . . . I hadn't understood . . . sometimes she'd just go there."

Nena had started to cry.

"And what did you do there?" Tommaso's voice had grown ever deeper.

"We'd chat."

"Chat? You and Costanza? What about? That's impossible." Magdalena had tensed up, offended by the notion of that contact.

With a slow, implacable movement, Grimani approached the boy, ready to crush him with the full weight of his authority.

"We've welcomed you into this house like a son." Tommaso had a paternal tone. "Tell me the truth, Alvise. I don't believe Costanza would have given you a lock of her hair . . . That's something lovers do . . . "

"It's you!" Magdalena screamed, beside herself. "Did you abduct her? Where are you hiding her? Speak!"

Everything was going very, very fast. Edgardo tried to understand what logic was prompting the mistress to this conclusion, other than an obtuse desire to find a thread of hope.

"No, Signora," Alvise whimpered, "it wasn't me, I swear it."

Nobody dared raise objections, and Magdalena's accusation

was almost welcomed with relief by the other servants, who, this way, saw the shadow of suspicion diverted from them.

"If you've hurt her I'll scratch your eyes out," Magdalena threatened.

The boy was shaking his head violently, like a bull led to slaughter.

"It wasn't him, Signora, he's incapable of doing anyone any harm, he's a good, a sensible boy . . . "

Weeping, Nena grabbed Magdalena's dress, but her mistress pushed her away with a jerk of the arm and walked up to Alvise.

"Speak, you animal, what have you done with her!" she screamed.

The young man's head was a complete muddle of words and thoughts at odds with one another: he couldn't understand what they wanted from him or what was happening.

They were dragging him into their nightmares and obsessions, ready to sacrifice him just so they could find an explanation.

"If I may speak," Edgardo's calm, deep tone managed to restore a glimpse of light into the diseased shadow that had fallen over them. "Emotions tend to run away too fast and overtake the mind. May I please ask everyone: let's not get too ahead of ourselves but remain anchored in reality as it is, and not allow ourselves to be cheated by appearances." His own words surprised him, seeing how he was guilty of living by dreams. "So far we don't have any definite information about Costanza's disappearance, and none of us have lost the hope of finding her safe and sound. That is why we must still concentrate our efforts on the search." He went up to the boy, almost as though trying to suggest a way out. "That which now casts a shadow of suspicion on this *garzone* is but a vague, imperfect clue that can lead us to the wrong conclusions. We have no proof that he's abducted her. He says the hair was a gift. From what I've seen of him all these years, I am inclined to believe him and trust him." Edgardo turned to Tommaso. "I beg you, Signore, let's take the time to carry on investigating and searching."

"With every night that goes by I see my hope drain away." Magdalena's voice was broken. "If Alvise was involved and would talk, we could save her."

"Even at the cost of making him confess to something he hasn't committed?" Edgardo remembered his father, who, although a hard, inflexible man, had passed onto his sons a deep sense of justice.

Nena dropped to her knees before the master. "I beg you, Signore."

Tommaso started rubbing his eyes. A sign that he was torn by conflicting thoughts. He slapped his chest, as though trying to remind everybody how big and generous his heart was. "In consideration of the long time you've been at the service of this household and of the love we have for your mother, we'll examine the suggestion to take time and carry on the search. However, if we don't get definite news soon, we'll take the only possible way and report you to the gastald." Tommaso gave Alvise a stare full of pain. "Remember, boy, that you still have time to save your soul. Our Lord forgives those who mend their ways."

A man's magnanimity reveals itself when life's accidents become more distressing, Edgardo thought.

Annoyed by her husband's decision, Magdalena stiffened and pursed her lips in a sour grimace; she was not allowed to contradict him, and knew she had to accept that act of generosity as a sign of the greatness of their family.

Edgardo smiled, proud to be in the service of a man of noble, equanimous spirit. Justice had to take its course, and the culprit would be punished. Tommaso would wait, then strike ruthlessly. The only way to exonerate Alvise was to find Costanza as soon as possible.

The naked body, lying on the bed, wrapped in the fur blanket, reminded Magdalena of an old, lifeless seal, tossed by the waves, that she'd seen as a little girl on the beach in Bruges.

Her husband, however, was alive, breathing in his sleep, absorbing into his powerful chest the malevolent humors that seemed to have taken possession of the household.

There was a wreath of bad luck on her head. She'd got married in mourning and heartache. But she wouldn't give in. Women from Nordic countries are made of ice and rock. She would find her sister and give her husband an heir.

She undressed. Her barren nudity revolted her.

She took the wad she'd purchased from the apothecary out of the chest where she'd hidden it.

Tommaso was sound asleep, so wouldn't notice anything. She brought the stool close to the oil lamp and sat on it. She thrust her pelvis forward and spread her legs as far apart as she could.

She wasn't sure the subterfuge would work and was also afraid her husband would notice the presence of a foreign body inside her. But there was no other way.

She folded the wad, which she'd softened with a little honey, and gently inserted it into her vagina. Not too deep, for fear of not being able to take it out again. She closed her legs and tried getting up. She felt slightly off-balance, and a kind of nausea.

She joined her husband under the marten fur blanket, and the wild animal smell grabbed her by the throat. She'd never been able to work out if it was the fur or Tommaso's skin.

During the early years of their marriage, his body smelled of sea water and rigging, then, ever since he'd stopped spending the long summer months at sea, his scent had changed, and become more akin to soil and wilderness. Or perhaps it was Luca's death that had made his hips heavier, and left the stench of pain in the folds of his body.

She reached out to his penis and began stroking it, bringing back to memory the days of her youth, when she used to run across fields of tall grass, during the brief springs of Bruges.

When his cock stiffened, Tommaso rolled onto his back, panting, his mind clouded over: had the demon of lust come to visit him in a dream, or was it a real sensation? He half opened his eyes and glimpsed Magdalena's luminous face as she bent over him, her small, pale breasts brushing against his chest.

"Sleep, don't think of anything, close your eyes," Magdalena whispered.

Tommaso groaned, wishing he could take his body back and free his mind from the spell. A layer of sticky pitch stopped him from moving, and sleep was dragging him into the abyss.

"Abandon yourself to me, let me cradle you," she said.

Tommaso grunted. Magdalena climbed on his belly, opened her legs, and with a decisive move that surprised even her, slid his penis into her vulva. She felt him pushing against the wad pressed inside her. Tommaso let out a moan. Magdalena smiled with satisfaction. He'd noticed nothing. He was in her power.

She started rocking, gently at first, drowning that alien flesh in the stringy humors generated by her belly. It was a new sensation, one of omnipotence, as though she was swimming deep in the sea without needing to breathe.

Then the movement became more intense, a succession of foamy waves crashing against the cliffs.

She looked at him, stunned: who was this man, lying beneath her, a being that was now lost, drifting through inaccessible waters?

Only she, wife, mother, woman, was firmly anchored to the earth.

She struck deeper into her guts, without pity. She had all the power to conduct the game as she pleased.

"Don't resist, forget, it's just a dream."

One final, deep, decisive push, and a bolt of lightning pierced her mind. A cold, bright light tore through her soul. She felt her body come apart, her bones shatter, her flesh yield to a never-before tasted intoxication. It was the first time in her marriage that she had felt such ecstasy.

Tommaso gave a start, curled up, gave a deep wheeze, like the agony of a slaughtered pig, and emptied his scrotum, filling her vagina.

Magdalena broke away from him immediately, trying to plug the entrance to her vagina with her hand. Then she rushed to the little privy, crouched over the pot and, very delicately, took out the wad.

As she had expected, it was completely soaked in Tommaso's sperm. She took the glass bottle she'd prepared and wrung the piece of cotton. One by one, the pearly, stringy drops landed at the bottom of the receptacle. She managed to collect a large quantity, much more than she'd anticipated.

A triumphant light flashed in her eyes. Women always find a way. Now all she had to do was deliver the precious substance to Abella, and wait for the outcome.

E dgardo just couldn't believe that Alvise was guilty.
Picturing him as an abductor, a murderer, a rapist of
young girls was a stretch of the imagination. True, he'd
lied, probably carried away by ignorance and fear, and now he
was at the edge of the precipice.

Although everyone was pushing him toward the abyss,
Edgardo wanted to prove his innocence.

He made an effort to analyze the results of his research and
was sorry to discover that he possessed nothing tangible.
Costanza's and Tataro's servant's disappearance might not be
connected. The only element in common was the vague coincidence of the location: the canal around San Zaccaria, where
she'd been abducted, and where the young man's abandoned
boat had been found. Perhaps he would discover more if he
spoke to the Jewish steward the *garzone* had been going to
meet in order to show him the glass pieces.

He was just about to leave Ca' Grimani when Nena came to
say that the Signora wished to see him immediately. What
could Magdalena possibly want from him? She'd never used
his services, considering him as an immediate employee of her
husband and, ultimately, Costanza's tutor. And now, after what
had happened . . .

"I must ask a favor, Edgardo." This time, he sensed a
crack in Magdalena's usually icy tone. "It's of paramount
importance that Magister Abella get this bottle in Torcellus as
soon as possible." She showed him a receptacle made of

opaque green glass. "I would be most grateful if you took it to her."

Edgardo couldn't conceal an expression of astonishment.

"I realize this task is not part of your duties but, in the circumstances, I don't feel it would be appropriate to ask Nena, so I'm forced to ask you to do this, as a favor. The bottle must reach Abella as soon as possible, perfectly preserved." She paused for a second. "You're the only one in this house who can guarantee me the necessary discretion . . . I'd rather nobody knew you're doing this."

She underlined the word "nobody," implying that the "nobody" included her husband Tommaso. Edgardo was highly surprised by this request: Magdalena had never considered him as her ally, and now she was asking him to share a secret that excluded Tommaso, his benefactor. What did the bottle contain? He wanted nothing to do with that quack's trafficking.

However, he was certainly in no position to refuse, so he lowered his head in obedience and took the bottle.

At times, he had the impression that Magdalena forgot her suffering at her sister's disappearance, and became absorbed by other thoughts. So he felt it his duty to remind her cunningly. "I was about to follow a lead to gather more information on Costanza's disappearance. I'll go to Torcellus as you ask, then, on my way back, I'll carry out my mission."

Magdalena stared at him, offended: how dare he remind her of her pain! "Costanza is always in my thoughts. Not a moment goes by that I don't pray to God for her safety."

The subtle crease in her lips expressed all her annoyance.

His last journey through the senseless labyrinth of the islands in the north of the lagoon had been with Kallis, over ten years earlier. The only sailor aboard his miserable *scaula*, Edgardo advanced slowly, pushing his boat with heavy strokes of the oar on the leaden surface of flat, slimy waters, amid shoals, fords, small islands, fishing pools and enclosures.

He'd left the Rivus Altus, going along the long canal that connected it to the shipyard, then turning toward the open marsh, in the direction of Amurianum.

The deeper he ventured into the industrious islands surrounding the Silis estuary, the more he felt he was penetrating an unknown, wonderful world suspended between heaven and earth. The vivid natural colors dissolved into magical reflections that transformed the landscape into an otherworldly vision that gave the inhabitants the illusion they belonged to a divine dream.

Through the threads of pale blue fog, he suddenly thought he saw Kallis, evanescent, regal, an amber-colored thread of wool pushing her *scaula* on the surface of the water with determined strokes of the oar. A ravenous longing devoured his heart.

He shouldn't have come back to these islands. And yet these places, so heavy with a painful past, still managed to give him an unexplainable sense of calm, a luminosity of the soul he couldn't find anywhere else.

The city rising around Rivoalto looked so alien to him, crisscrossed as it was by passions and desires, longings for power and wealth that did not belong to him, while one could breathe the grace of God amid these strips of land.

Leaving Amurianum behind him, he entered the throbbing heart of the islands, Majurbium, Burianum, Costanciacum, Aymanas, and Torcellus, which, according to legend, derived its name from a door of the ancient city of Altinum, on the mainland, when, following an invasion by the Lombards, its inhabitants abandoned it and fled to the sea.

He immediately noticed how much the landscape had altered since his last trip. New monasteries and churches had been erected everywhere, in an even higher number than in the past.

Towers, belfries, and crosses seemed to rise out of nothing through the mist. A dense forest of offerings to the glory of Our Lord.

It was Terce, and the tolling of the bells was like an echo that seemed to be repeated ad infinitum. He felt that the to-ing and fro-ing of boats, trade, and exchanges he'd seen blossom so much in the past had given way to spirituality and prayer. As though the Venetian people had wished to move the heart of productive, political, and commercial life to Rivoalto, and leave the islands in the lagoon only to religious life.

The barges still crossed natural and artificial canals, but they no longer carried merchandise, timber, and animals, but rather salt and crops produced from the countless vegetable patches scattered all over the islands.

Approaching Torcellus, he was surprised to see a group of workmen taking apart the remains of an ancient crumbled church. Up to their hips in water, they were loading onto a barge all the salvageable material: precious marble slabs, blocks of Istrian marble, bricks, wooden beams, and pieces of mosaic that could be re-used for new buildings in Venice.

In recent years, the water level had constantly risen, flooding land that was once totally above water, making some places of worship unusable and forcing the monks to abandon them. Extensive works had been launched to counter the invasion of the tides: embankments, dams, *fondamenta*. Even so, many seemingly unassailable small islands had been submerged, swallowed by the mud of the lagoon.

He reached Torcello via the large upper canal that ran at the back of the basilica of Santa Maria Assunta, the most direct route to Altinum, on the mainland.

He tied the *scaula* to a branch of a fig tree and made his way to the main square, walking around the watchtower that had been turned into a belfry. Outside Santa Fosca, many craftsmen were exhibiting their work: objects made of horn, bronze buckles, glass pieces very similar to the ones he'd seen at Tataro's foundry. All the items had been manufactured on the island.

Blending in with the crowd, he made out various foreigners, Saracens and especially Africans. This mix of races was however but a memory of the *emporion mega*, as Constantine VII, emperor of Constantinople, had called Torcellus two centuries earlier. The island could obviously no longer compete with the new commercial center in Rivoalto or with the docks at San Marco.

Outside the baptistery, once a hot spring with running water that poured out of the mouths of gargoyles, he asked a woman if she could point him toward Magister Abella's house.

"Who? The witch? She's by San Giovanni Evangelista," she replied, hesitating, then indicated a path running alongside a canal.

Not the least reassured by that description, Edgardo walked along the Torcellus canal. The houses there looked tidier, more even than those in Venice: they looked out onto the canal on one side, and onto a courtyard equipped with a well on the other. They were timber buildings, two stories high, with four doors: on the ground floor the storerooms and hearth, built from clay; on the upper floor the family rooms. There were vegetable patches in the gaps between the houses.

All around, there was a large number of monasteries and churches. Edgardo had counted seven. The surrounding fords were covered in dense woods with oaks, alders, and cypresses. There was an atmosphere of peace, and Edgardo thought that perhaps, someday, he could live here, serene, removed from the tribulations life had dealt him until now.

He went past the ancient church of Sant'Andrea and the Benedictine monastery of Santa Margherita, walked over two narrow canals across swaying planks, and finally reached a large island where rose up the Benedictine monastery of San Giovanni, the oldest in the lagoon, founded in 640. The surrounding fields were cultivated as vegetable patches, and there were long rows of vineyards extending as far as the lagoon.

Behind the monastery, there was a small cluster of huts inhabited by fishermen and men working in the salt pans nearby.

Edgardo couldn't imagine Abella living in one of those humble abodes. Then, on a small island, separated from the monastery by just a narrow canal, he noticed an unusual, eccentric looking building. The front part, made of brick, one story high, was nestled in a round block of white Istrian marble with a domed roof.

He cautiously approached. It looked uninhabited. Several times, he tried to call out. Nobody answered.

He was thirsty, his back was aching, and his mind seemed sucked into a vortex of chaotic drunkenness. His nerves were frayed for no reason. He sat under an oak tree to regain strength. His eyelids felt heavy and his limbs felt strangely numb.

He was about to give in to sleep when he heard a rustle coming from the reeds, followed by a kind of dirge or lament. Behind the building, he saw an indefinable figure, half woman and half forest demon, with a thick bush of tousled curly hair, like an eagle's nest, and soft, bare, rosy arms. She wore a short dress, low cut, that didn't conceal her soft, large bosom, and a large, perfectly round behind that seemed to immortalize every prophetic vision of a garden of delights.

Around her neck, almost breaking any illusion of a celestial vision, hung two shreds of shiny, bleeding meat, which Edgardo couldn't identify at first. When the creature drew closer, he was able to solve both riddles at once: the face belonged to Magister Abella, unrecognizable without her physician's headdress and outfit, and the shreds of meat were two skinned rabbits, on show like an ermine stole.

Abella stopped, surprised to see the scribe who looked like a hermit prey to the temptations of Saint Anthony the Abbot in the Thebaid desert.

She welcomed him in her usual, hospitable tone. "You look dreadful!"

"Madonna Magdalena Grimani has charged me with delivering you a bottle," Edgardo said, coming straight to the point and taking the precious relic out of his bag.

"I didn't think you'd come all the way here just for the pleasure of meeting me." Abella took the bottle. "Can I restore you to life with a glass of wine and some rye bread? Or would you like to go back immediately and face certain death?"

The Magister flung open her door and went in without waiting for an answer. Although he didn't want to give in to her, Edgardo felt too weak, so he followed her inside.

The only room, bare and without adornments, contained what was necessary for survival: a fire, a table, and a bed.

With a graceful gesture, Abella took off the rabbit necklace and hung it on a hook, then took a jug and some bread and slammed them on the table.

Despite her confident, masculine gestures, the pink folds in her flesh, her full lips, and all her bulges oozed a femininity Edgardo couldn't help but be overwhelmed by. Her body smelled of warm milk, freshly drawn, frothy, sweet, with a slight aftertaste of aromatic herbs from the Alps.

"I must return to Venice right away, but thank you for your hospitality." Edgardo sat at the table.

"The obligation to treat the dying is part of the physician's oath."

Edgardo smiled. His tormented, emaciated appearance had become his daily outfit since he'd lost Kallis. "I knew better times when I was a cleric," he said in self-justification.

"I'm sure you did." Abella poured two glasses of wine. "The nuns make it. It's excellent," she said, drinking hers in a single gulp. She looked more like a hunter than a physician. "What happened to make you abandon the habit?"

Such a direct question made him suspicious. "Painful events which I do not wish to recall."

"And don't you have any more friends among the monks?"

Why was she so curious? Edgardo finished his wine and stood up, swaying. "I really must go."

"Why such a rush to go back to Ca' Grimani? Does your master keep you on a leash?"

"My only master is my conscience. I promised I'd find Costanza. I feel responsible for her disappearance."

"You harbor the illusion that after so many days she's still alive?" Abella wet her lips to collect the last traces of wine.

"I hope so. Alvise is in serious danger."

"You really believe that boy is innocent?" Abella's tone was almost scornful.

He wanted to answer yes, but a sudden weakness wound around his tongue, wrapped around his throat, and went down to his legs. He felt his head come apart from his body, and his ass sink into the void. A blanket of pitch blurred his vision.

When he came to, the first thing he knew was the pungent scent of mandrake and henbane, herbs the apothecary often mixed with opium in order to make the concoction even more powerful.

He tried to open his eyes, which felt coated in birdlime. After several attempts, he finally succeeded. He then realized that he was horizontal, lying on a slab of cold, shiny stone. Above him, the sky was torn by a ray of blinding light that illuminated the thousand-colored feathers of a huge peacock as it flew out of a stormy sea. The bright plumage and cheerful look of the bird that stared at him from above for a few seconds made him think he'd abandoned the world of the living and ended up in paradise.

"You're awake, finally."

That voice called him back to reality.

He was no longer in the room where Abella had received him. It was a totally different place. There was a high ceiling with a circular opening at the top, from whence came a beam of light. The surrounding walls were slightly curved, made of light-colored stone, with narrow slits, most of which were decorated with brightly colored drawings. They represented scenes of hunting in the lagoon: a boat carrying men armed with bows they were pointing at birds with colorful plumage. A boar was peering out of the bushes.

Only then did he realize that the appearance of that miraculous peacock was a painting in the vault, and the discovery made him feel devastated.

"Take a deep breath." Edgardo recognized Abella's voice and saw her hand bring a soaked sponge to his nose.

"What happened?" he stammered.

"Your humors lost their balance and you passed out. The phlegm has given way to black bile. Go on, take a deep breath."

Edgardo obeyed, and the healing vapors invaded his brain.

"You use opium, don't you?"

Edgardo said nothing.

"When the body is impregnated with a stimulant substance, it can no longer go on without it except by triggering a serious imbalance. I didn't have any opium but I've compensated with other similar herbs."

Edgardo tried to get up.

Abella stopped him. "Lie there for a while longer."

Only then did he realize that he was naked from the waist up. His left arm, dangling at his side, had a cut that was still dripping with blood.

"I bled you: you have the frothy, purple blood typical of drug users." Abella gave him a strict look, then leaned over him. "And you've been carrying around this pretty excrescence since birth, have you?" she said, examining the bump on his chest with a professorial air.

"Yes, but it's gotten worse in the past few years, and turned purulent. Our Lord decided to brand me for reasons He hasn't yet given me the grace to reveal."

"May I?" Magister Abella examined it. It was shaped like an enormous tick, stuck to the chest right over the sternum. It was covered on the outside with a callous mass, with dark hair here and there, streaked with deep, narrow cracks that gave off a nauseating smell. It was purple, with gray tones, and flabby to the touch. Abella tried prodding it on the side: the fleshy inflorescence bobbed about, letting out a thick, yellow humor like congealed mucus.

"Interesting. I've never seen anything like this," she said. "It doesn't seem rooted to the bone. It's independent and has a life of its own that doesn't interfere with other internal organs. Does it hurt if I press?"

"No, it's as though it belonged to someone else."

"Just as I thought." Abella's face was leaning so close to him that Edgardo could smell the milky fragrance of her skin. For a moment, he was carried away by the memory of sensations he thought he'd lost.

"I don't want to mislead you, but I think I can safely assure you that, if you so wished, this foul leech that sucks your lymph and your energy could be removed."

Edgardo looked at her in disbelief.

"The School of Salerno was the first to recognize and practice the art of surgery, taking it away from charlatans and barbers who operate without any knowledge, often causing patients irrevocable damage."

"So you think this gift from God could be removed?" Edgardo stroked his bump like the head of a loyal dog.

"We possess the knowledge and experience, even though I

confess I've never performed this kind of operation before. A tumor of this size," she felt the protuberance, "is something new for me too."

Edgardo bent to the side and slid to the floor.

He saw strange tools hanging on the walls: scales, straps, scalpels, pointers, tweezers, scissors, saws, needles, syringes, and, on the shelves, earthenware vases with various writings on them.

"I'll think about it," he said, far from comforted by what he saw. "You live in an odd place."

Abella looked around with a naive expression. "It was once a tomb, perhaps of some Roman tribune. There were quite a few on this island. The fishermen added a room at the front of the building. I turned this space into my *studium*. They say Santa Maria Assunta was once a military facility, and that Santa Fosca too was a funereal monument."

"I must go now. There's a Jewish steward in San Lorenzo who could give me valuable information. I've wasted enough time already." Edgardo took a step but swayed, almost losing his balance.

Abella held him up. "Wait." He felt her full breasts press against his arm. "You'll never be able to row as far as San Lorenzo. You're still very weak."

"Thank you, but I think I can manage." Edgardo walked to the exit and collided with the table in the front room.

"Don't stand up. I'll come with you," Abella said and, without waiting for a reply, took him under the arm, almost lifting him bodily.

First the offer of removing his hump, and now she even suggested accompanying him. Edgardo couldn't account for this sudden change in attitude on Abella's part. What was her aim? Was she hoping that the operation would rid her of him or was it just pity for a poor cripple?

## XII.

## JUDEUS

It was like flying over the water. His mind, still numb, was swaying between dream and reality. More than once, instead of Abella, he thought he saw Kallis's threadlike form at the oar. Rather than nourishment, love had turned into a devastating disease. He had to get rid of her, erase her from his heart.

He was so wrapped up in thought, he didn't notice that they'd reached San Lorenzo. They left the boat by the steps leading to the palazzo of the merchant from the East.

"What do you intend to do?' Abella asked, trying to make him see reason.

"I want to question the steward of the owner of this palazzo. He'll certainly remember the servant boy Tataro sent him with the merchandise. He disappeared on his way to him."

"And what if that was the case?" Abella said. "May I remind you that it's Costanza you're looking for. I can't see the link between these two events."

Edgardo stared at her, impatient. "Look, I didn't ask you to come here with me. I am, however, very grateful to you. Now you can go back to Torcellus. You must have patients waiting."

"None of my patients is worse off than you are," Abella replied, getting out of the boat.

They went to the front door. It was shut, as were all the blinds.

Without affording her so much as a look, Edgardo started knocking. They waited in vain.

"There's nobody here. Let's go. I'll take you back to Ca' Grimani." Abella took Edgardo by the arm and tried to drag him away.

"He's out. He'll be back," he stated confidently.

Abella snorted. "What makes you think he will?"

"An impression, a feeling . . . "

"You're damned stubborn." Abella was losing her temper. "You'll never get anywhere this way. You must follow logic in your actions. No doubt you're familiar with Aristotle's Topics, with the commentary of the great philosopher Avicenna. Well, you should follow the reasoning of syllogism: there's a principal premise, a secondary one, and a conclusion. You, on the other hand, are talking nonsense."

"I'm following my intuition. I imagine you've read Plotinus . . . "

"This isn't intuition! You're scrambling in the dark like a blind man!" Abella sounded aggravated.

"You could well be right. Even so, I'll use these leftovers," Edgardo pointed at his ailing eyes, "to take a look around."

"What are you hoping to find?"

"Don't you understand yet? Giacomo, the servant boy, goes to meet the steward of an Eastern merchant, and vanishes into thin air. And where does this steward live? Just a few steps away from where Costanza disappeared. Moreover, Giacomo's *scaula* is found nearby, outside San Lorenzo. Everything revolves around this building, it can't be a coincidence . . . Don't you think?"

Abella hadn't followed much of what he'd said, but still she had to admit that there was a certain series of unexplainable coincidences. "You mean that Costanza's disappearance, as well as the *garzone*'s, revolves around the palazzo of this hypothetical Oriental merchant whom no one has ever seen?"

"You said it."

"But why should a merchant abduct young people?"

"That's something I haven't worked out yet. Perhaps to sell them as slaves in some country in the East. It's a thriving market."

"Yes, but what could be the connection between Costanza and the servant boy? They're so different. Besides, why pick a girl from a noble family when there are so many servants' daughters in the city? It's much riskier."

The succession of questions was making Edgardo nervous and insecure. "That's what we must find out."

Abella smiled, pleased with herself. "Did you say we?"

"Look." Edgardo was leaning over the canal. "You see those windows, on the mezzanine floor, that open onto the water? They have no shutters. We can look inside through them. Quick, we can reach them by boat."

Abella went along, not very convinced.

They came under the openings, which were barred with iron gratings. Because the water level was low, you had to grab hold of them and lift yourself up to them.

Edgardo looked at the Magister's build, which was much sturdier than his own. "If you support me, I can reach the grating."

"Do you expect me to lift you in my arms?" Abella said, irritated.

"If you don't mind. I'm sure you've done worse in your capacity as a physician."

Abella grumbled something about the duties of a scholar, then opened her arms. "I warn you, I'll have to put my arms around you."

"I'll close my eyes."

The Magister came forward like a wrestler about to crush a bull, but when her arms enfolded Edgardo's body, he felt as though he was being wrapped in a warm, soft cloak, stuffed with chicken feathers and scented with lavender. She lifted him with apparent effortlessness.

"Is this alright? What can you see?'

Edgardo clung to the gratings. "It's dark . . . Wait." He tried to focus, but his shaky vision couldn't make out shapes. "It all seems empty."

"No chained young maiden?"

"It looks like there are some kind of chests at the back . . . "

"Hurry up. I can't hold you up for much longer."

"Just a moment . . . one of them is partly open, and there's something shiny inside. Unfortunately, my eyes . . . "

"The devil be damned . . . I can't hold you up anymore," Abella hissed.

The scribe's body slipped out of her arms and landed in the boat, making it rock violently.

"So what did you see?' Abella asked, panting.

Edgardo looked disappointed. "I don't know. I didn't have time to see exactly. It was shining. Perhaps it was a blade . . . weapons . . . "

"Doesn't sound like an amazing discovery to me." Abella caught her breath. "Can we go now?"

Digging his fingers into his tousled hair, his cerulean-blue eyes staring into space, Edgardo was desperately trying to give all the elements a meaning.

The boat traveled down the canal until it reached the side entrance of the palazzo.

"Stop," he suddenly said. And, with a surprising leap, he got out of the boat and onto the steps.

Abella watched him bend down and take a closer look, pinching with his fingers the steps that were shiny with algae, as though searching for molluscs, then suddenly get up and raise his arms to the sky, lit up by a childlike smile.

"*Mentis lumen!*" he cried out. "I understand everything. Do you know what that chest contains? Glass, drinking cups, bottles."

"What makes you so sure?"

"After Costanza disappeared, I came to search for clues around the convent. And right in front of this building I find tiny specks of straw like the ones they use in stables, and I couldn't work out why, since there were no animals inside. These specks of straw are also used to protect glass and crockery during transportation. It's therefore obvious that the reflection from that chest must be caused by the glass."

It was the first time she'd heard him put forward a theory that was, if not entirely logical, then at least sensible. Abella nodded. "Perhaps . . . So?"

"Are you never happy, woman?!" Edgardo exclaimed. "It's proof. Tataro's servant was supposed to deliver glass, his boat was found nearby, and the glass is inside the building: obviously, the boy had dealings with these people. Whether he is now alive or dead, I couldn't say, but—" he stopped. "Look! That must be him," he suddenly said. "It's Lippomano. You see? He came back."

A short, stout man was approaching the palazzo. He had a goatee and a round skullcap. He was skipping like a lame cat.

Whistling merrily, he stopped at the front door. He was carrying a full sack over his shoulder.

"Didn't you want to talk with him? This is the time to do it."

"You're right." Edgardo went toward the Jew.

"I beg your pardon, sir, if I dare bother you." He gave a half bow.

"How can I help you?" Lippomano's voice was sing-song, and matched his chubby face and lively eyes perfectly.

The scribe was about to embark on the full story about the disappearing *garzone*, ready to see his reaction, when his eyes accidentally drifted to the sack. You could clearly see that it contained fine fabrics embroidered with pearls and gems, like those used to make women's dresses.

"I'm lost, signore. I need to get to Rivoalto. Could you show me the way?"

"It's very easy." Lippomano began a long, tortuous explanation, which allowed Edgardo time to examine the bundle with his eyes. It was obvious that these were very expensive women's clothes.

"You're very kind. My deepest thanks."

Lippomano inserted a heavy key in the lock and opened a gap just wide enough to sneak inside.

"It all makes sense. Intuition drinks from divine light," Edgardo said as soon as he'd joined Abella in the boat. "There's no more doubt now."

The Magister snorted. She couldn't bear to have to follow this dreamer's improbable cogitations.

"We have evidence that Costanza is being kept a prisoner in the merchant's palazzo."

"What evidence?"

"The man was carrying a sack of women's clothes."

"So? They could be for anyone—his wife, his daughter."

"The building is always locked, the windows shut. He has no family."

"And you think a jailer's primary concern is to supply his prisoner with luxury clothes?"

"Of course, if she is to be sold to an Arab prince as a concubine."

"Enough, I'm not following anymore." Abella pushed the *scaula* to the middle of the canal and began rowing. "I've already wasted enough of my precious time on you. I'm a physician. I have patients who require my presence."

"Then I will leave you to your patients, and never was it more appropriate to say that you truly need to be patient to put up with you."

"You have the grace of an elephant!" Abella hissed.

She was arrogant and acerbic, but one had to admit that,

dressed up to the nines, with the scarlet robe and the head-dress, she commanded respect and awe.

It was that very robe and imposing build that gave him the idea. Edgardo pretended to think aloud. "We must find a way of getting inside the palazzo."

"You said we again."

"Yes, because now I need your illustrious persona to succeed in my enterprise," he said, trying to flatter her.

"You're crazy. I've already told you, I want nothing to do with your fantasies," Abella replied.

"I can't show myself. Lippomano has seen me. I have a plan, but I could never get inside that house without your help."

"I'm not your assistant," Abella replied.

"Do you want to let Costanza die? It'll be on your conscience both as a physician and as a Christian."

Abella grumbled something to herself in incomprehensible Latin.

"Listen, it's very simple," Edgardo began, then outlined his strategy.

"A very cunning plan." Abella's face stretched into a smile heavy with mockery. "My role is very clear, but I can't quite understand yours."

"I'll be by your side."

"Then you must come up with a disguise."

Edgardo looked at her, perplexed.

"I know!" Abella exclaimed. "I know what you'll wear so you won't be recognized."

The Magister had an evil expression on her face.

# XIII.
## SMALLPOX

It was a morning of high waters and the *scaula* was gliding easily over embankments, down *calli*, and along flooded *fondamenta*.

The light reflected by the stretch of water gave Magister Abella's robe even more solemn majesty. The purple mantle that went down to her ankles emanated a luminous halo that vibrated in the brilliant light of that March day.

Edgardo, however, harbored an ambiguous, contradictory feeling in his soul. He'd reacted to Abella's suggestion like a blow below the belt, but had yielded in the end.

"Didn't you say you were once a cleric at Bobbio? You'll disguise yourself as a monk."

This habit brought him no regret but, on the contrary, a deep sense of peace, a gentleness he hadn't felt for a long time, but, simultaneously, the feeling that he was playing a part that had nothing to do with the sense of spirituality that habit had represented for him in the past.

"So, are you ready?" he asked Abella as they reached the shore.

"I've followed you in this illogical enterprise only so no stone would be left unturned in the search for Costanza. I should tell you, though, that I consider all this a jest," Abella replied.

"Thank you for your kind words. Now will you knock on the door?"

The taps echoed all the way up to the loft. After a while, a gap opened and Lippomano's goatee swayed through.

"May God keep you, Signore," she said. "I am Magister Abella, *clarissimus medicus* of the School of Salerno and most humble servant of the duchy of Venice, and this," she added, indicating Edgardo, "is a holy monk who assists me in my work with his prayers and his faith."

Lippomano smiled. "I am very honored."

"We're taking the liberty of bothering you because of a very serious issue. We have reason to believe that there's currently a smallpox epidemic in Venice among the confraternity of tailors." Abella gave an exhausted sigh. "And we heard that you've recently collected some garments."

Lippomano's face stiffened. "Yes, that's right."

"It's as I feared. We have a well-founded suspicion that there are pustules, scabs, and traces of infected pus stuck on those clothes."

"Merciful God, that would be terrible!"

"It's just a suspicion, mind you. That's why I've come to ask if it's possible to examine you to check if there are any symptoms of contagion on you, and if so, intervene immediately to save your life."

Lippomano was sweating profusely.

"May we come in?" Edgardo asked, camouflaging his voice with a high-pitched tone, like that of a hungry hen.

"Yes, of course, come in."

The door opened wide. An atmosphere of stale humidity wrapped around them, making it hard to breathe. There were no ceilings or walls: the darkness was so dense that it even erased the anxiety that had gotten hold of them. Accompanied only by their echoing footsteps, they walked as far as another door, beyond which they were suddenly immersed, as if by magic, in a reverberation of light oozing an infinity of different greens. They were absorbed by a luxuriant garden stretching around a well made of pink stone. Edgardo had never seen such vegetation in Venice. He remembered miniatures in

Arabic manuscripts he'd leafed through in Bobbio: they must have been palms, papyruses, and every kind of aromatic Oriental plant giving off a sweet fragrance.

Around the garden, a network of stone stairs led to the eaves on two floors.

Lippomano led them into a salon on the ground floor. Edgardo looked around, trying to work out the layout of the house. Although it maintained the character of Venetian homes, its staircases, eaves, and garden paths gave the impression of something akin to a labyrinth.

"What must I do?" Lippomano asked anxiously.

"I should examine you." Abella came closer to the Jew's goatee, which stank of stale sweetmeats. "I need to check if a smallpox pustule or a purulent wound has developed in a cleft of your body. This is a dark room. Could you bring me an oil lamp?"

"I'll run and get one right away."

No sooner had Lippomano left than Abella pulled Edgardo toward her. "Hurry up, I don't know how long I can keep him busy. I'll say you went to pray for his safety."

"The prayers of a Christian monk won't mean much to him. He's a Jew."

"Hurry up!"

Edgardo vanished into the shadows. His first thought was to find the storeroom. It was difficult to find your way in the tangle of staircases that went through the garden. Bearing in mind the height of the window over the canal, through which he'd looked, it must be located on the mezzanine.

He crossed the portico, hoping to hear the soft sound of Costanza's voice. The house seemed uninhabited. Nothing but the swishing of the waves against the water door and the gloomy hiss coming from the well.

On the other side of the entrance, a half-staircase led to a raised floor. The door was ajar. He pushed it open. There was

a smell of stables. A faint light filtered through a window grating. Slowly, his ailing eyes got accustomed to the semi-darkness. The reflection of the canal waters, projected on the ceiling, created dancing jellyfish.

He groped his way forward, dragging his feet on the dirt
floor. It really did look like a storeroom. There were wooden
chests stacked up, and wicker baskets. Every step was accompanied by a sinister rustling: straw, made rotten by the damp.
In a corner, he noticed a plank held up by two trestles, on
which lay abandoned a moldy blanket. It may have been used
as a bed. He lifted the blanket to his nose and breathed in
deeply. His sight might let him down but his sense of smell had
become more acute. He was hoping to pick up a clue that
Costanza had been here.

Dried fish and salt: certainly not the young girl's fragrance.
He moved to the window. If this was the room he'd seen from
the canal, then he should be able to find the chest he'd noticed.
He collided with it: it was long and narrow, like those used to
bury the bodies of noble ladies and gentlemen. The lid was
raised. Inside, there seemed to be nothing but a mountain of
straw. Overcoming repulsion, he plunged his hand up to his
elbow. For a moment, he was afraid he could feel the flabby,
icy consistency of a lifeless body.

His fingers slid over a smooth, clean object. He gently lifted
it out.

It was a skilfully manufactured chalice made of clear, transparent glass. He rummaged further: bottles, glasses, vases, all
perfectly packed away.

He'd found them: they were the pieces Tataro had
entrusted to his *garzone*, so he could show them to
Lippomano. He had proof that Giacomo had been here, or at
least that the merchandise had been snatched away from him.
This didn't mean that Costanza had any connection at all with
the young man's disappearance, but if the merchant was

involved in an abduction, there was a good reason for suspecting him.

He took the chalice, wrapped it in a rag, and stuffed it into the inside pocket of his habit. Then he rushed to the exit.

There was no sign of life in the inner courtyard. Lippomano must still be in Abella's expert hands. He had time to carry on searching.

He went back up the stairs that led to the first floor. He came across a series of closed doors. He went from one to the other, looking into empty salons decorated with frescoes of flowery, arabic-style patterns that reminded him again of the miniatures in the manuscripts that had come to the abbey from Constantinople.

When he was sure that his search would yield no result, he had a surprise.

In the last room, surrounded by walls covered in indigo silks, a regal bed stood prominently, carved out of oak trunks, decorated with figures embossed in gold, representing monstrous creatures feeding on people enveloped by the flames of hell. The blankets were in perfect condition, tight, immaculate. There was a desk and a stool by the window. A huge closet, decorated in gold, stood against a wall. A lavish decor that indicated the owner's noble origins. He drew nearer, hoping to find some clue. The door opened with a squeak. A sweet scent of amber came over him.

He found various women's dresses, decorated with gemstones and pearls, arranged in perfect order. So he was right to believe that there was a female presence in the palazzo . . . Costanza?

A creaking sound gave him a start, and he heard footsteps echoing beneath the loggia, coming toward the door to the room. His back was suddenly covered in sweat. He felt the customary feeling of void and powerlessness take over his mind. He was lost. They'd discover him.

He tried to keep hold of his senses.

He looked around. There was no way out. The footsteps grew closer. The only possibility was the closet. There was plenty of room under the shelves with the dresses. He curled up and managed to pull the door of the closet shut before the door to the room opened.

A tentative shuffling filled the room. He heard the rustling of garments a few steps away from his hiding place. He pressed his eye against the gap between the two shutters. From where he was, he could see only a fraction of the room. He saw a shadow. Then a louder shuffle, very close. It was a moor, most probably a servant. He was placing tiny bottles, amphoras, and phials, probably containing ointments and perfumes, on the desk. He was putting them down gently, arranging them tidily.

Who were these cosmetics for? Edgardo had trouble breathing, and because of his position, excruciating pain was radiating from his back. He moved a leg slightly. There was an imperceptible squeak. The moor turned and looked in his direction, listened out for a moment, then took a step and moved out of sight. He was plunged into an eerie silence. Was the man still in the room? Was he waiting for him? Or had he left after doing what he had to do? The uncertainty didn't allow him to leave his hiding place. He was trying to breathe without a sound, inhaling slowly through his nose.

And so, like a bolt out of the blue, a hidden image of the past flashed, that smell he knew so well: the fragrance that had nurtured him and given him moments of sublime joy in his unhappy life.

Cabbage juice, copper sulphate, gall with arabica gum, and beer: the ink he had used when copying manuscripts in Bobbio.

That scent, in addition to the habit he was wearing, suddenly hurled him into regret for a serene, simple life without worries, entirely dedicated to copying manuscripts; hunched over lecterns with the other brothers, surrounded by parchment, miniatures, shielded by words, seized by the ecstasy that only copying could give him.

He had nothing left from those happy times. He'd abandoned the abbey and the habit, and his writing had been reduced to a list of goods and banal calculations.

Why had he been so foolish as to let himself be dragged down into the abyss by insane passion?

He fervently hoped that the body of the woman found in Metamauco was that of Kallis, so that he could once and for all be done with those memories that still weighed heavy on his soul, depriving him of a real life.

No more sounds seemed to be coming from the room. He cautiously pushed the door open and looked around. The servant had left. With difficulty, he managed to free his poor bones from the slot where he'd been crammed. He was about to close the closet door when he froze.

Where was the smell of ink coming from? Had he dreamed it? He slipped his head between the shelves. He smelled again. He couldn't be wrong.

Seized by a kind of frenzy, he started rummaging through the clothes, searching thoroughly. In the end, he found it. An ink horn like the one they had used in the scriptorium. He opened it and the fragrance spread around him. There it was, thick and palpable, soft, the creator of worlds, of dreams, the end and the means of free human expression.

How come it had been put among women's clothes? He kept looking and the rest appeared: the goose quill, two perfectly preserved blank pieces of parchment, a pumice for erasing. Everything a skillful scribe could need.

He couldn't see a connection between that equipment, the place, and the clothes.

He sneaked out of the room and went to the salon on the ground floor.

He found Abella holding a lamp, examining Lippomano's half-naked body lying on the table. He approached her cautiously.

"Where have you been all this time?" she hissed.

"The palazzo is a labyrinth," Edgardo replied in self-defense.

"So, Magister," Lippomano whimpered, "say something. Have you find any smallpox pustules?"

Abella slapped his lumpy belly. "No, no smallpox. Get dressed and God be with you."

And, without another word, they scurried away, leaving Lippomano to tidy himself up in a state of joy.

"I get the feeling your intuition has played a dirty trick on you," Abella said provocatively, walking to the boat.

"That's not quite true." Edgardo pulled the glass chalice from his habit. "I found one of Giacomo's glass pieces in the storeroom."

Magister Abella pulled a sceptical face.

"Not only this . . . In a wardrobe, I discovered writing tools as well as women's dresses."

"Interesting . . . This makes everything clear." Abella had that annoying smile of hers stamped across her face.

But of course! Edgardo rubbed his curly hair. How come his mind hadn't made the connection? "They're Costanza's!" he blurted out.

"What?"

"The ink, the parchment, the quill! Who else would have made such an unusual request? How many women do you know who practice writing? No. I'll tell you how things stand. Costanza was in that palazzo while waiting to embark, or perhaps she's still there, a prisoner."

The Magister gave him a sideways glance. "Nothing proves this is the case. Did you perhaps find something that belongs to her?"

"Not yet."

"Another one of your fantasies."

"Is the glass chalice also a fantasy?"

"Do you still think it may have something to do with Costanza?" Abella asked.

"Yes, and I know someone who can confirm it," he concluded, darting her an angry look. He couldn't stand it that this quack always wanted to have the final word.

# XIV.
## THE FORMULA

He got out of the boat that had brought him to Amurianum full of hope and perhaps, for the first time, proud of his achievements. If Tataro recognized the chalice, then his theories would be confirmed and thus become tangible proof.

At the foundry, he was told that the master was ill, "with his guts in great turmoil," and that he'd find him at home.

Getting to the San Donato canal, beyond the church of San Salvatore, he found Tataro's palazzo.

He'd seen it in the process of being built, and was stunned by its grandeur. The marble of the façade, both white Istrian and multi-colored, glowed with the dying light of the sunset, which played in the empty and filled spaces of the *polifora*, its rays exploding in alabaster splinters, bouncing off the round stained glass panes that shielded the windows.

The glassmaker had made his dream come true: to be able to shut his windows, like the abbey at Montecassino, with circles of glass held together with molten lead.

He was shown up to the main floor. Tataro received him in bed. He looked ill and jaundiced.

"I've got two wolves tearing at my kidneys day and night," Tataro moaned, grinding his teeth. Then he took a glass from a stool and drained the contents with a grimace of disgust. His lips were stained with blood.

"I have to drink this muck that makes me sick: the blood of a kid fed on diuretic herbs . . . And that's not all. I have to eat boiled newborn puppy meat—physician's orders."

He pursed his lips and made a kind of painful whistle.

"God keep you. I'm sorry for your illness." Edgardo was surprised by his own monastic tone, which he thought he'd forgotten.

The glassmaker motioned to him to approach. "What do you want?"

"I think I may have found your glass pieces, the ones you entrusted to Giacomo so he'd show them to Lippomano."

Despite his illness, Tataro gave a start of curiosity.

"They're in his palazzo storeroom," Edgardo added.

"What about Giacomo?"

"I found no trace of him."

"Are you sure they're my glass pieces?"

"I've brought you one to make sure."

The glassmaker lifted himself up with great difficulty. Edgardo slipped his hand under his cloak, and began to unwrap the rags.

Pierced by the rays of the dying sun, the chalice lit up, making the crystal glass vibrate with the most perfect light.

As though shaking off his amazement, Tataro livened up, and, trying to gather all his remaining strength, reached out to the object and brushed it with his fingers, like a loving caress.

"Is it one of yours?" Edgardo asked quickly.

The glassmaker didn't reply straight away, but stared at the chalice, spellbound. "Where did you find it?" he asked in a broken voice.

"I told you, in the merchant's house—"

Tataro's face turned purple, his fingers shaking, and the veins in his neck were swollen and throbbing. "You're lying, you damned scribe!" he shouted. "Are you trying to make fun of me? Do you take me for a madman? I've been a glassmaker all my life and I'm not going to let a disrobed cleric take me for an ass!"

Edgardo looked at him, unable to comprehend. "I don't understand, really—"

"Are you trying to make me believe you know nothing about the glass this chalice is made of?"

As though caught red-handed without knowing why, Edgardo lowered his head. "For heaven's sake, I don't know what you're talking about."

Tataro's chest shook with a phlegmy laugh. "You're a terrible actor. You know perfectly well this chalice can't possibly be mine. The glass it's made of is pure crystalline glass, transparent and clear like rock crystal. The only ones who knew the formula of perfect crystal were Segrado and . . . " he stared at him with hatred, " . . . and a scribe to whom Segrado dictated the formula before he died, and that scribe was you!"

Edgardo felt the glass scorch his fingers as though suddenly molten. A chalice manufactured according to Segrado's instructions. How could that be possible? The tragic events of twelve winters earlier flashed before his eyes.

His arrival in Venice from Bobbio Abbey after a long journey down the Medoacus. The hope of finding out about the eye stone mentioned by his friend Ademaro. The illusion that the miraculous medication could cure his ailing eyes that no longer allowed him to perform his much-loved work as a copyist. The magic that had overwhelmed him as soon as he'd arrived in this miraculous city rising from the waters, his first contact with the world of glassmakers and glassblowers. Meeting Master Segrado and his young slave, Kallis.

Segrado had worked his entire life to obtain the perfection of pure glass, crystalline, exactly like rock crystal, without that green shade that always made glass paste dull. After many attempts, he'd succeeded in discovering the correct formula.

It was this discovery that had led him, almost by chance, to invent the "eye circles," the round pieces of glass that would accomplish the miracle of restoring Edgardo's sight.

It was the formula for crystalline glass that had triggered the war between Segrado and Tataro, and Edgardo—an innocent cleric—had been dragged into a battle between glassmakers that had led to horrible murders.

Reliving these moments made Edgardo realize that it wasn't those tragic events that had upset his life at the time. They were nothing in comparison with the devastating power of passion, and the discovery of the sensual world. His love for Kallis had made him abandon his monk's habit, just like that, overnight, relinquishing all privileges, finding himself hunted, renounced by everyone, wandering without any hope.

When, in the end, Segrado had asked him of all people to transcribe the secret formula for crystalline glass, the demons of evil had been unleashed in all their might. In just a few hours, the world had turned against him, leaving him in the darkest pit of despair.

Tataro's words had reawakened the slumbering beast beneath the mud of the lagoon. It was obvious that the glassmaker was convinced Edgardo had shared the formula with another master craftsman, and was trying to work out why.

That wasn't the case, he wasn't lying, and he too was surprised to discover the existence of crystalline glass. Who could have come into possession of the formula? He was the only one to have transcribed it, and the copy had been lost in the sea before his very eyes.

"Do you want to know the truth?" Edgardo said, smiling. "Yes, Segrado dictated the formula to me, but then the parchment was lost and I . . . you know, my mind isn't what it used to be . . . it wavers, wanders . . . I've forgotten it. I can't remember it anymore."

"That's not true, I don't believe you!" Tataro cried. "You're lying. You know the formula for crystalline glass but it's of no use to you. You're nothing but a blind, crippled scribe!"

"I'm telling you, I know nothing about this glass. I found it in the merchant's storeroom. I have a witness who was with me, an eminent physician, Magister Abella."

Tataro grimaced with disgust. "The canker take me—that woman's a first-class crook. I know her well. She came to see me at the foundry, she'd heard I was suffering from colic, and wanted to offer her services for some strange treatment, and insisted on seeing my piss, as if I'd show it to a woman . . . And then she also asked my *garzoni* lots of questions."

Edgardo started ruffling his messy shock of ruby-colored hair that looked like a whirlwind of autumn maple leaves. "So you know Magister Abella?"

"Of course, and I swear I wouldn't use a woman doctor even if I was dead, no way I'd trust her . . . Magister of my balls."

A worm of suspicion crawled into Edgardo's ear and, digging its way forward, was sliding in with remarkable speed. "Tell me, when did Abella come to see you at the foundry?"

"I can't remember—what's the difference? She was a woman then, and is a woman now."

"Was it before or after Giacomo disappeared?"

"Before, definitely before. It was before the high autumnal tides, the weather was still warm."

"Do you remember if she also spoke with Giacomo?"

"I don't know, she might have . . . she questioned more or less everybody, she wanted to know about their ailments, if they were healthy."

Perhaps it was mere coincidence, an odd gut feeling like the ones you often get when you're a wretch who takes too much opium and hallucinogenic herbs, but Edgardo couldn't help but connect the two events.

Giacomo had vanished after meeting Abella. So had Costanza, who'd disappeared two days after the physician had entered the Grimani home. In both cases, she'd inquired after the young people's health. Perhaps it didn't mean much, but that little worm of suspicion was aiming to turn Edgardo's brain into a permanent home.

"So, scribe? Let's forget about Abella and your fantastical story, and get back to business. How much do you want for the formula?" The old man was aggressive. "I'm ready to shower you in gold. I don't know to whom you've entrusted your secret, but I could do much better than this amateur," he pointed at the chalice, "and we'll become rich."

"You really can't get any peace, can you, my poor Tataro?"

"What do you hope to achieve by keeping the secret? Segrado is nothing but dust now, and we too will soon be eaten by worms, so your promise is pointless now. Foolish scribe. Go to hell and may the devil eat your soul. You'll end up in hell very soon . . . very soon . . . "

Edgardo turned his back on him and left the room. Tataro's cries slid over the lagoon, in vain.

The tolling bells announcing Vespers were muffled by the clatter of stone shutters bolted over windows. An atmosphere of stagnant resignation and defeat had taken over Ca' Grimani. Days passed and Costanza's fate was increasingly linked to a feeling stripped of pain, to a predestined event that would remain shrouded in mystery.

The suspicions regarding Alvise were still hanging, floating in the air. Magdalena watched the servant boy, studied him, and although she couldn't find anything to confirm the nasty thoughts that troubled her mind, she couldn't suppress the deep resentment that corroded her soul.

And so she felt relieved when, that evening, she saw her husband return with a glimmer of light on his face, softened by a gentleness she'd long forgotten.

"I have good news, wife," Tommaso said. "Come, sit by my side." He took her hand.

Sitting on the high-backed chairs standing against the wall

covered in Flemish *arrases*, lit up by wavering flames that made their motionless bodies quiver, they were the faded fresco of a family struggling against its undoing.

Magdalena looked at him lovingly: he'd put on weight, seemed tired, his skin had turned gray, and his hands purple.

"We'll soon have an infallible medicine that will allow you to conceive."

Magdalena froze.

Tommaso continued. "I've heard of an extraordinary medicine, very expensive, that has already given many women the joy of a pregnancy." Then he leaned toward her and stroked her hair. "Are you happy?"

"Yes, of course," Magdalena said, trying to stall, "but how can you be so sure? Aren't you afraid this might be one of those falsely miraculous remedies sold by sorcerers and charlatans?"

"These are neither quacks nor crooks. It's a formula Romano Marzolo brought back from his trip to Alexandria. It's taken from *The Canon of Medicine* by Avicenna, the most illustrious physician of the Arab world."

Even though she trusted Magister Abella and her advice, Magdalena didn't want to contradict her husband. "I will gladly accept your medication, even though Magister Abella has advised me to—"

Tommaso's face twisted into a pained grimace. "I've asked you not to mention that charlatan." His tone was calm and icy. "Surely you won't compare a woman of unknown origins and training to the most illustrious Arabic physician. I am asking you: don't utter her name again in my presence, and forget her." Tommaso leaned and kissed his wife on the head. "Trust me. Do you promise?"

Magdalena gave her husband a final look of despair. "I'll do as you command."

Tommaso embraced her excitedly. "You won't regret it. I

can assure you that a year from now, the cries of a newborn baby will once again echo through this house."

Magdalena lowered her head.

"Now smile. The time for mourning is over, and it's now a time for hope. With God's help we'll also find your sister, I'm sure."

She'd never seen him so full of confidence. His eyes lit up with an expression of light-heartedness.

Tommaso let go of the embrace and left the salon. Magdalena sank into the high-backed chair in turmoil. She wished with all her heart that she could believe him.

She heard his footsteps on the stairs, then in the inner courtyard, grow increasingly distant.

He'd retired to his much-loved pantry, to that secret room to which only he had the keys. Lately, he would shut himself there more and more often, and stay there for hours. Nobody else had access. The last time—she couldn't even remember when it had been—that she'd visited the room, she thought it looked just like a simple, bare cabin, with no furniture, almost like a cell. But now, whenever she got close to it, she'd be seized by deep anguish. What did her husband do, locked away in that room, all alone, all that time? Why had he categorically forbidden anyone from entering?

Magdalena listened intently. There wasn't the slightest sound coming from the mezzanine floor. The long, unstoppable waves of the lagoon were crashing against the front gates with a sinister rumble.

A fetid taste of death tightened her throat. She was undecided, confused, and needed to speak with Abella to find out the result of the research conducted on her husband's sperm. Only the scribe could organize a meeting with the Magister without arousing Tommaso's suspicions.

Edgardo felt the infection of a new failure burn in his mind.

Tataro's negative response with regard to the origin of the chalice had undermined the theory of Giacomo's abduction, and so made the hope of finding Costanza more remote. Maybe Abella was right, and he'd sunk into the state of a destitute man ruled by excess, a prey to stimulant spices that removed him more and more from reality.

His suspicions about Abella increased his anxiety further.

Facing Magdalena, he tried to gather his lost dignity and strived to give her a glimmer of hope. He told her about the women's clothes and the writing tools in the room.

"Are you really convinced that Costanza could be kept prisoner in that house?" Magdalena asked, upset.

"The palazzo is very large, so I couldn't search every room, but it's a possibility I don't want to rule out."

Edgardo felt he was uttering these words more to absolve himself than because he was truly convinced.

"So what are you thinking of doing?"

"I'll go back. I must find a way to enter the palazzo again and rummage everywhere, so I need enough time."

"Will Magister Abella help you?" The physician's presence represented a new source of hope for Magdalena.

A veil of melancholy descended over the scribe's cerulean-blue eyes, saddened by suspicion. "I don't think so," he replied.

Magdalena put her hand on his. It was the first time the mistress had allowed herself such a familiar gesture of affection. "There's bad blood between you," she whispered, without concealing the suffering in her voice.

Torn by conflicting feelings, Edgardo said nothing.

"You must agree that she's a talented physician who possesses unique and exceptional qualities," Magdalena added.

The scribe nodded.

"You must inform her that I urgently need to meet with her, in a place that doesn't arouse suspicions . . . at the apothecary's."

Edgardo bowed his head, but couldn't stop himself from saying, "May I ask you to do something, Signora? When you meet with Magister Abella, please be prudent."

Magdalena straightened up, abandoning her intimate attitude, and considered him from the height of her superiority. "What do you mean?"

Edgardo had to find a way out without revealing his suspicions. "In this city many skilfully practice the art of listening, and words then bounce from one *calle* to another, across canals, flying over the waters, so it's not always appropriate to trustingly open one's soul."

Magdalena stared at him with a severe expression. "You're getting stuck in a tangle of obscure, tenuous concepts that conceal instead of clarify."

"I don't wish to alarm you, Signora, but life has taught me that we sometimes put our trust in people who then turn out to be very different from what we imagined."

His mind raced back to his friend Ademaro, his loyal companion while at Bobbio, and to the dramatic circumstances that had put an end to their friendship.

"If you mean Magister Abella, know that I have the highest respect for her, but she is just my physician, not my confessor."

Her words reassured him. Edgardo bowed his head and took his leave.

He didn't have time to notice the change in Magdalena's face: her tight lips, pale and bloodless, the gold-flecked eye now darkened, her long fingers outstretched in the void, trembling. Signs of a deep turmoil she could not conceal.

# XV

# THE TRAFEGO CONVOY

By of the laws that govern the universe," Sabbatai grumbled, "this man's as hard as an oak."

The blade had gotten stuck between the rump and the thigh, and the leg refused to come away from the trunk of the body.

Sabbatai threw the knife on the table and took from the wall a large-tooth saw, which hung on display alongside other tools: scalpels, pointers, scissors, hooks, syringes, cauterizers, and pliers of all lengths.

"Now we'll see who the winner is." With renewed energy, he took to pushing and pulling the saw through the long-suffering flesh. The soft parts, lubricated by their own blood, yielded immediately; ligaments and cartilage took a few more pushes but in the end, amid creaking and wet hissing, the limb came away from the body and rolled on the ground.

"So, you ass, you thought you could have a laugh at Sabbatai's expense? Ha!" the apothecary exclaimed with satisfaction.

Then he picked up the leg, approached the boiler, and dropped the limb into boiling water.

Animated by the energetic seething, two arms, a head, and two feet were already chasing one another in that small space, so much so that the leg struggled to find room. Sabbatai had to push it down to the bottom with a stick.

All he had left to do was saw off the other leg, and the bulk of the work would be done. The trunk was too large, so he would get another boiler ready for it.

The process was well under way, the soft, gray flesh had come away from the bones, dissolving into a thick, fat broth that was in no way inferior to tasty boar soup.

The laboratorium at the back was steeped in a sour, sickly-sweet stench that poured out into the small external courtyard, fortunately located next to a narrow, smelly canal.

He was about to tackle the last limb when he heard his shop door slam.

"Is anybody there?" he heard someone shout.

He didn't like to be disturbed when in the process of delicate operations.

"Damn it! Who's calling me?" He put the saw down, wiped his bloodied hands on his apron, and went into the shop.

Because of his height, which did not allow his head to be higher than the counter, he couldn't make out a face straight away. The hem of scarlet he saw undulating over well-made shoes left no doubt. He climbed on the footboard and found himself face to face with Magister Abella's ruddy complexion.

"I must speak with you," Abella said in a detached tone.

Sabbatai did not reply but simply glanced to the side and went to the back. Abella followed him.

The vapor emanating from the broth had now spread through the low, narrow room, floating in mid-air like a layer of fog. Abella glanced at the dismembered body that was waiting on the table, and turned up her nose in disgust.

"A devoted Christian," Sabbatai explained. "A Tanais merchant who came to drop dead here in Venice, poor devil . . . "

Abella gave an understanding nod. It had become customary that when someone died in a foreign land, he'd state in his will the wish to be buried in the country of his birth. To comply with his wishes, it was common to boil the body in order to recover the bones, then send them to even faraway countries without the risk of their rotting.

"I need some fresh meat," Abella said abruptly, in a professional tone.

The apothecary looked at the dismembered body and gave an angelic smile. "That's not an easy task," he said.

"Come now, I have no time to waste. Tell me how much you want," Abella replied.

"Twenty dinars."

"You're a thief."

"I am your servant." Sabbatai bowed, and his outsized head brushed against his boots, almost making him roll to the ground.

"Very well, then. Will you deliver it to the same place? Let me know when the goods arrive."

"Don't worry, Magister, you'll have what you wish. You can trust Sabbatai."

The stench of human flesh gave an aftertaste of steaming dung, making the air unbreathable. Abella put a handkerchief over her nose. "Listen, I must meet a noblewoman in your shop. Do you have anywhere private we can talk?"

The apothecary looked around, bewildered, then clicked his tongue like a whipcrack. "In the courtyard next door, by the canal. You can access it only through the shop. Nobody'll see you there."

Abella nodded. "That'll be fine. I'll wait for her there."

As she was walking to the Crowned Wolf, Magdalena kept mulling over what Edgardo had said about Abella. Why had he warned her? What did he know about the Magister that he didn't wish to reveal?

Escorted by Nena, she arrived at the apothecary's in a state of intense agitation, shaken by events she could neither control nor understand.

Outside the entrance there were the usual Theriac sellers, surrounded by servants from noble households, sent to buy the wondrous remedy.

Leaving Nena to watch the entrance, Magdalena went in. The stench of what was boiling, mixed with the scents of spices, had created a deadly air that tickled her throat and made her nauseous.

Sabbatai skipped out from behind the counter and greeted her with exaggerated bowing and scraping. "I am so immensely happy when your grace brings a little light to my humble shop . . . How can I serve you, Signora?"

Magdalena looked around, hoping to glimpse Abella, then took her time to reply. "I've heard high praise about a perfume from Tunisia. Apparently, it can give the mind celestial visions."

"The Trafego convey has brought us myrrh, burning bush, mastic, mustard, marjoram, and sandalwood. Blended together, they form an essence that has miraculous properties, releases all worries, and rekindles both male and female organs."

Magdalena looked down, as though caught red-handed. "Could you prepare some for me?" she said, looking around again.

"Sabbatai, the apothecary, receives essences from every country, through the convoys from Syria, Egypt, Tanais, Northern Africa, Southern Spain, and Aigues Mortes. And from each of these, I draw fragrances that are able to stir a woman's soul deeply. It will be an honor to serve you, Signora." Seeing her agitated, he added, "Perhaps you're expecting someone?"

Magdalena gave a weak smile.

"If you would follow me."

He made his way, in small steps, to a side door hidden between two sets of shelves. Magdalena didn't stir, as though turned to stone.

"Trust me."

The door led to the inner courtyard. Magdalena found Abella waiting for her by the well. The physician and Sabbatai exchanged a meaningful look, and he disappeared, leaving the two women alone.

"I'm so grateful to you for coming at my request," Magdalena said, immediately regretting her overly warm greeting.

"I have good news for you," Abella replied with an open smile that dispelled all suspicion.

How could this frank, learned woman be involved in anything that required caution?

"Tell me, I beg you."

"I've examined your husband's sperm very carefully." Abella weighed her words, articulating every one. "*Nullum impedimentum manet*. The humor is warm and dry, runny and frothy. The taste is citrusy, in other words, there's nothing to stop your husband from procreating."

Magdalena's face dropped with astonishment. "Then, if we're both in good health, how is it possible that . . . "

"You're right, and I've also asked myself the same question. There is only one answer: the influence of the stars. As you know, all the medical schools, Salerno especially, claim that there's an interdependent relationship between the human body and the signs of the zodiac. That is why medicine has assigned a sign of the zodiac to every organ. The belly, where the reproductive organs are situated, is ruled by Virgo, and all this year it has been under the negative influence of the Moon. You'll see: as soon as you're free of the shadow cast upon you by it, the virgin in you will blossom again, and your belly will go back to generating."

"So what should I do?" Magdalena asked in a faint voice.

"Wait," Abella replied.

Magdalena stared at the brown waters of the lagoon. How many times had she heard that word during her son's illness? The doubt Edgardo had sowed in her suddenly resurfaced. She had placed her last hope in this physician, a woman, and immediately trusted her, feeling something akin to friendship toward her, and now everything seemed to be coming apart, because of that one word. Why had she deceived her? What secret interests were guiding her actions?

"It's no longer possible to wait. My husband is expecting a wondrous remedy from the Orient, a medicine that will give my belly new life. As soon as he receives it, I'll have to take it. I can't refuse."

"Let me know when this happens, and I'll try to analyze it. Meanwhile, let's hope time is on our side and that the Moon turns favorable."

"May God hear you."

Magister Abella noticed the bewildered, disillusioned expression weighing on Magdalena's face. She came up to her and squeezed her hands. "You must have faith. You can be sure that I won't abandon you."

She couldn't say anything else because she could not reveal the truth deep inside her heart: that even she hadn't been able to work out the cause of their sterility. So she turned to the stars, without much conviction, as a last resort. The experience she'd gained after treating many women had taught her that there was always a physical impediment, always—except in this case.

Magdalena hid her face in the fur of her cloak, and went back into the shop. Sabbatai came toward her and obsequiously handed her a bottle with a yellow glow. "Here's your perfume, Signora."

His soft smile froze at the icy look she gave him as she furtively took the bottle and concealed it in her cloak. As though she felt stained by having to share a secret with that treacherous being.

"Oh, here you are. I was looking for you."

Grimani's voice gave him a start, and Edgardo looked up from the parchment and put his precious eye circles down on the lectern. "I'm writing down the inventory of all the goods you brought back from Flanders."

Edgardo knew the master insisted on order and demanded with obsessive precision that all revenue and expenditure should be recorded. He didn't want him to think that his search for Costanza, no matter how important, made him neglect his work.

Tommaso Grimani had been the first merchant in Venice to introduce the compulsory written record of the amount of goods that went into the storehouses, as well as the ones that were loaded onto chelandions bound for the harbors of Romania, Tanais, and Trabzon.

"My wife has told me of your intentions regarding the search for Costanza." Tommaso almost humbly brushed his fingers against the contraption with lenses that allowed Edgardo to magnify words. "I appreciate your efforts and am very grateful to you." He rubbed his eyes. "Only I suggest you exercise prudence. Secretly breaking into a private home, especially that of a foreign guest, is a crime. It goes against our laws and is severely punished. If I were to find out about it, as a member of the Council, I'd be obliged to report it to the judges. Do you understand what I mean?"

"Of course, Signore." Edgardo put down the goose quill. "Have no worry." He turned his head until he met Tommaso's gaze. "May I ask a question, Signore?"

"Do."

"Tell me frankly . . . have you lost all hope? Do you think we will not find Costanza alive?"

There was a long silence, while Edgardo's mind was sucked in by the swish of a wave crashing against the steps.

The awaited answer wasn't coming.

Tommaso kept rubbing his eyes, as though absorbed in the memory of faraway places. Then he suddenly turned around, as though no question had ever been asked, and said, "I'd be grateful if you could come with me. I'd like the opinion of a man of letters with regard to a project I hold dear. The accounts can wait."

Then he walked out, promptly followed by Edgardo.

The mist rising from the water was drifting in mid-air in the narrow *calli*, creating sudden jolts of shadow and light. A layer of icy humidity coated the green mane and branches of the oaks in the fields. Tommaso huddled in his fox-lined cloak.

They were proceeding with difficulty, sinking in the slimy mud of the path, forced to circumvent ruins and step over wooden beams that had come crashing down during the earthquake that had struck Venice a year earlier. Many small houses and churches hadn't been rebuilt yet, and their inhabitants had moved to other districts, where the tremors had caused less destruction.

They crossed a rickety wooden bridge and reached the field behind the church of Saint Ermagora and Saint Fortunato, or rather, what was left of that holy place, one of the city's oldest, established by the first refugees who had fled the mainland during the Lombard invasion. A fire that had broken out during the earthquake had destroyed it almost totally.

Among the ruins of Ca' Memmo a stretch of grass sloped toward Rivus Altus, where iron crosses rose like twisted branches. In front of one of these, on a slab of granite, a name and a date were engraved: LUCA GRIMANI, 1117.

Tommaso walked past his son's grave without even a glance. Edgardo had noticed this strange behavior before. Despite all the love he'd had for the prematurely dead boy, he'd never seen him pray at his grave, almost as though he didn't believe in its Christian importance.

They came to the bank of Rivus Altus. The muddy waters blended with the ash-gray reflections of the winter sunset. Their eyes silently followed the swaying of a solitary gondola bobbing in the middle of the canal.

"You were a cleric, so tell me something." Tommaso was staring into space. "Do you believe that a man's soul can pass into the body of a newborn baby?"

Edgardo tensed up and fiddled with his clothes, visibly embarrassed. Never had the master broached such a delicate, deep subject with him.

"It's not easy to answer your question, Signore. I'm no more than a scribe. You'd need a Church scholar for this. From what I've read in the Christian doctrine, there's no mention of souls being reborn." Edgardo stopped, then spoke again with renewed energy, almost as though he didn't want to disappoint him. "However, a few years ago, I copied Porphyry's transcription of Plotinus's *Enneads*, and the text mentioned that souls can be reborn many times, always in different bodies."

"I have great faith in our merciful God," Tommaso said, "and I know He will make up for the misfortune that has befallen our home. I am certain that Luca's soul will be born again in the new creature Magdalena will conceive." Tommaso's face took on an inspired expression. "I've spoken to him, and Luca has promised."

Edgardo did not dare reply. Pain and faith were mixed in Grimani's mind into a kind of delirium one could not but respect.

"The Memmo and Lupanizza families have decided to provide the funds to rebuild the church of San Ermagora and San Fortunato. They've asked me if I want to contribute to the works," Tommaso added, looking at Ca' Memmo, the splendid façade of which, just beyond the graveyard, was mirrored in the waters of Rivus Altus.

Possibly the most magnificent house in Venice, it had been built by the doge Tribuno Memmo, after the Doge's Palace had been burned down during an uprising against the doge Pietro Candiano IV in 976.

"I gave my word on condition that I may be allowed to

erect inside the church a marble sepulcher next to the high altar, to contain the remains of my beloved son, a tomb that's worthy of him." Grimani put his hand on the scribe's shoulder, as though to seal a pact. "You're the only one who knows, Edgardo d'Arduino, not even my wife knows the secret of Luca's return. If anything should happen to me, I entrust you with the task of erecting my son's tomb."

"I thank you for the honor you pay me. I promise that if it comes to it I will do everything possible to fulfil your wish."

Grimani crossed himself. Edgardo wanted to do the same but was held back by a kind of modesty. He had the feeling there was something blasphemous about that oath.

"Come, let's go back now. The sun is setting and Magdalena will have already given orders to bolt the shutters and doors."

A stench of rotting meat was rising from the internal canals.

"The wind has changed. We'll have high tide tonight. Let's hope it drops before dawn. Tomorrow, we're displaying the body of the virgin of the beads in the gardens of San Geminiano."

The body . . . tomorrow . . . in the gardens! A deadly chill went through Edgardo's chest and ran down his limbs.

"That young woman is making trouble even dead . . . "

"It's going to be displayed . . . shown to the whole of Venice?" Edgardo asked.

"Of course. Everybody has to see with their own eyes that it's just a well-preserved corpse and nothing more. It's essential to put an end to the fanciful rumors that have been running through the city for too many days now, stirring up all kinds of trouble."

"What rumors, Signore?"

"There are charlatans who have fun spreading senseless gossip, saying it's the body of a Byzantine princess who died during the Metamauco cataclysm, and who will rise with the new moon to become Venice's new doge. It sounds very much like a fairy tale, don't you think?"

"Yes, you're right, a fairy tale," Edgardo murmured in a thin voice.

"We'll display her, and then burn her. Better not leave any traces likely to fuel disrespectful cult practices."

Edgardo huddled in his cloak, his eyes welling up with emotion. Just one night, all he had to do was wait for the dawn, and he'd know. The end of a dream, the end of a nightmare.

# XVI.
## THE VIRGIN OF THE BEADS

The darkest hours of the night had become dense, turning sleep into a hope of rebirth. As though making his way through a thick forest, fighting against brambles and vines step by step in an agonizing search for a clearing or a glimmer of light that would show him the way, Edgardo passed those hours of waiting: a path of suffering and the illusion of attaining the truth and putting an end to a nightmare that had gone on for far too long.

He woke up at matins, a leftover of the habit he'd had as a cleric at Bobbio Abbey, and got ready for the event.

He imagined a large crowd forming in the gardens outside San Geminiano in order to see the body of the virgin of the beads on display, and wanted to be one of the first in line.

A blanket of pitch still shrouded the contours of the huts, the profiles of the belfries, and the edges of the boats moored along the canals. The only sound escorting him was the viscous swish of his footsteps in the mud, which had been softened by hoarfrost.

His mind was clouded, as though affected by the opium vapors. Consequently, when he approached the Rivoalto, he didn't immediately notice the horrifying spectacle before him.

In a niche next to Santissimi Apostoli, he noticed, faintly lit by an oil lamp, a dark, hairy mass streaked in bright ruby-red. Over it he could make out a form, leaning forward, with unclear contours.

A slimy sound was coming from the creature, like a thousand leeches at work on the carcass of a skinned cat.

Edgardo drew a few steps closer. What he saw made him think he was still immersed in the nightmare of an endless night.

On the ground, an animal was lying on its side, possibly a bull or an ox; the belly was ripped open, showing the bowels. A little farther was the head, which had been cleanly severed from the body, its sad eyes staring at him.

Hunched over the deep wound, her head plunged into the belly, into the intestines, Edgardo recognized a woman's form, even though it was hidden by a dark tunic. She was avidly digging out the animal's tripes and, after tearing out shreds of meat and insides, she was lifting them to her mouth, swallowing them with an eerie sound, like the sucking of a whirlpool.

What made the apparition incomprehensible at first sight was a kind of unreal extension behind the woman.

Behind her, as though generated by her back, rose a kind of bush, made of branches and boughs, through which you could make out wide areas of pink skin and a pair of hairy legs.

The bush man had lifted the woman's dress, exposing a large, white backside, and, his penis inserted into the ravenous creature's cleft, was pushing and charging into it over and over, forcing the woman's head to sink deeper and deeper into the animal's belly with every thrust, although this didn't seem to bother in any way the God-fearing woman who, unperturbed, carried on sucking a piece of bowel full of shit.

Repelled, Edgardo moved away, leaving the night shadows to repossess that monstrous vision.

What was happening to his beloved Venice? Her morals seemed to be degenerating by the day, and perhaps even darker times awaited him.

Drawing nearer San Marco, walking down the long Calle delle Merzerie, he came across other extraordinary-looking individuals. Lying on the ground, in the mud, their faces were covered with masks of pigs, stags, and bears. They weren't disguises manufactured by skilled craftsmen but real animal heads emptied of brains, with two holes in the place of eyes. Many were snoring loudly, and others were regurgitating food and wine, leaving no doubt that they were drunk.

Only then did Edgardo realize why this deforming epidemic seemed to be taking possession of the city.

Shrovetide had started, the period preceding Lent, when celebrations, disguises, dances, music, and abuse of wine and food grew out of all proportion, condoning all carnal excesses.

Even though the celebrations had started right after Saint Stephen's Day, during those so-called Carnival days the entire population seemed prey to an uncontrollable desire to transgress every rule. Perhaps in this Year of Our Lord, since Venice was still without a doge and afflicted by great scarcity, the desire for excess had reached previously unknown heights, so much so that, rather than joy, it suggested a deep sense of despair and mourning, like wanting to enjoy oneself while waiting for death.

Edgardo reached the *brolo* and walked across the Batario canal. Outside the church of San Geminiano several people had already gathered, waiting to see the remains of the virgin.

He got in line. Next to him, a wrinkled, bony old woman with a face made up like that of a young girl sported a swollen, disproportionately large, fake belly that made her look like a goatskin. She was laughing boisterously, showing her gray, toothless gums.

The time was drawing near. As soon as the gates opened, the truth about the virgin's identity would finally be revealed, and his torments would cease.

Once again, Edgardo asked himself what feeling dominated

his heart. His mind was wandering from one thought to another, and the wait was becoming increasingly unbearable.

He felt deeply offended by the jokes and disrespectful comments bystanders were making about the virgin's face, treating her like a curiosity at a fair, displayed to the people on the occasion of the Carnival.

The line was growing, and didn't just contain ordinary people but also noblemen and ladies accompanied by their female servants.

In all that confusion, Edgardo had no trouble recognizing, concealed under the large, ruby-colored cloak, the imposing figure of Magister Abella; she was standing in line, just like everybody else.

He watched her attentively, wondering why she was there, looking all innocent, with a pure smile. She turned to look in his direction, and Edgardo tried to hide behind the pregnant old woman. Too late. She had recognized him.

Quicker than the time it would have taken a frightened lizard to find shelter in the crack of a tree, she appeared before him, imposing, ruddy, bursting with energy to the point of being irritating.

"I never imagined I'd find a learned scribe standing in line since dawn in order to enjoy the kind of spectacle one sees at a fair," Abella said, taunting him.

"I never imagined I'd find an illustrious physician among all these people in the mood for celebrating, either," Edgardo replied. "In any case, I hear that it's not just some monstrous invention held up to be ridiculed, but a real corpse that has remained intact for many years."

"Yes, I heard that rumor too. That's why I'm here. My profession demands that I study all extraordinary events." Abella stared him straight in the eye. "How about you?"

Edgardo shook his curly head, clearly embarrassed, naturally unable to tell the truth. "Simple curiosity," he stammered.

The Magister swelled her cheeks and emitted a kind of whistle. "So you've given up searching for your Costanza, if you find the time to go after a simple oddity."

The insinuation made him flare up. "I haven't forgotten Costanza in the least, and you know that very well. I'm convinced she's held prisoner in the Alexandria merchant's house. I must find a way of exploring it again, more carefully."

"Without my help," Abella said.

"I haven't asked you."

At that moment, a shudder ran through the crowd, there was confusion, then a group quickly thronged the front door of the church, outside which two soldiers of the doge had appeared alongside the parish priest.

In the middle of all that bustle, Edgardo saw the deformed, warty head of Sabbatai, who, taking advantage of his height, was sneaking between people's legs and reaching the front position, next to the entrance.

The soldiers pushed back the throng with sticks, allowing the parish priest to open the door just enough to let one onlooker in at a time.

The virgin was being displayed in the crypt beneath the high altar at the end of the nave.

Just a few more minutes, and Edgardo would see the body.

He let himself be tugged, pushed, and crushed, and finally stepped inside San Geminiano. Intimidated by the sacred nature of the place, the line was now moving slowly and silently, as in a procession.

Edgardo reached the altar and went down the narrow steps that led to the crypt.

The stone walls were oozing cold moisture and a smell of diseased flesh. Once underground, he stopped.

A circle of people of all ages was standing around an open stone sarcophagus, supported by four pillars.

Everybody's eyes were glued to the tomb and a spectral silence was infecting the air.

Edgardo went forward. For a moment, he felt his legs go weak, and he closed his eyes. Finally, he would know the truth . . .

Trembling, he leaned forward and opened his eyes.

An icy wind froze his heart: the sarcophagus was empty.

## XVII.
## CARNEM LEVARE

S he's resurrected!"
"Go to hell, you fool, she was never dead, she didn't even smell."

"Listen to me, you ass, it's a well-known fact that during Carnival, corpses escape from coffins and go around playing tricks."

The voices interrupted one another, each putting forward its theory, but the one certainty was that the virgin's body had disappeared.

In addition to the fantastical hypotheses circulating among the people, the authorities were inclined to believe that the corpse had been purloined overnight by some criminal, through the gratings that were found uprooted, even though the reason for such an act could not yet be fathomed.

An act that, per se, was not all that serious, since the girl was a total stranger and didn't belong to any noble family; what was unacceptable was the offence to the authorities, the obvious proof that, without respect, one could mock power and its representatives.

In addition to this, the very rumors that the display of the corpse aimed to contradict were growing: that the young woman was a demon capable of being born again, possessing supernatural powers able to deeply undermine the government of Venice, already deprived of a doge and afflicted by serious scarcity.

All this prompted the Great Council, and Tommaso

Grimani was among the most adamant to order that all military forces should be used to find the virgin of the beads.

So they began to comb every district, beat the canals, check every kind of boat, and search houses and shelters.

This event also caused concern in the Grimani family: another worrying, obscure sign in addition to those that had already appeared. As a representative of the authorities, Tommaso took the outrage personally, and Magdalena couldn't help but look for a connection between her sister Costanza's disappearance and that of the Metamauco girl's body.

The person who suffered most in body and mind was Edgardo, numbed as though he'd been in armed battle with a band of barbarians.

The illusion of finally having done with the past, and the hope of touching his Kallis's beloved face one last time, had vanished.

Edgardo had built around that presence a dream of rebirth that had been dissolved in the blink of an eye. He was ashamed of himself, he, the former cleric, a skilled and learned copyist, carried away by the fantasy that the virgin of the beads had come back to life and was wandering through the streets of Venice.

Was there any truth in the age-old superstition that during Carnival some of the dead came out of their graves and walked among the living? And if that was Kallis's body, why had she returned? Was it to see him one last time? To atone for the terrible sin that had stained her soul? To ask for forgiveness?

He could not believe his mind could indulge in such thoughts. The dead do not come back. Only Our Lord was resurrected.

Even so, while roaming near the Alexandria merchant's house, hoping to detect any suspect goings-on, he harbored the illusion of miraculously coming across Kallis's ghost.

Celebrations were at their height and the city was prey to all kinds of excesses.

Outside the convent of San Lorenzo, his attention was caught by a strange company that was coming forward, dancing along the bank.

A monstrous creature, half goat, half human, was leading the group, his head hidden inside the muzzle of a ram with antlers, wearing heavy hooves over his feet. He was holding a long stick at the extremities of which hung a bag full of water, which he used to strike anyone who happened to pass near him. The rest of the procession was formed of shapes wrapped in large black cloaks, their faces hidden under a thick layer of white ceruse that erased all their features. They were swaying about, dragging their feet, as though under a spell: they were like larvae, supernatural beings from the hereafter.

The procession crossed the *campo* outside the convent in a chilling silence. There was something gloomy and dismal about that presence.

Anxious, Edgardo stood aside and let them overtake him.

He was about to resume walking when he noticed a detail that had escaped him earlier.

He saw something shining around the neck of one of the larvae: it was a small bead necklace like the one Alvise said he'd seen on the virgin of Metamauco.

An image flashed before Edgardo's eyes which he thought he'd forgotten: Kallis in her refuge on the abandoned island of San Lorenzo, opening her little box and pouring out a myriad of colorful beads like the ones in that necklace.

Was it her? Was that half-dead, half-living larva Kallis come back to life?

A second later, the dismal group had already moved away.

Abandoning any shame for his paradoxical, blasphemous thought, Edgardo ran after them.

It was hard to make his way through the crowd. The *calli*

were swarming with monsters, deformed shapes, scary animal masks. It seemed that all the inhabitants of Venice had poured out of their houses, seized by a kind of frenzy that was dragging them from one bank to the other, from one *campo* to the other, as though in search of something that would give this folly a meaning. Everybody was pursuing excess just for the sake of breaking all the rules.

Along the canals, a few steps away from the soldiers who were checking every passing boat, Edgardo saw people sitting at makeshift tables with the little food they'd been able to find in those lean times. They were all stuffing themselves unrestrainedly with smelly leftover fish, bones of lagoon birds with the flesh stripped off, and shreds of rancid pork.

Barely had some gulped down the food with large sips of watered-down wine than they suddenly turned around and vomited in one jet everything they'd just eaten.

Edgardo was struggling to advance, risking slipping on that slimy carpet of food leftovers that irreverent stomachs had just brought back up to the light, and every kind of excrement abandoned by intestines devoid of any dignity.

Without any shame, on the contrary, with a large dose of provocative excitement, between courses, the table companions exhibited asses of various shapes and colors, and were shitting without restraint in every corner, or competing as to who could piss farther into the water. It was as though you were watching a universal blend of fluids and human matter going in and coming out of every orifice in a kind of perpetual dance.

Engulfed in that chaos, Edgardo was afraid he'd lost them, but, as though by miracle, the larvae reappeared, mingled with *gnaghe*, corpulent, hairy men dressed as matrons, who went about shouting obscenities or miming unnatural mating acts.

He elbowed his way to the larva with the bead necklace,

who was moving in a light, slinky way, brushing against the ground like a thread of wool.

Under the thick ceruse, he thought he recognized Kallis's oriental features, her high cheekbones, her eyes like crescent moons.

He reached out with his hand until he was nearly touching her, and even thought he could smell her amber scent.

"Kallis . . . Kallis . . . " he called softly, but the larva was dragged away by the band and disappeared once again.

They were now all advancing in single file, down a narrow alley between houses made of rotting timber, in a kind of procession that had slowed their pace. At the end of the bottle-neck, Edgardo understood the reason for the slowing down. As they reached the final hut, every member of the line had to perform the ritual of the *osculum infame*.

From the ground-floor window of that den was protruding not a beautiful girl's face, but an enormous naked, shriveled behind, the only treasure of an old shrew. Every passer-by was obliged, on pain of being caned, to bend over and kiss the holy orifice.

Everybody seemed to subject themselves to this shameful kiss with much hilarity and enjoyment, but Edgardo didn't like this ritual at all.

When his turn came, he tried to sneak away, but a broad-shouldered *gnaga* grabbed him by the neck and forced him back in line.

He bowed his head, held his breath, closed his eyes, and plunged his face between the two flaps of flabby, hanging flesh that stank like baked eel vomited by a dog.

Never would he have imagined that he, the first-born son of a noble family, would have to humiliate himself in such an abject act. Still, they said that the ritual heralded wealth and honor for the year to come. He certainly needed that.

He wondered if, with that act, he'd touched the pit of his abjectness.

He paid homage, the throng dissolved, and, once he'd left the narrow path, he came to a wide, green *campo* with trees.

They'd arrived at Santa Maria Formosa.

The place brought back sweet memories: there, with Kallis, he'd been to the Feast of the Marys, and that same day, a little later, in a *scaula* in the middle of the lagoon, he'd asked her to be his wife. Twelve years had since passed, and yet that moment was still so vivid in his mind that he might as well have lived it a few days earlier.

He looked around for her ghost. The *campo* looked very different than before. It was bursting with people, like for the Feast of the Marys, but the atmosphere had very much altered.

He was right in the middle of a bull hunt, a cruel, very violent game, one of the people's favorites during Carnival.

At that moment the *tiradori*, dressed in short black velvet dresses and red jackets, were entering. They were dragging the animal into the middle of the square, among the crowd, with ropes tied around its horns. Here, other *tiradori* started provoking the bull with straw fires, tying them to his horns and ears. Frightened and in pain, the animal was arching its back, kicking and howling, struggling to free itself.

After a number of times when the bull was dragged along, still tied with ropes, they set the dogs on it, which had been especially trained to bite its ears.

The fierce mastiffs surrounded the animal, taking powerful leaps to attack the poor creature's muzzle.

The crowd was laughing and encouraging them, delighted with the spectacle, while Edgardo wondered how such a cruel game could bring so much enjoyment.

The bull's almost human laments, mixed with the growling and howling of the dogs, seemed to generate a heartfelt cry, a prayer to Our Lord.

But the ferocious ritual was only just beginning.

After repeated attacks, a mastiff managed to grab the bull's ear. However much the bull shook his muzzle and arched his back, the dog wouldn't let go, was tossed in every direction, until the animal finally managed to rid itself of it with a more powerful jerk. The dog rolled on the ground, the hairy ear between its teeth. The bull's muzzle was flooded with blood.

Then, all of a sudden, the crowd fell silent, and a quietness charged with anticipation enveloped the entire *campo*.

A bare-chested, muscular young man slowly approached the bleeding bull. Holding a saber, he stared into the animal's eyes. The wretched bull looked down, as though apologizing for existing.

A deep sense of grief stifled Edgardo's chest.

The sword was raised high, the young man stood with his legs apart to take his position and remained so, accompanied only by the raucous breathing of the bull.

A sharp whistle cut through the air. The blade fell, luminous and inexorable on the blood-soaked neck. The head came away from the body.

A roar of satisfaction rose from the crowd in praise of the hero who'd detached the head with a single blow, his sword not touching the ground.

Blood flooded out, and the dogs ran to lick the delicacy, while the young man was carried off in triumph.

Defeated and repelled, Edgardo lowered his head. How could this same crowd, now drunk on violence, sing hymns full of faith to Our Lord during processions?

The *campo* slowly emptied, and what was left of the bull was tied by the legs to two cart horses, and dragged, like a trophy, to Rivus Altus, followed by a celebrating crowd.

The group of larvae with Kallis's ghost had vanished. Perhaps that vision had been merely the fruit of his sick mind, burned up by opium.

He carried on wandering aimlessly, letting himself be dragged, in a daze, by groups of *gnaghe* and wild men.

When he heard None being rung, he went back to Ca' Grimani, exhausted.

The hours of sleep passed in apparent calm, with a humid, sticky wind running through them, spreading a veil of fog over the soft land that peered out through the surface of the lagoon.

Venice was sunk in a surreal silence. After the celebrations and clanging of the last day of Carnival, the people had been overwhelmed by an animal sleep full of regurgitations.

Lying atop one another in *campi, calli,* church porticos, inside gondolas and cogs, in shelters, and storerooms, the exhausted bodies looked like corpses abandoned in a battle-field. Death, more than life, seemed to have become the mistress of these muddy lands.

Matins rang in vain, echoing from district to district, but nobody stirred. Only the monks in the monasteries scattered between Venice and the islands in the lagoon left their cells to go to church for the first prayers.

Then, gradually, a mother-of-pearl light flashed illuminated splinters on the horizon, and the expanse of water lit up with scales of silver.

The new day was approaching from the Orient with small steps, defeating with great effort the army of shadows.

Edgardo was awoken by a succession of blows that reverberated in the interior courtyard.

For a moment, he thought they were just in his head, then he came to: they were coming from the front door. He put on his breeches and ran to the ground floor. None of the servants had heard anything.

"Who's there?" he shouted without opening.

"I'm here on the orders of the gastald. I must speak with the illustrious nobleman Tommaso Grimani . . . It's important."

"Wait, I'll go call him."

He was about to go when he saw Tommaso walking toward him.

"What's happening?" Tommaso asked, in a state of agitation.

"A messenger of the gastald is asking for you."

Without delay, Tommaso lifted the iron bar that blocked the door and removed the chains.

"Are you the nobleman Tommaso Grimani?" the messenger asked.

"I am, you may speak."

"The gastald asks you to follow me to the Doge's Palace."

"What happened?" Tommaso asked.

"I couldn't tell you much, Signore." The man gave Edgardo a suspicious look. "If I might speak . . . " Tommaso nodded. "It seems that during last night's patrol, the body was found."

"The body?" Grimani said, surprised. "The body of the virgin of the beads?"

"I have no other news, Signore. They just ordered me to come and call you."

"Very well, I'll follow you."

Edgardo's face had turned purple, blood had rushed to his head, triggered by powerful emotion.

She hadn't been resurrected. She wasn't roaming around the streets of Venice like a larva without peace. Nature had reinstated its laws. The dead shouldn't be confused with the living.

"Edgardo, tell my wife. Let's go," Grimani said, leaving the *palazzo*.

Edgardo bowed his head. He wanted to follow him. The identity of that mysterious young woman would finally be revealed.

# XVIII.
## NATRON

He went down the steps leading to the cellars of the Doge's Palace slowly, uncertainly, as though his robust body wished to rebel against the resolve of his mind.

The nobleman Tommaso Grimani, illustrious member of the Great Council, was about to do his duty on this dawn clouded by shreds of fog.

When he walked into the domed salon, beneath the main courtyard, his footsteps sounded to him like the drumroll before a death sentence.

Standing in front of a long table, in the middle of the basement, he recognized the gastald, as well as the nobleman Morosini, who immediately walked toward him, looking attentive.

"Come," Morosini said, sliding a hand under his arm, as though to support him.

Tommaso immediately saw that the laid-out body, totally naked, was that of a woman. The milky whiteness of her skin gave off a chilling, otherworldly aura. It was an adolescent, with just a hint of breasts, narrow hips, and long, frail legs.

A veil of deep sadness filled his chest. He rubbed his eyes again and again, then the gastald moved aside to let him see the face.

Morosini's hand held his arm more firmly.

Tommaso took a step forward and recognized her: it was Costanza, his Costanza, his beloved wife's sister.

The gastald thought Grimani's face looked like that of a

knight who, convinced his life is safe after a long battle, suddenly feels an icy blade pierce his side.

The muscles of his face hardened and, astonished, he turned to Morosini, then to the gastald, as though seeking confirmation for what lay before him.

"The soldiers found her at dawn, at a checkpoint set up to look for the virgin of the beads," the gastald explained, holding his breath.

Tommaso didn't utter a single word, but reached out and caressed Costanza's face. The girl did not have a suffering expression.

"Poor, innocent Costanza," Tommaso whispered.

"She was at the bottom of a cog, covered with rags, naked," the gastald continued. "The boat had been abandoned."

"Where?" Tommaso asked.

"In a canal behind San Lorenzo."

"San Lorenzo . . . very near where she was abducted."

"We think the murderers were in the process of moving the body," Morosini said, "but then they must have gotten scared by the checks we'd ordered for the virgin, so they abandoned the boat when they saw the guards."

"And do we know anything about the body of the Metamauco girl?" Grimani asked.

"No, nothing." Morosini shook his head. "Fate has played a trick on us."

"You said 'murderers.'" Grimani had a hard expression. "Do you know how she was killed?"

"As a matter of fact, we've found no traces of violence or cuts on her body," the gastald explained. "The flesh is intact, only of an unnatural whiteness."

"She could have been poisoned . . . or suffocated," Morosini added.

Tommaso's warm breath, as he leaned so close to her face, seemed to restore a touch of life to Costanza's cheeks.

"I see no sign of strangulation on her neck. Nor the blue caused by some poisons on her lips . . . but for this we need to consult a physician or an apothecary," Tommaso said, caressing her face and arranging her loose hair.

"Look," the gastald exclaimed.

A fine white dust had risen from her hair, and floated around her face, like a halo.

"What could this possibly be?" Morosini asked.

The gastald tested the consistency of the dust. "It feels like flour, only much finer. Her hair is steeped in it." He ran his hand down her arms and legs and raised the same dust. "The entire body is covered in it."

"She must have lain somewhere in the middle of this mysterious substance," Morosini suggested.

Tommaso nodded. "So it would seem."

"Collect a small amount," Morosini ordered the gastald, "and I will personally ask an eminent apothecary monk who lives at San Giorgio's Abbey for his expert opinion. Naturally, if you agree, Grimani."

"Nothing will bring her back to life. Do as you see fit." Tommaso suddenly covered his face with his hands. "Merciful God, how will I break the news to my wife?"

"Have we sinned? Tell us, Lord, how have we sinned? What are our faults? A child, an innocent, pure young girl: what were her sins? Speak to me, Lord, so I may understand why Thou hast decided to send us this test. Reveal Thyself to me, enlighten me, so that I might accept Thy will and bear the death that has come among us."

Everyone had expected Magdalena's desperate screams to fill the rooms and spread through the house but, instead, there was that whisper, that litany she obsessively mumbled, roaming around like a madwoman. She'd repeated her pained dirge for hours, and it was unbearable, soul-destroying.

"Have we sinned? Tell me, Lord, how have we sinned? What were my sweet, innocent sister's faults?"

Magdalena dragged herself from room to room, biting her arms and slamming doors as though she'd lost her mind.

They'd all rushed in at the news: servants, Nena, Edgardo, and found their mistress broken by grief in Tommaso's arms as he tried to give a little relief to her heart, torn to shreds.

Nena had thrown herself at her feet and burst into sobs, while Edgardo had remained frozen, his chest in pain, like an abscess swollen with bad humors.

He'd promised, he'd sworn, and he'd failed once again. He should have dedicated himself more attentively to searching for Costanza, instead of chasing after a ghost among the Carnival crowd. In the end, Lent had come, the time for penitence.

Magdalena had given him a look full of resentment. That death was also his responsibility. Edgardo had lowered his head. Would he ever find the courage to look his benefactors in the eye again?

"We'll bury her in the monastery of San Zaccaria," Tommaso announced. "She'll rest in a marble sarcophagus. I'll ask the abbess for permission to place it in the crypt, where Costanza prayed for the last time."

Magdalena let out a dull howl.

"As for the culprit, or culprits, I will use all my power to find them wherever they may be, and their punishment will be terrible and exemplary. The violence in this city is spreading like an uncontrollable disease. We must react and do everything in our power to defend honest, righteous citizens."

It sounded like the speech of a future doge and, for the first time, Edgardo had the suspicion that Tommaso wanted to use this terrible murder for his personal gain.

Magdalena, on the other hand, seemed relieved by these words, as though the public recognition of her sister's death made her suffering less acute. Seemingly calmer, she told her husband that she was going to her room to pray.

Alone with Tommaso, Edgardo finally managed to express his feelings. "You know how much affection and esteem I had for Costanza; my pain is equal only to the shame I feel for not having been able to protect her and save her. I assure you that I will not stop fighting at your side until we discover the perpetrator of this abominable act."

"You have been unforgivably neglectful . . . " Tommaso sighed, "but then, afterwards, you did everything in your power."

"No, I didn't do enough. And I cannot find peace."

At that moment, a servant announced the arrival of the gastald, who was asking to be admitted.

"Signore, we discovered what the dust found on the girl's body is," the gastald stated proudly. Tommaso gave him a sign to carry on. "The apothecary monk recognized it immediately. In the Benedictine monastery where he grew up they had a small foundry for manufacturing glass. It's natron. It's used by glassmakers as a flux in the production of glass. You find it in many foundries."

Foundries, glassmakers: the words thrust Edgardo back in time. Everything seemed to be happening all over again.

"So the body came in contact with this substance?" Grimani asked.

"The girl was most probably kept prisoner in a glassmaker's foundry, or her body may have been hidden there," was the gastald's theory.

"I can't understand what Costanza would have had to do with glassmakers," Tommaso wondered.

Edgardo's mind was a whirl of all the elements of an insoluble riddle: Tataro, the disappearance of his assistant Giacomo, the Alexandria merchant and the pure glass pieces found in the storeroom, and now the natron powder on

Costanza's body. He couldn't find a thread that would link such seemingly distant events.

Grimani was absorbed in thought. He was slowly pacing up and down the salon, rubbing his eyes.

Suddenly, he stopped, rooted, as though about to attack.

"Edgardo, please call back my wife. I want her here immediately, as well as all the servants, Nena, Alvise, everybody here." Then he turned to the gastald. "Please be kind enough to wait too. I'd like to ask your opinion on a suspicion that's wormed its way into my mind."

The bells of San Leonardo were starting to ring Sext. By the time the bells had struck twelve, they were all assembled in the salon once again.

Magdalena, worried and surprised, had her eyes fixed on her husband, trying to guess his thoughts.

"I can't see Alvise," Tommaso exclaimed.

"He's gone out to fetch logs for the fire," Nena said apologetically.

"I wanted to gather you here so that you might all be aware that our souls are crying out in pain over the death of our dear sister Costanza. At the same time, our souls are crying out for justice. Therefore, we will pursue the culprit with all our might." Grimani looked at all present one by one. "I've just heard from the illustrious gastald here that Costanza's hair and body were covered in a very fine powder called natron." Everyone in the room looked at one another, quizzically. "It's a substance used by glassmakers to prepare glass paste."

For a moment, Edgardo thought that, because of his past, the master assumed he was involved in the murder.

"Therefore, the gastald and I have deduced that the body must have been kept prisoner in a foundry." Tommaso took a deep breath to muster the strength for one final burst. "So I wondered who, among those close to Costanza, may have had anything to do with glassmakers now or in the past."

Edgardo thought he was in a trap.

"If memory serves," Grimani continued, "during the last search, glass beads were found in . . . in Alvise's room." He turned to Nena, who looked blank with fear.

"It's nothing, Signore. His master gave them to him. Two winters ago, Alvise worked as a *garzone* in a foundry . . . "

Unable to continue, Nena swallowed saliva in a desperate attempt to stuff back down her throat the words that had just come out of her toothless mouth.

The nauseating breath of suspicion eddied among those present and turned into a sigh of relief. It was now clear to everyone what Grimani was getting at.

At that moment, a cheerful whistling came from the canal, then the sound of wood hitting the steps.

Alvise's footsteps resounded loudly in the inner courtyard. When he walked into the salon, the boy looked around, bewildered, at all those people staring at him.

"Come forward." Grimani's tone was persuasive. "Now, I'm going to ask you a few questions, and you'll answer as truthfully as if you were with your confessor."

Alvise swallowed.

"Where were you on the last night of the Carnival . . . where were you yesterday at dawn?"

The young man looked at his mother, then Edgardo, as though hoping to be prompted. "I don't know, I went around, here and there, drinking and joking . . . I fell asleep in a *campo*."

"Which *campo*?" Tommaso asked.

Alvise's eyes opened wide. "The one behind San Severo, I think."

"Did you sleep until dawn?"

"Yes, Signore."

"Were you with a friend? Did anyone see you?"

"No, Signore, I was alone."

Nena was twisting her fingers as though trying to tear them off.

"Come now, Alvise. Remember, you're speaking with your confessor. Is it true that two winters ago you worked as a *garzone* for a glassmaker?"

"Yes, Signore, it's true."

"Where's the foundry where you worked?" Tommaso pursued.

"In Luprio."

"How long did you work there?"

"Just for the summer."

"And you haven't been back to that foundry . . . not even recently?"

"No, Signore, the foundry closed down. The glassmaker moved to Amurianum."

"So the foundry is abandoned, then?"

"I think so, yes."

The silence in the room was disturbed only by the waters slapping against the *fondamenta*. Grimani took a deep breath, then continued. "Alvise, do you know what natron is?"

"I think it was used for melting the glass."

"So there was natron in your foundry?'

"Yes, I think so, Signore."

Tommaso slowly walked around the perimeter of the salon, and stopped in front of the gastald.

"You've heard." His tone suddenly became forceful. "Once before I decided to trust this boy I consider a godson, even though irrefutable evidence, one of Costanza's ribbons, was found in his boat . . . Then there was the lock of hair found in his room, and now there's been a new, definitive discovery: Costanza's body was covered in natron, and natron can be found in foundries. Alvise has worked in a foundry and that's where he kept her prisoner until . . . " he stroked his forehead, closed his eyes, then boomed, "Alvise, son of Nena, I accuse you before witnesses of having abducted Costanza with the intention of abusing her and, when she tried to resist, of killing her!"

The words vibrated in the air, silencing the deep gurgle of the lagoon. The accusation had been uttered. A member of the Great Council had spoken, and nothing would ever be the same again.

"I will ask the gastald to take the boy away with him and lock him up in the cells of the Doge's Palace to await trial."

With inhuman cries, Nena threw herself at her son's body and pressed it against her. "No, no, it's not true! It wasn't him! Merciful God, help us!"

The servants were shocked.

Magdalena remained with her mouth half open, perhaps wanting to say something, but stunned by the speed of events.

Edgardo tried to search his master's soul: the relaxed expression, the frank look, head high, as though he'd received divine investiture.

He'd just accused a boy of having committed a murder, which almost certainly meant a death sentence, and yet his face betrayed no emotion. For a moment, Edgardo felt envy, wishing he could have even just an ounce of Tommaso's certainty, he, who was always full of doubts, of insecurities, and prey to emotion.

The only person who didn't seem to realize what was happening was Alvise. He was looking around as though all this chaos had nothing to do with him.

Only when the gastald approached, took him by the arm, and dragged him away did he feel that this gesture contained his destiny, and that his life would be changed forever.

# XIX.
## INSPECTIO

T he body of her beloved sister was coming back home. It was proceeding slowly, rocked by the soft waves of the lagoon, across Venice, to be reunited with its blood. Magdalena was waiting.

The Grimani household would receive her and get her ready for the final farewell before she was buried in the crypt of San Zaccaria.

Magdalena would wash her, dress her, and hold her in her arms one last time.

The body of her beloved sister.

The more time passed, the more she felt something growing in her belly, a feeling she couldn't—didn't want to explain because she was too ashamed. A feeling more invasive than the deep sorrow caused by Costanza's death.

She heard the *scaula* bump against the steps, and men discussing how they'd organize the transport of the body to beneath the loggia.

The body had entered her home, the body of her sweet, tender, generous sister.

The feeling she didn't want to see born was swelling her belly. It was stirring and pushing.

Why, merciful God? Why had such dark ghosts been let loose in her?

The footsteps resounded on the stairs. They'd already reached the upstairs loggia, just a few more seconds and they would lay the body on the virginal bed upon which she had spent so many peaceful nights.

Magdalena remained obstinately seated in the high-backed chair by the window and let herself be blinded by the sun reflected on the water. She should get up and go to her. Costanza's body was waiting.

Instead, she was frozen, unable to move, and that feeling grew more and more forceful until it exploded and obliged her to name it: anger.

Anger, resentment toward her sister, as though her destiny had been her fault.

This body was carrying another sorrow, another death in a house devastated by mourning. Magdalena felt that this pain would dry up forever her belly that was incapable of conceiving, that the sight of Costanza's body would decree the end of every hope, the impossibility of bringing into the world a new Grimani heir.

Why had they brought it into this house, what did they want from her? She had no more tears, no more pain to offer the world!

Enough of death, Magdalena wanted life.

Wracked with shame for having these thoughts, she mustered the strength to lift her fragile body and head to Costanza's room.

When she saw her, her glowingly white face, her dusty hair, her long fingers protruding from the linen canvas in which she was wrapped, she momentarily recovered the outline of her sisterly sorrow, and the anger vanished.

She approached, kissed her forehead, and kneeled.

Nena was sobbing at her side. She hadn't stopped crying since Alvise had been taken away. Now, the tears she was shedding for her son mixed with those for Costanza.

Magdalena's prayer spread through the room: a soft, monotonous chant.

Edgardo paused at the door, waiting for a sign that would allow him to approach. Seeing the body threw him into an abyss: the sense of guilt and the confirmation that he had failed blended with deep sorrow for the loss of a young girl barely at life's threshold.

He took courage and kneeled near Magdalena, who didn't let that distract her from her prayers even for a second.

"I humbly beg you to forgive me, Signora. I'd made you a promise and I failed," Edgardo whispered.

"I can't forget that Costanza was abducted because of you."

"You're right to hate me . . . I also hate myself, I hate my ineptitude, and my weakness. If you wish me to leave this house, I will respect your decision."

Overwhelmed with grief, Magdalena tilted her head slightly. "What purpose would that serve?" Edgardo thought he saw a hint of compassion in her eyes. "You've been a cleric. Can you explain to me why God is raging against me so?"

Her tone sounded cold and detached. Edgardo said nothing, searching for an answer he couldn't find, then, almost without realizing it, replied, "The ways of Our Lord are unfathomable." And an image suddenly flashed through his mind: he remembered those very same words spoken by Ademaro, his friend and a monk at the same abbey, on the top of the tower, after he'd dissuaded Edgardo from seeking his own death.

Magdalena gave him an angry look. The same reaction that he had once had. It's too easy to attribute everything to the mysteries of God's will.

"Tomorrow we're going to bury her . . . and I will never see her again," Magdalena whispered.

Nena's sobs turned into a hoarse cry.

"Quiet! Enough! You've no right to weep," Magdalena suddenly railed. "Your son has taken her life and now I have to put up with your sniveling on top of everything else!"

Nena prostrated herself on the floor. "No, no, it's not true. Alvise is innocent. It wasn't him."

"Quiet. Don't speak."

"He respected her. He never, never would have touched her." Nena dragged herself to Edgardo. "You tell her, I beg you, for the love of God, you know Alvise is innocent."

Edgardo had stood up for him once before, but now it would seem disrespectful and cowardly to go against his master's decision again. "Alvise will have a trial, and if it's as you say, the judges will acknowledge his innocence."

He immediately felt ashamed of having spoken so insensitively.

"What do the judges know? Tomorrow, Costanza will be buried and Alvise condemned."

Edgardo searched for Magdalena's gaze. He had to try, then she could go ahead and throw him out.

"Have they investigated the cause of death?" he asked.

Magdalena said nothing.

"They said Alvise killed her because he was trying to rape her, but it's not true!" Nena cried.

"Has rape been established?"

He took the slow lifting of her chin and the glow in her eyes, which seemed to emit incandescent scales, as a sign that his question had made a breach in Magdalena's mind.

"No," she replied harshly.

"Don't you think, Signora, that before making such a serious accusation, it would be fairer to find out the truth? How can we say that Alvise raped or killed Costanza when we don't even know how she died?"

"And how can we have the certainty that the accusations are founded?" Magdalena asked without betraying the slightest emotion.

Taken by surprise, Edgardo ventured further. "One would have to get the body examined now, right away, before it's buried."

Magdalena slowly got up. Nena stopped sobbing, as though

aware of a chink of hope, and followed her lady with her eyes as she went to stand pensively by the window.

"Send someone to fetch Magister Abella immediately," she suddenly commanded Nena. Then she looked at Edgardo defiantly. "She's an illustrious physician. She'll be able to give us an answer."

This was an unexpected and unwelcome conclusion for Edgardo, but he raised no objection. Alvise's life was at risk.

Nena was already on her way, glimpsing a favorable outcome in that decision. "She must come as soon as possible," Magdalena added. "Tommaso won't be back before nightfall, and he mustn't find her here."

She sought the scribe's gaze, openly requesting his complicity. He lowered his head.

When he saw her come in, Edgardo couldn't help noticing that Abella's face had acquired a new glow that made it unexpectedly amiable. The ruby-red robe hugged her curves, and her hair cascaded softly over her shoulders.

Why was he noticing these details? It was an ambiguous attraction, since his doubts about her had certainly not been dispelled.

Abella greeted him with a nod and approached Magdalena. With an unexpected, irregular gesture, and without a word, she pressed the lady of the house to her in a rough, masculine hug.

As though this hug had untied a tight knot that pressed on her chest, Magdalena abandoned herself, unrestrained, to desperate weeping, resting her head on the Magister's shoulder.

At that moment, Edgardo sensed that the pale, puny feelings of a man were nothing in comparison to the immeasurable, powerful universe of female emotions.

"You must tell me how she died but, above all, I want to know if her virginity is still intact," Magdalena whispered through sobs.

With a wide, regal gesture, Abella tossed off her cloak. "I will proceed according to the rules of the illustrious master Galen, following the teachings of my guide and mentor Trotula de Ruggiero, *magistra mulier sapiens.*"

Her display of knowledge always irritated Edgardo, and made him suspicious as well.

"I'll begin work immediately. I wish to spare you an unpleasant sight," Abella added, addressing both. "I'll send for you as soon as I've drawn some conclusions."

A polite way of sending them out, Edgardo thought. Abella wanted to be alone while examining the body. Why?

"Signora," Edgardo butted in rather daringly. "Please allow me to assist our illustrious physician. My duty to you demands that I represent your eyes during this painful moment."

"A scribe, and former cleric on top of that, seems like an unusual . . . and useless assistant," Abella immediately replied.

"Far be it from me to want to interfere with your work. It was simply my intention to write down, under your dictation, your comments about the body. I think they will be useful in view of the trial."

Taken by surprise, Abella couldn't find any argument against Edgardo's point.

"Unless, illustrious one, you would rather write down your comments yourself," Edgardo added smugly.

"That is not how I normally work. I have a prodigious memory."

"*Verba volant, scripta manent.* As Caius Titus said in the Roman Senate." He bit his lip: he too had shown off his useless knowledge.

"You may stay," Magdalena said abruptly, putting an end to the ongoing tension.

"Thank you, Signora, I'll get the necessary writing tools immediately."

"Please be gentle," Magdalena added, caressing her sister's

face. Then, realizing the absurdity of her words, she said, "Do whatever you need to."

Edgardo came back with parchment, a quill, and a horn filled with ink. He brought the lectern closer to the bed, took his precious eye circles out of his pocket, and adopted a waiting pose, flashing a provocative, defiant smile.

"I can't see what you're hoping to achieve," Abella said, getting ready.

"I only wish for Alvise to have a fair trial," Edgardo replied.

That wasn't all and Abella knew it: the scribe harbored a suspicion, a distrust toward her, which she couldn't account for.

She bent over Costanza and removed the canvas from her body.

The underdeveloped breasts, the narrow hips, and the long, skinny legs: naked, she looked even more frighteningly white. She'd examined countless women, many of them victims of rape, others already ill or about to leave this world.

Costanza was different. Even though at least two nights had passed since her death, there was no sign of decay.

"It's natron," Edgardo explained when Abella noticed the veil of white dust. "Glassmakers use it during the melting stage. Her whole body was covered in it. That's why they've accused Alvise. He's worked in a foundry."

Abella picked up a small amount of the mineral with her fingers and placed it in a handkerchief which she put back into her pocket.

"Alright, let's begin the *inspectio*. *In primis*, we'll analyze the top part," she announced with authority. Then, with a skilled gesture, she took the head between her hands and bent it right and left, examining the insides of the ears, feeling the nape, and checking the neck.

"Write down: *nullum signum* of strangulation, nor of a blow with a rod, a sword, or a club. *Calva intacta est*. There is no smell of decay from the flesh, so she can't have been dead for more than three days."

She prized open her jaw, parted her mouth, stuck two fingers in, and rubbed inside, going down to the throat. Then she took the damp fingertips up to her nose and breathed in deeply, before licking them with enthusiasm.

"It smells of lamb suckling meat, thick, slippery humors, a slight scent of . . . " she paused thoughtfully, " . . . I'd say of juniper. There's no trace of venomous vapors, or of toxic herbs, or deadly substances. So I'd rule out poisoning."

"You're going too fast," Edgardo interrupted. "My hand can't keep up with your voice."

"I didn't ask you to write down my words, and I thought you were more skilled. Instead, I see you are slow and boring and, besides, that strange contraption to help your eyes is slowing you down. You're not much of a scribe."

"At Bobbio, I was considered one of the best."

"Perhaps that was many years ago."

Edgardo decided not to respond. She was right. His season for writing was inevitably heading toward a long, harsh winter.

Magister Abella's hands went up the shoulders, lifted the frail arms, tapped on the breastbone, rose up to the heart, then went down to the abdomen. The physician looked, pressed, kneaded.

"There's an unusual, unnatural swelling and hardness in the area where third-region organs reside, such as the liver, bile, stomach, spleen, and intestines." She paused and looked at Edgardo. "I've never seen anything like this. It's almost as though the organs are swollen."

"What can it mean?" Edgardo asked.

Abella did not reply and carried on with her inspection.

"And now let's move to the fourth region, to the genital organs." And, with a decisive gesture, she parted the girl's legs.

There was soft, luxuriant hair sprouting over the pubis.

Abella bent down, searched for the entrance to the *collum matricis* and delicately inserted two fingers into the vulva.

She pushed, felt, turned, took them out and raised her fingers to her nose and mouth, tasting it as she'd done earlier.

"It smells of eel skin dried in the sun, a slightly salty, crackling taste of strong spice." She looked up at Edgardo, who kept writing, holding the goose quill with one hand and the eye circles with the other. "I can say for certain that there has been no penetration . . . *pulcra illibata est.*"

The scribe stopped writing and drew a deep breath of relief. "So the hypothesis that Alvise may have raped her before or after her death is not plausible. Moreover, there are no signs of struggle."

"You're right, but what makes me perplexed is that I've found nothing that would have caused her death . . . except for the strange swelling in the third region."

"Maybe she was suffocated," Edgardo said.

There was a shared look of understanding that surprised them both . . . they were working together, and it was as though they'd decided that at the same time.

"Help me turn the body over."

Somewhat reluctantly, Edgardo approached Costanza.

"Lift her legs, and I'll take the shoulders," the physician commanded. Seeing him hesitate, she sneered. "It looks like you're not very used to corpses . . . "

Edgardo took the wretched girl's feet. He made an effort and found himself looking at Costanza's skinny behind.

Paying no attention to him, Abella started examining the rest of the body: shoulders, arms, back, legs, feet.

She was about to cover the body with the canvas again when she stopped, puzzled by a red spot that spread between the buttocks.

She bent down and, with two fingers, spread the flaps to fully expose the anus. "By the Hippocratic oath . . . " She fell silent for a fraction of a second. "I've never seen anything like this before! Come closer, look."

The scribe hesitated.

"Oh, I beg your pardon, perhaps I'm embarrassing you. I forgot you used to be a cleric. It is a sight, totally new to you, which could upset your sensibility."

Stiff as a dried sea bass, Edgardo approached the Magister without saying a word.

"Here, look between the buttocks." She seemed to be deliberately trying to provoke him. "You see, the anus has been sewn up very skilfully, by the hand of an expert."

Because of his poor sight, Edgardo couldn't really see what Abella was pointing at, so, without even thinking about it, out of habit, he went to fetch his eye circles and came close to the orifice.

"Can you see properly now?"

"Yes, it's horrible, it's sewn up like the gash of a wound." He read the same terrible thought in Abella's face. "You mean to say that—" he stopped, ashamed.

"I don't know . . . It's certainly the first hypothesis that comes to mind: that the murderer performed violence against nature."

They both took a step back, almost as though trying to push the thought out of their minds.

"It's monstrous, poor Costanza . . . " Edgardo stammered. "But who . . . I can never believe that Alvise could have performed such an act. Besides, why then sew up the orifice?"

Abella puffed her cheeks, breathed out, and shook her head. "I can't account for it. It's as though the murderer wanted to put the body back together after death . . . I don't understand."

They remained without speaking, as though in silent prayer.

"I think our work is over," Abella concluded.

They turned the body over again, then picked up the cloth to cover it once more.

"Wait." Edgardo bent over the girl's face. "I'm certain that she is already with God, illuminated by His love."

He kissed her forehead and gently touched her cheeks and her lips.

It was just a second, the feeling of something hard: he thought he felt a swelling under her nose. He instinctively brought the glass circles close to his eyes and examined the nasal cavity.

As a matter of fact, there were two lacerations inside; small cuts caked with blood, as though a tool had been inserted into the nose.

How come? What could these unusually situated wounds mean?

"Have you seen something?" Abella asked, seeing him bend over the girl's face.

"No, nothing . . . I was dazzled by her beauty, which has outlived death."

Why had he lied?

"So can we cover her now?"

Edgardo nodded.

Why couldn't he entirely trust Abella? What reasons did he have to doubt her?

The Magister stood before him and gave him a severe look. For a moment, he thought she'd read his mind.

"I want you to be totally honest with me."

Edgardo stiffened, ready to take the blow.

"Do you think it really necessary to tell Magdalena the whole truth?"

They buried her in a great rush. The sun had set only once since she had been found. Grimani said the corpse was decaying. That wasn't true. Miraculously, Costanza's body still looked as it had on the first day: luminous, white, with no nauseating smell; on the contrary, it had the scent of aromatic herbs.

They wanted to be rid of her, of her macabre presence that had brought so much sorrow into the house and Magdalena's already devastated spirit.

Edgardo could understand his master wanting to have done with this business and go back to facing the future.

When he and Abella had reported, and lied about the results of the examination, Edgardo had realized with sadness that the only piece of information Magdalena cared about was her sister's virginity. She hadn't been raped, and that was all that counted.

Other observations that could cast doubt on Alvise's guilt had been dismissed with total indifference; he saw that Magdalena wasn't listening, lost in the maze of her own despair.

Edgardo was tempted to reveal the cruel truth, thinking this could somehow help Alvise, but then realized that it would only increase their desire for revenge. How could he prove that the *garzone* was unable to perform such a procedure? It would be useless, and the hatred generated by an act of such violence would have exploded uncontrollably.

During the ceremony in the crypt of San Zaccaria convent,

on a late winter's day stifled by an impenetrable cloak of hoar-frost dripping from the Istrian marble, Edgardo thought he could see in his master's face a detachment he'd never noticed before. He got the impression that he was treating him with unusual coldness. He assumed this was due to the circumstances and the place, even though deep in his heart he feared that Tommaso, having been made aware of Edgardo's doubts regarding Alvise's guilt, somehow wanted to punish him and push him away. Edgardo felt guilty, as though he had disappointed him.

The same feeling he'd experienced when he'd let down his father's hopes, when the latter had expected to have a son who was a knight and, instead, had gotten a deformed creature unable to fight.

So much time had passed since then, and yet the twisted game in his fragile soul was always replayed in the same way, ever more painfully.

Would he therefore never be free of the feeling of ineptitude that had shadowed him since birth?

Once night had fallen on this day of mourning, Edgardo retired to his room with the need to put some order to the confusion of thoughts and feelings stirring in his mind. He had a decision to make.

He put out the oil lamp and went to bed. His bones always ached when he lay down on the straw mattress.

The blackness of the night had erased all points of reference, and the only glimmer of light came from the collision of his thoughts, which generated lightning bolts and glows, and dragged him deeper into the eye of a devastating storm.

If he really wanted to prove Alvise's innocence, he would have to oppose Tommaso's will when the latter already seemed to have found the man responsible for the crime.

It wasn't easy to go against the one he considered his benefactor. Besides, he would have to find a new culprit in order to make his certainty credible. He did not have much confidence in himself. He'd followed his intuition, vague feelings, convinced that he would bring Costanza back home alive, but instead . . .

Places and faces were muddled in a tangle with no head or tail: the Alexandrian merchant and his mysterious palazzo, the very pure glass he'd found in the storeroom, Tataro and the disappearance of his *garzone* Giacomo and, finally, discovering natron on Costanza's body, which led back to glass . . . And now the unexplained sewing up of her anus and the cuts in her nose.

And then there was Abella, so tough and decisive, an expert in her art, capable of generous, unselfish acts—what was she truly looking for? Was she simply in the service of Magdalena, or did she have something to do with Costanza's abduction and death?

His head was pounding and sleep was eluding him. He didn't want to give up. He tried to resist the temptation although he knew that his willpower was more fragile than a newborn baby's body.

He slipped out of bed, took a small purple glass bottle from his trunk, poured a few drops of thick liquid over an old sponge, and breathed the vapors in deeply.

Ah, opium, saving, heavenly substance, divine food, nectar of the gods, whirlpool of pleasure, providential light . . . The muddle of thoughts was immediately dissolved, his ailing feelings lit up with hope, and his anguish and sorrow vanished. He'd shaken off the burden of his actual life, and past failures appeared as no more than a bad dream after too much drink. He closed his eyes and finally fell asleep.

A flicker of light piercing through the roof tiles and the beating of an invasive seagull's wings heralded the birth of a new dawn.

He woke up lucid and full of energy. In his clear mind, one

thought shone bright. He had to go forth and carry on fighting. If there was one lesson he'd learned from his failures, it was that he must never flee before the enemy, not even when fear dwelled within him.

He went down into the inner courtyard. The servants were already at work around the well. Drawing water for the day was their first task. He found Nena in the kitchen, poking the fire. The air smelled of resin and smoked reeds. The wretched woman looked at him with surprise, fearing bad news.

"You said your son worked for a glassmaker two summers ago, didn't you?" Edgardo asked.

Nena's mouth mumbled a few senseless sounds, perhaps some kind of prayer, then the words took shape. "By the blessed Virgin, God almighty, Saint Mark who watches over the poor, Alvise is innocent. You know that. Alvise is a good boy, oh, blessed God."

Edgardo shook her. "Answer me, Nena, where was this glassmaker's foundry? I want to save your Alvise, do you understand that?"

The woman opened her mouth wide and, amid her sparse teeth, her tongue took a moment's rest, then she continued. "By merciful God, by the holy Apostles, by the prayers of all the martyrs, I don't know . . . I think in Luprio, near a salt pan . . . he was a good *garzone.*"

"In Luprio, near a salt pan?" Edgardo repeated. It couldn't be.

As far as he knew, there was only one foundry in the district of Luprio, the one he knew well, the one that Segrado, the great master glassmaker, who had given him his precious eye circles, had rented from Zoto, the crystal maker.

He'd been keeping away from the district for many years, far away from memories, from the past . . . and now the past had returned. It was always this way.

They were all dead: Segrado, Zoto the crystal maker, his

beloved Kallis, even though her ghost, in the body of the virgin of the beads, fueled the illusion of rebirth.

He was scared, but at the same time curious to discover how his heart would react to seeing these places again.

With Carnival over and the start of Lent, the appearance of the city had totally altered: the dark breath of poverty, hunger, and despair had penetrated everywhere, and with every step you took, you felt as though you were advancing into a decomposing body.

When he reached Rivus Altus, Edgardo rushed across the canal over the bridge made of cogs built between the shores.

That place, which only ten years earlier had looked like a flourishing market, rich with produce from the vegetable patches of the lagoon islands, had turned into a miserable market of the scarce crops that the countryside, invaded by the waters, still managed to yield. The cabbages, kale, and fennel displayed in the baskets were corroded by rot and mold.

The makeshift stalls gave off a nauseating stench from mounds of mussels and dead crabs. Eels, sardines, and even gobies were a rarity. There was still a great bustle, especially of beggars, bigots, penitents, and lepers, rooting on the ground in search of leftovers. Two cripples were arguing over a fish head snatched away from the paws of a cat.

The deprivations of the Year of Our Lord 1118 were striking violently the land of the wide rivers, and hunger prompted the poorest people to commit crimes in order to survive.

He walked past the little church of San Giacomo di Rivo Alto and ventured into the narrow streets and canals, into the district called Luprio.

How many times had he taken this trip? He thought he could have walked with his eyes shut, but noticed that the landscape had changed greatly. You could still see everywhere the ruins of houses that had collapsed during the earthquake the year before. Bridges thrown down into the canals had been swept away by the currents, and many paths submerged by high tides; sand banks and fords had taken over once luxuriant fields. He struggled to walk, his boots sinking into treacherous slime that, with his every step, gave off a sharp stench of moldy dung.

When he reached Campo San Giacomo di Luprio, he almost couldn't believe his eyes. Every spot was overgrown; tall cordgrass concealed every path. Heaps of leaves, dried branches, and brambles were rolling around, dragged by the tramontana wind; alders and oaks, too leafy, were concealing the light, so that to reach the church you had to walk through a kind of forest.

The disaster hadn't even spared the house of God. Part of the bell tower had collapsed, the portico outside the entrance was roofless, and the surrounding brick wall was full of cracks. A desolate sight that filled him with sadness: the city of Venice hadn't managed to pick itself back up yet.

Just a little farther, and he would find Segrado's foundry, the place that had witnessed the events that had overturned his life.

There, he had first met Kallis, watched Segrado's attempts to discover the formula for crystal glass, and, from that very foundry, had received from Segrado the eye circles that had saved his ailing eyesight.

In the nearby salt pan, he had seen Kallis for the last time before she disappeared in the billows during the terrible storm that shook Venice and erased Metamauco in the Year of Our Lord 1106.

Afraid and anxious to discover how his heart would respond, he walked the last few steps.

He turned around a hut and . . . an excruciating pain, like the blow of a sword, tore through his chest. Almost nothing remained of the place he remembered.

The larch beams of the walls had snapped; only the skeleton

remained of the roof, covered in thatch and reeds; the front door had collapsed, and the furnace had been razed to the ground.

Climbing over charred beams and mounds of soil, he made his way through the tall grass and entered what was once Segrado's workshop.

For a moment, he thought he saw him at work, the bald bear, bare-chested, hairy-backed, handling the blowpipe with his huge hands, with Kallis's help. Kallis, strong, decisive, wrapped in her amber-colored cloak, with those sharp eyes, full of pain and passion.

He rummaged in the ruins and searched around the fireplaces. There was no trace of natron. The only dust was the one brought over by the wind from the rubble. No sign of Costanza's presence. How could anyone think that Alvise had kept her a prisoner and killed her here? This foundry hadn't been active for a while. Another piece of proof that the accusations against the boy made no sense.

He went out and saw that the workshop of Zoto, the crystal maker, was also abandoned; of those times and those men there was nothing left.

He went toward the salt pan that bordered the foundry and was surprised to see that the blinding glow that used to reverberate from the basins was much weaker, and had turned from icy white to a sickly gray.

The reason for this became clear when he reached the edge of the dams. The muddy sea, which rules over all of Venice, as well as the islands in the west and in the north, had swelled out of all proportion in recent years, erasing everything. The water level had risen to the point where it had submerged small islands and fords.

The salt pan had turned into a huge pool: the glistening crystal just beneath the water surface produced splinters of light that flickered and chased one another, creating a cloak strewn with precious gemstones. The sea seemed dressed up for a celebration.

Edgardo could not enjoy this brilliant sight; his heart and mind were immersed in the past, in the memory of that final image, of Kallis bending over Segrado's bloodied body . . . then her desperate flight, tossed about by the billows in the storm, before being submerged.

He looked up at the horizon: a thin blue line was caressing the lagoon, rippled by the wind, and, in the middle, there was a dark whirlpool joining the sky and the sea, which was coming fast, approaching the land like a messenger rising from the depths of the waters. He followed it, waiting for it to reach the shore and drag him into the eddy together with the memory of Kallis.

However, a few yards away from the land, struck by a blade of light, the whirlpool dissolved and dispersed in the air.

Edgardo hung his head: had God sent him a sign? Was it too early to put an end to his existence? He felt like praying, but couldn't muster the courage to do so. He had no right to. God must still be very angry with him.

He heard a noise behind him. It was a boatman, dragging a sackful of grain toward the *dominicum*, the thatched hut of the watchman.

The old windmill had undergone a powerful transformation: with the waters rising, it had been turned into a watermill that used the lagoon currents to activate the grinder.

The watchman came out and took the sack.

"God be with you," Edgardo called out to him.

The weary old man didn't as much as grant him a look.

"Forgive me for interrupting your work," Edgardo insisted. "I saw that old abandoned foundry. Do you know who owns it? I'd like to get it started again," he lied.

The man looked at him with suspicion, undecided whether or not to reply to a stranger.

"I heard it once belonged to a man called Zoto, a crystal maker," Edgardo persevered.

As though, by uttering that name, Edgardo had been endowed with credibility, the old man made up his mind to speak.

"Zoto is not even food for worms anymore," he smiled, pleased, "nothing but bones. The foundry has been taken over by an illustrious and powerful glassmaker."

"Do you know his name?"

"Tataro. You'll find him im Amurianum, but I don't think he wants to part with it. He rented it out for a while, but then he closed it down, and there's been no smoke from that fire ever since . . . he'd rather let it go to ruin."

"Thank you, you've been very kind," Edgardo said, walking away.

Tataro again. His name sprung out like an infection that can't be eradicated.

The missing *garzone*, his relationship with Abella, the crystal glass, and now the foundry that used to belong to Segrado. How were all these events connected? Edgardo was trying to weave a canvas, to tie together threads that kept slipping out of his fingers.

The only certainty was Alvise.

The fact that he'd found nothing at the foundry was new proof of his innocence. What could be done to spare him an unjust sentence? Face Tommaso? Clash with him? Would he ever admit his error? That was unlikely. The pride of power does not admit failure.

Maybe Magdalena could intercede, at least out of duty toward justice. She had welcomed Nena's son into her home, and before condemning him, she had to grant him a chance.

However, the word of a poor scribe was not credible enough. He had to find a voice of authority, someone she trusted blindly.

He tried to push away the first spontaneous idea that came to him, but the more he tried to avoid it, the more convinced he was that there was only one person who could persuade Magdalena to plead the case with her husband. And he now harboured too many suspicions about her!

# XXI

## THE FAT MAN AND THE MAN FROM BERGAMO

Bloody hell, may the worms eat your balls, your mother's ass, and the ass of that whore, your daughter!" swore the fat man, whose bulky body made it hard for him to move.

"Take it by the head, you incompetent ass," the man from Bergamo shouted. "It's about to break, it's coming apart."

The two porters lifted the large bundle wrapped in a jute sack and unloaded it from the cog, anchored along the canal, onto the ground.

"Watch it, you fool, you'll drop it into the canal," grumbled the large man who had the neck of a bull and hands as large as the gates of hell.

With difficulty, they lifted the load onto their shoulders and walked uncertainly in the dark, behind the convent of San Giovanni Evangelista in Torcellus.

"Son of a whore, damned ass . . . you can't see a thing," complained the slimmer one, who had under his chin a goiter the size of a pumpkin.

"Get a move on, you Bergamo pig."

"It stinks like shit that's been shat twice."

"Just keep walking and shut up, fool."

They followed the path and, when they reached the entrance, they knocked. A few seconds later, the door opened.

Magister Abella was wrapped in a kind of sky-blue caftan that left only her face uncovered.

"Where do we dump this?" the fat man asked.

"Come inside, quickly." Abella motioned with her head.

"You should be pleased, Signora, it's fresh meat, a luxury."

Abella felt the weight of the package, which was dripping with a thick, dark liquid.

"So I see."

They went through the front room to the laboratorium at the back.

"Put it there," she said, indicating a stone table in the middle of the room.

"One, two, three." They swung the load and placed it on the table, paying no attention to the sinister creaking of bones.

"Gently, you wretches. It's delicate stuff." She took a pouch from under her caftan. "So it's seven dinars, as usual."

"No, Signora, ten . . . It was a dangerous bit of work," the fat man replied.

"Venice is crawling with soldiers," said the other one, in support.

"Hey, Bergamo man, don't try and be clever," Abella interrupted, putting the seven dinars into his hand. "Your merchandise certainly isn't worth any more than that. Let's see if the meat is as fresh as you say."

"I swear it on my stinking mother. You'll see if I'm telling the truth."

The stocky man took the reward and signaled to his companion. They mumbled something incomprehensible, then left the house.

Abella went back into her laboratorium. The package seemed less swollen than before. It had changed shape, lying limp on the stone surface.

She wasn't proud of what she'd done, but she'd had no choice. Acting in the dark and breaking the law meant dealing with not very commendable people: these weren't the rules she'd agreed to follow when she'd embarked on practicing the art of medicine.

She'd found herself forced to do this—this was the truth—in order to build her name and reputation. A woman physician certainly didn't have an easy life, not even in a city like Venice, where travelers, merchants, artisans from all over the Earth were generously welcomed . . . as long as they were male, complete with cock and balls; otherwise they were seen with suspicion or, worse, not seen at all.

Women were all very well if submissive or used for humping, but if they dared philosophize or discuss illnesses and remedies, they were considered witches or liars.

And so Abella had learned not to have too many qualms about it. The odd subterfuge was unavoidable. Like, for instance, doing some research about the patients in order to astonish them at first sight by guessing their ailments. The path to her goal was tortuous, and there was no point in being squeamish.

She estimated the weight of the merchandise with her eyes. It was late at night and tiredness had taken possession of her limbs. She would postpone the heavy work till tomorrow.

"There's an evil wind blowing." The boatman pushed the oar hard, and the *scaula* finally managed to turn into the large canal in Torcellus.

Edgardo looked up at the lead-gray sky. The waters of the lagoon were rebelling against him, and nature itself seemed to be hostile toward him.

They struggled to land at the dock outside Santa Maria Assunta. There were cogs anchored along the *fondamenta*, some loaded with wine and oil, others covered in sacks of salt or timber from forests on the mainland. Slaves and servants were coming and going between the storerooms and the boats that were to transport the goods to the freight ships anchored in the bay outside San Marco.

Near the baptistry, outside the Cathedral, he came across a

small procession of women heading to Santa Fosca, carrying a tiny coffin that must have contained the body of a child.

When he'd reached the convent of San Giovanni Evangelista, he made his way to the laboratorium.

The door was shut and the windows barred with heavy planks. No one responded. He looked around and noticed a Benedictine nun hoeing a small vegetable patch at the back of the monumental church with three naves.

"God be with you, sister," he called out.

"God is always in my heart," the nun replied.

She had a soft voice and a body so frail that Edgardo wondered how she could lift such a heavy tool.

"I've come to meet Magister Abella. Do you know her?"

"Abella, *magister mulier sapiens*. We hold her in great esteem."

"Do you know if she's coming back or if, by any chance, she's gone on a long journey?" Edgardo asked.

"They call for her from all over the lagoon, she's very much in demand, especially among women. She possesses special qualities . . . She'll be back, be patient, you just need to wait."

The nun stopped working and, panting, leaned on the hoe.

"Would you like me to help you or bring you some water?"

"May God bless you, son. Don't let my body deceive you. What counts is the spirit, that's where true strength comes from." The nun looked at the fields surrounding the convent. "We now have to do everything ourselves, the vine, the vegetable patches, the orchard. Now we only get help with the salt pan in the marsh of San Gerolamo," she sighed. "Able-bodied men are all moving from Torcellus to Rivoalto. They say there's no more work here. The cogs that come down from the Silis now all carry on to Venice. They've forgotten us. The masters no longer care about Torcellus, Aymanas, Costanciacum, Majurbium, Burianum . . . only Rivoalto exists now, the doge wants all the power close to him." She crossed herself. "You'll see, all that'll be left here is us nuns and just a few fishermen." She wiped her forehead and resumed her hoeing with renewed energy.

Edgardo kept looking at her with admiration, then retraced his steps to the laboratorium, intent on waiting for the Magister's return.

A blanket of cloud had risen and a wan winter sun was filtering through the gaps. He sat on the front door step and stretched his neck like a tortoise in search of warmth.

The threshold was lit by a beam. Edgardo noticed that a few irregular spots of a vague ruby-red were glistening on the stone. He tried their consistency with his fingernail. The substance was dried up and his weak eyes didn't allow him to investigate further. An idea crossed his mind. It had worked once before, so why not try it again?

He took from his pouch the case inside which he jealously kept the miraculous contraption.

He brought his eye circles close to his eyes and bent down: irregular edges, circular shapes, purple in color. They looked like drops, the drops of a dense, viscous liquid . . . there was no doubt: it was blood. The traces led inside the house.

Perhaps an injured man had sought help at the physician's house. He examined the green patch outside the front door: there were other, even more copious traces of blood, and the grass was crushed as though a load had been carried to the door.

The tendency of delirious imagination to roam down twisted paths led him to a rather rash decision.

He made up his mind to go in. He'd never been able to dispel the shadows gathered around that quack's behavior.

The door was firmly shut. He walked around the house. On the side facing the lagoon, the protective beam of one of the windows had a long crack. It wouldn't be hard to take it off its hinges. He managed to open a gap with a blow, climbed through it, and slipped inside.

Light spread from the reed roof. He first recognized the front room, with the bed and the hearth. He looked at the floor beams and, albeit with difficulty, found the same purple drops that continued to the second door, which led to the laboratorium.

He hadn't forgotten the specific arrangement of the place, the rounded walls decorated with marvelous paintings and the stone table lit by a beam of light raining down from the circular hole in the ceiling dome.

Finally, there were the frescoes, the aura of healing fascination emitted by the blue peacock that glowed with colors and gold sparks as it took flight from a stormy sea toward a clear sky. He couldn't fathom why this image triggered such a strong emotion in him.

He followed the traces that went across the whole house and stopped in front of a shabby arras hanging on the wall.

He tried to push it apart and saw a low, arched door concealed in the wall.

He pulled the bolt across and pushed the door.

A whiff of sick, putrid air, like the breath of an old leper woman who eats too many sweets, made him choke. The place was plunged in darkness. He went back to the laboratorium to look for an oil lamp, and lit it.

His mouth was suddenly filled with a sour terror that rose from his stomach. He plucked up the courage to go into the room.

The stench grew more intense and nauseating. It looked like a church chapel, with a dirt floor and brick walls. He raised the light so as to see to the end of the room.

Merciful God! He took a leap backwards. His stomach churned, he bent double, the taste of bile in his mouth.

Never had he seen such a spectacle.

Hanging from a hook that protruded from the wall, held up with ropes, dangled a bleeding mass of unrecognizable shape.

Shreds of intestine were hanging out of the belly; the official organs, liver, spleen, and stomach, had been removed and neatly arranged on a beam; the chest, ripped open, displayed the heart. The limbs, cut along orderly, precise vertical lines, revealed the streaks of the muscles and the shape of the bones. No recognizable element of the face remained. The skin had been torn off and the bones stripped so that they showed the white outline of the skull and the arch of the teeth giving a malicious smile amid that mass of murky, opaque humors.

The eye sockets, from which the eyeballs had been pulled out, were waiting disappointedly for someone to restore some of their dignity.

Not far from there, the two now hopeless eyes were floating in a yellow fluid inside a glass jar.

Next to them, in another recipient, to keep them company, was a flabby, ash-colored mass; Edgardo thought it must be the cerebral mass, seeing that the cranium, sharply sawed, looked totally empty.

Never had he seen such butchery, not even when the hunters at his father's castle skinned and slaughtered deer or boars after the hunt.

He brought the light closer to what remained of that wretched body, trying to work out the sex and the age.

There was no suggestion of breasts on the opened thorax. Only in the lower part of the belly did he think he saw what could have been the memory of female genitalia, two female testicles, the *vasa seminalia* and *os matricis*.

It must have been a woman, a young woman, judging by her hips and build.

The humors and blood dripping from the body had formed a puddle that the ground was slowly absorbing. The air was unbreathable and made his mind numb.

He was right to have suspected Abella. What terrible rituals, what experiments did that witch perform, that she had reduced a human being to such a condition?

And who was the young girl? He immediately thought of Costanza and her abduction. Was she perhaps destined to meet the same horrible end?

An absurd thought suddenly flashed through his mind, plunging him into despair. And what if this long-suffering body belonged to the virgin of the beads?

Was this shapeless mishmash of bones, organs, and muscles all that was left of his sweet Kallis?

He did not have time to provide an answer. An excruciating pain in his head made him lose consciousness.

## XXII.
### ARZANÀ

When, with a huge effort, he reopened his eyes, the first thing he saw was the muzzle of the boar watching him, surprised, leaning out of the center of the dome in the ceiling.

"Still here?" it seemed to say. "This slab of granite has now become your bed."

Edgardo slowly turned his head, blood throbbing in his temples. He located the blue peacock and greeted it like an old friend. He was in Abella's laboratorium. What had happened?

The image of the corpse, cut open and hanging in this sort of chapel, flashed through his mind. He must run, go to the gastald, and report the incident. With difficulty, he managed to sit up, and tried to get down.

Before he even put his feet down, he pulled them away in fear.

The floor was moving, undulating. Lively snakes with dark, shiny skins were leaping out of everywhere. They were moving in bursts, winding around the counter, slapping against the walls, slithering with a slimy hiss.

The excesses of opium had compromised his wretched mind, which wandered in foreign lands populated by gruesome visions.

There was a thud in the room, then the sound of footsteps. "So, scribe, still feel like snooping?" Abella's voice was calm and cheerful. "Oh, look, dinner is off for a stroll. You turn your back for a minute and these eels start crawling all over the place."

She started chasing after the snakes and, having caught them, threw them into a basket.

They were eels, simple eels. Edgardo propped himself up. The Magister didn't look the least worried.

The scribe confronted her. "I know everything. I never imagined you could be capable of such cruelty."

Not even as much as giving him a look, Abella continued hunting for the eels.

"Who was that wretched girl?" he insisted.

"I have no idea."

"How can you speak so carelessly of a human being after reducing her to such a state?"

The last eel was finally in the basket. Abella looked at the scribe with defiance. "Are you perhaps thinking of reporting me?"

"It's my duty. Will you try to stop me?"

Abella approached with a threatening expression. "I'm very tempted to string you up next to the girl. Nobody will miss a crippled scribe devastated by opium."

Edgardo leaped to his feet in a flash, ready to defend himself.

"Unfortunately, I don't think even fish would enjoy your flesh, you're too indigestible."

Abella drew even closer. Edgardo was dazzled by her lips, her soft skin, the fragrance of her sage-smelling breath, and by the pleasant weight of her chest pressing against his hump.

"Tell me honestly," she continued, "what advantage would you get from knowing that I am in prison? Or is it just because you hate me?"

"You've killed and cut open a stranger and Heaven knows how many other people you've treated the same way. Perhaps you're also involved in Costanza's death—"

"Just a moment!" Abella said aggressively. "What are you raving about, you demented, hallucinating scribe? I haven't killed anybody. I purchased the corpse you saw in an above-board transaction. It was most probably the body of a woman sentenced to death."

"Are you trying to tell me that you spend money to have a corpse delivered to your home and then cut it to pieces?"

"Exactly. I know the law forbids it but I have no choice. If we physicians want to study the human body, learn how organs function, the density of humors, the combination of primary elements, we have no choice but to cut up the bodies of the dead. The Holy Church forbids it, so we're forced to use crooks who obtain the goods with the help of subterfuge. Many of my colleagues do the same as I, secretly, to increase their knowledge." Abella drew breath, and was about to walk away like a member of the Roman Forum after an oration, but then changed her mind and added, angrily, "A woman who practices medicine must prove she has more knowledge than her male counterparts, so she can gain patients' trust, and I'm ready to do everything in order to establish my knowledge and my name. Have you got something against that? Now if you want to report me, go ahead . . . the gastald is waiting."

The castle of theories he'd built was crumbling wretchedly. It was always like this: his imagination would gallop, creating plots and weaving threads that would then dissolve into nothingness. Still, Edgardo didn't want to give in so quickly. "Are you trying to say that you do this just for the love of knowledge?"

"Do you think it's fun for me to dissect corpses?"

"That's the point: I can't equate the sacred urge for knowledge with the work of a butcher."

"You see, you're making the mistake of seeing the world as a huge parchment: it's only by investigating matter, testing, and experimenting that we can discover how the laws of nature are governed. It's only through the study of organs that I've understood how diseases manifest themselves and how I can treat them."

Edgardo stroked his beard. "I guess I must apologize to you." He uttered the words softly, hesitantly.

"So you've decided not to report me?"

"Yes, but in exchange, I'll ask you to help me," Edgardo replied in counterattack.

"Again?"

"It's for a noble cause."

"You're always chasing after noble causes, but without much success, it seems to me."

"This time I can't fail." Edgardo stood up. There was a little demon lashing out obsessively in his head, sticking a peg right between his eyes. "Do you have some water?"

Abella handed him a goatskin. "It's from the nuns' well, so it doesn't taste of salt."

The scribe drank greedily, then rinsed his face.

"You look like a drunken toad," Abella remarked.

"Thank you. Only you can highlight my qualities in such an appropriate manner."

"So, what do you want from me?"

"I'm convinced Alvise is innocent. There's nothing to prove his guilt, that unexplainable operation on Costanza's body cannot be his doing. Besides, I went to the foundry where he worked: there's no trace of the natron found on her body . . . and also he adored her."

"Perhaps that's precisely why he abducted her and then . . . "

"No, Alvise wouldn't be capable of that. He's a simple soul . . . I know him well."

"So why did you come here?" Abella asked.

"The only authority figure who can guarantee a fair trial is Tommaso Grimani," Edgardo continued.

"But he's the accuser!" Abella replied.

"He's blinded by grief, so he wanted to find someone to

blame at all costs . . . And then I think his position forces him to prove to the people that the *boni homines* cannot let such horrific crimes go unpunished."

"There's certainly no love lost between that man and me . . ." Abella remarked.

"Magdalena trusts you, listens to you, has great respect for your opinions. If you could intercede with her . . . " Edgardo's voice was heartfelt and sincere. "The only person who can find her way into Grimani's heart is, after all, his wife."

A light, cold rain began to fall through the hole in the dome.

Abella remained silent, watching the pillar of water in the middle of her laboratorium. "Are you absolutely sure?" she suddenly said. "Magdalena is a strong, determined woman, at least she appears to be, yet she shows a compliance toward her husband that seems at odds with her personality . . . Something doesn't quite add up in my mind."

"It's a wife's natural desire to go along with her husband, perhaps you've no experience of that . . . " Edgardo added with a dart of malice.

"As far as I know neither have you, and yet you pontificate about marriage feelings somewhat confidently. It's not something you learn from manuscripts."

"Anyway," Edgardo interrupted, "will you help me or not?"

Abella examined the scribe carefully. His body left much to be desired: that horrible bulge on his chest, the crooked bearing, the excessively pale skin, and that untidy bush of red curls that blended with the scruffy beard, made him look like an angry hedgehog. And yet there was something about him, a kind of aura that suggested suffering, an age-old pain in search of redemption, a longing to free himself from the weight of matter, a quest for lightness, that made him worthy of attention and kindness.

"I can't guarantee it'll be a successful enterprise, but I'll try," Abella said.

"I'm very grateful. Your generosity will magnify your soul and your knowledge." Edgardo hadn't forgotten the teachings of the Abbey.

"You may be right about my soul, but I think my mind needs other nutrients."

The quack always wanted to have the final word. Edgardo smiled.

"Come, let's prepare something to eat. Would you like an eel pie?"

Abella went into the front room, followed by Edgardo.

It was a flash. He hadn't paid attention before, but looking at the shelves in the laboratorium and then the living quarters, he noticed that there was no sign of any parchment, manuscript, or tables in any corner or closet; nothing that had anything to do with the work of a physician or the activities of a scholar. It was strange.

He watched Abella as she tried to keep an eel still so she could strike it: her build and manner were more akin to those of a hunter than a physician. Still, he had to admit that it was precisely what he liked about this woman.

He'd spent the early hours of the morning, from dawn to Terce, shut away in the pantry, asking not to be disturbed, so when Magdalena saw him come into the salon in an unnerving silence, she thought he looked like an apparition.

Tommaso was wearing the Oriental nobleman's outfit he used for ceremonies: a jacket made of expensive cloth embroidered with silk and gold, held by a belt with a silver clasp. Over it, he had a cloak of fine wool trimmed with ermine, clipped with a golden clasp. On his head, he sported a mitre-shaped beret.

He had a luminous, peaceful expression she hadn't seen for

a long time. She was even more surprised when Tommaso asked her to stop what she was doing and go with him on an important visit.

Following the Biria canal, which linked the Rivus Altus and Olivolo, the gondola crossed a city in the grip of hunger, at the mercy of muddy waters that drew closer, like an army of Barbarians, dragging into the abyss the Venetians' attempts to build on this mushy, treacherous land.

Moreover, in recent days, despite the freezing weather, some purple aquatic plants had multiplied, stifling canals with a gelatinous mass that smelled like rotting hay.

Once they'd passed the church of San Biagio, Magdalena realized that the boat was taking the canal that led to the *Arzanà*—the Arsenal.

Even though she was the wife of one of Venice's most powerful merchants, it was a place she'd never visited.

Everything looked grand and awe-inspiring to her.

There were crenelated walls surrounding a pool as large as the *brolo* of San Marco. On the east side was erected a watchtower, and a wide canal connected the Arsenal to the open lagoon.

The first isolated shipyards gathered around the parish church of San Martino had multiplied, and were now all within the protective walls, in the bay dug out on one side of the lake of San Daniele.

Carpenters, specialist workers, sawers, oar makers, and blacksmiths were working hard around the hulls of various ships in the process of being built. It was hectic work, and Magdalena was surprised by the large number of men engaged in this activity.

The main shipyards produced the larger ships: galleys, chelandions, dromons; from the minor ones came the smaller vessels, such as *scaulas*, gondolas, and *sandolos* as well as all the flat-bottomed boats used in the muddy sea.

At one of the shipyards, Tommaso invited Magdalena to step out of the boat. The workmen stood aside to let them pass.

Grimani had abandoned the older, more renowned arsenal of Terranova, which looked over the bay of San Marco, near the Calle dei Fabbri, putting in charge a new foreman whom everyone praised and who also cost much less.

"Look at the new galley that's going to make the Grimani fleet even wealthier," Tommaso said proudly. "There is no ship as large as this in the whole of Venice."

Magdalena looked up and, for a moment, was blinded by the milky whiteness of the sky.

What she saw before her looked more like a floating fortress than a ship. A galley three times as long as its width, with two masts almost as tall as the vessel itself, armed with lateens. It had two decks, a quarterdeck at the stern, and one at the bow as well as a warship crow's nest.

The sails that came down from the poles and interwove with the hawsers created a kind of forest with crystal reflections.

"It must be ready for the spring convoy," Grimani added, giving a nod of greeting to Romano Marzolo, his associate, who was talking nearby with an odd individual dressed in Oriental clothes, with sunburned skin and a shiny skull.

It was Marzolo who would take on the responsibility for the journey, putting to the test his skill as a sailor at the risk of his life. Suppliers, such as Tommaso, would invest the capital and remain safely in Venice.

The ships would leave, loaded with timber, iron, and salt, then, once they'd sold them and reinvested in spices, silk, gold, and slaves, would—wars and pirates permitting—return home, where the earnings would be split equally among the partners.

"I want to call it Luca, like our son," Tommaso announced, seeking his wife's eyes. "It will travel to the ports of Acre, Tyre,

Alexandria, and will venture down new routes beyond the Pillars of Hercules. We'll increase our trade until we become the wealthiest, most powerful family in the Dogado."

For a moment, dazzled by her husband's dreams of power, Magdalena found herself imagining fleeing toward the Orient, far from the slime of the lagoon that clung to her and kept her prisoner.

"I've brought you here so that you may see the symbol of our rebirth."

Tommaso took her hand and pressed it to his chest. It gave her a start, since it was a gesture he'd never made before.

"We must remain united and start living again. The season for mourning will give way to fruitful times. God will grant us peace and fertility. Let's throw grief and dark memories behind us." He looked into his wife's eyes. "Are you ready to come with me on this new path, and follow my advice with trust and hope?"

Magdalena wanted to give in to the impulse of embracing him, since never before had he uttered such words. "Yes, my lord, with all my heart and soul, I am ready to follow you, and begin anew."

"As you see, this vessel has wide, capacious hips, and can contain grain, salt, wine, oil, everything our generous soil yields . . . It's therefore just like your womb, which will soon give life to our new heir."

"I wish that above everything else," Magdalena whispered.

"You needn't be afraid anymore, trust me, we're close. In a few days' time, the miraculous medicine I promised you will arrive, and you will once again have the joy of motherhood."

Magdalena remembered Abella's advice, but she was ready to do anything in order to have a child.

"God willing," she replied.

"God is willing. I must give you some important news that proves it," Tommaso announced, pressing Magdalena's hand to his chest.

# XXIII.
## TATARO

S he had decided to meet her in the crypt of San Zaccaria, where she would go and pray at the tomb of her beloved sister. Tommaso wouldn't object and the conversation with Abella would take place away from prying eyes.

Magdalena kneeled and began reciting her prayers.

Gusts of icy wind filtered through the slits, making a gloomy sound, like the screams of the nuns who'd been burned alive down below, during the fire that had destroyed the church several years earlier. The souls of those wretched women were still wandering around in search of some peace.

She turned around when she heard the rustling of footsteps behind her. She thought that, in her scarlet garment, Magister Abella projected a luminous, almost holy aura. For a moment, she regretted having agreed to meet with her.

"My most esteemed lady," Abella said, "I asked to see you urgently because I cannot ignore the desperate call of my conscience."

Magdalena interrupted. "Come here and kneel with me at the grave of this innocent."

Abella obeyed.

"I have the highest esteem for you and I trust your knowledge," Magdalena continued. "Sometimes, however, there are events and misfortunes that call for definitive, quick choices, and we cannot afford to please our hearts. I promised to follow your instructions to cure the sterility that has taken residence in my womb, and wait. Now I must be honest with you

. . . I can't, and will not . . . since Costanza's death, my husband has been closer to me with feelings of love I'd thought vanished. I don't want to disappoint him, nor do I wish to antagonize him."

The Magister listened without displaying any sign of anxiety.

"Tommaso has assured me that the miraculous medicine arriving from the Orient will enable me to conceive once again. They say many women in those countries have benefitted from it, and I have no reason to doubt my husband's words. I have therefore decided to make him happy. I wanted to let you know, out of honesty and because I respect you."

"And I thank you for your consideration and understand your reasons. Even so, please be careful. I know of many cases where, in order to reach their goals, women have undergone treatments that have endangered their very lives."

"Don't worry, my husband cares about my health above all else." Magdalena reached out for her. "Help me stand up, I'm feeling so weak."

Abella lifted her with a determined gesture. It seemed to her as though that fragile body had been totally drained of the will to live.

"You must eat and go out, you must rebuild your strength."

"It's what my husband says. To be reborn, to rise again . . . perhaps if a new life were to blossom inside me . . . " Her words remained suspended, as though broken off by a premonition.

"Signora, as I was saying, I asked to meet with you because of a question of conscience." Abella searched for the right words. "I do not claim to cast doubt over the decisions of those who have the authority and skill to make the judgement; and it is precisely because I believe that the government of the city of Venice is recognized in every foreign country for the wisdom with which it administers justice and for the fairness of its tri-

als that I must intercede for the fate of your servant Alvise."
Abella took on a scholarly tone. "The study I conducted on
your sister's body and the investigations on the substance
found on her skin have triggered many doubts as to the boy's
guilt."

Magdalena raised her hand in front of her eyes, as though to
stop the sound of these words. "Enough, say no more. It's all
useless. Have no concerns for his fate: Alvise has confessed."

"Confessed?" Abella repeated, astonished.

"My husband brought me the news a few hours ago. It's
been a heavy blow. We've treated that boy like a son. We would
never have imagined him capable of such a horrific action."

"Confessed," Abella muttered to herself, as though unable
to make sense of the word.

"He'll pay for his crime with his life. He'll be blinded,
hanged and quartered. The execution will take place outside
the Doge's Palace, in the presence of the people of Venice, as
soon as the sentence pronounced by the judgement court is
confirmed by the Great Council and the Arengo."

"So there's nothing to be done?" Abella asked naively.

"Nothing. Only a new confession could annul the first sentence. God's will has been done, and Costanza will be avenged.
Alvise will pay for his sin."


"They've extorted a confession under torture, I'm certain of
it." Edgardo couldn't find peace. The news brought by Abella
had opened an abyss: there wasn't much time left, and if they
wanted to save the boy, they had to find the real murderer and
prove to the judges who was the guilty party.

They didn't have many tangible elements and could only
rely on a few unexplained facts.

"Let's follow the natron," Abella suggested. "Costanza's body
was covered in this substance. If we find out who uses it, or
where it's kept, perhaps we'll discover where the body was hid-

den. We must track down all the glassmakers who use it, and that won't be easy."

"There's only one person who knows all the secrets and workings of our master glassmakers, and that's Maestro Tataro," Edgardo exclaimed. "I don't suppose he'll welcome me as a good friend, but we must try. Let's take a boat to Amurianum and question him."

Abella was suddenly overwhelmed by a feeling of futility. Why should she follow the scribe? Why did she always allow herself to get involved? Her mission was to cure the sick, not save those who'd been sentenced to death.

At the same time, she felt she could not leave Edgardo alone in that impossible struggle to save a *garzone* who had perhaps been chosen by the authorities as a scapegoat. She could smell the stench of injustice and, as a *magister mulier sapiens* in constant war against superstition and prejudice, she was ready to fight.

They found Tataro at work in his foundry. Bare-chested, bathed in sweat, he was blowing through the pipe, swelling his chest like the belly of a pregnant cow. Edgardo thought he looked even more gaunt and tired, his rough skin burned by the heat. He sneered as soon as he saw them.

"You make a lovely couple. The fat woman and the cripple." His laugh was now even more like a rattle. "So, scribe, have you decided how much you want for revealing the formula of pure glass?"

Edgardo did not answer and addressed Abella instead. "Maestro Tataro is obsessed with the notion that I possess the formula for perfect crystalline glass."

"And isn't that the case?" Tataro replied.

"I tell you once again, I remember nothing of the formula Segrado dictated to me."

"Then where do those pure glass chalices you brought me come from?" Tataro insisted with an arrogant tone.

"I can't explain that."

The glassmaker spat in the furnace, wiped his mouth, and went to sit on a chair. He was panting. "What do you want?'

Tired of skirmishes that did not concern her, Abella stepped forward. "We want to know which glassmakers in Venice still use natron for making glass." Her tone was determined.

"And what would you know about natron?" Tataro asked, looking at her with contempt. "Didn't you say you were a physician? Or are you thinking of changing profession?"

"Remember the missing girl? She was found dead and covered in natron," Edgardo explained.

The old man closed his eyes, and Edgardo thought he detected a wince of compassion.

"So that's how they murdered her." His voice was almost gentle. "This city is sinking, it will be submerged by evil. I wonder if Giacomo, my *garzone*, met the same end."

"So what can you tell us?" Abella said.

"By the devil's tail, even children know that no glassmaker in Venice uses natron anymore, that it's too expensive. Ever since antiquity, it used to come from the dried up lakes in Egypt, near Alexandria, and it cost a fortune to bring it over. Nowadays, everyone in Venice uses cathine alum."

"So it's impossible to find natron in a foundry?"

Tataro shrugged.

"And where else would you find natron in Venice? Who uses it?" Edgardo asked.

"I'm a glassmaker. How am I supposed to know who uses certain substances? Ask an apothecary, he'll certainly have some in his shop."

Egypt, Alexandria, natron, transparent glass: all these tiles were forming in Edgardo's mind a precious mosaic that, once again, took him back to the same image, the one of the mysterious merchant from Alexandria and his *palazzo* in San Lorenzo.

"We'll go to the Crowned Wolf, the best-supplied shop in the city," Abella said. "I know Sabbatai, the apothecary, well. I get my medicines from him."

Edgardo too knew Sabbatai well, although for different reasons, but he chose not to say anything.

"We're grateful for the information." Abella even managed to produce a smile and Tataro seemed pleased.

Old age softens muscles and feelings, Edgardo thought.

They were already on their way out of the foundry when they heard Tataro's voice, loud, behind them. "Scribe!"

Edgardo turned and saw him just a few steps away. A stench of rotting teeth and putrefied mussels swept over him.

"An odd fellow, short, stocky, with a goatee, came to see me." Tataro came close to Edgardo's ear, as though not to divulge the secret to too many people. "He asked if I wanted to sell the Luprio foundry, the one where Segrado worked in, remember? He said he was the steward of a merchant . . . " He paused, watching the scribe's reaction.

"Who could possibly be interested in those ruins?" Edgardo asked with false naivety.

"I was hoping you'd have the answer to that question," Tataro replied. "You have a deep connection with that place, so it might be someone you know."

There was no doubt about it. The description corresponded to Lippomano, the steward of the merchant from Alexandria, but Edgardo took care not to reveal that to the glassmaker. "There's a hopeless mess in my wretched mind; recollections, images, names, all over the place, tossed in a corner, covered in dust and cobwebs. Give me time. I'll come back when I've put some order in this cesspool," Edgardo said, hitting his head with his fist several times.

At the end of the bank, Abella stood firmly rooted, waiting for him. She exuded a primordial strength. It occurred to Edgardo that he was lucky to have met her.

*

When Edgardo and Abella reached the Crowned Wolf, daylight was about to fall into a thicket of darkness. The clear sky was invaded by an army of ashen clouds that were advancing fast and relentless, heavy with storms.

Sabbatai's warty face was peering from behind the counter, lit up by a lipless sneer that tried, in vain, to look like a welcoming smile.

In front of him, a poor woman, still young but consumed by tiredness and salt, was accompanying a girl so skinny that her bones were sticking out through her scarce flesh. Her wan face damp with sweat, her lips cracked, and she had thin straw-colored hair hanging behind elephant-like ears that were red like embers.

Around her neck, hanging from a ribbon, was the heart of a small animal, dripping with blood.

"She's had quartan fever for two new moons now," the woman explained. "A crone told me to hang the heart of a hare around her neck." She pointed at the bleeding organ that still seemed to throb. "But the fever isn't dropping. The poor thing is suffering so much."

The curls of Sabbatai's beard quivered as he leaned forward as though to check the state of the hare's heart, then he shook his huge head, looked up at Abella and Edgardo, and nodded, satisfied.

"For the quartan fever, I have a miraculous herb that heals the body totally. Unfortunately for you, it's a very, very expensive herb."

Sabbatai opened his arms like a helpless sparrow, seeking approval from the Magister, who had stepped forward to look at the girl.

Without saying a word, Abella rubbed two fingers on the girl's clammy forehead, brought them up to her lips, and tasted them with the regulation clicking of the tongue.

"It's malaria," she said, addressing Sabbatai. "Give her quinine and molasses. Make an infusion. She has to drink it at dawn and at sunset." She gave the woman a piercing look of stern disapproval and tapped the hare's heart. "And take this rubbish off her neck and give it to the cat!" she boomed.

The woman muttered a few words of thanks, took the herbs, and slipped out of the shop. Edgardo smiled, proud to have such a talented physician for an ally.

"Illustrious Magister, how can I serve you?" Sabbatai said sentimentally, giving Edgardo astonished looks, trying to understand the odd pair.

Abella approached the shelf and examined the jars full of spices, powders, animal, mineral, and vegetable remedies, plain and mixed.

"Tell me, apothecary, among these substances, do you have a particularly rare one called natron?"

As though stung by a tarantula, the dwarf leaped out of his shelter and improvised an involuntary dance, skipping and shaking his enormous hump.

"I trade in alum, borax, chalcedony, quartz, sapphire, and saltpeter, I sell aloe vera, poppy, plantain, liquorice, gentian, and saffron, and I'm not above using duck meat, dog testicles, billy-goat bile, fly ash, snake broth, mouse ears, and a hoist of cicada powder . . . but of this natron you're asking about, I know absolutely nothing," he said, repeating like a refrain, "*Natrum no, natrum nunca, natrum usquam vidi.*"

"It's a fine, whitish powder that tastes sour but has no smell, and that was once used by glassmakers," Edgardo added. "Have you ever heard of it?"

"*Usquam no, nunca none, substantia ignota est.*"

"We understand, we understand, you know nothing about it," Abella said, staring into the apothecary's slug eyes.

"And do you know anybody who could tell us who uses it?"

At Edgardo's question, the apothecary produced the sweet expression of someone who has long forgotten his earthly worries.

Not intending to waste any more time asking questions that brought no answers, the two associates left the shop.

An increasingly strong breeze was blowing along the canals.

"Did he look sincere to you?" Abella asked.

"It's hard to tell, since I don't believe the concept of sincerity is something he's familiar with. Rather, he looked unhealthily agitated.

"This natron isn't leading us anywhere," Edgardo continued. "I keep thinking about those stitches . . . What reason would the murderer have had to close the orifice with such care? It must have been at least a barber or a surgeon," he added, and Abella darted him a black look suggesting he had offended her personally.

"If we rule out glassmakers," Abella was now following her own thread of thought, "who else could be using natron? Tataro said the Egyptians had been gathering it from the Nile Valley since antiquity. What did they do with it?" Abella wrinkled the tip of her nose. "You were a cleric, do you perhaps know someone who studies Egyptian customs and professions?"

"No," Edgardo replied. Then he suddenly spread open his arms, as though to take flight. "Or rather yes, I do!" he exclaimed, excited.

"And could we meet with him?"

"I fear not. He departed this world before Our Lord was born. But he left some extraordinary writings." Abella looked at him, exhausted. "Herodotus . . . Herodotus of Halicarnassus. In his *Histories*, an entire volume is devoted to Egyptian customs. I remember copying it many years ago, when I was still living in Bobbio Abbey."

"And you don't recall if it says anything about natron or what?"

"You expect too much from my memory."

"So we're back at the beginning."

"No," Edgardo replied. "There's always a copy of Herodotus's *Histories* in every important library. It's not easy to access the parchments but I know someone who could help us. He's a talented translator. He knows Spanish, Arabic, Latin, and Greek. In other words, he's a great scholar. His name is Ermanno d'Istria." Edgardo's face clouded over. "And perhaps he's the only one in there who harbors no hatred or resentment toward me."

"Good. Go and talk to him." Abella had recovered her usual energy and was walking briskly.

"I'd rather keep away from that place."

"Unhappy memories?" the Magister carelessly asked.

"Memories, always memories . . . I'm tired of living besieged by the past. In any case, I think I know where to find him. I've already seen him a few times near the *brolo*, all engrossed in his favorite activity."

"Didn't you say that this monk drank only human knowledge?"

Edgardo laughed. "You're right . . . but even more than knowledge, he drinks something that's much more pleasant to the palate. You'll see for yourself. Come with me."

# XXIV.
## AT THE GOLDEN HEAD

I t was Quadragesima Sunday. A light, irregular rain, like a veil of humidity coating the city, had started to fall from a reluctant sky since dawn. In the beginning, nobody paid attention to it: it was no more than the death rattle of winter.

It was still raining at sunset when Edgardo left Ca' Grimani, and the liquid cloak that was dropping from the sky gave the gondolas and *scaulas* rocking by the shore a surreal glow. He knew where he'd find Ermanno d'Istria. He'd happened to see him sitting on Calle delle Merzerie, at the table of an inn, drinking wine, alone, as he passed by after Vespers.

After a day of arduous work, hunched over parchments in the scriptorium of the Abbey of San Giorgio, translating Arabic manuscripts, he deemed it his just reward to devote himself to his favorite pastime, away from the prying eyes of his fellow brothers.

Edgardo immediately found himself immersed in the usual throng that flowed down the *calle* connecting San Marco and Rivoalto. Apprentices, servants, slaves, merchants, craftsmen, and soldiers on horseback crowded together, pushing one another.

Outside shops, sellers displayed every kind of merchandise, taking up the space necessary for the walkway, which was consequently reduced to a narrow path turned by the rain into a stream that washed all the goods away: soaked vegetables, fruit peel, animal bones, excrement of every color, shape, and size, mussel shells that floated like tiny boats, fish heads, and dead sewer rats.

Just before reaching the *brolo*, between a blacksmith's and a barber's, was the conspicuous sign of the Golden Head inn. A room blackened by smoke and corroded by salt.

Edgardo found it difficult to get accustomed to the darkness of the room, which was barely lit by a few oil lamps on the tables. The waterlogged dirt floor seemed to give under every step. The air was steeped in a sickly-sweet, nauseating fragrance that made it hard to breathe. He'd already smelled this odor before, but couldn't remember where.

He searched among the customers. He noticed a darkskinned young woman at one of the tables, wrapped in a short tunic that was open on the front and thus left little to the imagination, sitting with a soldier. Next to them, lying on a bench, a *garzone* dressed in rags was snoring. At the back, somewhat concealed, he thought he recognized a monk's habit. He approached.

He hadn't the least changed, not even after ten years or more. Rounder, crimson-faced, graying hair covering his shoulders, he was hunched over a carafe.

"Father, may I sit at your table?"

Ermanno's lively eyes darted in search of the origin of that voice. "You'll make me happy, my son. Wine drunk alone has a bitter taste."

Edgardo sat down. "Don't you recognize me?" he asked, leaning forward toward the lamp.

"Now, now," Ermanno muttered, "let me look at your features: ruby hair, scruffy beard, cerulean-blue eyes, milky complexion, an abundance of freckles . . . "

"I too once wore the habit," Edgardo added.

"By Jove, God keep you!" Ermanno exclaimed, slamming the carafe on the table. "You're that excellent Bobbio scribe who came with Ademaro . . . your name escapes me."

"Edgardo d'Arduino, known as The Crooked."

"God Almighty, whatever happened to you? You vanished, and we never saw you on the island of Memmia again."

"Our Lord chose not to grant me a life free of trials and tribulations . . . or perhaps it was I who was unable to follow the path He had shown me."

"By the devil, we must celebrate. More wine!" he shouted.

There was a bustle in the semi-darkness, followed by a phlegmy grunt; a curtain swelled, and a wave of that nauseating smell of cedar, amber, camphor, and myrrh came crashing down on the wretched men.

Edgardo saw before him a shapeless mass, flabby and ivory-colored, full of folds, clefts, and flaps of fat, which one would have strained to describe as being female.

"Teodora," Edgardo whispered to himself, "that's who that perfume belonged to—the oriental wife of that unfortunate merchant Karamago."

"How can I satisfy the desires of the most illustrious and scholarly father who graces us with his presence?" Teodora asked in her sing-song voice, wiggling the superfluous flesh on her chest.

"More sweet Cyprus wine," Ermanno ordered. "We must celebrate the return of a long-lost friend."

The woman gave Edgardo an absent-minded look and left.

She hadn't recognized him. Perhaps it was the beard. Edgardo heaved a sigh of relief. He remembered her husband, who'd sacrificed his life in order to save him from the angry mob, and felt very moved.

Widowed, Teodora had obviously stopped the trade and devoted herself to the comfort of the traveler's stomach. And, judging by the half-naked young girl sitting at the table, not just his stomach.

"And do you have any news of the other fellow brother,

your friend Ademaro? He never came back to our monastery, either."

"Ademaro?" Edgardo half-closed his eyes, as though to focus on a recollection. "No, I never saw him again after I gave up the habit."

His friend Ademaro: could he call him that after what had happened?

Ademaro had lied to him, betrayed him, and yet uttering his name still triggered a strong emotion. Could he still call the feeling that persisted in his heart friendship?

In Bobbio, he'd shared with him years of study, suffering, sacrifice, dreams, conquests, but then, after their trip to Venice, their ways had irremediably parted, each one following his own beliefs, his own fate.

And yet he could not bring himself to feel any resentment, let alone hatred. On the contrary, a feeling of closeness, of solidarity had developed in him, which he could not explain.

Was that true friendship? To close one's eyes before the suffered wrongs, to forget the differences, the clashes, and go beyond them? When does such a deep feeling take root in our hearts? There's something that acts in spite of ourselves . . . it is time, the passing of time that creates and anchors a friendship. Disappointments and betrayals amalgamate in the slow flow of time and dissolve, making room for forgiveness.

Yes, Edgardo concluded, he could still utter the word friendship when thinking of Ademaro.

Ermanno noticed the veil of melancholy that had overtaken the face of his guest, and raised his glass. "Let's drink to Abbot Carimanno, who has passed over to a better life. Now he's wandering freely across the pastures of absolute knowledge—lucky him." Then he emptied the glass in a single gulp. "We have a new abbot, the library is growing, go forth and multiply . . . that's what I'm always saying to my manuscripts. New volumes arrive from the Orient, the work is never-ending, and I'm old. What about you?" Ermanno indicated Edgardo's clothes. "You've left the habit!"

"I'm a scribe for a merchant."

Ermanno nodded. "I understand. I won't ask what prompted your decision . . . it can't have been easy."

Edgardo picked up the carafe and poured himself a glass of wine. His hand was shaking. "This isn't a chance encounter, my illustrious friend," he continued, trying to shake off the deep melancholy that had enveloped him. "I need your help."

"You can count on me in anything that is lawful."

"I hope you'll consider it so. The *garzone* of the merchant for whom I work has, in my opinion, been accused of a crime he did not commit. I'm trying to save his life. The only element in my possession, which may lead me to a solution, is natron, a substance found on the body, but I can't find out how it's used nowadays. However, my memory has come to my aid: many years ago, when I was still at Bobbio, I copied all Herodotus's *Histories*. One of the books concerned Egyptian customs, and it's from that country that natron comes, because Egyptians use it in abundance."

"Yes, of course, it's in Book Two . . . a treasure trove of knowledge, is our Herodotus."

"I wouldn't like my request to be inappropriate but, unfortunately, it's no longer possible for me to access your library. May I ask you to track down this book and, if it's not too much trouble for you, check if it talks about natron and in what context? It would be precious information for me."

The lively eyes groped in the void in search of a foothold, then Ermanno's face lit up. "We can do even better, my dear friend: I will look for the manuscript and read Book Two. If I find passages that mention natron, I'll copy them for you. Come by the inn in four days' time, and if you see me sitting at this table in the company of this faithful friend," he indicated the carafe of wine, "then you can shout victory."

"Would you really do this for me? I shall be grateful to you for ever. But isn't it forbidden to get copies of manuscripts out of the abbey?"

"Of course, it is, but I've always considered it a silly rule. Knowledge should circulate, travel, go from mouth to mouth . . . like good wine." He gulped down another glass with satisfaction and stood up.

Leaning over the counter, intent on proffering the cuts of meat that burst out of her tunic, Teodora was staring at the scribe. They exchanged looks by the door, and Edgardo got the impression she recognized him.

The image of that hag still before his eyes, Edgardo plunged into the throng of Calle delle Merzerie. The drizzle had turned into a downpour that, pushed by the wind, was slamming against the planks of the huts. Everybody was running for shelter in shops or under porticos. The only one apparently careless of the deluge was Edgardo. He walked slowly, trying to untangle himself from twisted, oppressive thoughts.

Ermanno had said four days. Confirmation of Alvise's execution could arrive at any time. Time was flying. He felt powerless. A deep melancholy had taken a grip of his soul: the memory of Ademaro had reawakened the feeling of emptiness that increasingly assaulted him.

When he'd reached Rivoalto, he happened to pass by the Crowned Wolf. Until that moment, it hadn't occurred to him to resort to the apothecary in order to find some peace. All of a sudden, the demon had reawakened, and he felt he was being dragged into the shop, as though clutched by a hand.

When Sabbatai saw him, dripping, his hair and beard stuck to his pale face, his eyes feverish, he knew immediately why he had come.

"The load that's crushing you is unbearable, brother," the

apothecary said by way of welcome. "You need a pinch of paradise, don't you?"

Edgardo lowered his head guiltily.

"Wait . . . I'll be as quick as lightning." Then he vanished at the back of the shop.

There was violent roaring over the lagoon, the fords, the submerged land, and the muddy shoals amid the reeds and the rushes; such a shuffling of water and currents between the sea and the sky that it was difficult to tell the difference between above and below, east and west. Even Edgardo felt as though he was turning liquid and dissolving into nothingness.

The apothecary returned with a pouch full of very fine powder. "For you, brother, a very special blend. It's a little expensive but very powerful, You must dissolve two pinches in water and swallow, then," he gave a long whistle, "you'll feel your heart swell with happiness."

Edgardo took the pouch, paid almost without realizing it, then made his way back to Ca' Grimani.

As soon as he was back in his room, in the grip of an insane frenzy, he poured a little water into a bowl and took the pouch. His hand was shaking like that of an old madman. He put in a dusting of powder, which immediately dissolved in contact with the water. He gulped it down, like a traveler who has just crossed the desert, and abandoned himself on his bed, exhausted. He closed his eyes, waiting anxiously for the saving journey that would erase all suffering and open the doors to paradise before him.

He didn't have the time to dream of the coveted pleasure before he felt a widespread sensation of burning on his skin, then a feeling of choking, as though his tongue had swelled so much it was obstructing his throat. He tried to get up, but was prevented by the fatigue. His muscles were flabby, his bones broken, his blood turned to water, and he opened his mouth wide in an endless wheeze.

All his pain disappeared, and his entire being was dragged into a deep sleep.

Suddenly, a violent knock made him jump, almost as though a mysterious force had pried him away from his actual body.

He felt a comfortable warmth in his chest. He got the impression of floating in the void. He opened his eyes.

And he saw him. He saw Edgardo d'Arduino, called The Crooked, lying on his bed, pale as death.

He watched him as though he were above him, up on the ceiling.

He felt so sorry for that human being, loaded with suffering, with a frail body and soul, deprived of every hope.

He tried to bend down so he could touch him, but discovered that his limbs had no substance, that they were made of air and light. And, unwittingly, he began to mentally utter a prayer for that being who was lying down below, all alone in the world, forgotten. For a moment, he felt pity, and forgave him all the errors he had committed.

The light within him turned liquid, his eyes filled with tears, and a drop slipped out, a luminous drop that fell into the void, as slow as the thought of a newborn baby, and came crashing down onto the chest of that wretched being lying down below, right on top of the fleshy hump that protruded from his chest.

That's when he saw what he could never have imagined ever seeing.

In contact with the tear, the wrinkled skin became alive, quivered, gave a start, turned indigo and, in a heartbeat, tore open like a voracious mouth, the muzzle of a monster writhing in a terrible rattle, as though gasping for breath. Then, after the final spasm, a winged creature flew out of the gash. It was brightly-colored, with turquoise wings, emerald-green talons, and a large open fan-shaped tail with gold and blue circles.

It was a peacock. A splendid blue peacock.

The bird lingered awhile on the fleshy hump, turned its head toward Edgardo, almost as a greeting, then flew up and vanished in the air.

## XXV.
## THE HUMP

The bells of San Leonardo had already rung Terce and none of the servants had seen Edgardo appear yet.

Nena was surprised. The scribe had kept his habits from when he was a cleric, and as Prime tolled, he was usually seen already busying himself between the study and the storerooms.

A servant was sent to knock on the door of his room, but there was no response. Nena then made sure she informed the Signora, who rushed to tell her husband. A few seconds later, there was a small gathering outside Edgardo's door.

Tommaso knocked energetically, without result, so he made up his mind and flung the door open.

Illumined by a ray of pale light that filtered through the beams of the roof, Edgardo's face, wan and marble-like, was peering out of his dark clothes like a funeral mask.

"God almighty!" Nena exclaimed.

Tommaso bent over him.

"Is he dead?" Magdalena asked in a whisper of a voice.

"I can't feel his breath," Tommaso said.

Nena stifled a moan. Grimano put his ear against the hump. "I think I can hear a faint heartbeat."

"Then he's alive," Magdalena said, and turned to Nena. "Run fetch a physician," she urged, then paused and looked at her husband. "May I please have your permission to call for Magister Abella?"

Grimani stiffened, and raised a hand as though to place a barrier between himself and his wife's request.

"I beg you. I have great trust in her knowledge, and I'm certain she can save him. Other physicians have brought nothing but sorrow to this house. Grant my request and I promise I will fulfil all your wishes. I promise Abella will not influence my decisions in any way . . . She's the only one who can save Edgardo, believe me."

He huffed, sighed, and covered his eyes with his hand as though to seek a reply in the darkness. In the end, Tommaso agreed and a servant ran to look for Abella.

The rain, which hadn't relented in stifling the city, had gone back to a thin, dense veil that penetrated every crack and slid even into the strongest spirits.

Magdalena and Nena watched over the scribe while waiting for the Magister.

Edgardo's body gave no sign of life: his arms were limp, his face as though carved in stone, and even his red hair and beard seemed to have faded into a tow gray. The women prayed that the shadow death had spread over the house be pushed away.

By the time Magister Abella arrived, they'd lost all hope. His heartbeat had become like the fluttering of a moth's wings.

"This is how we found him when we woke up," Magdalena explained.

Without saying a word, Abella immediately set to work. With a few confident gestures, she disengaged Edgardo's body from his tunic. Magdalena couldn't suppress a grimace of disgust. Never had she seen that bumpy protrusion, now reduced to a mass of open meat, crossed by purple, smelly cracks.

His body was covered in a layer of cold sweat, his limbs were blue, and his eyes rolled back. Abella managed to open his mouth. She examined his tongue: it was covered in a thick, white patina.

She noticed a bowl next to the bed. There was still a thin layer of white powder at the bottom. She took a pinch and put

THE APOTHECARY'S SHOP · 237

it in her mouth, clicking her tongue. "We must void him of all bad humors: he's been poisoned! Help me," she commanded Nena, "we must turn the body on its side. Now you keep his mouth open, and I'll attempt to trigger the emptying of the *stomacus et iecur*."

She took a goose quill from her cloak, inserted it into Edgardo's mouth, and began tickling his throat.

His body didn't seem to want to react.

"Open it more, I must go in deep."

After much tickling, his upper body was shaken by a powerful jolt and, as well as the coughing, a green, oily, sour-smelling liquid began pouring out.

"Thank you, God!" Abella exclaimed. "Keep his head forward."

After several jolts, Edgardo opened his eyelids slightly and moved his eyes but didn't seem to recognize the faces leaning over him.

"Go get some theriac."

Nena rushed out.

"He must drink it with an infusion of milk and swamp clover," Abella said to Magdalena, "every day at Prime and None."

"Will the breath of life come back into his veins?" she asked.

"I hope so. He's strong, even though it was a very powerful poison."

"You said he's been poisoned. Who could have wanted his death, and why?"

The Magister's eyes narrowed. "I don't know . . . but I have a idea." Then she covered the body without completing her thought.

Twice did the dawn caress Edgardo's sleeping body. When he woke up, rain was pelting down from the leaden sky, lashing out at the city. The canals had turned into torrents of soil.

A single yellow, shitty expanse surrounded Venice, penetrating even the innermost waterways.

When he opened his eyes, Edgardo saw Abella's sunny face at his side. She'd come to visit him every day.

"What happened to me?" he asked in a whisper of a voice.

"You slept for two days," Abella replied.

Edgardo grimaced. "Yes, I remember now . . . I must have overdone it with—" he stopped. "My guts are turned inside out and my head is like an anvil."

"Would you be so kind as to tell me what happened to you?"

"You just want to humiliate me . . . you already know. The other night, I went to Sabbatai. I felt the need to empty my mind . . . I took opium powder."

"It wasn't just opium. There was also a large quantity of mandrake, henbane, and white poppy. A deadly mixture. They tried to poison you," Abella said categorically.

"Poison me?" Edgardo managed to prop himself up. "Why? I don't understand. Sabbatai? He's the only one who—"

"Exactly."

"What reason can the apothecary possibly have to wish for my death? He'd only lose a good customer."

"I have no idea. The only thing to do is go and ask him."

Edgardo tried to stand up.

"Lean on me." Abella gave him her arm. It smelled of sage and was as sturdy as a hundred-year-old oak.

"It's the second time you've saved my life . . . I am deeply grateful to you," Edgardo muttered with a hint of gallantry.

"Alright, alright, but make sure it doesn't become a habit," she replied abruptly.

"I fear your mission isn't over yet."

"What do you mean?"

Edgardo's face lit up with a glow Abella had never seen. "While I was dead, I had a dream. Perhaps not a dream even but a vision, a journey." He looked inspired. "The time for waiting is over. Perhaps the events to come will force me to face serious risks and dangers, and death may be at my side. If my time comes, I want to appear before the Almighty at peace." He took a deep breath. "At peace with myself, in my soul and my body.

"All my life I have humbly accepted my monstrosity without complaining, as an unfathomable mark of divine will. This purulent hump I've been carrying on my chest has prevented my spirit from flying freely, crushed my heart, and put a stain on my love for my fellow men.

"Our merciful and infinitely just God wanted to punish me for some sin that I don't know about . . . Well, now I've paid for it, I have been cleansed and I too have the right to rise, take flight, and be born again." He stared at the Magister. "You once said you could remove this horrible excrescence that deforms my chest. I've made up my mind: take off this hump, even at the peril to my life."

Abella had listened in silence to what sounded to her like an authentic confession. Edgardo had bared his soul, told her of his torments, and the suffering he'd carried with him since birth.

"I'll be honest with you, scribe," she replied. "I've never performed this kind of operation. I learned my art from distinguished masters in Salerno, according to the teachings of the most illustrious surgeon who ever lived, the outstanding Abulcasis. You will do me great honor if you put your trust in me. For that I am grateful and promise I shan't disappoint you." Overwhelmed by emotion, she fell silent.

"Then so be it," Edgardo said, surprising himself. A few days earlier he'd been full of suspicions about the Magister's abilities, and now he was placing his life in her hands.

The stone slab had become his bed. Lying on it, his chest

uncovered, Edgardo looked among the patterns of the fresco on the dome for his guide, the blue peacock, and felt reassured and confident once he'd located it.

"Drink this," Abella said, handing him a bowl. "Opium no longer has any effect on you so I've added a little nightshade, henbane, and poppy juice. They'll keep the pain at bay. We must act cautiously, since you're still very weak. Are you sure about your decision?"

"I don't want to wait any longer, but if life were to abandon me, promise me you'll save Alvise," he said after drinking the mixture in a single gulp.

"Do you have such little faith in my art?"

"It's your first time, you said so yourself."

"Now close your eyes and breathe deeply."

The last image Edgardo saw was the boar on the dome, which, frightened by the appearance of a hand holding a long, sharp blade, was hiding his muzzle in his paws. Then nothing.

Magister Abella had never seen such a large fleshy protuberance. It stuck out of the chest like a deformed mask. The bumpy, chapped flesh was covered in deep cracks that seemed to push past the bone, and oozed a white, oily fluid that gave off a smell like urine after a large consumption of asparagus.

"If I weren't a physician, I'd say this is Beelzebub's hump," she muttered to herself, trying to pluck up her courage.

She had to cut, and had never done it before. The swelling looked like a continuation of the formal organs. A wrong move could kill him.

She decided to tackle it at the base, and cut along the perimeter. Her hand was shaking. She took a deep breath and put her trust in the great Abulcasis.

The point penetrated as softly as into a block of lard.

She pushed in deeper and began to slide the blade. There was no blood coming out of the wound, and she considered this a good omen.

Fast asleep, Edgardo showed no sign of suffering.

The bumpy protuberance shuddered and jumped at every stroke, releasing only stinking fluid.

Once she'd detached the base, she had to tackle the central part, which was more compact and dangerous.

She tried to test the consistency of the matter. The point of the blade encountered resistance: an impediment of a horn-like nature.

She took a saw from among her instruments, the one she used for amputations. She slid it between the flaps of the wound as delicately as she could, and began to move the tool back and forth against the hard, resistant substance that refused to be sawed.

Every move of the iron provoked a kind of lament, a dull, gloomy cry that gushed out of the chest. It was as though she was sawing through his soul.

She stopped. Not a drop of blood. The consistency of the surface had become paler and more languid. The cracks were dry. There was no turning back.

She looked at Edgardo. He was breathing.

She gathered her strength and prepared to deliver the final attack. A sharp blow, then another. There was a terrible creaking sound that echoed throughout the whole body.

It was yielding. The root of evil was yielding. She pushed the saw further in. The cry grew sharper and more desperate. An infant in swaddling cloths crushed by a club. She pretended not to hear. A burst of oily fluid suddenly splashed her face and, after the last blow, there was a distinct crash, as though all Edgardo's bones had been broken at the same time, and the fleshy being rolled to one side.

Abella looked at it with disgust. It seemed to be breathing.

Edgardo's chest, where the protuberance used to be, was covered by a transparent membrane, like soft, shiny skin. In the centre, there was a bleeding wound.

She took a triangular needle and some silk thread, and put in a few stitches.

She put her ear closer to his body. The heartbeat was frequent, in double rhythm, as though there were two hearts.

An expression of horror disfigured her features. She pulled her hands away. Was another heart beating from the eradicated excrescence? It was alive, refusing to die.

She grabbed a thin blade and, with a clean blow, cut along the hump, which opened up like a cracked apple.

She found no heart wedged in that flabby mass of fat, but something equally disturbing: a lock of hair, bits of fingernail, roots of teeth, all perfectly preserved.

They were the remains of another Edgardo, whom the scribe had carried with him since birth like an unborn brother, his monstrous double that had prevented him from taking flight.

He reawakened through flashes of lucidity and opaque sleepiness. When he finally managed to open his eyes and regain consciousness, Edgardo realized that a deep melancholy had taken hold of his mind. A dull pain, an incomprehensible anger that had no beginning and no end.

He lifted his head slightly. His chest was wrapped in white, blood-stained strips.

The hump had disappeared.

His eyes filled with tears, as though he'd lost a much-loved companion. Monstrosity can be a faithful friend, a guide, a counselor, a defense against the world. Side by side all his life. And now it was gone.

Abella saw him awake and approached.

"Am I alive?" Edgardo asked.

The Magister smiled. "So it would seem. Alive and free of all oppression."

"I have no more arrows in the bow of commiseration."

"Look." Abella took the excrescence split in two and showed it to him. "You had another Edgardo stuck to your chest."

Teeth, fingernails, hair . . . The scribe's eyes caressed the remains of his monstrosity.

"Now I must go forth alone. I thought I would be happy. Instead, I'm afraid."

Never had Abella seen in a man's eyes this mixture of nostalgia, bewilderment, and deep loneliness. She wanted to put her arms around him, to comfort him, the way one does with children. But a physician cannot give in to feelings and emotions.

She tried to find a solemn, detached expression. "You'll feel better when the new day comes." And she touched his wound, almost caressing it.

"Do you still think we should pay the apothecary a call?" Edgardo asked.

Abella looked at him in surprise. "Surely you're not thinking of roaming around the city in your current state?"

"I must." He touched his chest. "That excrescence was draining away my life force, now I am reborn . . . and thanks to you."

"For now, content yourself with a nice bowl of milk and a goose liver pie, to replenish your blood."

Edgardo received the offer with a disgusted grimace.

## XXVI.
## HERODOTUS OF HALICARNASSUS

And the sea of stone generated a forest. As a result of the devastating rainfall that had afflicted the Venetian lands, the Medoacus maior, the Silis, and the Plavis had swelled beyond measure and, in addition to soil and mud, had vomited into the lagoon chunks of mountains, forests, and huts. Sailing from Torcellus, Edgardo saw wrinkled tree trunks slicing through the waters like battering rams. Brambles and roots that dragged carpets of leaves, bushes, and grass covered the entire lagoon, so much so that the boat steered by Abella seemed to be gliding over a woody pasture just devastated by a tempest.

It took great effort to reach the Crowned Wolf, struggling against a slimy bog that swallowed your feet with every step, refusing to give them back.

The front door and windows were shut. Edgardo knocked and called out but there was no answer. "Maybe he's at the back of the shop and can't hear us."

"Or he's not happy that we've come to call," Abella said "Don't forget that according to his plans, you should already be underground."

They leaned out on the bridge over the canal near the shop.

"If we walk on the boats moored along the little canal, we'll get to the courtyard at the back," suggested Edgardo, who had by then regained his strength.

"I'm used to these ventures with you."

They lowered themselves onto the floor of the first boat,

then, leaping from one to the other, they reached the courtyard. The expanse of grass had turned into a pool. They went
to the door. It was shut.

"Perhaps Sabbatai has left Venice," Edgardo said.

"If so, then it's proof his conscience was dirty."

At that moment, it stopped raining. Edgardo sat on the
steps of the well, absorbed in thought. "However much my
mind tries to explore the most twisted arguments, I can't find
a reason to explain why Sabbatai should want my death."

"Maybe it's not Sabbatai who wants your death, and somebody may have used him."

"That's even worse," Edgardo said. "Why hate me so
much?"

"It has nothing to do with hatred. You're looking for the
person responsible for Costanza's death, and somebody doesn't
like it."

Edgardo hadn't considered this. He admired Abella's iron
logic.

He was about to get up when his attention was caught by a
shiny fragment on one of the steps by the well. He picked it up
and brought it closer to his eyes.

"What have you found?" Abella asked.

"I have no idea," he said, bringing it even closer. "I can't
see."

"Use your circles," she suggested.

"You're right." He took the contraption out of its case, and
placed it before his eyes. "Ah, finally!" he exclaimed. "It's glass
. . . colored glass . . . it seems . . . it looks like . . . "

"Come on, tell me."

"It's incredible. I'd venture a theory that it's a piece of a
bead."

Silence fell. Abella looked at the scribe. "So?"

Edgardo closed his eyes and remained still as a civet that,
sniffed out by a wolf, pretends to be dead in order to save its

life. Then, suddenly . . . "Help me remove the iron plank that covers the puteal."

With some effort, they pushed the plank to the ground. Edgardo leaned over the cistern flue. A sickly-sweet breath blew in his face. He picked up a stone and threw it down. A loud thud echoed up to the opening of the well.

"Did you hear that? With all the rain over the past few days, the cistern should be full, and yet a stone has just fallen on bare ground. The well is empty," he explained, proud of his deduction.

From the hook he took down the rope on which the bucket hung and climbed onto the crown of the puteal.

"What are you trying to do?" Abella asked, worried.

"I want to go down to the bottom."

"Where do you get this insane passion for climbing into every cleft?" Abella was trying to disguise her anxiety. "Are you sure you feel strong enough?"

"I have more energy than a lion."

As a matter of fact, Abella thought, he really did look like a lion with that red, bristly hair that blended in with his beard like a huge mane.

"Do you have a piece of tow, or a bit of tallow?"

"I don't carry the whole house in my pocket." Abella searched the pockets of her tunic. "Perhaps this will do the trick." She handed him a woven ribbon.

Edgardo clung to the rope and began his descent, propping himself with his feet. Despite the excruciating pain in his bones, he touched the bottom. His feet landed on a compact, dry surface. As he had anticipated, there was not a trickle of water. The air was steeped in a sickly-sweet, moldy stench.

He tried to find the flint to make some light.

He bumped into something, pulled away, then reached out gingerly with his hand.

A stringy, soft substance was coming out of a hard surface.

He felt it again and came across something flabby, fleshy . . . like a mouth.

He let out a raucous cry.

"What happened?" Abella cried from above.

"There's a presence down here," Edgardo replied uncertainly.

"What kind of presence?"

"I'll tell you in a minute."

He rubbed the flint on the ribbon. After a few attempts, it caught fire and the place slowly lit up.

A shock shook his chest and he felt his stomach liquefy. He leaned back against the wall as far as he could. A step away, right in front of him, hung a woman . . . a woman with perfect features, with a youthful, appealing form, full breasts, a silky belly, soft hair, and fleshy, almost rosy lips. Only her eyes, which you could glimpse beneath the lids, had lost their original sheen. She looked asleep.

Edgardo stood staring at her, entranced by such beauty. Around her neck, she wore a copper thread with a row of beads.

An unexplainable feeling of overwhelming emotion rose to his throat. His eyes filled with tears. It looked to him as though in its perfection, that being had won man's eternal battle against death.

At the same time, he felt relieved: it was not Kallis's body, it was not his ghost. He could continue to hope that she would return from the land of the dead.

"Have you discovered the substance of that presence?" Abella shouted from above.

"I've found a dream, a vision, the image of man's immortality."

"This is not the time to turn poet, come back up."

He stroked the angelic face one more time, and climbed back up to the opening of the well. When she saw him come out, Abella thought she was before a living corpse. "What did you see?"

"We've found the virgin of the beads, the girl stolen from the church of San Geminiano. They've hidden her in the well. I can't understand why."

"Evidently, Sabbatai is involved in the trafficking of corpses . . . this one was too tempting. I'm not the only one in Venice who practices anatomy on lifeless bodies." Abella looked upset, as though someone had stolen the secret of a remedy from her.

"This could explain why the apothecary has tried to send me to heaven before my time," Edgardo said.

"Possibly. Though I can't see why you would represent a danger to his trafficking." Abella stared at him, lost in thought. "Strange. You look as if you've prematurely aged . . . your hair and beard are completely white."

Edgardo shook himself: a cloud of dust rose in the air.

"Your clothes too . . . and your hands . . . " Abella said.

The scribe was about to rub himself.

"Stop!" She blocked his hand and tried to pick up a pinch of the strange dust. Then she lifted it to her lips and, with the tip of her tongue, raised it to her palate for a taste.

She rolled, clicked, knocked, gurgled and, in the end, forcefully announced, "It's natron!"

"Natron? Like what we found on Costanza's body? Are you sure."

"Absolutely certain."

"By the horns of Beelzebub and the tail of Titivillus, now this is a discovery!" Edgardo was as excited as a little boy fascinated by the tail movements of a lizard that writhes even after it's been cleanly severed from the body.

"It means that there's a secret link between the virgin and Costanza," he added.

"Sabbatai lied to us. He swore he knew nothing about natron."

"God almighty!" Edgardo suddenly exclaimed. "How many nights have passed since my poisoning?"

"Three."

"Ermanno d'Istria assured me that if he found the pages in Herodotus about the use of natron, he'd wait for me at the Golden Head Inn after four days. We must go there as soon as possible."

And they smiled at each other, like two associates who'd just sold a load of counterfeits to a Turkish merchant.

The tavern was heaving with customers. Edgardo wondered if it was because the weather was bad. They looked around for Ermanno: Persian merchants, Mamluks, Slavonian sailors wrapped in thick furs, all in the company of provocative young girls with sad eyes. No sign of the monk.

"We're too late," Edgardo said, downhearted.

"Let's ask the owner," Abella suggested.

"No, it's no use, she's an old shrew with a confused mind," Edgardo replied abruptly, not wishing to reawaken unpleasant memories.

They were about to leave the inn when, at the door, Abella collided with a protruding belly advancing in a rush.

"I beg your pardon, illustrious Magister," said the man, noticing the physicians' scarlet robe.

"Ermanno!" Edgardo cried.

"My young friend, thank God I've found you. For an entire day, while waiting for you, I've had to engage in what seems like an ever-losing battle to keep sober."

Ermanno gave him an affectionate hug.

"I am with an esteemed physician of great knowledge, whom I have the pleasure of presenting to you," Edgardo said. "Her name is Abella."

Ermanno's face widened in an exaggerated smile. "A female scholar . . . oh . . . what a surprise, I didn't know they existed, let me look at you closely, I am honored to make your acquaintance. Do you come from a land beyond the Pillars of Hercules?"

"She studied medicine at the School of Salerno," the scribe added to increase Abella's credit.

"Really? Many years ago, I met one of your colleagues, Bernardo di Provenza, who taught at Salerno."

Abella interrupted him in a way Edgardo found almost discourteous. "I've heard of him. I'd left the school by then."

"Of course, of course," Ermanno said, looking around. "There's the mid-Lent crowd here today, and so many attractive Circassian girls. Come with me, I know this hovel's every secret."

He pushed them into a small room at the back of the inn, behind the counter.

"My respects, sweet Teodora." Ermanno produced a musical tone. "A carafe of sweet Cyprus wine for my friends."

The innkeeper grunted in return and, with a huge effort, lifted the outsized behind she was resting on two stools. For a moment, she stared at Edgardo, then wobbled her flabby flesh in the direction of the barrels.

"Good news," Ermanno said. "I've found it. In the Second Book of Herodotus's *Histories,* there's something about natron."

"Really?"

"Natron, a powder that looks like salt, with a faint smell and a savory taste, can be found in crystal form in the sands of the Natron Valley, situated between Alexandria and the Al Qattara desert," he continued. "For Ancient Egyptians, it was a miraculous substance, essential for embalming the dead."

Edgardo and Abella exchanged inquisitive looks.

"You've been very helpful," Edgardo said.

"I'm glad. Here," he said, handing him a rolled-up parchment. "I've copied the whole passage. Read it, it's very instructive . . . These Egyptians had strange rituals."

Abella and Edgardo stood up.

Ermanno stopped them. "A favor. I would be grateful if you could settle the bill with that harpy for this divine nectar. A translator's life is a very wretched one."

Edgardo bowed and kissed his hand, and, while Abella went toward the exit, he looked for Teodora. It wasn't hard to find her. All he had to do was follow the nauseating scent of myrrh and civet. He quickly handed her the money. The woman looked up at him, then remained staring, like a statue of salt. "The more I see you, the more you look familiar . . . By all the relics of Saint John and Saint Paul, you're that timid scribe, that shitty coward, with no faith or compassion, who sent my lovely husband Karamago to the gibbet! You Judas . . . you could have saved him but you ran away as fast as you could!"

She grabbed him by the sleeve. Crushed with shame, Edgardo tried to leave.

"Repent! Repent!" the hag shouted.

The customers turned to look. The scribe managed to disengage himself with a tug and ran out, pursued by coarse screaming.

Teodora was right. That act of cowardice belonged to his past. He'd done nothing to save the merchant who had given him shelter and saved his life. After all this time, the gravity of that sin still weighed on his conscience.

He caught up with Abella, shaken and embittered.

"You took a long time! Did the lady ask you to marry her?" This time, Abella's sarcasm was painfully annoying. "We've made giant steps," the Magister continued. "We know that natron is used in embalming . . . and since Costanza and the virgin's bodies were covered in it, I assume that most probably that's the treatment they were intended for."

"True." Edgardo tried to calm down. "But I can't imagine why. To abduct, rape, and kill a girl, sew up her anal orifice and then embalm her is, I'd say, incomprehensible behavior. Who could have concocted such a plan?"

"The virgin of the beads was also about to undergo the same treatment. What's the connection between the two girls?" Abella paused, deep in thought. "Sabbatai has disappeared, but maybe I know where to go for more information about this business of mummies and corpses. Come with me."

They picked up the pace, splattering mud all around.

She knew where to find the fat man and the man from Bergamo. They lived on the island of San Serviglius, in a hut behind the hospice built by Benedictine monks to accommodate the droves of pilgrims who came to Venice prepared to face a long and perilous journey in order to visit the holy places in Jerusalem and, in this way, earn eternal salvation.

Some of them would get sick, even seriously sick, and quickly yield their souls to God.

The monks would bury unclaimed bodies behind the church, and that was where the fat man and the man from Bergamo would go to gather what for them was manna from heaven.

Corpses that were still fresh, dug up at night, and immediately delivered to the houses of physicians, alchemists, sorcerers, all those—and they were many—who would ask for them. A lucrative and not too strenuous trade about which they couldn't complain.

Magister Abella went straight to the point. "I want to know about the mummies."

The two men looked at each other in amazement, with the most innocent air in the world.

"In the well of Sabbatai's shop we found the Metamauco virgin covered in natron. We know it's used for embalming,"

Edgardo said. "Have you heard any rumor, any hint, even a whisper, about the abduction from the church of San Geminiano?"

"Forgive us, Signore," the man from Bergamo replied, "we're just poor devils, we know nothing."

Abella stood in front of the fat man. He had a good build for fighting, but one had to admit that the Magister outshone him in boldness and agility. "You'd better search your memory if you don't want to lose a good customer," she threatened.

"Well, actually, yes, it's true . . . now that I think about it, we have on occasion done business with Sabbatai."

"Go on."

"The dwarf started trading in corpses, just for a joke, and sometimes we get him the odd mummy . . . when we have to, you see."

"Who needs mummies?"

"I don't know. We're working men. He orders a corpse and we take it to him. Sabbatai gets some nice bodies—because of his shop he knows all the dying people in Venice."

"Sabbatai tried to kill me, if I report him you'll also be involved, and the trade will be exposed," Edgardo said aggressively.

"There's a merchant who keeps going back and forth between Venice and Alexandria with good corpses . . . I've also heard something about mummies."

The fat man gave him a dirty look.

"A merchant from Alexandria? Do you know his name?"

"No, no, all we do is give Sabbatai a hand to carry them . . . we're just working men, we know nothing else."

"A merchant from Alexandria," Edgardo repeated, calling for Abella's attention. "You see, everything starts to make sense, and the mosaic is taking shape."

Abella was always a little astounded by the scribe's sudden deductions.

"We must go back to where it all began, to the Alexandria merchant's palazzo in San Lorenzo. The circle is closing."

"Are you sure?" Abella replied, perplexed.

"And I even know what stratagem to use in order to get straight to the merchant," Edgardo added proudly.

The fat man and the man from Bergamo had listened to the whole exchange with moronic smiles, pleased that their situation wasn't deteriorating.

"So, illustrious Magister, as soon as a pilgrim drops dead, we'll bring it to you as usual," the man from Bergamo said, as though to seal a pact of non-aggression. "We'll give you a special price.

Abella did not reply. She wasn't convinced by Edgardo's confidence. The days were passing, and the announcement of Alvise's execution could arrive at any moment.

# XXVII.
## THE CONTRACT

The sun had already risen, and the bell tower of San Giovanni Evangelista was casting its shadow on Abella's house when Edgardo woke up. Still groggy, he turned onto his side and looked around. He'd slept in Abella's bed. He remembered nothing of the night that had just gone by, but he felt a deep sense of sweetness filling his flesh, and the scent of sage stuck to his hair.

He mechanically touched his bandages. A chest like any other man's, and a feeling of lightness, a desire to be reborn.

"You're finally awake," Abella said, walking in with an energetic step. "You're quite at home here now . . . " For a moment, she thought how pleasant it was to have a man around. "I'm just back from the *brolo*. I saw the commendatore outside the Doge's Palace announcing Alvise's execution with my own eyes. '*Post diem quartum, iudicium capitis agetur,*'" Abella said solemnly.

"Only four days!" Edgardo exclaimed.

"Then he'll be blinded, hanged, and quartered before the crowd."

"That's horrible."

"They want him to be an example to anyone who abducts aristocratic Venetian girls."

"Alvise is innocent."

"That's what you and I think. But it's useless unless we can find the culprit."

"We must get to the Alexandrian merchant. That *palazzo* conceals too many secrets."

"It won't be easy to meet him. Do you at least know if he's currently staying in Venice?"

"We'll find out soon enough, I've thought of a way . . . "

Abella pulled a face, worried.

"Maestro Tataro," Edgardo announced. "I wouldn't exactly say we're friends, but I think I have a good argument to convince him."

"Him again! That man seems to hold a strange attraction for you," Abella said carelessly.

She was right, Edgardo thought. In his search for the truth, Tataro seemed to represent an unavoidable component, as though in the end, he always had to come to terms with him.

A dried prune, wrinkled by the fire of the furnace. He was sitting on the chair, bent double, the blowpipe abandoned between his legs.

He had no more breath left, the omnipotent bolus had won the battle, it no longer wanted to be molded, it was the stronger of the two. Tataro had been defeated, old age had surrendered to the substance he'd tried to tame all his life. He was panting, desperately searching for his lost energy.

Seeing him in this condition, Edgardo felt deeply sorry for him: the hunger for power and glory and the hunt for wealth had all crumbled inside a body eaten away at by disease.

At the start, he refused to help them, so Edgardo played his last card: if they managed to get inside the merchant's *palazzo,* they'd be able to discover the origin of the pieces of pure glass, and probably get the formula of crystalline glass he'd been pursuing his whole life.

At this possibility, Tataro came alive. "And how could I help you?" he finally asked.

"You told me that Lippomano, the merchant's steward, asked to buy the abandoned foundry in Lupo."

"That's right."

"Agree. Tell him you're willing to sell it but on one condition: that the contract be signed personally by the merchant, before a notary, in his *palazzo*. We'll face him and force him to talk. There are many things he'll have to explain."

"And if he refuses?" Tataro asked.

"We have witnesses who've told us of a traffic of corpses between Venice and Alexandria, in which the merchant is involved."

"You're getting ahead of yourself here," Abella interrupted. "Those two body snatchers never mentioned any names, so we don't know if it's exactly that merchant."

"There are too many signs, too many coincidences leading to the *palazzo* . . . I have a feeling we're about to unravel the knot."

Edgardo was overwhelmed by excitement, and Abella didn't dare reply, but the inexorable power of logic had raised a wall of doubt in her mind.

The scribe's intuition and suppositions had so far proved to be slippery paths that had led to nothing but failure.

The prow of the gondola was struggling to slice through the carpet of leaves, bushes, and clods of grass covering the surface of the lagoon. The thick mantle exhaled a cloud of putrefying, rancid vapors that stifled any life form, and made the minds and movements of Venetians sluggish.

Silent and uncertain about their enterprise, the passengers were turning things over in their minds while waiting for the boat to drop them off at San Lorenzo, outside the Alexandria merchant's *palazzo*.

Tataro had difficulty breathing, his eyes lowered, wondering whether it was still worth getting himself involved in this new tribulation. Crystalline glass? He'd pursued it his whole life, and now wasn't so sure it was all that important, after all.

Abella, on the other hand, was wondering why she was

there, why she'd agreed to go with them. Was it to be near Edgardo? She thought he was frail and vulnerable, determined to follow a seemingly shaky hypothesis.

The only one who looked confident was the scribe.

He was savoring the trappings the past: the monk's habit, which he was wearing because that's how he'd introduced himself to Lippomano at their first meeting, filled him with sweet nostalgia, and he felt a sense of vigor, of freedom whenever he looked down at his chest, where he'd been used to seeing the invasive bulge, now vanished.

They were about to pass the stretch of open lagoon to the east and take the canal of San Zaccaria when their attention was caught by a ribbon floating above the emerald glow of the waves, which was gliding along the line of the horizon.

The wind had raised an eddy of water, boughs, and leaves, and was taking a stroll, lit up by the reflection of the sun.

It was the last thing they noticed before disembarking on the steps outside the *palazzo*.

Tataro had agreed directly with Lippomano. He'd bring two witnesses. It was up to the buyer to choose a trusty notary who'd draw up the contract.

When the Jew opened the door, he did not conceal his surprise at seeing the physician and monk who'd arrived when rumors of a smallpox epidemic had started circulating. Tataro immediately explained that it was his personal physician and his confessor.

They went through the dark, stuffy entrance hall and came into the internal garden. Tataro stared in disbelief. Huge, fleshy leaves were dripping with drops large as Oriental pearls, and vines and threads of ivy were hanging from the second-story loggia. The glassmaker walked with his face turned upward, enchanted by the spectacle—unusual in Venice—of such an abundance of exotic greenery.

In the ground-floor salon, they were received by a little man as lean as an anchovy, squeezed into a long, black robe that came down to his feet, with a face as sharp as the tip of an arrow and two little eyes that darted after each other like cats and dogs.

Without a word, the notary handed them the parchment. "The contract has already been drawn up," Lippomano explained, addressing the glassmaker. "Would you like to look at it," he gave a slight cough, "or would you prefer me to read it out?"

"I am perfectly capable of doing it myself," Tataro replied, peeved. "I can read." He brought the document close so that his witnesses could see it.

With a haughty gesture, Edgardo took out the case where he jealously kept his eye circles and brought them up to his eyes, triggering Lippomano's curiosity.

"I beg your pardon, I see that you use a strange contraption in order to read. If I'm not being indiscreet, may I ask what its function is?"

"It magnifies words . . . to help my ailing eyes."

"How ingenious. I could do with this too. As I get older, my eyes are failing. Could you tell me where I can find it?"

"First and foremost, you need to obtain very pure crystalline glass. Right, Father?" Tataro replied with an angry expression.

Edgardo bowed his head.

They started reading the document. Abella kept a distance, almost irritated by the comedy in progress.

"It all seems correct," Tataro said. "The figure agreed, the limits—"

"If you'd like to sign . . . " Lippomano handed him a quill and ink horn.

"Just a moment," Edgardo intervened. "I don't see the other contracting party, the buyer."

Lippomano looked embarrassed. "Yes, of course . . . he'll

join us presently . . . he's been delayed by a temporary indisposition. If, in the meantime, you'd like to sign . . . "

Edgardo wanted to stop him, but Tataro had already grabbed the quill and was writing his name. As soon as he'd finished, the Jew smiled with satisfaction and reached out for the parchment. "I'll go call—"

Edgardo swiftly put his hand on the parchment, and held onto it. "We're impatient to see him!" he exclaimed decisively.

Lippomano had no choice but to let go of it. "I'll be back immediately."

They were left alone, the notary suddenly looking like a mullet about to be tossed into a frying pan. While waiting, Edgardo's attention was caught by the horn filled with ink. It had an unusual shape, long and twisted, like a sickly root. It reminded him of another horn he'd had occasion to use many years earlier, when he was a monk. Its shape was unforgettable.

Preceded by a grumbling bustle, Lippomano reappeared. He was bent forward in sign of reverence, and dragged his feet in small steps. "His most illustrious magnificence, his excellency Ibrahim al-Fazari," he announced.

A long, slim figure, without edges, emerged from the semi-darkness. A stain floating through the air. It was impossible to glimpse its features. The body was wrapped in a black caftan of coarse texture, without embroidery or embellishments. The head was covered in a veil that came down below the chin. And the face . . . the face made everyone give a start of surprise and repulsion: a mask of mottled skin, like that of a snake, clung to the face, concealing the features and giving it an eerie stillness and coldness.

An icy silence had fallen on those present. Edgardo heard clearly Tataro's wheezing breath and Abella's heartbeat.

The merchant stopped in the doorway. Edgardo thought he gave a start. Perhaps he felt cornered and had a premonition of the blow that was about to strike him.

"The magnificent Ibrahim al-Fazari welcomes you to his home. He apologizes for being unable to greet you warmly in his own voice, but . . . " Lippomano looked at his master, who responded with a nod. "A very serious form of smallpox has completely disfigured his face and his mouth can no longer perform the role it was created for." He fell silent. Ibrahim had listened motionlessly. "However, he will have no trouble signing the document," Lippomano added, bringing a high-backed chair close to the table.

The robe rustled, giving off a scent of myrrh and frankincense.

They stood before each other: Edgardo tried to pick up some sign that would reveal to him this individual's identity. However, nothing showed through that mask of dark, iridescent scales.

Lippomano handed him the quill, and the merchant began tracing his name, revealing long, tapered fingers wrapped in white bands.

Edgardo watched the position of the hand, the movement, and the angle of the arm.

When Ibrahim had finished, he put down the quill, bent his head, and made an imperceptible sign to Lippomano, who put a leather purse down on the table.

Tataro immediately grabbed it, opened it, and, without standing on ceremony, started to count the money.

The merchant had already stood up, ready to leave the room.

Edgardo stopped him. "Your Excellency, allow me to take advantage of your hospitality and of the great honor you paid me by asking a favor." He hesitated for a moment, sought Abella's eyes, then continued. "Two young people went missing near your palazzo: Giacomo, the *garzone* of Maestro Tataro here, and a few days later Costanza, a relative of Tommaso Grimani. The girl was found dead in a boat not far from this

place, and a young man has been falsely accused of her murder. I was wondering if anybody in your household, perhaps a
servant or a slave, has seen any suspicious characters loitering
in the area. I know you're often traveling between Alexandria
and Venice in order to trade your very pure glass pieces . . . "
Edgardo was hoping to trigger a reaction.

At these words, Tataro stopped counting the money and
Lippomano's mouth fell open.

"The contract is sealed," the notary announced solemnly,
and those were the only words he emitted.

Lippomano offered his arm to the merchant, who walked
toward the exit.

"I know you can't utter a word," Edgardo continued, "and
for that I am sorry, but perhaps your steward could speak for
you."

The merchant turned his back on him, indifferent.

"Moreover, I should be honored to admire your merchandise," Edgardo persevered. "They say your glass pieces are of
superior quality, more transparent than any other glass, and
they also say that you don't just trade in glass . . . " He glanced
at Abella for approval, but she gave him a look of dismay.
"They say, although I'm sure it's just malicious gossip, that you
trade in slaves, young girls, and corpses . . . "

Everything came to a head, and Lippomano began to stammer something that made no sense.

Abella closed her eyes, overwhelmed, and sank into a chair.

The merchant looked about to respond to Edgardo's accusations, leaned toward him and spread open his arms like a
frightened bat, but then turned away and quickly made for the
exit without saying a word.

At that point, Edgardo impulsively decided not to let go of
his prey and leaped beyond the table, intent on stopping him.
In response, Lippomano grabbed him by the habit, trying to
hold onto the scribe.

"You must answer my questions!" Edgardo cried, and with a tug, he disengaged himself from Lippomano's grip and ran after him.

The garden swallowed them in its greenery.

Ibrahim's black caftan appeared and disappeared amid bushes and vines, blending in with the shadow of the enormous fleshy leaves.

For a second, Edgardo glimpsed him on the staircase leading to the upper loggia. He disentangled himself from the vegetation with a leap and went up to the second floor. There was a series of doors opening onto the long corridor. He was about to throw one of them open when he was stopped by a loud crash. It came from the garden. He rushed to the parapet in time to see the caftan vanish through the arch leading to the steps.

He went back down into the garden, then ran to the platform that connected to the canal.

In the sparkling air, cleansed by a light northerly breeze, a *scaula* was struggling to slice through the surface of the lagoon.

At the stern, the merchant was maneuvering the oar with smooth, precise movements. The wind swelled the caftan, turning it into a black shadow.

Without a moment's hesitation, Edgardo jumped into a gondola and reached open water.

Not without difficulty, they reached the bay outside San Marco.

The *scaula* had taken the direction of the open lagoon, slicing through the dark leaves. Edgardo was forcing the oar, determined to catch up, but the distance between them never seemed to decrease.

The farther he went, the more he felt as though that man would drag him to the edge of the known sea, into an abyss that would swallow him forever.

They went past the compact shores of Dorsoduro. The signs of human presence were diminishing. Edgardo started feeling tired and his body grew heavy, while the merchant's energy seemed inexhaustible: the arm movements, the leaning of the torso, like a perfect dance.

For a moment, a distant memory numbed his mind, then he was overcome with fatigue.

The gondola slowed down, collided with a trunk, and stopped with a sinister rustle. He'd lost, once again.

The scribe looked up and was extremely surprised to realize that the merchant's boat was also slowing down.

Like a knight who raises his lance before the start of a tournament, the merchant raised his oar to the sky.

If this was a challenge, then, Edgardo thought, this was the opportunity for him to redeem himself. Free from the weight of monstrosity, he felt like a new man, reborn, the knight his father had always dreamed of having for a son.

He mustered his strength and spurred the gondola on, standing straight at the stern, going to face the enemy.

The merchant was waiting for him, motionless, his face shining with serpent scales.

They studied each other for an moment. The two boats were turning in front of each other.

Edgardo crossed himself, not knowing why, perhaps a memory of his past life.

And, almost as a signal, a gust of wind pushed his gondola against the *scaula.*

Edgardo raised the oar, as though it were a spear. "Confess!" he cried, full of anger.

The merchant's oar, pointing up at the sky, did not move.

"Confess!" he repeated.

It was an instant. "Yes, I confess." The merchant's voice hovered in the air. And everything blended and blurred. The wind slid over the lagoon, the sky turned ruby, and a wave of heat came over his chest.

He abandoned his oar, exhausted. He felt the merchant's

eyes, under the mask, piercing through him. He thought his heart would burst.

That voice, the unmistakable sound of that voice he could never forget . . . It was not a man's voice.

## XXVIII.
## THE RETURN

A sudden current pushed the *scaula* away. The merchant remained motionless at the stern, his robe swollen like a sail in the storm.

Edgardo was stunned, unable to move, clinging to that voice he'd never forgotten: a sharp, vibrant sound, a breath of wind through the rushes.

Could he really believe it was . . . or was it just an illusion, the ghost of a memory, desire toying with his imagination?

He clutched the oar and, with two strokes, brought the gondola back into position. Now *scaula* and gondola were bobbing next to each other, gently tapping each other.

"I am guilty and you know that perfectly well," the voice said again.

Edgardo couldn't restrain himself. He leaped onto the *scaula*. The two bodies were now a step away from each other. In the air, as well as myrrh and frankincense, there was an ancient scent of amber.

"God almighty, don't let this be the hallucination of a sick man, slave to opium," he prayed. Then he addressed the merchant. "Signore, I fear my mind is upset by delirium: I'm hearing lost voices, seeing ghosts floating in the water. My desire is so overwhelming that it is giving substance to my memories. My soul is very confused, so I beg you, make yourself known, reveal your identity."

He thought he saw a smile crease the serpent skin. Without a word, the merchant took off the caftan, revealing a slender body covered with a tortoise-shell-colored tunic.

"A thread of wool, delicate and sinuous, made by the hands of a Mongolian weaver," Edgardo murmured. A strong sense of burning was ravaging his chest. "I beg you, take off your mask too."

The merchant bowed his head, hesitant.

"Your steward said your face is disfigured by smallpox," Edgardo insisted. "He also stated that you couldn't utter a word, and yet that's not the case . . . I therefore beg you."

A long sigh full of sorrow and desolation, then the hand rose and, with a determined gesture, the merchant tore the serpent skin from his face.

Not even a poet, a magician, and a madman put together could have described what Edgardo felt the moment he recognized that face: dismay, bliss, the miracle of resurrection, a dream incarnate, a ghost acquiring its body anew, the revelation of a mystery, and, at the same time, fear, revulsion, God's punishment. Everything got mixed up in a vortex.

Dark eyes slit like a blade, obsidian hair, amber skin, the face of a Mongolian slave ravaged by the disease that had left deep furrows and lines of damaged skin.

It was her, the woman he'd loved, dreamed of, waited for, pursued during all those nights. "My God, Kallis . . . " he murmured.

"I have returned."

She came closer. He felt her chest heaving. He was about to embrace her but she pulled away, lowering her face.

"As you see, Lippomano wasn't lying. The mask conceals a monstrous face. Keep away."

Edgardo violently brought her close to him, hugging her, kissing her ravaged face, her cracked lips, caressing her hair. "Don't ask me that, you who have loved a twisted, crooked being when you were the most beautiful creature in the universe. Do you really think that the love I feel for you can be undermined by the weakness of the flesh? I thank God for bringing you back to me. I saw you vanish amid the waves, I thought you were lost forever, and yet you're here, you've returned from the realm of the dead."

"I've dreamed of this moment so many times." Kallis spoke in a thin voice. "I wanted to see you sooner, but I didn't have the courage after soiling myself with all those sins . . . I am evil, Edgardo, don't forget that."

He hugged her tighter, again and again, almost suffocating her. "If this is evil, then God has chosen to make fun of us. For over ten years I've hoped you would rise from the waters that swallowed you, and prayed for a miracle . . . God has answered my prayer, and God wants no harm for His children."

Kallis pulled away and looked down at his chest. "It's gone." She stroked his tunic. "How is this possible?"

"An illustrious physician called Abella has freed me from the horrible excrescence."

Kallis touched the scars on her face. "God's ways are unfathomable. Those without faith struggle to accept the wounds inflicted by life. Our bond seems to be indissolubly linked to deformity."

The boats had started to drift.

"We must go back now," Kallis said. "And find an explanation so as not to arouse suspicion."

Still confused, Edgardo brought his gondola closer, and tied it to the prow with a rope, then stood at the stern of the *scaula* and began to navigate. Kallis was looking at him, moved. "You've become a good sailor. Remember? When we first met, you were surprised by how I could sail a boat."

Edgardo couldn't get enough of drinking in Kallis's face. "Do you remember this place?" he asked.

"You asked for my hand here?"

"And you didn't reply."

Kallis closed her eyes. "It all belongs to our past lives."

Suddenly, Edgardo put down the oar, came close to her, and embraced her. "I'm bursting with happiness . . . you're here, you're alive, you've returned forever. Nobody can ever pull our destinies apart."

He brushed his mouth against hers. Her lips still tasted of almond, like they used to. "But tell me, how did you save yourself from that terrible storm, all those years ago? What happened?"

"When I fled from the shore of the Luprio salt pan, I found myself surrounded by the scariest tempest ever known on the Venetian seas," Kallis began. "My *scaula* capsized not far from Metamauco. I was almost submerged by the waves, but I managed to cling to a plank and, with great difficulty, managed to go back to my island.

"There was devastation everywhere, waves as tall as towers came crashing on the harbor, the bishop's palace had been razed to the ground, boats were stacked up on top of one another like firewood, galleys folded, with sails tossed by the waves, the fishermen's huts nothing but a heap of beams. There were fires burning everywhere. It was as though long tongues of fire were coming out of the earth, burning everything.

"I walked through ruins and desolation on a soft, hot soil that gave at every step. Everything seemed to be sinking into an abyss. The inhabitants of Metamauco were running, terrified, trying in vain to stem the power of the wind and the waters that were simmering as if in the mouth of a volcano.

"I managed to reach our hut. I found nothing left, not even the goat. Everything had been swept away by the violence of the waters. There was only a little box stranded on the beach, which contained just a few things." Kallis looked at him with great tenderness. "The goose quill and the horn you'd given me."

"So I wasn't wrong . . . It was the same horn Lippomano brought to sign the contract."

"It's been with me through all my tribulations."

"So in the end you learned to write," Edgardo exclaimed.

"I had a great teacher who initiated me into the art."

"And the pupil was stubborn."

"I knew," Kallis continued, "that after the sins I'd soiled myself with I was marked forever and had to leave Venice as soon as possible. For two nights, I hid amid the ruins of the huts. Then I heard that a Paduan merchant was organizing a journey to the Orient, to Alexandria. I went on board as a slave.

"It was a long, dangerous crossing. We were attacked by Narentine pirates, struck by two tempests but, in the end, with God's help, we disembarked at Alexandria.

"I was alone, I didn't know anyone, I had nothing except my arms and . . . " Kallis paused, as though uttering that word caused her enormous pain. "And a formula, the formula for pure glass, crystalline glass, that Segrado had discovered."

At these words, a deep sadness overcame their hearts and Kallis's eyes filled with tears.

She let the swish of the waves against the keel sweep away the weight of their memories, then continued.

"Nobody in Alexandria knew the art of glass-making as I did. I offered my services as a servant in a foundry and, even though I was a woman, after putting me to the test, they hired me immediately. And so began my apprenticeship, and my new life. After three winters, I managed to have my very own foundry . . . only then did I decide to try experimenting with the crystalline glass formula. It was an unexpected, over-whelming success. I began to manufacture every piece out of transparent glass: cups, phials, vases, bottles—"

"Even eye circles?" Edgardo interrupted.

"No, never eye circles . . . I didn't feel worthy enough." She looked at him. "Do you still have them?"

Edgardo took out the case from his tunic. "Here they are, I'm never without them, they're my salvation. And so . . . carry on."

"My products were in demand everywhere. Merchants sold my glass pieces to Mamluks, Persians, Armenians, and even Mongols. I started two new foundries, and became wealthy and respected. Everybody forgot I was a woman and formerly a slave."

Edgardo rowed, unable to take his eyes away from her, full of loving admiration.

"Not a day went by when my thoughts didn't return to Venice . . . and you. I knew nothing of your fate. I gave a steward the task of buying me a *palazzo* in the city, and so every so often I started coming back, incognito, as an Alexandrian merchant called Ibrahim al-Fazari."

"So that explains why I found the glass pieces in your storeroom," Edgardo said.

Kallis was surprised. "Did you sneak into my *palazzo*?"

"I had to. I thought you were—I mean the Alexandrian merchant—was involved in the disappearance of two young people and in Costanza's death." He paused. "You have nothing to do with the abduction of these young people, have you?"

Kallis looked toward the Lido of Spinalunga. "That's not entirely true."

Edgardo shuddered.

"When I returned to Venice, my first concern was to redeem myself from the harm I'd done. I immediately tracked down Niccolò's family, remember Niccolò, Segrado's servant?"

Of course. Edgardo still had before his eyes the ghastly details of that day.

"Well, I tracked down his younger brother, who was still a child then. He'd become a talented *garzone* at Tataro's foundry, his name was Giacomo."

"So you met him?"

"No, I never met him in person. Lippomano took care of everything. He managed to see him with the excuse of an order of glass, and made him a proposition on my behalf: I would hire him as an assistant at double the pay. However, the agreement had to remain a secret, and nobody could know about the position. He agreed. He is now working, very content, in one of my foundries in Alexandria."

"That's why he vanished into thin air."

Kallis nodded. "But that wasn't enough. I decided to buy Segrado's old foundry. I didn't want it to remain in Tataro's unworthy hands. I want to make it active again, and give it as a gift to Giacomo, when he becomes a skillful master. I'm also looking for poor Balbo's family."

"You're repaying all your debts."

"I was blinded by hatred. " Kallis sighed. "I'm looking for a glimmer of light, even though it's not easy to forgive completely."

"What about Costanza? Do you know anything about her? She was found near your *palazzo*."

"I know nothing about this girl. Did you say she was killed?"

"I have reason to believe that they wanted to turn her into a mummy, even though I don't understand why. An innocent man is about to be executed for her murder."

They were approaching the city. As though a deep sense of shame prevented her from showing herself in public, Kallis hid her face under the hood of her tunic. "Too many innocents pay unjustly for the folly of men." These words concealed the torment that was tearing her to pieces.

At that moment, as the *scaula* was went past the far strip of Spinalunga and came into view of the bay of San Marco, Edgardo grew self-aware.

He'd thrown himself blindly, certain he'd solve the riddle of Costanza's death by following the tracks of the Alexandrian merchant, and now he had to start his search from the beginning. Had his intuition tricked him again?

His instinct, the visions overwhelming him, his strange deductions, were worthy of the ravings of someone who entrusts his body to opium as its only food.

He looked up at Kallis. She was there before him, resplendent, and he realized that his intuition hadn't tricked him at all, on the contrary, it had led him safely to his coveted aim: that of finding Kallis. That had been his first task. His heart, without his knowledge, had guided him to the light.

Now he had to immerse himself in the darkness again, in order to save Alvise.

Advancing with difficulty through the grassy lagoon, the boat had reached the entrance to the canal of San Zaccaria. A few more instants, and they would arrive at the *palazzo*. Kallis covered her face with her mask.

"Nobody must know I've returned," she said. "It's not time yet. It could be dangerous."

"I'll say that we've explained everything to each other. That you provided evidence that you have nothing to do with these events. And that I was wrong." Edgardo smiled. "They'll believe me. They're used to it."

"Beware of Tataro. He's very cunning."

"When can we see each other again?"

"We're safe in the *palazzo*. Lippomano and my servant can be trusted."

"The thought of leaving you throws me into despair. I fear something might happen that will separate us once more."

Kallis squeezed his hand. They were already going down the canal, and, in the distance they could see, cold and imposing, the palazzo of the merchant Ibrahim al-Fazari.

# XXIX

# THE NEST

Edgardo's immense joy at Kallis's return from the under-world had generated a sense of omnipotence in him. Two miracles in just a few hours: freedom from the horrible excrescence and Kallis's resurrection. He was convinced he'd now be able to succeed in every venture, including the impossible one of saving Alvise.

The yarn he'd spun to those present when he returned to the palazzo had left them all perplexed. Edgardo had cleared the merchant of all responsibility, and explained that he'd made a blunder. There was no involvement in Costanza's death or the disappearance of the *garzone*; Ibrahim traded glass that he himself purchased from foundries in Mesopotamia.

Tataro's mouth had twisted in anger. Edgardo had used him, tricked him with promises he hadn't kept. The formula for crystalline glass was still a secret.

Abella too was surprised. "That you should want to dupe me, scribe, is something I really can't tolerate," her expression seemed to say.

In the end, they'd left the palazzo silent and dejected, mulling over what they considered to be a sack of lies.

"You look extremely happy," Abella said as soon as they were alone. "An incomprehensible attitude after the umpteenth failure. May I remind you that Alvise is about to be quartered for the spectacle of the Venetian people?"

"I haven't forgotten," Edgardo replied. "What you're seeing in my face is the determination not to abandon the struggle."

"That may be the case but listen carefully: let's abandon your so-called intuition and get back to the facts, to concrete things, and reasoning. The first evident symptom, as we physicians would say, through which to track the origin of the disease is still Sabbatai. First of all, he tried to kill you, then we find the corpse with the natron, like Costanza, at the bottom of his well. All this makes me think that the apothecary is deeply involved in this business . . . What does your intuitive mind say?"

"It agrees."

"Excellent. Then we must go back to Sabbatai and grill him."

"He's vanished."

"That's what it looks like. At times, symptoms can be deceiving. There are rumors concerning his return. Tonight, we'll get inside his shop, like a probe in the guts of a sick man, and see if the rumors are true."

There are nights when the lagoon conceals the glassy reflections of the moon and the flicker of lights; it stifles the gurgle of waves against the shores; wraps in silence the sighs, the whimperings of pleasure, the songs of the drunks, the screams of sinners shaken by night terrors of death, allows itself a well-deserved rest, and abandons itself serenely into the arms of darkness.

The muddy waters, fords, sandbanks, and stretches of reeds and rushes blend into a single thick, motionless expanse. Nothing has any more shape or substance, and even the edges of the buildings, churches, and towers on the Rivus Altus blur into that flow of pitch that envelops everything.

It seemed this night had chosen to be their ally.

Edgardo and Abella's *scaula* sliced the surface of the canal like a swallow's flight, skimming the water without a sound.

The perfect night to circulate unseen.

They left the boat alongside the stream that lapped the internal courtyard behind the apothecary's shop, and disembarked.

Edgardo gave Abella a bewildered look. "We can try going in through the roof, but we have to climb all the way up there."

"That won't be necessary." Abella took out of her tunic a strange device with two arms in the form of a cross, made of curved iron, shaped like a spoon, and looking like an enormous pair of pliers.

"What the devil is that?" Edgardo asked.

"You use it to extract a dead fetus from the mother's womb," the Magister explained, "and it will be useful to us now."

She slid the points into the gap between two planks and squeezed the handles. There was a soft creaking sound, followed by a painful squeak, and the plank came off.

"I hope you don't put in as much strength with those poor women," Edgardo said.

"Come, let's go in." Abella lit a tallow.

A rotten stench caught their breaths in their throats: a mixture of moldy spices, dried meat, and powder of putrefied dog innards, kept closed in a barrel to be marinated for seven nights.

"Worse than a gangrenous leg," Abella grumbled. "You can't breathe in here."

Raising the flame, Edgardo shed some light on the back of the shop.

The utensils and clay and ceramic pots were well-organized on the shelves, as though they hadn't been used for ages. In a yellow glass jar swam a kind of monstrous-looking fetus, with a human bust and octopus-like tentacles.

They looked into the shop. It looked abandoned, the spices giving off a slightly stale smell. No sign of Sabbatai.

"Maybe he's not back," Edgardo suggested.

"Let's go upstairs."

Abella was trying to move softly, but her stout body announced her presence at every step with creaking, rustling, and grumbling.

In the first room, where you could smell acrid, extinguished embers with a generous watering of piss, they found no sign of human presence.

However, Edgardo noticed on the table half a salted sardine drowned in white semolina.

He sniffed and examined it. "This hasn't been here long. There aren't any worms yet."

The Magister stuck her finger into the mush, then lifted it to her mouth.

With a delicate flick of the tongue, she sent part of it down her throat. Edgardo couldn't repress a grimace of disgust.

"It was cooked no later than yesterday evening at Sext, with too much rosemary and very little salt. Revolting," she pronounced.

"So he's been through here."

"Perhaps he's still here."

Slithering like snakes, they went into the second room: there was a trunk, a chest, a bed thrown on the floor, and a stench of curdled goat's milk that grabbed one by the throat.

Abella grimaced. "It's like being in a stable."

"Except that the animal has bolted."

A pointless expedition; the chances of saving Alvise were growing slimmer. Only two nights left before the execution.

They were about to leave the house when they heard a regular, hiccupping chirping. They weren't sure where it was coming from, because it seemed to be raining down from the sky. They thought perhaps a sparrow had been caught in the reeds.

Edgardo raised the candle and saw a kind of nest hanging between two beams. It was quite large, made of cloth, and held up with ropes. Inside, there must be more than a sparrow, a larger bird, a big fat goose, for example.

The two partners gave each other a look of understanding, then Edgardo took a pole that was standing in a corner and, without much ceremony, began to poke the mysterious guest.

The chirping suddenly turned into miaowing, then a grunt, and finally into incomprehensible swearing. "By that whore of your mother who stinks like rotten shit, and that pimp of your father, may his dick fall off . . . " The sweet song ended with a loud thud.

At their feet lay a strange kind of bird, short, without wings, without hair, with a head like a watermelon, full of bumps, and which they had no trouble recognizing: it was Sabbatai.

Edgardo grabbed him by the shirt that covered his repulsive nudity and put him on his feet.

"For the love of God, what do you want from me?" Sabbatai mumbled.

"Why did you try to murder me?" Edgardo said, coming straight to the point.

"Murder you? Absolutely not, Signore, you're mistaken . . . "

"You added an excessive quantity of henbane and white poppy to the opium," Abella said with all her authority.

"No, no, forgive me."

Edgardo let go of him. Sabbatai stood up. He looked terrible, the bump over his eye was as large as a duck's egg. "I can explain . . . It was a very special blend. Stronger, better . . . the usual mixture wasn't enough . . . you needed something magical . . . "

"And you didn't think I could have given up the ghost?"

"No, Signore, really, I swear."

"I don't believe you. That kind of mixture leads to death, and you know it." Abella lifted him bodily and sat him on the chest, like a child. His little legs were swinging like two tired intestines. "And what about the well-preserved body you keep hidden in your well?"

The apothecary's face, hard as it is to imagine, grew even more distorted into a devilish grimace, and began dancing about on his neck as though trying to abandon its body to find an escape route.

"You told us you knew nothing about natron, and yet your well is full of it," Edgardo said.

At this point, Sabbatai decided to keep his head on, and shielded himself from the blows of destiny by hiding his face in his little hands. "Natron, natron, I know nothing about this natron . . . and the virgin of the beads has nothing to do with me, I swear."

"Did she walk here by herself?" Abella said.

"No, no, I was forced . . . they threatened me, the city was full of soldiers, they didn't know where to hide her."

"Who? Who didn't know?" Edgardo had a fierce expression that allowed no way out.

"Those two, the fat man and the man from Bergamo . . . they dumped her on me, I didn't even know it was the virgin."

"And what's your business with those two cutthroats?"

"Trifles, small trade, a little dead body every now and then . . . corpses of no importance that nobody wants, people sentenced to death, lepers, slaves. We fix them up and sell them to scholars like yourself," he said, pointing at Abella.

"And do you also trade in mummies? What were you supposed to do with the virgin's body?" Edgardo insisted.

"Mummies are a gift from heaven, a lot of money, but the virgin was just here temporarily . . . the man from Bergamo and the fat one were really scared."

"Where's the virgin now?"

"Down in the well."

"And what do you mean to do with her?" Abella asked.

"Me, nothing. They'll come and get her."

"And take her where?"

"I don't know . . . to whoever ordered them to steal her."

A flash of light illuminated Edgardo's eyes. "And when are they coming to get her?" he cried.

"Tomorrow night, when there's no moon."

The night before Alvise's execution outside San Marco.

"Tomorrow we will wait for these two gentlemen here, hidden in your shop," Edgardo said.

"And if you play any trick, I'll report you to the judges for poisoning," Abella threatened. "The word of a physician is highly esteemed."

Sabbatai nodded, terrified.

## XXX.
## LITUS MERCEDIS

They crouched behind the shop counter while Sabbatai waited upstairs. The lagoon was calm, still, like the night before. The black waters had ebbed away, dragged by the northern currents.

In the dark, Edgardo was unconsciously smiling. The thought that he might have to face dangers, fights, and use force couldn't keep from his face the ecstatic expression and the new sensation he could have described as courage. Kallis's return made him feel reborn.

They'd met for a few minutes, after None. He'd slipped into the palazzo like a thief. He couldn't resist the desire to hug her. Kallis's presence had unexpectedly reawakened a wave of sensations and emotions he thought had been dulled forever. A frenzy was burning in his chest. He needed to see her, caress her, kiss her, hold her body tight against his. He hadn't felt anything akin to this since they'd parted.

A confused rumbling came from the internal courtyard, then a sinister scraping at the door that led to the back of the shop.

The skipping steps of the apothecary on the stairs were interrupted by the hissing voice of Abella, who'd practically lifted him up by the neck. "Remember . . . don't try and be clever."

Sabbatai disengaged himself and rushed to open the door. The fat man and the man from Bergamo were waiting for him, looking tired.

"So, where have you hidden her?" The man from Bergamo stank of curdled milk.

"In there," Sabbatai replied, pointing at the well.

"In the cistern?" the fat man exclaimed irritably.

"And where was I supposed to put her, on the shelf in the shop?"

"Damn rotten, stinking luck," the man from Bergamo swore, and went to lift the iron plank that covered the well. "Will you go down?" he said to the fat man.

"What? So I get stuck in there?" his partner replied.

They looked at each other in silence, expecting heaven to nominate someone.

"Come on, hurry," Sabbatai said.

Still swearing, the man from Bergamo went down into the well. When he heard him reach the bottom, the fat man leaned over. "So, what can you see?"

"Nothing, it's pitch black."

"Is the girl there?"

"Of course she is."

"Does she stink?"

"No, she doesn't stink."

"Is she rotting?"

"No, she's nice and dry, dry as a salted sardine."

"Then tie her and I'll pull her up."

A moment later, the body was tied to a rope, and the fat man began to pull. "She's as light as a chaffinch," he said to Sabbatai, looking pleased.

The apothecary helped him lift her. While the man from Bergamo was climbing out, they wrapped her in a torn sail.

Abella and Edgardo had followed the entire procedure hidden behind the window of the back of the shop.

"And this concludes our business," Sabbatai said. "I don't want to hear anything more about this girl."

"Go on, you know you'd have liked to have a little go with

her, she's still in good condition," said the fat man, who started laughing.

They placed the body at the bottom of the boat and, with a quick maneuver, pushed away from the shore.

Abella and Edgardo rushed to their own *scaula* to go after them.

The cog of the two crooks was advancing in a dull, almost surreal silence, as though the lagoon wished to pay the virgin of Metamauco a final homage.

After going down the Rivus Altus, past the bay of San Marco, they went along the Riva degli Schiavoni, toward the Lido.

Sitting on the boat floor, Abella wondered where the two villains were taking the mummified body, and why. Once again, she'd let herself be involved by the visionary scribe. She studied him while he rowed, absorbed in his thoughts, and unexpectedly had to admit that she had begun to feel something she couldn't quite describe: a rush? A way of feeling that was in tune with his? Affection?

In the distance, in the east, they saw the line of battlements erected in defence of San Nicolò and the watchtower. The calm, flat waters of the lagoon gave way to the lapping of waves caused by the open sea currents.

The cog turned north, in the direction of the island with forests brimming with vegetable gardens and vines that was dedicated to the holy martyrs Saint Erme and Saint Erasmus, known as *Litus Mercedis* because of a legend according to which, during the construction of the church, a large quantity of gold was supposed to have been discovered.

They followed the coastline and docked on an isolated shore near the Amurianum harbor.

The two villains unloaded the body and went down a path in the midst of a bed of reeds. The Magister and the scribe kept a safe distance.

After just a few steps, they reached a tall, round building in poor condition, and easily identified it as an abandoned water mill.

Hiding in the rushes, soon afterwards they saw the two men leave the mill empty-handed and return to their boat.

Abella gave a sign, and they set off.

They didn't know what to expect: there could be dangerous people in there, and they could be risking their lives.

They walked around the building, trying to pick up the slightest sound from inside. The creaking of their footsteps was a sign that the mill was built on the border of a saltpan.

The acidic, metallic smell that rose from the basins burned their lips and throats. A breath of wind rose, bending the reeds.

Built, like so many others in the lagoon, next to canals in order to use the tides, the water mill had been used to mangle salt and grain, but it looked long-disused; the large wooden wheel was covered in algae. Because of the rising waters during the past few years, many saltworks had been abandoned.

They went to the door. It was ajar. They pushed it open.

In the pitch dark, they were greeted by a singular stench: a warm, repugnant mixture of aromas and rotten meat.

They groped their way forward. They made out the dark shadow of a huge millstone standing vertically over another one, and the long wooden arm that connected them to the outside mechanisms.

Abella took a few steps forward and collided with a stone plank. "Light a candle, quick!" she said.

Edgardo took a tallow from his jacket and, with the help of his flint, managed to bring a faint light to the place.

Right in front of Abella, on the stone slab, lay the body of the virgin of the beads: totally naked, covered in that powder that gave her an icy, supernatural glow, still looking healthy and unexplainably beautiful after all those days.

"It's the natron that keeps her intact," Abella whispered. Edgardo raised the flame to have a more comprehensive look at the place and was astounded.

In the room of the mill, various, ancient stone sarcophagi were laid out in an orderly fashion, some with their lids removed, other sealed with marble slabs. They approached. The stench of rot and aromatic herbs made the air unbreathable.

They leaned over the first sarcophagus. A horrifying sight that even Abella, in her experience as a physician, had never come across. A body that had been quartered, with no hands or eyes, sewn back together as well as could have been, covered in natron, its skin and flesh dried up in places, dripping a thick, sticky, green liquid that gave off an unbearable smell.

"Judging by his state, he must have been sentenced to death," Abella remarked.

They went to the sarcophagus next to it. Inside were the remains of a somebody who must have been a nobleman. His skull was smashed but the body, wrapped in pale linen bands, maintained a certain dignity, and gave off a scent of cedar and myrrh. It looked like an ancient Egyptian mummy.

In the other sarcophagi, they found other corpses, some in a state of putrefaction, others part-mummified, others perfectly preserved. A graveyard of mummies of all kinds and ages.

Next to the stone slab on which the young girl lay, Abella recognized a few surgical tools and various terracotta receptacles, some of which surprised her. "It's the workshop of an embalmer," she said.

"An embalmer in Venice?"

"Evidently, as those two villains told us, there's a blossoming trade in corpses in Venice, which someone transforms into mummies . . . But for what purpose?" She looked around. "There's something I don't understand."

Edgardo leaned against the millstone, lost in thought. He suddenly noticed a heap of rags thrown in a corner. Something was shining among the fabrics. He started rummaging. They were poor jackets, torn breeches, tunics, perhaps clothes that had belonged to the victims.

Among them a quality garment stood out, fine wool embroidered with gold thread, which had certainly belonged to a member of the nobility. Edgardo picked it up. "Look."

Abella approached.

"It's a refined dress, very expensive." Edgardo turned it around, studying it. "I've seen this dress before . . . of course . . . this dress belonged to Costanza."

"Costanza?"

"Yes, I have no doubt. She often wore it on feast days."

The flash that lit up Edgardo's face didn't have time to turn into an exclamation of victory before they heard footsteps outside.

Fingers tight on the wick, and darkness came back to reign over the abandoned mill. Abella and Edgardo quickly climbed up a ladder that led to a gallery. They crouched behind sacks of salt that had been long forgotten there.

The door opened and the sound of panting took possession of the surrounding space. After some bustling, the light of a lamp revealed the features of the man who'd just entered. He had the dark skin of a resident of the African coast, and was wearing Arab clothes. His skull was shiny and his body strong and muscular. He moved with phlegmatic slowness amid the tools, as though getting ready for a procedure. In the end, he approached the body of the virgin, and placed the lamp on the stone slab.

With a light, expert touch, he felt the consistency of the flesh and tissue. Then he remained in contemplation, as though prey to a dream, listening to the creaking sounds caused by a sudden northerly wind.

With unexpected energy, he set to work.

From his tools, he picked a thin rod, curved, which ended in a hook. With infinite delicacy, he inserted it into the nasal cavity. He pushed it in and twisted it with skill until he managed to extract a gray, flabby, gelatinous substance. He repeated the procedure over and over. His movements were precise, always the same, his eyes inspired, as though he were celebrating a ritual.

When he thought nothing more was coming from digging, he turned the body on its side.

He picked up an enema syringe from his tools. It had a long, twisted tube. He immersed it into one of the receptacles next to him, and sucked up some liquid. A fresh scent of cedar spread through the air, so much so that, for a moment, it was like being transported to the shores of the Nile.

When the syringe was full, he carefully looked for the girl's anus, inserted the tube, and emptied the entire liquid into it.

He repeated the operation until, feeling the belly and stomach, he felt no more tension in them. He then took a curved needle, threaded it with silk, and, with the grace of a woman, went about carefully sewing up the anus that had just been filled with the liquid.

Edgardo squeezed Abella's arm: it was the same treatment Costanza had received.

Therefore, it hadn't been violence against nature, but an embalming procedure. All the elements concurred: the stitches in the orifice, the small cuts in the nasal cavity, the swollen belly. If to this you added finding the dress, there was no more doubt. The embalmer was Costanza's murderer.

Not allowing his heart to consult reason, gripped by an unstoppable impetus, Edgardo lunged down the ladder and fell on the back of the man, who, overwhelmed, rolled on the ground.

The struggle turned immediately fierce. The Saracen,

although caught by surprise, managed to grip the scribe's lean body, and tried to crush it.

Strangled screams, dull blows, wheezing.

Abella rushed down from the gallery and threw all her weight on the embalmer in order to immobilize him, but the Egyptian's strength was beyond her expectations. Edgardo had been too impulsive.

The bodies rolled, knocking against the sarcophagi.

The wind had started to whistle, shaking the reed roof.

The Magister tried to block one of the Saracen's arms in order to free Edgardo, but the maniac was stronger than a bear. She received a fist in her face that left her on the ground, unconscious.

The grip loosened and the scribe managed to disengage himself, trying to grab a stick that was leaning against the wall. In vain. The Egyptian came up behind him like an avalanche, and crushed him against the base of the millstone.

The violence of the wind had raised the waters of the lagoon and the tide was rapidly rising.

There was a sudden crash, and the mill wheel began to turn, activating the vertical grindstone that turned around its axis.

Edgardo's body was lying on the stone base. Panting, blocked by the man's weight he saw the granite mass inexorably approaching . . . In a few seconds, he'd be crushed. He smelled salt in his nostrils, and his final thought went to Kallis. Theirs was an adverse destiny. He prayed to God and asked forgiveness for all his sins. He closed his eyes.

A sudden tear, as though he'd been lifted in the air by a vortex. A blow, a wheeze, a thud. Before him, still dazed, Abella was holding a stick.

The Egyptian's body was lying on the millstone. The wheel was advancing, implacable.

They almost didn't realize it in time. Edgardo leaped to his feet.

A sinister creak of mangled bones, a mix of dull and flabby sounds. A bloody mush. The man's head had been crushed like a melon that was too ripe. The grinder slowly pursued its course.

Abella and Edgardo took a step back, disturbed by the horrifying spectacle.

Almost automatically, the scribe's hands made the sign of the cross in the air.

Drowned by the wind, the matins bells drifted across from Torcellus.

"He shouldn't have died. He was our only proof," Abella murmured.

"The night is about to give way to a new day. We haven't much time left."

Edgardo picked up Costanza's dress and gave the embalmer's body one final look. "We must reach the Doge's Palace before dawn."

"A nything interesting this morning?"
"A quartering, with gouging of the eyes."
"Oh, good. And who's the lucky man?"
"Alvise, Nena's child."
"Poor boy."

The crowd in San Marco, outside the Doge's Palace, had been growing since dawn, awaiting the execution.

On the main floor, where the doge's Curia gathered, Edgardo and Abella were waiting with trepidation to meet the representatives of the Great Council.

In his cell, Alvise was reciting his final prayers, wondering why Our Lord had reserved him such an unjust fate for him.

The bells of the basilica rang Prime. The fateful moment had arrived.

A few footsteps resonated in the salon and Grimani appeared at the bottom of it, followed by the nobleman Morosini.

Edgardo and Abella immediately went toward them. "Illustrious gentlemen," Edgardo said, going down on his knees, "you must suspend the execution. Alvise is innocent."

The hostile look Tommaso gave Abella did not bode well.

"We've discovered Costanza's true murderer," Edgardo continued.

"So who could that be and where is he?" Morosini immediately asked.

"We left him in a water mill in Litus Mercedis. Alas, dead."

"Did he confess?" Tommaso asked authoritatively.

"No, Signore, he didn't have time. However, there are many unequivocal signs of his guilt." Edgardo made a sign to Abella. "We found this in his house."

The Magister showed them the dress.

"Do you recognize it?

Tommaso examined the dress attentively. "It's Costanza's," he said.

"Moreover, we discovered that he killed other people in the same way," Abella added.

Morosini's eyes narrowed so much they almost disappeared.

"He was an embalmer," Abella explained. "He arrived *cum aliqua verisimile ratione* from Egypt. He abducted and killed the victims, then turned them into mummies. We found various bodies treated this way in the water mill."

"Are you sure it really was an embalmer?" Morosini asked.

Edgardo took out the parchment Ermanno d'Istria had given him. "The procedure coincides perfectly with Herodotus's description in Book Two of his *Histories*. Listen." And he began to read out the text. "Herodotus says that there are three kinds of embalming: the first for the rich and powerful, the second for those who are less rich, and the third for the poor wretches.

"In the first one, on the first day, the body is washed and the brain extracted with an iron hook through the nostrils. Then one of the embalmers, also known as the quarterer, uses an obsidian knife to make a long incision in the left side of the abdomen to remove the stomach, intestine, lungs, and liver. Not the heart, which remains where it is. Then the quarterer, being impure, is sent away. The organs are carefully washed and the belly filled with myrrh, cassia, and various aromas, then sewn up. The corpse is then covered in natron and left to dry out for forty days. Subsequently, the corpse is coated with juniper and cedar oils and aromatic resins, and wrapped in linen bands soaked in resin. At that point, the mummy is ready to be shut in a sarcophagus.

"And now we get to the second type of embalming, which is less costly. In this case, the organs are not removed, but repeated enemas with salt, wine vinegar, and aromatic herbs are administered, and the intestines are washed until they are clean. Then, still by means of enemas, a solution of natron is inserted through the rectum, which is then sewn up to stop the liquid from pouring back out, so it can act inside and dissecate the organs." Edgardo stared at them. "It's what we saw the man do with the virgin's body."

"And the same treatment was performed on Costanza," Abella added. "I saw it with my own eyes."

"God Almighty," Tommaso exclaimed. "And why would he have attacked poor Costanza like this?"

"We know there's a secret, highly remunerative trade in mummies between Venice and Alexandria," Edgardo explained.

"Buying and selling mummies. I don't understand why." Nobleman Morosini looked increasingly upset.

"We haven't found an explanation either, but there's no doubt that the embalmer abducted and killed Costanza in order to make her into a mummy. The dress is proof, as well as the natron on her body. It's a salt ancient Egyptians used in order to dry meat and heal wounds."

"Alvise confessed," Tommaso said, turning to look at Morosini.

"Under torture," the nobleman replied.

"It's true," Tommaso squeezed Costanza's dress in his hands, "but we cannot ignore this new element."

The *boni homines* exchanged unfathomable looks, then Morosini said to Grimani, "I think we could suspend the sentence while we wait for new and more accurate details about this case and about this Egyptian's trafficking."

"We'll send guards to the water mill," Tommaso replied.

"I'll run and give Nena the news," Edgardo exclaimed, forgetting all etiquette.

"Remember, it's just a suspension. The magistrates will decide whether there's a case for holding a new trial," Tommaso repeated with austerity.

Edgardo and Abella took their leave.

"It's a first victory," Edgardo whispered as they were leaving.

"We've only tripped death up," Abella said, not looking quite so confident.

So many times he'd gone through *calli* and shores, crossed fords, slipped away like a thief in the hope of merging into the silver glow of the lagoon, of turning into a rush, of sinking into the muddy slime of that uncertain land. So many times, over those years of desolation and solitude, he'd dreamed of a slow death while dissolving in the vapor of opium; so many times, he'd clung to the faint hope, the illusion that Kallis hadn't sunk into the abyss of the muddy sea.

Now, as he brushed against huts, hiding in the shadows, plunging into the thickest vegetation, looking for deserted paths amid sand banks and pools, ponds and little islands, now that he avoided prying eyes like the pustules of lepers, Edgardo wished he could shout his joy to the world, shout to strangers the warmth his new-found love had generated in his soul, the huge desire to build a new existence.

Nobody was supposed to know, nobody was supposed to see him going into the palazzo of Ibrahim al-Fazari. That's what he'd agreed with Kallis. Revealing herself would have been too dangerous, and the past could still crush her.

The Moorish servant opened the door. He crossed the garden, which looked even more luxuriant, and went up to the loggia. Kallis was waiting for him in her room, the same room where he'd hidden and where he'd found feminine traces he'd then connected to Costanza.

He saw, standing by the window closed with an oilskin, a mercurial form undulating in a stretch of light. She was wearing the tortoise-colored tunic she'd had on when they'd first met.

"God Almighty, how I've dreamed of this moment. I've even hoped to get some evidence of your death, so I could keep your memory alive in my heart. I couldn't survive in a state of doubt." He approached, and was inebriated by the amber scent of her body. "And how have you lived these past years?"

There was a shudder of uncertainty, a shadow. "I've worked every day to build this return." Kallis touched her face. "When I felt death sleeping at my side, I thought God wanted to punish me for my terrible sins. Then salvation appeared on the horizon, and I understood that, in the end, I would win my battle, because God wanted me to atone for my guilt: I had to return to Venice, to the city where I was born a slave, where I died as a slave, and was then born again thanks to you."

Edgardo stroked her face, her lips, her earlobes, the cut of her obsidian eyes.

"Don't I horrify you? It's not my face anymore . . . "

"Horror? You of all people talk of horror, when you made love to a cripple bent over by a purulent hump, you who chose to love a monster?"

"You're free now." Kallis lifted his jacket. A red line marked his chest where flesh once grew.

"The signs of our struggle with death are what our lives have in common." Edgardo pushed her onto the bed and lightly placed his mouth on the scars that ravaged her face, one by one, as though to heal them. "Do you remember when you stole my soul with a kiss?" he whispered.

Kallis laughed. "Even when I was far away you were inside me."

"You can give it back to me now. I am here, body and soul. Nothing can separate us."

Deep in the Mongolian slave's eyes, there was a flash of dismay the scribe couldn't grasp.

"After all that's happened, despite all the sins with which I soiled myself, do you really love me so much you can imagine being able to cross the tempestuous sea of life with me? Aren't you afraid of God's judgement?"

It was a question he'd asked himself many times. "I'm scared to admit it but I love the whole of your being, I even love the evil in you."

Kallis clung to him and held him as tight as her slave arms allowed.

The memory of when their bodies had blended in divine ecstasy had never been erased. As though not even a season had passed, the memory of the skin, gestures, and tastes bloomed again, and Edgardo was reacquainted with the incomprehensible, magic words Kallis had whispered, swept by pleasure, and the almond taste of her sex, the amber tones of her skin; Kallis was reacquainted with the hardness of his member, and the tousled passion of his kisses, and the cry of ecstasy he emitted at the moon, like a stray wolf. How could two people, after all these years, find each other again as though the handwriting of their love had never been interrupted?

"I must leave, you know, even though that makes me very sad," Edgardo whispered. "I managed to postpone the execution of the *garzone*, but his life isn't safe yet."

"So he's innocent, then," Kallis said with a kind of venom. "I am envious of the innocent." An expression of repressed anger flashed through her eyes.

Edgardo looked at her, perturbed. "I believe it, and I must convince the judges that I am right."

"Are you so sure that justice is always after the truth? Truth has many faces."

Edgardo felt that hatred he'd known so well resurface in Kallis's words. "The murderer was involved in a traffic of mummies, but unfortunately he is no longer alive, so he can't confess. It seems that this traffic takes place between Venice and Alexandria. Did you hear anything about it when you were there?"

Kallis stared into the void. "I heard the sailors who were transporting my glass mention it. They were talking about this lucrative and successful mummy trade, but from Alexandria to Venice, not the other way around."

"Why would anybody buy mummies in Venice?" Edgardo felt on the brink of a gut feeling, and that frightened him.

"I don't know. I heard that many thieves would go plunder ancient Egyptian tombs and then purloin them, to sell them at a high price."

"From Alexandria to Venice," Edgardo repeated. "In that case, why kill and mummify Costanza if she wasn't going to be sold in the Orient?"

"Are you saying that Alvise isn't guilty?" Magdalena murmured.

"Nena only hears what she wants to hear." Tommaso was fidgeting in the semi-darkness of the bedroom, wrapped in a fur cape. "The execution has merely been suspended. They're conducting more enquiries."

"I only want for this business to be over as soon as possible." Magdalena's voice was faint and exhausted.

"You mustn't worry about it anymore, it's all over. We can begin anew."

Tommaso sat on the edge of the bed where his wife lay wrapped in fox fur blankets.

"This is the beginning of our new life." He showed her a small bottle. "The miraculous medicine I told you about. It's finally arrived."

It was an oily, cinnabar-colored liquid.

"Are you sure?" Magdalena asked, worried.

"Many women in the Orient have become pregnant after taking this potion, and given birth to strong, valorous sons."

Magdalena remembered Abella's words, trying to warn her.

"And is there no danger?"

"Trust me. I care about your health above anything else."

"Even above another son?"

Lowering his head almost as though trying to hide, Tommaso began to rub his eyes. "Above anything else," he replied, then removed the stopper from the bottle.

A stale, rancid smell wafted out into the air. Magdalena pulled away.

"Drink it," he commanded.

Her hand shaking like that of an old woman, Magdalena clutched the bottle and lifted it to her mouth. A foreboding of death spread through her chest.

"A new life will be born," Tommaso said, encouraging her.

She closed her eyes and drank the sticky liquid.

An itchy effervescence burst in her throat, while a sickening taste of festering water remained glued to her tongue and palate; then a flinching, a stirring of her internal organs, as though the body was rejecting this substance.

Magdalena lay down, holding her chest and, gradually, the turmoil subsided. There seemed to be a fidgeting demon in her belly that was tickling her vagina.

Tommaso was undressing to lie down next to her. She knew what awaited her.

He turned her on her front and spread her legs as though tearing two strips from a cloth. "We'll have a new heir . . . and it will be as though Luca has returned."

Magdalena closed her eyes tight and clung to oblivion. She felt herself penetrated by a member as hard as granite, resolute, devastating, which shattered the sweet memory of her dead child. She took his blows, praying to God to hear her prayers and make her pregnant.

When, in the end, the sperm carrying humor spread through her belly, she felt as though it mixed with the tincture she'd just drunk, and the image appeared to her of a ram with a siren's head and a swollen belly staring at her from the top of a mountain. She wondered if it was a good or a bad omen.

## XXXII.
## AVICENNA

All night, Abella had followed the path of the moon lighting sand banks and fords around Torcellus. A demon had gotten a grip on her mind, tormenting her with doubts and questions that had given rise to a deep sense of guilt in her soul.

She couldn't remain indifferent to the thrust of questions without answers, even if that meant endangering her own life.

Alvise wasn't safe yet, and what she'd seen at the mill could throw light on many corners that were still dark in that affair.

She remained in uncertainty until dawn, when she saw a heron take flight in front of the monastery of San Giovanni and cross the horizon, skimming over a glowing lagoon that radiated hope.

She went back into her laboratorium. In her trunk, she kept her most precious memories: a woollen dress that had belonged to her mother, an arrowhead used by her father when he hunted, a wooden wheel carved from a tree trunk, the only toy she'd had as a little girl . . . and the manuscript.

She picked up the volume, untied the ribbon, and opened the first sheet: Avicenna, *Liber Canonis Medicinae*.

She stroked with her eyes the Carolingian minuscule that made up the page in a magical pattern. She touched the manuscript with her fingers, like a caress.

She'd never left it behind, but taken it with her from Salerno, as she wandered from city to city, like a relic, the cornerstone of knowledge. She was convinced that, sooner or later, God would punish her for her sin: purloining, or rather stealing, such a precious text from the library of the School of Salerno, thus betraying the trust of all those who had welcomed her, taught her, and given her their knowledge. When she'd run away, she'd been unable to resist it. And she still felt guilty about it.

For years, she had admired it, leafed through it, caressed it like a baby in swaddling clothes, her baby.

She placed it delicately on the stone table. Now all she had to do was wait.


Edgardo arrived at the chimes of Terce, as agreed. He felt full of energy and, for the first time, his view of the world shone with light. His mind was crammed with future projects with Kallis and he couldn't think of a single obstacle that couldn't be overcome. He even felt on the right path as far as Alvise's fate was concerned.

He found Abella sitting outside the door, staring into space.

"I heard from a merchant—" Edgardo started without even greeting her.

"What merchant?" Abella interrupted.

The scribe fell silent, unsure whether to reveal at least part of the truth to the companion of his adventures.

"The Alexandrian merchant."

"So you continue to frequent him?" Abella said, suspicious.

"I met him by chance," Edgardo lied. "He told me that the trade in mummies is conducted from Alexandria to Venice. It's here that the goods are picked up, and we need to discover why."

"Come in, I might have the answer." Abella's tone was weary, almost melancholy, like someone about to undergo a difficult trial. She took him into her laboratorium. "Look," she said.

The manuscript seemed to be floating on the gray stone.

"It's a rare copy translated in Toledo of the *Liber Canonis Medicinae* of the great Avicenna. Do you know him?"

"I heard his name mentioned when I was a copyist at Bobbio."

"Ibn Sinà, known as Avicenna, is the most illustrious Persian physician. This manuscript comprises all his knowledge: the classification of diseases, causes, remedies, anatomical studies, new medicines. Everything a scholar of medicine must know." Abella paused and bit her lip, betraying uncontrolled tension. "I have reason to believe that we'll find the answer to our questions in this manuscript."

She was confused, unsure. Edgardo couldn't understand the reason for this hesitation.

"In the embalmer's mill I noticed tools I know well, because they're used in the laboratoria of physicians and apothecaries . . ."

"So tell me, what did you find in the manuscript?"

"Let me drink a bowl of water first."

Abella went to the jug. She was exhausted. She was about to place her life in the hands of this illogical scribe: why? Why face such a grave danger? Why sacrifice her whole tormented existence for the sake of sincerity? To save young Alvise? That wasn't true, and she knew it. It was for Edgardo. She wanted to submit her pure soul to his judgement . . . what an absurd feeling she had for this frail, limping creature with a confused mind. She didn't want to give what she felt a name, or perhaps it would be more accurate to say that she couldn't find a name for what she had never felt before. Was it perhaps that feeling some call love?

She took a sip of water, and that perked her up. "Alright, now I can explain but, before that, let me add a few words to what I'm about to say." She was ready to open up her soul and disclose all her feelings. "I've decided to be totally honest with you. After all, we've been walking side by side for many days now, so the time for subterfuge and lies is over, don't you think?"

It was like a knife through his heart. Edgardo didn't expect to hear that, not from Abella.

He'd always considered her a strong, decisive, learned woman and, throughout all their adventures, he'd always neglected to notice her moods, to appreciate her generous thoughts, her words of affection. He had stuck to appearances and felt like a nonentity, a man without principles, because he had not been totally honest with her.

"Wait. Before you bare your soul, it is I who must beg your humble pardon. I was the first to deceive you. I don't want there to be any shadow to darken the transparency of our friendship.

"I must confess a secret: the Alexandrian merchant we've just met isn't called Ibrahim al-Fazari, he has another identity. It's a woman called Kallis. She disappeared from Venice over ten years ago and I thought she was dead . . . and now she has returned, she lives in Alexandria. She was a slave when I met her, and we were deeply in love. It's for her that I left the habit and the monastery . . . Now she's here and I don't want to lose her again. I've bared my soul to you, and I beg you to keep this a secret."

While pouring out the feelings oppressing his chest, Edgardo didn't notice the deep transformation in Abella's face: her rosy cheeks had turned to an icy pallor, her eyes swelled with tears, and her mouth tightened to repress a suffering grimace. Edgardo noticed nothing, and Abella somehow managed to conceal her burst of anger, disappointment, and torment. She said nothing.

"So, what did you want to confess?" Edgardo said.

"Nothing, nothing of importance," the Magister replied in a thin voice.

"You were saying that we would perhaps find the answer we are looking for in Avicenna's manuscript."

"Maybe." Abella pointed at it. "Look for yourself."

"There are many sheets. Where should I look?"

"Look in the book that deals with medicines."

Edgardo leafed through the parchment. "Why waste more time? Tell me yourself," he added, irked.

"I want you to realize for yourself."

Only then did Edgardo notice the tension that had altered Abella's face. "I don't see why you insist. I trust what you say." He stopped, and a thought flashed through him that made him give a start. Then he continued. "As you wish, I'll look through the manuscript." He began searching his tunic pocket. "I need my instrument. Without the circles, I'm wretchedly blind." He rummaged in his inside pocket, then in the breeches one. "I don't understand, I always carry them with me." He looked at Abella, bewildered. "I fear I may have left them in my room, in the palazzo. I hope I haven't lost them. There are no other circles in Venice."

A layer of sweat had appeared on Abella's forehead, which made her face look even more ghostly.

"I'm afraid you'll have to lend me your eyes." The scribe pushed the manuscript toward her. "Tell me what it says in the colophon."

Edgardo waited, watching her with a treacherous smile.

Abella brought her hand close to the volume, opened the first sheet, and gently caressed the characters that filled the page, her eyes running along the lines.

"Go on," Edgardo prompted.

Abella parted her lips as though to take her final breath. She closed the sheet again and turned to the scribe.

Her face had disintegrated in an expression full of such deep sadness that Edgardo was upset by it.

"I can't help you," Abella murmured. "I can't read."

Edgardo stared at her, motionless.

"I've lied to you, and I'm sorry." Abella's voice was like the song of a little girl. It revealed a part of her soul deep inside her being.

"I suspected as much," Edgardo replied.

"You knew?"

"There isn't a single manuscript in your laboratorium, and you've always avoided having anything to do with reading, even during the signing of the merchant's contract. Also, you've never wanted to go into detail when anyone mentioned your teachers at the School of Salerno."

The Magister got up abruptly. She seemed relieved. Her cheeks recovered a brighter color.

"I really did live in Salerno, and was at Trotula de Ruggiero's side. I learned everything from her. I spied on her, watched her every gesture, memorized every formula. I was her servant. My parents worked the land and were very poor; they were afraid I'd die of starvation, so they left me in a Benedictine convent.

"I was raised by nuns. From them I learned the usage of herbs and spices. They said I had a talent for it. That's when I discovered the supernatural power my mouth possesses: to taste, with my palate and tongue, the composition of substances so precisely that I am able to place the origin of diseases.

"When I was a little older, the nuns sent me to work at the School of Salerno, and there I put the most illustrious scholars and renowned physicians out of a job."

"Without ever studying the texts."

"Never. I always managed to find a way around it." She gently touched the parchment. "When I left Salerno to go seek my fortune, I stole this manuscript and promised myself I'd learn to read. This contains all knowledge. Avicenna is a great master . . . I dreamed that one day . . . " She stopped and put a hand on Edgardo's shoulder. "What do you mean to do now?" Abella uttered those words, aware that the answer would contain her future, her life.

"Nothing," Edgardo replied bluntly. "You know my secret, and I yours. You're a great *magister medicinae* and I am living proof of that." He touched his chest, where his hump had once protruded.

A soft light appeared in Abella's eyes, which could have been taken for gratitude, but it was much more than that.

"But now let's get back to work." Edgardo took the manuscript. "You said we had to look in the book of medicines?"

"Yes, but what will you do without your eye circles?"

"Of course, I forgot." Edgardo put a hand in his pocket. "By the devil, look, they were here." He took out the case. "I'm very absent-minded," he added in a cunning tone.

Abella's face twisted in anger, but then immediately relaxed into a smile of complicity.

"Come on, read," she said, spurring him on.

Edgardo brought the contraption up to his eyes, and the miracle took place again: the writing appeared clear and sharp.

The work was divided into five books: theoretical and practical medicine; the *Materia medica*—on simple medicines; specific diseases and particular parts of the body; non-specific diseases; the composition and administration of medicines.

"Go to the *Materia medica*."

The list was long and complex.

"What should I look for?" Edgardo asked, alarmed.

"A reference to embalming and mummies."

Edgardo got down to work: mineral drugs, animal drugs, vegetable drugs, composite drugs, powders, pills, syrups, poultices, ointments, balms, a sea of remedies you could get lost in.

"I can't find anything like that," he said impatiently.

"And yet the tools and instruments I saw at the embalmer's were similar to the ones used for making medicines. Read on."

The scribe persevered. Abella followed him with apprehension and envy for his ability and speed at reading.

"Just a moment." Edgardo took the circles away then brought them close again, as though to make sure his ailing eyes had seen correctly.

"*Mumia calida est in fine tertii sicca prout creditur in primo. Inest autem ei proprietas omnem spiritum confortandi,*" he read out loud.

"Wonderful!" Abella cried out joyously. "I'd seen correctly. Avicenna considers the mummy as a medicine."

"He also says that 'the mummy' is very effective against a large number of ailments: abscess, outbreaks, fractures, bruises, paralysis, epilepsy, cough, palpitations, liver and spleen disorders, and any kind of poison. There's the black, common mummy, the one found in sepulchers, and then there are spiritual mummies that have supernatural powers."

"In the mill, on the millstone, I noticed remains that looked like bone splinters, and from that I deduced that the stone was used to mince the cut-up mummies, and turn them into thin powder. Then I saw a pot filled with wine vinegar, where one usually leaves substances to marinate from which one wants to extract the medicine."

"That's why there were all those mummies in the embalmer's mill." Edgardo was excited by the discovery. "They were for extracting the medicines which are apparently in great demand, enough to organize a trade between Alexandria and Venice."

Abella interrupted. "But since mummies from Egypt are very rare . . . some cunning person decided to create new ones, using local corpses, and then sell the medicine as original. A very profitable business."

Edgardo stood up and took a few steps, lost in thought. "There's a question to which I still can't find the answer: why kill Costanza, the relative of a Venetian nobleman, to turn her into a mummy, when they could find servant girls and slaves at a much lower risk?"

"Perhaps revenge against the Grimani family?"

Edgardo did not reply. His mind was absorbed in a labyrinth of conflicting theories and conjectures.

# XXXIII.
## THE CRYPT

They emerged from the depth of the lagoon and overran streams, canals, and the dock. The waters turned silver. In one night, struck by an unfathomable evil spell, all the fish in the muddy sea decided to die and, pushed by underground currents, eyes wide open and gills palpitating, they surfaced and floated, their lives finally draining away.

At first, the inhabitants of Venice interpreted the event as an ill omen that the city would soon come to an end. Then the poorest, hungriest, and most destitute took it as a sign of divine intervention to fight the starvation that was decimating the population. As early as the first light of dawn, the waterways through the city filled with *garzoni*, fishermen, mothers, and children, who, by any means, were trying to grab the charity God had chosen to send.

They picked everything: parrotfish, soles, diplodus, bass, goby, as well as never-before-seen monstrous fish.

The hungriest, fearing they wouldn't be able to gather enough, were stuffing themselves there and then with raw fish, filling their bellies like a storeroom.

By the time Vespers rang, shores and *campi* were covered in a carpet of shiny scales that shone in the fading light and were beginning to give off a nauseating stench that made the air unbreathable.

Her face buried in a handkerchief soaked in civet perfume, Magdalena walked around the palazzo, ordering that every gap be closed that could let in the disgusting stench. However, there was nothing to be done. The miasma of rotting fish seemed to be released by the earth itself, walls, and wells.

Ever since Magdalena had been taking the medicine imposed by her husband, her senses had become overly sharp. She was abnormally sensitive to tastes and smells, and even her hearing seemed to have grown more acute. Moreover, she had put on weight in a short space of time, her skin was unnaturally stretched, and she had acquired a pink tone: rather like an artificial youth, which Tommaso saw blooming with immense pleasure.

Two nights had passed since reading Avicenna's manuscripts when Edgardo was summoned by the Signora to her chambers. He was very surprised that she should receive him in private.

"It wasn't my husband who suggested I see you." Magdalena had a dark expression. "I'm doing it of my own initiative. I want you to know that what you have done for Alvise has served no purpose. The magistrates have considered the results of the new enquiries about the embalmer but, as my husband has said, they did not find any elements to prove that he was guilty of Costanza's death." She sighed. "We're very aggrieved, believe me, my husband has done everything possible . . . but there's a confession."

Edgardo lowered his head. He couldn't accept defeat just when, after the latest discoveries, he thought he was only a step away from the truth.

There was a shuffling behind him, as well as dry wheezing. Nena, hunched by sorrow, was dragging herself to the bed with one of the Signora's dresses. She walked slowly in the semi-darkness, the Flanders cloth dress in her arms, like the limp body of a child.

Her brief journey never seemed to end.

Upset, Edgardo closed his eyes. A picture, a faded memory suddenly appeared in his mind, very similar to the reality of that instant, but which had happened in the past.

He opened his eyes again. Nena was still on the same spot, as though she hadn't moved.

There was a palpitation in his chest, a flutter in his soul, and he was assailed by a deep anguish: the thought that was forming in his mind, the gut feeling from a horrible abyss, dragged him into a diabolical design. It couldn't be true, and yet he couldn't not believe it. He was, once again, willing to trust his instinct.

"Holy Mother of God, this stench of rotten fish could even kill a pig." The young nun at San Zaccaria crossed the central nave of the church with a quick step, covering her face with her veil. She bolted the central entrance, holding her breath, then went back to the refectory.

"Has she gone?"

"I think so."

Huddled behind the main altar, Edgardo and Abella waited, motionless.

"Let's wait for nightfall before we start on our work," Edgardo whispered.

Abella nodded. This was perhaps the first time she had shared Edgardo's gut feeling. She was somewhat confused, but the scribe's explanation, his suspicion, and his terrible doubts had seemed so convincing to her that she had agreed to take the risk.

Alone, close to each other in that sacred place: she felt that an affinity, a common tension had arisen between them that she could not define. Even though Edgardo loved another woman, she couldn't bring herself to feel resentment or jealousy, on the contrary, she felt an inspiration only the two of them possessed, and that nobody could oppose.

The shadows softly dispersed, giving way to a thick, dark cloak.

In a surreal silence, they left their hiding place and went

down the narrow staircase that led to the crypt beneath the altar.

A candle lit the urn containing the relics of various saints, donated to the nuns by Pope Benedict III.

Edgardo kneeled. "Here it is."

Abella handed him an iron bar. The tombstone was engraved with the name and year of death: Costanza Colyn, Anno Domini MCXVIII.

With a precise gesture, he slid the tip of the bar into the gap between the sarcophagus and the floor and prised it up with all the strength in his body. The marble slab gave a little shudder, moved, and was lifted.

"Help me push it to the side."

Abella's intervention was decisive, and, despite some difficulty, they managed to slide off the lid.

The coffin, laid there only recently, still gave off the scent of pine, and no unpleasant smell came from the casket.

Edgardo went down into the grave. He felt like a defiler of tombs, but Abella made a sign that he should carry on.

The coffin lid came off at the first attempt, as though it hadn't been nailed expertly.

"Bring the candle closer."

Abella leaned over. The scribe's face was tense, prey to profound agitation.

"Please God we don't find what I think we will."

With a clean movement, he pushed the beam and opened the casket. The faint light of the flame lapped at the walls, Abella let out a kind of hoarse cry.

The coffin was empty.

"God almighty, why have You done this to me?" Edgardo threw himself into a dark lament. "As I feared, Costanza's body isn't here anymore. This means my most gloomiest theories have come true. For once, I'd hoped my instinct would let me down again."

The Magister made the sign of the cross. The human spirit sometimes sinks into such a dark abyss, in which even a physician can do nothing except entrust herself to God.

They went to Ca' Grimani early in the morning. Edgardo asked Nena to request an audience with the Signora. Even the servant sensed an unusual excitement in the air, pale faces, disconnected gestures.

Magdalena received them in her rooms and could barely manage to restrain her unease.

Sitting in front of her image reflected in the slate of polished metal, she continued, with exhausting slowness, to spread a thick layer of ceruse on her face, a barrier against the world.

"We asked to see you, Signora," the words came out tired from Edgardo's mouth, "to tell you about an extraordinarily serious discovery."

There was no reaction nor word. Another layer of mask that now made her unrecognizable spread over her face.

"Costanza's sepulcher is empty," Edgardo said. "Her body is no longer in the San Zaccaria crypt. It's disappeared."

The brush fell from her hands, she bent over, stiffened, but did not turn around. There was only breathlessness.

"Allow me to ask you a few questions, Signora, it's very important."

Abella approached. "Are you quite well?"

Magdalena showed her swollen, flabby face, ravaged by icy whiteness.

"In the mill where the embalmer worked, we found Costanza's dress. We showed it to the judges and to your husband. Do you know where that dress is now?"

Bewildered and cornered, Magdalena stammered a few words. "Costanza's dress . . . I don't know anything . . . "

"Are you sure?" Abella insisted.

She rolled her head like a sick child.

"Do you remember which dress your sister was buried in?" Edgardo asked in a persuasive voice.

"Buried? In which dress?"

Abella wanted to shake her out of her torpor.

"I have a vague memory," Edgardo continued. "The day before the burial, just after we inspected the body, Nena came in with a dress in her arms."

Magdalena's absent eyes seemed to melt in a screen of tears.

"Perhaps it was the dress she wore to my father's funeral; in Bruges . . . I can't remember, I don't know . . . "

"Try thinking." Abella leaned over her until their faces nearly touched. "It all depends on you, make an effort."

"Enough!" Magdalena cried. "Why do you torment me? Have pity, I can't remember any dress!"

"I remember it." A voice behind them chilled their souls. Edgardo and Abella turned in dismay. "Flanders cloth, an excellent quality wool, embroidered with gold flowers all around the collar and sleeves . . . she looked so beautiful."

It was Nena's voice.

The description matched, there was no doubt about that. Edgardo turned to the Signora. "Was it that one?"

Magdalena nodded without conviction.

"And you haven't seen that dress since?"

"No."

"Are you sure?"

Magdalena gave Nena a desperate look, then lowered her head.

"Do you think it might be possible to see your husband to ask about this dress?" Edgardo had forgotten all prudence.

Magdalena suddenly stood up. "My husband? Whatever for?"

"Is nobleman Grimani at home?" Abella asked.

A sudden frenzy caused Magdalena's movements to become

uncoordinated. "I haven't seen him, he went out at dawn . . . he may be at the Dogado . . . he'll be back late."

"You know Alvise's life is at stake, don't you?" Edgardo was no longer willing to pander to her evasive behavior.

"The Signore is in the pantry." Nena's voice was even darker.

## XXXIV.
## REBIRTH

They proceeded slowly along the upstairs loggia, then came down into the internal courtyard as far as the mezzanine. The stench afflicting the city had turned sickly-sweet, like soaked flowers.

Magdalena gave a light knock at the door of the pantry, but there was no reply. She then turned to Edgardo and Abella, with some of her old pride. "He isn't here," she said.

They were about to leave, when they heard a creaking sound from within.

Without asking permission, Edgardo hammered on the door with more determination. "It's Edgardo, Signore, please open the door. We must speak with you."

When Tommaso's ravaged face emerged from the semi-darkness, Edgardo noticed that Magdalena's eyes contained all the despair of a woman who sees ruination advance in large strides.

"Why do you disturb me?" Grimani's eyes glistened with tears. "I was praying."

Bravely, Magdalena stepped forward and opened the door. Tommaso didn't stop her. She had never been to that room, her husband's exclusive refuge.

In the middle of a small cave lined with timber, like the pantry of a ship, stood a coffin covered in a velvet, emerald-green cloth. There was a *prie-dieu* before it. It gave the impression of a chapel with an altar.

"Forgive me, Signore," Edgardo said, plucking up the

courage. "We must ask you a question of vital importance that even your wife can't answer."

Tommaso didn't move, only his eyes briefly searched for a sign from Magdalena, who remained with her head lowered.

"Was the dress we handed you, and that you recognized as belonging to Costanza, the one she wore the day she was abducted, or the one she was buried in?"

His body gave a start, he glanced at his wife one last time, then approached the altar. "What difference could it make?" Tommaso replied, trying to control an outburst of anger.

Swaying, Magdalena approached and touched his chest. On her face, the ceruse was drying like a lake of salt. "Where is my sister's body?" Her voice was cold, metallic.

Tommaso's eyes ran to all present, in search of support.

"The sarcophagus in San Zaccaria is empty," Abella added.

"What are you saying?" Tommaso exclaimed, offended.

"We've seen it with our own eyes," Edgardo replied.

"What happened to my sister's body?" Magdalena screamed.

"My beloved wife, my life's companion." Tommaso gently stroked her hair. "What difference does all this make now? Costanza is in the Kingdom of Heaven, her body is dust."

Magdalena took a step back. The air had become unbreathable.

"My sweet wife, don't walk away. Come and see."

Tommaso took Magdalena by the hand and led her to the altar.

Edgardo and Abella leaned against the wall, as though wanting to disappear.

"Look." With a solemn gesture, Tommaso made the cloth slide to the floor.

Lit by the diaphanous light of a morning not quite materialized, in the middle of the room, before the horrified eyes of those present, an image took shape in which the real world and the fairy-tale world became blurred.

An enormous, turquoise-colored reliquary glowed with the iridescence of the deep sea. Inside, beautifully composed, beautifully dressed, perfectly preserved, a body seemed to float in the abyss.

"You see, it's our Luca . . . he is still with us."

Magdalena let out a desperate scream that tore through her chest, as though her heart had been smashed in two.

It was Luca, her son: his face, hair, his hands intact, perfectly preserved.

"Isn't it incredible? I had him embalmed, to have him with us always, while awaiting his return."

Never had Abella heard such a tender, loving voice.

Magdalena had approached the reliquary and, leaning over the glass, was trying to find the image of her lost son amid the emerald glow.

"Ancient Egyptians believed that in order to live on, the spirit needs a perfectly preserved body." Tommaso turned to Edgardo and Abella, indicating his son. "His spirit is here while waiting to be reborn, to transmigrate into the new body God will create in Magdalena's womb."

Tommaso noticed Abella's dismayed expression.

"You have the illusion that you have the knowledge of scholars and you don't believe this can happen, right? But you're wrong. Many Greek philosophers and Persian wise men support this truth . . . and besides . . . " He caressed the glass casket. "Luca has told me himself." He took Magdalena's face in his hands. "I can hear his voice, you know? He's promised me that he will be reborn in his brother's body."

In the grip of uncontrollable tears, Magdalena collapsed on the floor. Edgardo and Abella rushed to hold her up.

"You mustn't weep. You must rejoice. The rebirth is near." Tommaso's voice seemed to be coming from a body that wasn't his.

"Where is Costanza's body?" Magdalena repeated, kneeling in front of the reliquary.

"You mustn't get upset, she sacrificed herself for you, in an act of generosity. Her life was of no use, she would have ended her days in a convent."

Magdalena couldn't understand. Her husband's incomprehensible words seemed to her nothing but a cruel game.

"Signore." Edgardo's voice had taken on an authority that chilled Tommaso. "The dress you recognized was the one for the burial, you knew it perfectly well, but you chose to say nothing. And that's what prompted the question in my mind: how could it end up in the mill, and why didn't you report it immediately?" He paused, waiting for a reply that would never come. "Because you were the one who ordered that the body be purloined. Is that not the truth?"

Tommaso Grimani gave a start, as though his safety had suddenly been threatened by the word "truth."

He took his wife by the shoulders and embraced her. "I had no choice. When the path to resurrection is revealed to you, you must sacrifice everything, even what you hold most dear. There is only one medicine that can restore life to a barren womb. Oriental wise men know the miraculous properties of this substance: it's called mummy and is extracted from a mummified body."

Magdalena had turned into a deformed mask. "I don't understand . . . what do you mean? . . . that the medicine you've given me has been taken from a mummy?"

"Not from any mummy. I needed the best quality, the one they call spiritual, obtained from the mummified bodies of virgins who've died a violent death."

"Costanza . . . " she stammered, "you had Costanza killed?"

"Costanza was predestined, your own blood, she herself would have agreed to sacrifice herself for you."

Tommaso's calm precipitated them all into a vortex of horror.

With a scream that came from the depths of her guts, Magdalena threw herself on her husband and began to strike him with all her strength. "You're a monster! God almighty, you have fed my womb with the body of my sister! May God damn you, may He damn my womb and make it barren for all eternity!"

Tommaso suddenly took a step back, and fell backward.

The reliquary rocked and the timber stand slid on its side, depriving the sepulcher of its support. For a moment, it seemed to float in the air, then it fell to the floor with a terrible crash.

The glass shattered into tiny splinters, and the room was invaded by a dense rain of turquoise crystals that turned the walls and ceiling into a tempestuous sea.

Like a swimmer emerging from the abyss, little Luca's body came into contact with the air. It almost looked as though a final breath was exhaled through his mouth: a soul that was finding its freedom. Then, slowly, the skin began to fall apart, the hair became dull, the internal organs shriveled, and in a few instants, the mummy turned to dust, a heap of dust, fine and impalpable, that smelled of myrrh.

Shining like a statue of salt, turned to stone for all eternity.

Magdalena would have liked to remain like this forever, buried in her grief.

Motionless, Edgardo and Abella couldn't muster the strength to make sense of the events.

Disengaging himself from astonishment and agitation, Tommaso shook himself. His face lit up and he turned to those present with a wild expression and exclaimed, "You saw him. He's freed himself of his body. Now his spirit is ready to return to us."

It was his obsession; reason had given way to delirium.

Abella bowed her head, defeated. Only Edgardo found the courage to speak. "Signore, Costanza was killed by your order," he said, trying to bring him back to reality.

Grimani resumed the measured tone of ancient nobility. "I did what was right."

"You killed my sister, and you will pay for that," Magdalena murmured in fury.

Tommaso Grimani looked at the witnesses, one by one. "And who will report me? You, Magdalena, my beloved wife, who have nobody but me in the world? Or you, Edgardo, my faithful friend with a dark past? Or perhaps you, Abella, illustrious physician in search of fame and glory? Who will listen to you? For what reason? A dress?"

Edgardo interrupted him. "The body is no longer in the crypt."

"Purloined by one of the many body-snatchers," Tommaso said, confident. "To feed a blooming trade in mummies. The culprit has already paid with his life for this terrible commerce."

Abella couldn't contain her contempt. "And you would let Alvise die innocent?"

"Young Alvise?" Tommaso said. "No, we don't want to sacrifice another innocent. After all, we have a perpetrator and the missing body will bring further arguments in favor of the boy's innocence. I'm sure they will listen to my request for grace. Have trust in God, Alvise will be saved."

"If we hadn't unmasked you, you would have sent him to his death," Abella hissed.

Tommaso did not reply, accepting that theory as a trick of fate.

In the universe ruled by the noble Tommaso Grimani, every celestial body had found its position. Order had been restored, and nobody would dare upset it.

Edgardo and Abella turned to Magdalena, waiting for her reaction, but it didn't come.

"Don't be sad," Tommaso said to them, "but rejoice. We've used death to make life triumph. Death has been defeated."

## XXXV.
## THE FEAST OF THE MARYS

The April calends brought to the lagoon a gentle breeze that swept away miasmas, mud, epidemics, and the leftovers of the starvation that had afflicted the people all winter.

Our merciful Lord had bestowed new harmony upon the city, which presaged wealthy, peaceful times.

Venetia would soon have a new Doge. The Great Council had reached an agreement, and would choose between two noblemen of proven honesty and morals, God-fearing and brave condottieri: Tommaso Grimani and Domenico Michiel.

Life had resumed its natural rhythm: Sabbatai continued to sell potions in his shop; Tataro was increasingly ill and had left the foundry; Alvise, having been pardoned, had returned to the service of Ca' Grimani; Nena, devotedly grateful, served her mistress Magdalena, who had shut herself away in her rooms. Magister Abella practised her art with success.

Edgardo had left Ca' Grimani and found hospitality with the Alexandrian merchant.

In the clear air of a dawn that gave the waters an indigo hue, Venetia vibrated with lively activities, enveloped in a new hope.

Just a few nights were enough for the story of poor Costanza to be forgotten.

Edgardo and Kallis lived together, overwhelmed by a passion that fed on the fantasies of love they'd dreamed for too many years. In the eyes of strangers, they seemed to be leading a dull, insignificant life.

Ibrahim continued his trade in glass with Alexandria. Edgardo had been hired as a scribe to help Lippomano transcribe the accounts.

The burden of what had happened kept him awake at night, and his only relief was to feel Kallis's light breathing next to him.

He wondered if he and Abella had been cowardly or compassionate toward Magdalena, who had accepted living in the shadows, next to a man guilty of her sister's death.

This time, his instinct had led him to the truth. He'd saved the life of an innocent, but hadn't had the strength to do his duty all the way. And all the others had been his accomplices, nobody was without sin.

He avoided talking with Kallis about the past, and she asked no questions about the present. They lived intensely, burning these days that Edgardo felt could end as if by magic. Never was the word tomorrow uttered, and whenever Edgardo would indulge in plans, however vague, about their joint lives being lived in broad daylight, Kallis would smile and narrow her eyes, as though studying him to assess the consistency of his soul, the real weight of the love he had for her.

In that state, Edgardo felt breathless, as though his life was running along a steep, uncertain slope, constantly falling from one condition to another, without ever finding a firm landing, calm waters where he could stop and rest forever.

One morning that was ablaze with the glow that spring had placed on the waters of the lagoon, Kallis, protected by her mask and long dark tunic, asked Edgardo to accompany her to an event.

The *scaula* left behind galleys and dromons anchored in the bay outside San Marco, and took the direction of the islands in the north.

"Where are we going?" Edgardo asked.

"Follow the canal to Torcellus," Kallis replied without any other explanation.

They went beyond Amurianum, along Majurbium and Burianum, around Torcellus, and between Costanciacum and Aymanas, until they arrived within sight of an abandoned island, covered only in ruins.

That's when Edgardo remembered. Once before, in the past, Kallis had taken him there. The monastery of San Lorenzo had once been there, and it was where her mother was buried.

When they reached the shore, he realized with a sense of deep sadness how the power of the waters had transformed this place of prayer: abandonment and desolation were everywhere. Privet bushes, cordgrass, and brambles had invaded the inside of the church, reduced to a heap of debris. The slabs of marble that still covered the floor ten years earlier had been stolen, and the frescoed walls had collapsed. Only the broken altar still stood, alone, encrusted with algae, guarding the wooden statue of Christ bleached by salt.

"My shelter has also collapsed." Kallis indicated the tower where she sometimes liked to find a little peace in the past. The top of the bell tower had been reduced to a broken stump.

They walked around the ruins as far as the internal cloisters, where poplars stood out against the sky.

"Mind the snakes," Kallis warned him.

Edgardo smiled. "You also said this the first time you brought me here."

They reached the field behind the church. There was no more sign of the uprooted headstones. Kallis searched through the grass, dug, scraped. There was no trace of her mother's grave. So she kneeled and recited a prayer. When she stood up, her eyes were filled with tears.

She took Edgardo by the hand and led him to the broken altar, under the statue of Our Lord. "Do you remember when

I took you to Santa Maria Formosa to watch the celebrations of the Feast of the Marys?"

"Nothing has vanished from my memory about those days."

"When I saw the twelve brides go into the church, I told you that when I was little and I was sad, to comfort me, my mother would tell me the story of the marriage, and say that someday I too would marry. I never believed this dream could come true." Emotion was filling her chest. "Perhaps the time has come now."

She tore off her mask. Her amber face was radiant, the scars seemed to have disappeared, and her skin glowed in the morning light.

With meticulous care, she slipped off her large tunic and revealed a white dress, embossed with roses, decorated with gold, pearls, and diamonds. She smelled of frankincense.

"Can a knight marry a simple slave?" she asked in a thin voice.

Edgardo, forgetting that knights don't cry, abandoned himself to uncontrollable weeping, shaken by a joy he'd never known before.

Kallis, his bride . . . He'd had to wait over ten years since he'd first asked her to be his wife, and now the dream was coming true.

He took her hand. "A wretched knight is the man who falls at your feet, swears to you eternal faith, and is honored to take your hand."

"Now I really am one of the Marys," Kallis said in a child-like tone.

They kneeled before the altar, amid brambles and bushes. They had no celebrant, and their only witnesses were snakes.

Edgardo took Kallis's hand and raised it toward the cross. "I accept you in such a way that you become my wife and I your husband."

"I accept you in such a way that you become my husband and I your wife."

They had no rings. Edgardo tore off a blade of cordgrass, rolled it up, and put it on Kallis's ring finger. She did the same.

It was then that, like a rustle of wind in the reeds, they thought they heard a voice coming from the sky, "And thus I mean for these two to be married."

Is it man's destiny that happiness not last longer than a night, and that a diseased thought always creep into the mind and dig and fester, like a cruel demon?

Why had Kallis, by using that word, "knight," reminded Edgardo of a past he hoped was buried?

What kind of knight was someone who had never respected any of the fundamental guidelines of his position: honor, rectitude, sincerity?

His soul was pierced by many wounds. The deepest one, the one that prevented him from fully enjoying his supreme earned joy, was the thought of his cowardice, that he hadn't found the courage to report Tommaso to the law.

When he couldn't sleep, he would tell himself the fairytale about respecting Magdalena's wishes, and the terrible responsibility of destroying a family. But were those really the Signora's wishes, or was she also roaming in search of a courage she wasn't able to find?

What was the right choice for a knight? The answer was obvious.

He asked Kallis's advice.

"You must follow your conscience. But be aware that if you take the path of honesty and purity, you must go all the way. If you report Grimani because he's guilty, you must also report me. We have both gravely sinned."

Kallis could be so ruthless, so terrible in her simplicity.

She'd placed him at a crossroads: did pursuing truth mean sacrificing their love?

After a night spent roaming down streams and *calli*, getting lost in thick beds of reeds on the outskirts of the city, at the first light of dawn, he took a *scaula*, went to see Abella in Torcellus, and told her of his intentions.

He was relieved to hear that the Magister too lived torn by the same torments. So taking a decision wasn't hard.

They went to make a report to the magistrate and were surprised to be admitted immediately.

Perhaps this was owing to the procedures surrounding the appointment of the new doge.

In secret, given the noble origins of the accused, a detailed investigation was conducted and various witnesses heard.

The evidence of the young nun from San Zaccaria was crucial, as she confessed her part in the abduction of Costanza and the purloining of her body: the abduction had been staged in every detail, and would have been successful even if Edgardo hadn't been distracted. The confession of Tommaso's associate, Romano Marzolo, who admitted to the traffic in mummies that had long been conducted with Alexandria, also carried considerable weight.

Tommaso Grimani, nobleman, was found guilty of young Costanza's death, but not being the physical perpetrator of the crime, was sentenced to exile, under pain of beheading should he ever return to the city of San Marco.

His wife Magdalena was never called as a witness.

The church bells began to ring Prime in every district: the city was celebrating.

The new doge had been elected: the most illustrious and magnificent Domenico Michiel, a brave fighter and an honest man.

Magister Abella walked into Ca' Grimani, accompanied by the pealing that fueled the hopes of the people of Venice. She was very surprised when Magdalena had called for her. After that terrible day, she'd had no occasion to see her.

"I want you to examine me." Those were the only few words the Signora uttered.

Magdalena had very much altered. Her body had expelled the unnatural swelling and her flesh had recovered its natural glow. Her luminous face wore no ceruse, and her eyes were sparkling with life.

Abella asked for her urine. She observed it, studied it, checked its transparency, and sampled its flavor. Then she got Magdalena to lie down, felt her pulse, her belly, and conducted an in-depth investigation, with meticulous care, of the *os matricis*, the *collum*, and as far as the *vasa seminalia*.

"There isn't the shadow of a doubt," she concluded, "a new life is taking shape in your womb."

Magdalena remained impassive. No word came out of her mouth. Just a slight crease on her face that might evoke a grimace of horror.

Regal, almost as though her husband's authority and power had been transferred to her, Magdalena stood up. "I will call for you again," she said.

Abella bowed and, before she left, carefully studied the radiant aura emanating from the Signora, and couldn't help thinking, "Now that she's free of her husband's presence, her soul has begun to live again. That's why she couldn't get pregnant, she didn't want to, her body refused. Now that Tommaso is no longer with her, her womb is fertile once more."

The bells were still ringing when she left.

Outside the Basilica and the Palace, the people were singing the praises of the new doge who would bring prosperity and prestige to the city.

Edgardo had allowed himself to be dragged by the crowd, inebriated by this exceptional event. Around him, blended with the multitude, were all those who had been with him during those dark times: Abella in her blood-red tunic; Tataro, limping, supported by a servant; Sabbatai, who was sneaking reverently through the legs of the nobility; Ermanno d'Istria, who'd arrived from the abbey of San Giorgio; the innkeeper Teodora who struggled to drag around her flabby flesh; Alvise and Nena, finally carefree; and even the fat man and the man from Bergamo, half-drunk. Everybody was celebrating the new doge in front of the dock full of galleys, dromons, and chelandions.

Only Ibrahim, the Alexandrian merchant, had refused to participate. It still wasn't very prudent for him to be seen in public. Pushed around by the crowd, Edgardo suddenly found himself a few steps away from old Tataro. He felt his weasel eyes pricking his chest, a mocking, contemptuous grimace on his face. He raised his hands and with his fingers formed two circles in front of his eyes, like the eye circles, then added a gesture around his neck that left no doubt as to its meaning: the hanged man.

At first, Edgardo did not understand, almost bewitched by that toothless smile. Then a dismal thought, an omen, flashed through his mind: Tataro had discovered the true identity of Ibrahim al-Fazari.

He started running like a madman, pushing, kicking, until he'd reached the merchant's palazzo.

He was greeted by an unnatural silence as he walked through the vestibule.

He looked for Kallis in the salon, the garden, then went upstairs to the rooms on the main floor. They were deserted, in perfect order. In vain, he called her. Kallis had disappeared.

In her room, on a lectern, next to the goose quill and the horn, he found a parchment. In uncertain but clear handwriting, Kallis had traced just a few words:

"The day of absolution and peace hasn't come yet. The path to the truth is long and winding. I leave you so that I can continue seeing my reflection in your face. Wait for me. Your wife."

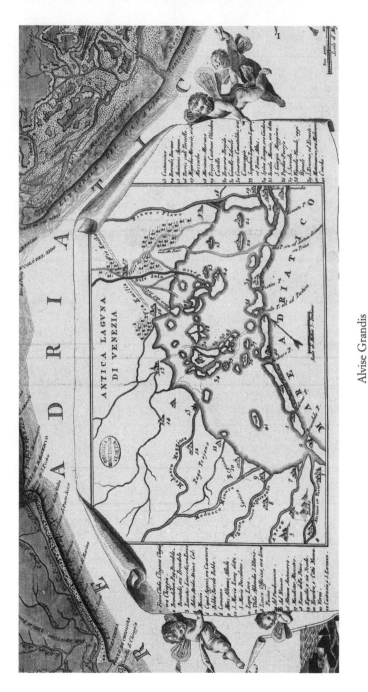

Alvise Grandis

*The Venice Lagoon, ancient and modern, newly outlined and distinct with its Islands, Valleys and Canals in the present day, as well as, in comparison, the Lagoon as it was at the time Venice was founded, with both the old and new names.*

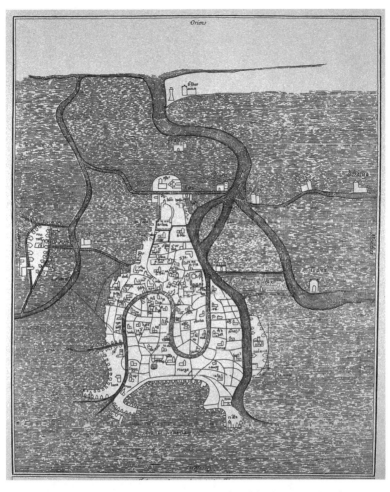

*Paolino da Venezia's map (1346), reproduced by Temanza (detail)*

# GLOSSARY

**Arengo**: General assembly of free men, citizens, and patricians, responsible for electing the Doge.

**Abulcasis**: Living in Cordoba at the turn of the 11th century, he was the most important representative of Hispanic-Arabic medicine in Islamic Spain.

**Brolo**: (vegetable patch) was the name given to Piazza San Marco in those days because it was covered in grass and trees.

**Ca'**: Short for "Casa" (house). In Venetian, it stands before the name of a house.

**Calle**: Venetian word for a narrow street.

**Campo**: Venetian word for a city square, which in the early days often had vegetation growing in it.

**Circassia**: Region in the Western Caucasus, extending as far as the Black Sea, currently part of Georgia.

**Consiglio dei Primates**: Group of laymen representing the Church and noblemen assisting the Doge in his decisions and in applying the law.

**Dogado**: Ancient Dukedom of Venice, which included the city and the lagoons.

**Domenico Michiel**: Doge of Venice from 1117 to 1130.

**Fondamenta**: In Venice, a stretch of road along a canal.

**Garzone (plural garzoni)**: Shop boy.

**Palazzo**: A large patrician house.

**Rivoalto**: The old name for the modern Rialto.

**Rivus Altus**: The old name for Canal Grande.

**Sandolo**: A light, flat-bottomed fishing boat widely used in the Venice Lagoon.

**Scaula**: A light boat, like a gondola, used internally in Venice.

**Trotula De Ruggiero**: Female physician who worked during the 11th century at the famous medical school of Salerno. Famous in the Middle Ages for her study of female ailments.

## About the Author

Roberto Tiraboschi was born in Bergamo, Italy. He is known as one of Italy's most stylish screenwriters and playwrights, having worked with Nobel laureate Dario Fo and written screenplays for a number of Italian directors, including Marco Pontecorvo, Silvio Soldini, and Liliana Cavani among others. His novels have enjoyed success with both critics and readers. *The Eye Stone* (Europa, 2015) was his English debut.